C. A. Chardenal

Complete French Course

C. A. Chardenal

Complete French Course

ISBN/EAN: 9783337400781

Printed in Europe, USA, Canada, Australia, Japan

Cover: Foto ©Andreas Hilbeck / pixelio.de

More available books at **www.hansebooks.com**

COMPLETE

FRENCH COURSE

BASED ON THE

First and Second French Courses

OF

C. A. CHARDENAL

BACHELIER ÈS LETTRES DE L'UNIVERSITÉ DE FRANCE

Boston

ALLYN AND BACON

CONTENTS.

THE NUMBERS REFER TO THE PAGES.

INTRODUCTION.

THE ARTICLE.

THE NOUN.

THE ADJECTIVE.

THE PRONOUN.

AUXILIARY VERBS.

REGULAR VERBS.

IRREGULAR VERBS.

THE SUBJUNCTIVE MOOD

THE INFINITIVE MOOD.

THE PARTICIPLES.

THE ADVERB.

THE PREPOSITION.

INTRODUCTION.

THE ALPHABET.

a	b	c	d	e	f	g	h	i	j
ah	*be*	*ke*	*de*	*e*	*fe*	*gue*	*he*	*i*	*je*
k	**l**	**m**	**n**	**o**	**p**	**q**	**r**	**s**	**t**
ke	*le*	*me*	*ne*	*o*	*pe*	*ke*	*re*	*se*	*te*
u	**v**	**x**	**y**	**z**					
u	*ve*	*kse*	*i*	*ze*					

The vowels have their usual French sounds. *Be, ke, de, e,* etc., have about the sounds of English *but, cut, dun, up,* etc., omitting the final consonant. The *u* in *gue* is silent. The *j* of *je* sounds like *si* in English *vision.* W appears in a few words taken from foreign languages, and usually has the sound of *v.*

ORTHOGRAPHIC SIGNS.

Accents. — Apostrophe. — Hyphen. — Cedilla. — Diæresis.

Three orthographic marks are called accents, — the acute (´), the grave (`), and the circumflex (ˆ).

The acute accent (´) is used only over the vowel *e* (é), which then has the sound of *a* in *late.* As **été, vérité.**

The grave accent (`) is used chiefly over the vowel *e* (è), which then has nearly the sound of *ai* in *air.* As **près, père.** It is used over *a* and *u* merely to distinguish certain words which are otherwise spelled alike, and does not alter the pronunciation. As **à** (*to*) from **a** (*has*); **là** (*there*) from **la** (*the* or *her*); **où** (*where*) from **ou** (*or*).

The circumflex accent (ˆ) is used on any vowel, which is then long. As **âge, tête, île, dôme, bûche.** It frequently indicates that a letter has been dropped.

These accents do not imply any stress of voice on the syllable where they occur.

The apostrophe (') indicates that one of the vowels **a**, **e**, or **i** has been dropped before a word beginning with a vowel or *h mute.*

a is elided only in the article or pronoun **la**; as **l'âme** for **la âme.**

e is elided in **le, je, me, te, se, de, ce, ne, que** (but when **je, ce, le,** and **la** come directly after the verb, either as subjects or objects, no elision takes place); in **jusque** and **lorsque**; in **puisque** and **quoique** before **il, ils, elle, elles, on, un, une**; in **quelque** before **un, une**; and in **entre** in compound words.

i is elided only in **si** before **il** or **ils.**

No elision occurs before **onze, onzième, oui, huit, huitième.**

The hyphen (-) marks the connection between two or more words or parts of a word.

The hyphen is used between the verb and the pronouns **je, moi, nous, tu, toi, vous, il, ils, elle, elles, le, la, les, lui, leur, y, en, ce, on,** when they are placed after a verb of which they are subjects or objects. The other cases of its use will be noticed as they occur.

The cedilla (ç) is put under **c** when it has the sound of *s* before **a, o,** or **u.** As **français, garçon, reçu.**

The diæresis (¨) is placed over the second of two vowels to show that it begins a new syllable. As **naïf, noël.**

PRONUNCIATION.

Simple Vowels.

a (short) has a sound between the *a* of *bar* and the *a* in *mat*. As **la**, *the ;* **quatre**, *four ;* **table**, *table.*

a (long) or **â** has the sound of *a* in *bar*. The mouth should be opened wide. As **âme**, *soul ;* **bâtir**, *to build ;* **sale**, *dirty ;* **fable**, *fable.*

a is silent in août, Curaçao, toast, Saône.

é has the sound of *a* in *late*. As **été**, *summer ;* **vérité**, *truth.*

è and **ê** vary in sound between the *e* of *met* and the *ai* of *air*. The mouth should be opened wide. As **près**, *near ;* **mère**, *mother ;* **tête**, *head ;* **même**, *same.*

e without an accent has a sound between the *u* in *but* and the *u* in *burr*. As **de**, *of ;* **je**, *I ;* **venir**, *to come.* At the end of words of more than one syllable it is silent; as **dame**, *lady ;* **farine**, *flour*. After two consonants, or at the end of a syllable and preceding a consonant, its sound is very indistinct; merely sufficient to pronounce the consonant before it; as **arbre**, *tree ;* **samedi**, *Saturday*. It has the sound of **é** (*a* in *late*) before final *d*, *f*, *r*, *t*, *z*, when mute; as **pied**, *foot ;* **clef**, *key ;* **parler**, *to speak ;* **et**, *and ;* **nez**, *nose*. It has the sound of **è** before *c*, *f*, *l*, *r*, *s*, *t*, *x* not mute, before a double consonant, and in the words **les**, **des**, **ces**, **mes**, **tes**, **ses**; as **bec**, *beak ;* **chef**, *chief ;* **sel**, *salt ;* **fer**, *iron ;* **net**, *clean ;* **ferme**, *farm.*

In **femme**, *woman*; **solennel**, *solemn ;* **hennir**, *to neigh ;* and in all adverbs ending in **-emment**, the first **e** has the sound of French short **a**.

i and **î** usually have the sound of *i* in *machine*. As **midi**, *noon ;* **île**, *island ;* **fini**, *finished.*

o (open) has a sound between the *o* of *not* and the *u* of *nut*. **Mode**, *fashion* : **mol**, *soft*.

o (close) has the sound of *o* in *note*. As **mot**, *word* ; **côté**, *side*.

o is silent in **faon, Laon, paon, taon.**

u has no equivalent in English; it can be formed by trying to pronounce French **i** with the lips in the position for whistling. **Lune**, *moon* ; **murmure**, *murmur*. It is usually silent after *q* and also when standing between *g* and *e* or *i*. As **quatre**, *four*; **guerre**, *war* ; **guide**, *guide*.

y following a consonant, or standing alone, has the sound of French **i**. As **type**, *type* ; **y**, *there*.

y standing between two vowels performs the office of **iy**, the *i* uniting with the preceding vowel. As **rayon** (*ray*) = **rai-yon** ; **appuyer** (*to support*) = **appui-yer**. (See below, Compound Vowels.) **Pays, paysan, paysage** = **pai-is**, etc.

Nasal Vowels.

m and **n**, when final or before a consonant, lose their value as consonants and form with the preceding vowel a nasal sound which is a true vowel. These sounds have no exact equivalents in English; and in pronouncing them, care must be taken that no consonant **m**. **n**, or **ng** be heard.

They are divided into four groups.

an **am** **en** **em**	= nasal **a** = French long **a** pronounced through the nose.

As **dans**, *in* ; **lampe**, *lamp* ; **enfant**, *child* ; **empire**, *empire*.

in
im
ain
aim
ein
} = so-called nasal **i** = English *a* in *man* pronounced through the nose.

As **vin**, *wine*; **important**, *important*; **pain**, *bread*; **faim**, *hunger*; **sein**, *breast*.

on
om
} = nasal **o** = French open **o** pronounced through the nose.

As **ponton**, *pontoon*; **nom**, *name*.

un
um
eun
} = nasal **eu** = French **eu** (see p. 6) pronounced through the nose.

As **brun**, *brown*; **parfum**, *perfume*; **à jeun**, *fasting*.

In words ending in **-ien** and in the verbs **tenir**, **venir**, and their compounds, **en** after **i** has the sound of nasal **i** As **bien**, *well*: **viens**, *come*. **En** is silent in the third person plural of verbs. As **ils aiment**, *they love*. Otherwise **en** nearly always has the sound of nasal **a**, as given in the first group.

Vowels are not nasalized before double **n** or double **m**, nor before **n** or **m** followed by a vowel or **h** mute. As **âme**, *soul*; **une**, *one*; **pomme**. *apple*; **inhumain**. *inhuman*.

But the nasal sound is heard in **ennui** and its derivatives, and in all words beginning with **emm**.

Compound Vowels and Diphthongs.

A compound vowel is the union of two or more vowels, with the sound of a single vowel.

A diphthong is the union of two vowels, both of which are heard in pronunciation.

ai at the end of verbs, in **gai**, **quai**, and in **je sais**, **tu sais**, **il sait**, has the sound of **é**; otherwise it has the sound of **è**. As **j'ai**, *I have*; **mais**, *but*; **vrai**, *true*.

In **faisant**, *doing*, and its derivatives, it has the sound of *u* in *but*.

au, **eau** have the sound of *o* in *note*. As **autre**, *other*; **beau**, *handsome*. In **Paul**, **mauvais** (*bad*), and before **r**, an **au** has the sound of open **o**.

ei has the sound of **è**. As **reine**, *queen*.

eu, **oeu** have no equivalent in English. The sound is somewhat like that of *i* in *sir*, and is longer in some words than in others. As **feu**, *fire*; **fleur**, *flower*; **œuf**, *egg*.

In all parts of the verb **avoir**, *to have*, **eu** has the sound of **u**.

ou has the sound of *oo* in *moon*. As **jour**, *day*.

oi has nearly the sound of *wa* in *wash*. As **moi**, *me*.

In all other diphthongs the first vowel is pronounced quickly and the voice dwells on the second. As **ciel**, *heaven*; **Dieu**, *God*; **bruit**, *noise*; **oui**, *yes*: **juin**, *June*.

Consonants.

Final consonants are generally silent except **c**, **f**, **l**, **r**. Otherwise they usually have the same sound as in English.

c before **e**, **i**, **y**, or with the cedilla (**ç**) has the sound of *s*. As **ceci**, *this*; **leçon**, *lesson*; **reçu**, *received*. Otherwise it has the sound of *k*. As **car**, *for*; **col**, *neck*; **avec**, *with*.

c final is silent after **n** (as **blanc**, *white*; **franc**, *frank*), and in **accroc**, **broc**, **clerc**, **cric**, **échecs**, **escroc**, **estomac**, **lacs**, **raccroc**, **tabac**. It has the sound of hard *g* in **second** and its derivatives.

ch has the sound of *ch* in *chagrin*. As **chat**, *cat*; **chercher**, *to seek*.

ch before a consonant, and usually in words derived from the Greek, has the sound of *k*. As **yacht** (*iak*); **orchestre**, *orchestra*; **choeur**, *choir*. It is silent in **almanach**.

d final is sounded in proper names (as **David**) and in **sud**, *south*.

f final is silent in **clef** (*key*), **cerf** (*stag*), **chef-d'œuvre**; and also in the plurals **bœufs** (*oxen*), **œufs** (*eggs*), **nerfs** (*nerves*), though heard in the singulars **bœuf, œuf, nerf**. In **neuf**, *nine*, **f** is silent before a consonant, and has the sound of *v* before a vowel or *h mute*.

g before **e, i,** and **y** has the sound of *s* in *pleasure*; before **a, o,** and **u**, the sound of *g* in *gag*. As **gingembre**, *ginger*; **gage**, *pledge*. **gn** sounds like *gn* in *mignonette*. As **agneau**, *lamb*.

h is not heard in pronunciation. It is called *mute* when the final vowel of the preceding word is elided before it; and *aspirate* when no elision takes place. As **l'homme**, *the man*; **le héros**, *the hero*.

Whether the **h** is mute or aspirate can be learned only by observation and practice. The following are among the most usual words in which the **h** is aspirate. **La hache**, *the axe*; **la haie**, *the hedge*; **la haine**, *hate*; **une halle**, *a market-place*; **les hardes**, *the clothes*; **les haricots**, *the beans*; **le hasard**, *the chance*; **la hâte**, *haste*; **le haut**, *the summit*; **le héros**, *the hero* (but **l'héroïne, l'héroïsme**); **la honte**, *the shame*; **le Hâvre**, *Havre*; **la Hollande**, *Holland*; **le huit**, *the eight* (but mute in **dix-huit** and **vingt-huit**).

j has the sound of *s* in *pleasure*. As **jour**, *day*; **joli**, *pretty*.

ill, not initial, and **il**, when final, form the so-called *liquid l*, with nearly the sound of *y* in *your*. As **péril**, *peril*, **fille**, *daughter*.

Any vowel standing before the liquid *l* does not form a diphthong with the **i**, but retains its own sound; **ue** and **oe** have then the sound of **eu**. As **paille**, *straw*; **soleil**, *sun*; **feuille**, *leaf*; **orgueil**. *pride*: **œil**, *eye*.

There is no liquid sound in **il, exil, vil, fil, mil, mille, civil, profil, nil, Achille, Lille, tranquille, pupille, ville, village, distiller, vaciller, osciller**, etc.

l is silent in **baril, chenil, coutil, fils, fusil, gentil, gril, outil, persil, pouls, soûl, sourcil**.

m and **n**, if the preceding vowel is not nasal, have the same sound as in English. **m** is silent in **damner** and its compounds and in **automne.**

p is silent in **baptême, compte, corps, dompter, exempt, temps, sculpter, sept,** and their compounds. **ph** has the sound of *f*.

qu has the sound of *k*. As **qui,** *who ;* **qualité,** *quality.*

In **aquarelle, équateur, équation, loquace, quadrupède, quartz,** and a few other words **qu** has the same sound as in English. In **cinq** followed by a consonant **q** is silent.

r is articulated much more distinctly than in English. As **rue,** *street ;* **rivière,** *river.*

r final is sounded when preceded by **a, i, o, u** (as **car,** *for ;* **finir,** *to finish ;* **dur,** *hard*), in monosyllables ending in **-er** (as **fer,** *iron*), and in **amer,** *bitter ;* **cuiller,** *spoon ;* **enfer,** *hell ;* **fier,** *proud ;* **hier,** *yesterday ;* **hiver,** *winter.*

In other words final **er** is sounded like **é**. As **parler,** *to speak ;* **dernier,** *last.*

Both **r's** are distinctly sounded in the future and conditional tenses of **acquérir, courir,** and **mourir,** to distinguish them from other forms with a single **r.** As **nous courons,** *we run ;* **nous courrons,** *we shall run.* It is always silent in **monsieur.**

s between two vowels has the sound of *s* in *please.* As **voisin,** *neighbor ;* **base,** *base.*

Except in **parasol, désuétude,** and in compound words, where **s** retains the hissing sound of its simple form. As **préséance,** *precedence* , **vraisemblable,** *likely.*

Otherwise it has the sound of *s* in *sister.* As **sensation,** *sensation ;* **prisme,** *prism ;* **héroïsme,** *heroism.*

Except in **transaction, transalpin, transiger, transit, transitif, transition,** and **balsamine,** in which it has the sound of *z*.

s final is silent, except in **aloés, as, atlas, blocus, cens, chorus, dervis, en-sus, fils, florés, gratis, iris, jadis, laps, lis** (though silent in **fleur-de-lis**), **maïs, mars, mœurs, ours, rébus, Rheims, rhinoceros, sinus, sens** (usually), **tous** (when used without a noun), **vis,** and in Greek and Latin names.

In **le Christ** both **s** and **t** are pronounced, but in **Jesus-Christ** both are silent.

t usually sounds as in *tutor*. It has the hissing sound of *s* in the combinations **-tion**, **-tial**, **-tiel**, **-tieux**, and in a few words ending in **-tie**, which in English end in *-cy*. As **situation**, *situation* : **partialité**, *partiality* ; **essentiel**, *essential* ; **factieux**, *factious* ; **démocratie**, *democracy*. Also in **balbutier**, **initier**, **patience**, **ineptie**, **minutie**, and in proper names ending in **-tien** ; as **Vénitien**, *a Venetian*.

In the past tenses of verbs, or when preceded by *s*, **t** retains its hard sound. As **nous partions, question.**

th always has the sound of *t*. As **théâtre**, *theatre*.

t final is silent, except in **brut, chut, dot, déficit, est** (*east*), **fat, granit, lest, mat, net, ouest** and most words ending in **-ct**. In **sept** and **huit**, the **t** is mute only before a noun or adjective beginning with a consonant; as **dans huit jours**. In **vingt**, **t** is always mute except in the numbers 21 to 29 inclusive.

x usually has the sound of *ks*. As **boxer**, *to box*. **ex** initial and followed by a vowel or *h mute* has the sound of *gz*. As **exil**, *exile* : **examen**, *examination*.

It has the sound of *ss* in **Bruxelles, soixante, six**, and **dix** ; but the **x** of **six** and **dix** is silent before a consonant, and sounds like *z* before a vowel or *h mute*. It has the sound of *z* in **deuxième, sixième, dixième, dix-sept, dix-huit, dix-neuf.**

The Union of Words.

The last consonant of a word, standing before a word beginning with a vowel or *h mute* and closely connected with it in sense, is often carried over to it in pronunciation.

In such cases **s** and **x** have the sound of **z**, **d** that of **t**, and **c** and **g** that of **k**. As **mes amis, ils ont, aux armes, grand homme, avec elle, rang élevé.**

This union of words, called **liaison**, is necessary in public speaking or reading; in conversation it is used only when the words thus joined cannot do without each other.

Division of Syllables.

In the body of a word each syllable must if possible begin with a consonant; as **mo-ra-li-té, a-ma-bi-li-té.**

If there are two consonants the division usually takes place between the two; as **hom-me, vil-le, par-tir, en-ten-du.** But if the second is **l** or **r** (and the first is neither **l** nor **r**), or if the two are **gn**, the division takes place before the two; as **é-glise, no-tre, vi-gne.**

As **h** is never heard in pronunciation, the consonant which precedes it is always carried, in speaking, to the following vowel; as **i-nhu-main, i-nha-bi-té.**

The compound consonant **x** (=**ks** or **gz**) always goes with the preceding vowel; as **ex-il.**

Capital Letters.

In French no capital letter is used, except at the beginning of a sentence, for the names of the months and of the days of the week; as **avril, lundi**: — for any word used as an adjective; as **un officier français**: — for any word used to signify rank or position; as **empereur, roi, duc, général, cardinal, docteur, abbé, maire,** etc.

EXERCISES.

1.

There are only two genders in French, the masculine and the feminine.[1]

Before a noun masculine use **un** for *a* or *an*, use **le** for *the*.

Before a noun feminine use **une** for *a* or *an*, and **la** for *the*.

Before a vowel or *h mute* use **l'** instead of **le** or **la**.

père, *father.*	**fils**, *son.*	**eau** (f.), *water.*
mère, *mother.*	**fille**, *daughter.*	**et**, *and.*
crayon (m.), *pencil.*	**grammaire** (f.), *grammar.*	**oncle**, *uncle.*
homme, *man.*	**ardoise** (f.), *slate.*	

1. Un père, une mère. 2. Une mère et un fils. 3. Un fils et une fille. 4. Le crayon et la grammaire. 5. Le fils et la fille. 6. Le père et la mère. 7. Le père et le fils. 8. Une grammaire et un crayon. 9. L'oncle, l'homme, l'ardoise, l'eau. 10. Le crayon et l'ardoise. 11. L'oncle et la fille. 12. L'homme, le fils et la fille.

1. A mother, a daughter. 2. A father and a son. 3. A son and a mother. 4. A mother and a father. 5. The

[1] Practice, and a general Rule to be found in the Appendix, will teach the gender of inanimate objects. In the meantime pupils are recommended, when learning a French noun, carefully to acquire with it the article denoting the gender.

grammar and the pencil. 6. A pencil and a grammar. 7. The daughter and the mother. 8. The son and the father. 9. The water and the slate. 10. The man and the uncle. 11. The uncle and the son. 12. The slate and the grammar.

2.

An adjective always agrees in gender with the noun which it qualifies. To form the feminine of adjectives, add *e mute* to the masculine.

Adjectives ending with *e mute* in the masculine do not change in the feminine.

petit (m.), **petite** (f.), *little, small, short.*
grand (m.), **grande** (f.), *large, tall, great.*
bon (m.), **bonne** (f.),[1] *good.*
mauvais (m.), **mauvaise** (f.), *bad.*

riche, *rich.*	**facile**, *easy.*	**est**, *is.*
pauvre, *poor.*	**aimable**, *amiable.*	**très**, *very.*

1. Le crayon est bon, l'ardoise est mauvaise. 2. Le père est grand, la fille est petite. 3. Un bon père, une mauvaise mère. 4. Un petit crayon, une grande ardoise. 5. Le père est bon, la fille est bonne. 6. Un bon fils et une bonne fille. 7. Le mauvais fils et la mauvaise fille. 8. Le bon père et la bonne mère. 9. La mère est riche, le père est pauvre. 10. La grammaire est facile. 11. La fille est très [2] aimable. 12. L'homme est riche.

1. The bad grammar, the bad slate, the bad pencil. 2. The water is bad. 3. A good son and a good daughter. 4. The slate is good, the pencil is bad. 5. A father

[1] The doubling of the **n** in this word is an exception which is to be explained in § 54.

[2] The last consonant of the words, **est**, **très**, **bon**, **mon**, **ton**, **son**, is always sounded upon the next word if it begins with a vowel, but the **t** of **et** is never sounded.

is good, a mother is good. 6. The mother is tall, the daughter is short. 7. A good grammar, a good pencil, a good slate. 8. The uncle is very rich, the father is very poor. 9. The son is amiable. 10. The man is rich. 11. The grammar is easy. 12. The son is bad, the daughter is very amiable.

3.

The possessive adjective *his, her, its*, always agrees in French with the thing possessed, and not, as in English, with the possessor. Whoever be the possessor, we put **son** before a masculine noun, and **sa** before a feminine. Therefore, before a masculine noun singular, use **mon, ton, son**; before a feminine noun singular, use **ma, ta, sa.**

son (m.), **sa** (f.), *his, her, its.*
mon (m.), **ma** (f.), *my.* **ton** (m.), **ta** (f.), *thy.*
a, *has.* **mais**, *but.* **aussi**, *also.*
perdu, *lost.* **vu**, *seen.* **plume** (f.), *pen.*

1. Mon oncle a vu son fils et sa fille. 2. Ma fille a perdu son crayon et sa grammaire. 3. Ta fille a aussi perdu son crayon. 4. Mon fils a perdu sa petite grammaire. 5. Son crayon est mauvais. 6. Sa petite ardoise est bonne. 7. Mon père est grand, mais ma mère est petite. 8. Ma mère est une bonne mère. 9. Ta fille est une bonne fille. 10. Ton père est un bon père. 11. Ton fils a une bonne grammaire. 12. Mon oncle a aussi une bonne grammaire. 13. Ton fils a un mauvais crayon et une mauvaise ardoise.

1. His mother is good. 2. Her son is good. 3. His daughter is tall, but his father is short. 4. Thy daugh-

ter has lost her pencil, her grammar, and also her large slate. 5. The man has seen his son and his daughter. 6. My uncle has seen thy father and thy daughter. 7. My son has a good pen. 8. My father, my mother, thy daughter, thy son. 9. My son has a good grammar. 10. My mother is poor, my uncle is rich. 11. My mother is a good mother. 12. My son is also a good son.

4.

The **e** of **je** is suppressed when the following verb begins with a vowel, and an apostrophe takes its place.

When the verb is interrogative, it is connected with the following pronoun by a hyphen.

je, *I.*	**ai**, *have.*	**j'ai**, *I have.*	**ai-je?** *have I?*
tu, *thou.*	**as**, *hast.*	**tu as**, *thou hast.*	**as-tu?** *hast thou?*

notre (m. and f.), *our.*	**votre** (m. and f.), *your.*
leur (m. and f.), *their.*	**difficile**, *difficult.*
exercice (m.), **thème** (m.) } *exercise.*	**le frère**, *the brother.*
	la sœur, *the sister.*

1. J'ai perdu votre crayon. 2. As-tu aussi perdu ma grammaire? 3. Tu as un bon frère et une bonne sœur. 4. As-tu une bonne mère? 5. J'ai un bon père et une bonne mère. 6. J'ai perdu une grammaire, une ardoise et un crayon. 7. As-tu aussi perdu ton exercice? 8. J'ai aussi perdu mon exercice. 9. Notre exercice est difficile. 10. Votre grammaire est facile. 11. Leur père est riche, mais leur oncle est pauvre. 12. Votre mère est une bonne mère. 13. Sa fille a vu notre oncle. 14. Leur sœur a une mauvaise grammaire.

1. Hast thou seen my little sister? 2. I have seen thy little sister and thy little brother. 3. Your sister has a

very good daughter. 4. Hast thou lost thy grammar? 5. I have lost my grammar, my exercise, and my pencil. 6. Hast thou seen my father? 7. I have seen your father, your sister, and also your uncle. 8. Our grammar is very easy. 9. Your exercise is very difficult. 10. Their son has a large slate. 11. Our uncle is rich, but our father is very poor. 12. My father has seen your mother. 13. Our daughter has a bad grammar.

5.

il, *he.*	**a**, *has.*	**il a**, *he has.*	**a-t-il?**[1] *has he?*
elle, *she.*	**a**, *has.*	**elle a**, *she has.*	**a-t-elle?**[1] *has she?*

la maison, *the house.*	**la tante**, *the aunt.*
le jardin, *the garden.*	**trouvé**, *found.*
le couteau, *the knife.*	**acheté**, *bought.*

1. J'ai acheté une maison et un jardin. 2. As-tu acheté une grande maison? 3. La maison est petite, mais le jardin est grand. 4. Mon frère a aussi acheté une maison. 5. A-t-il aussi acheté un jardin? 6. A-t-elle vu ma tante? 7. As-tu trouvé mon couteau? 8. Ta sœur a perdu mon crayon, mais elle a trouvé un petit couteau. 9. Tu as acheté une mauvaise grammaire. 10. Votre frère a un mauvais crayon. 11. Notre fils a aussi un mauvais crayon. 12. Leur maison est très grande.

1. He has lost his pen. 2. Has he seen my little sister? 3. He has seen thy little sister and thy little brother. 4. Your aunt has bought a house. 5. Has she bought a large house? 6. Have I seen your house? 7. Has she seen my garden? 8. Hast thou seen our garden and our house? 9. He has found their knife. 10. She has also

[1] The t placed between the verb and the pronoun does not belong to the verb, and its use is explained in § 53, 4.

found her knife. 11. Their uncle has a very good son and a very good daughter. 12. Hast thou a good sister and a good brother? 13. His sister has a large house.

6.

(1) When the nominative *it* stands for a masculine noun (such as **crayon**), translate it by **il**; when it stands for a feminine noun (such as **maison**), translate it by **elle**.

(2) The auxiliary verb *to do* does not exist in French and, in translation, you must change *did I* into *have I; did he* into *has he; did she* into *has she; did you* into *have you*, etc.

	la lettre, *the letter.*	**pris,** *taken.*
	le portrait, *the portrait.*	**où,** *where.*
	écrit, *written.*	**quand,** *when.*
nous, *we.*	**nous avons,** *we have.*	**avons-nous?** *have we?* or *did we?*
vous, *you.*	**vous avez,** *you have.*	**avez-vous?** *have you?* or *did you?*
	le livre, *the book.*	**la canne,** *the cane.*

1. J'ai vu sa maison, elle est très grande. 2. Quand[1] a-t-elle pris votre couteau? 3. Où as-tu acheté ta grammaire? 4. J'ai écrit mon exercice, il est très difficile. 5. Où ai-je perdu son couteau? 6. Où a-t-elle vu son oncle? 7. Avez-vous vu mon portrait? 8. Nous avons vu votre portrait, il est très bon. 9. Quand avez-vous vu ma mère? 10. Vous avez pris notre livre. 11. Votre sœur a trouvé leur lettre. 12. Où as-tu perdu mon livre?

1. When did he buy his garden? 2. Where did she lose her portrait? 3. When did I see your daughter? 4. I have seen your letter, it is very good. 5. She has written

[1] A **d** placed at the end of a word must be sounded like **a t** when the next word begins with a vowel.

a short letter. 6. Did I take their pen? 7. Has she lost her knife? 8. Where didst thou see my father? 9. Did you lose her book? 10. Have we taken their grammar? 11. I have seen his letter, it is very short. 12. Did you take my good pen? 13. Where did we lose their letter?

7.

The Possessive Case.

(1) The sign *'s* denoting possession is not used in French. Turn therefore *my brother's book, their aunt's garden*, and all such expressions, into *the book of my brother, the garden of their aunt*, etc.

(2) The prepositions **de** and **à** are repeated before each noun.

de, *of* or *from*. **à**,[1] *to* or *at*. **reçu**, *received*.
le mouchoir, *the pocket-handkerchief*.

1. Quand avez-vous perdu le livre de ma fille? 2. Nous avons écrit à notre tante et à notre oncle. 3. J'ai reçu une lettre de ma sœur. 4. Avez-vous écrit à la mère de votre oncle? 5. J'ai perdu le couteau de mon frère et le mouchoir de ma sœur. 6. L'exercice de mon frère est très difficile. 7. J'ai acheté la maison de votre frère. 8. Avez-vous vu le petit couteau de ma sœur? 9. Nous avons reçu une lettre de notre oncle et de notre tante. 10. Quand avez-vous écrit à votre sœur? 11. J'ai vu votre portrait, il est très bon.

1. Where is my mother's book? 2. Where did you lose your sister's knife? 3. My uncle's house is very large. 4. We have bought your aunt's garden. 5. She

[1] The preposition **à** is accented simply to be distinguished in writing from the verb **a**, but the pronunciation is the same.

has written to her father and to her mother. 6. I have received a letter from your father and from your mother. 7. She has lost her brother's grammar. 8. Where did you find my daughter's pencil? 9. We have bought our aunt's portrait. 10. Did she lose her mother's handkerchief? 11. We have seen your exercise, it is bad. 12. Where did she lose her knife?

8.

Qui, *who*, *which*, *that*, is nominative.

Que, *whom*, *which*, *that*, is accusative (or objective).

In other words, when the relative pronoun *which* or *that* is next the verb in English, translate it by **qui**. When it is separated from the verb by one or several words, translate it by **que**.

joli, *pretty.*	**utile**, *useful.*
haut, *high.*	**jeune**, *young.*
pour, *for.*	**dans**, *in.*

1. Nous avons vu une maison qui est très haute. 2. Le livre que vous avez acheté est très utile. 3. L'homme que nous avons vu dans le jardin est très jeune. 4. Elle a acheté pour sa tante une maison qui est très jolie. 5. J'ai trouvé une plume qui est très mauvaise. 6. Nous avons vu le jardin que votre père a acheté, il est très grand. 7. Le livre qu'il[1] a perdu est mon livre. 8. Avez-vous vu le jeune homme qui a acheté la canne de mon frère? 9. Avez-vous perdu le couteau que vous avez acheté pour mon fils? 10. Avez-vous vu le portrait qu'il a acheté?

1. We have bought the garden which you have seen. 2. Your brother has a grammar which is very useful.

[1] The **e** of **que** is always elided before a vowel or *h mute*, but the **i** of **qui** can never be suppressed.

3. The man whom you have seen in my father's garden is very tall. 4. You have an aunt who is very amiable. 5. Where did you see the knife which he has bought? 6. The garden which she has bought is very large. 7. She has written an exercise which is very difficult. 8. My uncle, whom you have seen in the garden, is very rich. 9. Did you take the small knife which I have bought for your brother? 10. I have taken a small knife which I have found in the garden.

9.

(1) Nouns form their plural, as in English, by adding **s** to the singular.

(2) Before all plural nouns use **les** for *the*.

SINGULAR.	PLURAL.
le frère, *the brother.*	**les frères**,[1] *the brothers.*
la sœur, *the sister.*	**les sœurs**, *the sisters.*
l'oncle, *the uncle.*	**les oncles**, *the uncles.*
la table, *the table.*	**mis**, *put.*
le fauteuil, *the arm-chair.*	**sur**, *on* or *upon.*

1. Notre oncle a vu la maison et les jardins. 2. Leur tante a aussi vu les jardins. 3. J'ai vu la table et le fauteuil. 4. J'ai vu les tables et les fauteuils. 5. Nous avons mis les livres sur votre table. 6. Où avez-vous vu les plumes de mon père. 7. J'ai vu le crayon, l'ardoise et les plumes de votre sœur. 8. Nous avons acheté les portraits que vous avez mis sur la table. 9. Avez-

[1] As the **s** put at the end of a plural noun is not sounded in French, the only way we have to show that a noun is singular or plural is the proper pronunciation of the preceding article. Pupils must therefore accustom themselves at once to pronounce **les**, and also **mes, tes, ses**, etc., long, as if they were written with a grave accent, **lès, mès, tès. sès.**

vous reçu les lettres? 10. Nous avons reçu les lettres et les portraits.

1. Where have you seen my sister's books? 2. I have lost my brother's pencils. 3. Did you also lose your sister's pens? 4. We have seen the house and the gardens. 5. Has he written his brother's exercises? 6. Where did you put the letters? 7. I have put the letters on the arm-chair. 8. Has she seen the portraits which I have put on her table? 9. We have seen my daughter's exercises. 10. She has lost her brother's pencil and pens. 11. Where and when did you buy your grammar?

10.

(1) An adjective always agrees in number (as well as in gender) with the noun which it qualifies.

(2) Adjectives form their plural, like nouns, by adding **s** to the singular.

SINGULAR.	PLURAL.
petit (m.).	**petits** (m.).
petite (f.).	**petites** (f.).
bon (m.).	**bons** (m.).
bonne (f.).	**bonnes** (f.).
méchant (m.), *naughty*.	**méchants** (m.).
méchante (f.).	**méchantes** (f.).
aimable (m. and f.).	**aimables** (m. and f.).

l'enfant, *the child*.
l'ami, *the friend*.
ils sont (m.), *they are*.
elles sont (f.), *they are*.
la chambre, *the room*.
la montre, *the watch*.
ils ont (m.), *they have*.
elles ont (f.), *they have*.

1. Les enfants de votre frère sont très aimables. 2. Les amis de mon oncle sont très riches. 3. Les

montres de notre oncle et de notre tante sont jolies. 4. Avez-vous vu les fils et les filles de notre ami? 5. Les fils sont aimables, mais les filles sont méchantes. 6. J'ai vu dans le jardin les enfants de votre frère, ils sont très jeunes. 7. Les mouchoirs que ma sœur a mis sur la table sont très jolis. 8. Avez-vous vu les petites cannes de mon frère? 9. Les enfants de ma sœur sont très aimables. 10. Les fils de ma sœur sont petits, mais les filles sont grandes.

1. You have taken the little books. 2. Did you see my uncle's little children? 3. My brother's pencils are good, my sister's pens are bad. 4. My friends' rooms are very large. 5. My father's houses are small. 6. We have seen your uncle's daughters, they are very pretty and very amiable. 7. Where did you see our friend's children? 8. Are they tall? 9. Are they pretty? 10. You have seen my son's exercises; are they good?

11.

(1) An adjective qualifying two or more nouns masculine, must be masculine plural.

(2) An adjective qualifying two or more nouns feminine, must be feminine plural.

(3) An adjective qualifying two or more nouns of different genders, must be masculine plural.

parlé, *spoken*. **souvent**, *often*.

1. Le père et le fils sont grands. 2. La mère et la fille sont grandes. 3. L'oncle et la tante sont petits. 4. J'ai vu votre fils et votre fille dans le jardin de ma tante, ils sont très jolis et très aimables. 5. Nous avons vu les

tables et les fauteuils de votre oncle, ils sont très hauts. 6. Où avez-vous vu les plumes de ma sœur ? 7. J'ai vu les plumes et les crayons de votre sœur sur la table, ils sont très bons. 8. Nous avons parlé à la mère, à la tante et à la fille, elles sont très bonnes et très aimables. 9. J'ai souvent vu le fils et la fille de votre oncle. 10. Sont-ils très jolis ? 11. Ils sont très jeunes et très jolis.

1. The daughter, the mother, and the aunt are very amiable. 2. The son, the father, and the uncle are very good. 3. We have often spoken to your uncle and (to) your aunt; they are young and amiable. 4. Are they rich ? 5. They are very poor. 6. I have seen your friend's arm-chairs and tables; they are pretty, but very high. 7. Your daughter's pens and pencils are good. 8. Did you often speak to your friend's aunt and mother? 9. Are they poor ? 10. They are poor, but amiable. 11. When did you see her book ?

12.

(1) The past participle of a verb[1] coming after any forms of *to be* agrees in gender and number, like all adjectives, with the subject.

(2) The following ten past participles are always used in French with *to be :* —

allé, *gone.*
sorti, *gone out.*
parti, *gone away, departed, set out, left.*
venu, *come.*
revenu, *come back, returned.*
devenu, *become.*
arrivé, *arrived.*
entré, *entered, come in.*
resté, *remained, stayed.*
tombé, *fallen.*

[1] See § 57 for the definition of a past participle.

Before any plural noun use **mes** for *my* : **tes** for *thy* ; **ses** for *his*, *her*, *its* ; **nos** for *our* ; **vos** for *your* ; **leurs** for *their*.

1. Où sont-elles allées ? 2. Mes frères sont sortis. 3. Leurs sœurs sont parties. 4. Nous avons vu votre oncle, ses fils sont venus. 5. Tes filles sont revenues. 6. Nos tantes sont entrées dans la maison. 7. Elles sont devenues très pauvres. 8. Sont-ils restés dans la maison ? 9. Les lettres sont arrivées. 10. Ma sœur est tombée dans le jardin. 11. Vos frères et vos sœurs sont revenus. 12. Nous avons acheté leur maison et leurs jardins.

1. I have seen thy sisters in the garden, they are arrived. 2. My uncles have become rich. 3. Has she come also ? 4. Our brothers are gone out. 5. My sisters have remained in the garden. 6. They are departed. 7. Have you seen my sons and my daughters ? they have become very tall. 8. Her exercises are difficult. 9. My sisters have fallen. 10. Where did they fall ? 11. Your brothers have entered (in) the house. 12. Their rooms are very large.

13.

Before a masculine noun singular beginning with a consonant, use **du** for *of the* or *from the* ; **au** for *to the* or *at the*.

le frère, *the brother.*
du frère, *of* or *from the brother.*
au frère, *to the brother.*

le professeur, *the professor.*
le médecin, *the doctor.*
le prince, *the prince.*
le cadeau, *the present.*
vendu, *sold.*
prêté, *lent.*
donné, *given.*

1. J'ai donné mes livres au frère du médecin. 2. Nous avons vendu notre maison à l'oncle du professeur. 3. Le jardin du prince est très grand. 4. Ma fille a reçu un cadeau de la tante du médecin. 5. Avez-vous parlé au prince ? 6. Elle a prêté sa grammaire au fils du professeur. 7. A-t-elle reçu une lettre du prince ? 8. A-t-il vendu ses livres au médecin ? 9. J'ai prêté ma canne au professeur. 10. Nous avons vendu nos maisons et nos jardins au fils du prince. 11. Nos enfants sont partis, mais vos sœurs sont restées.

1. The father, of the father, to the father. 2. The prince, of the prince, to the prince. 3. The garden, of the garden, to the garden. 4. The present, of the present, to the present. 5. The arm-chair, of the arm-chair, to the arm-chair. 6. My brother has lent his handkerchief to the doctor's son. 7. We have sold our house to the professor's brother. 8. Has she given her books, her pens, and her pencils, to the prince's son ? 9. He has received a present from the professor. 10. My brothers have written to the prince. 11. Did you speak to the prince's father ? 12. She has given a book to the doctor. 13. The son and the daughter of the prince have arrived. 14. The doctor's house is very small. 15. Did you receive a letter from the professor ? 16. Our daughters have become tall. 17. Your friends have arrived.

14.

Before a feminine noun singular beginning with a consonant, use **de la** for *of the* or *from the ;* **à la** for *to the* or *at the.*

la sœur, *the sister.*
de la sœur, *of* or *from the sister.*
à la sœur, *to the sister.*

la modiste, *the milliner.*	**offert,** *offered.*
la bonne, *the maid-servant.*	**accepté,** *accepted.*
la princesse, *the princess.*	**appartient,** *belongs.*

1. Nous avons offert notre maison au prince et à la princesse. 2. Avez-vous accepté un cadeau de la fille de votre oncle ? 3. Le petit livre que vous avez vu appartient au frère de la bonne. 4. J'ai vendu mon jardin à la modiste. 5. Avez-vous reçu une lettre de l'oncle de la princesse ? 6. Elle a parlé à la tante du prince. 7. A-t-il prêté sa canne au fils de la modiste ? 8. J'ai donné ma grammaire à la fille du médecin. 9. Elles ont vendu leur maison à la tante du professeur. 10. Avez-vous offert un fauteuil à la fille du prince ?

1. The mother, of the mother, to the mother. 2. The daughter, of the daughter, to the daughter. 3. The maid-servant, of the maid-servant, to the maid-servant. 4. The princess, of the princess, to the princess. 5. Of the father, of the mother. 6. To the father, to the mother. 7. The table, the arm-chair. 8. Of the table, of the arm-chair. 9. To the table, to the arm-chair. 10. The uncle of the prince and of the princess has departed. 11. I have lent my books to the son and to the daughter of the milliner. 12. The pencil belongs to the professor's daughter. 13. Have you given your knife to the maid-servant ? 14. Has she received a letter from the milliner ? 15. They have sold their house to the princess. 16. He has often spoken to the maid-servant's father.

15.

Before all singular nouns, whether masculine or feminine, beginning with a vowel or *h mute*, use **de l'** for *of the* or *from the* ; **à l'** for *to the* or *at the.*

l'enfant, *the child.*
de l'enfant, *of* or *from the child.*
à l'enfant, *to the child.*

l'omnibus (m.), *the omnibus.*
l'orange (f.), *the orange.*
l'arbre (m.), *the tree.*
la fleur, *the flower.*
le chien, *the dog.*
le chat, *the cat.*

1. Le livre que vous avez trouvé appartient à l'oncle du prince. 2. Avez-vous vu l'arbre que j'ai vendu à votre père? 3. J'ai donné mes fleurs à l'enfant. 4. Où ont-ils vu le petit chien et le petit chat de l'enfant? 5. Elle a offert une orange à l'ami de mon oncle. 6. J'ai donné mes fleurs à l'homme qui a trouvé votre livre. 7. Il a donné son petit chien à l'enfant du prince. 8. J'ai vu votre frère dans l'omnibus. 9. Où ont-ils vu les plumes de l'enfant? 10. J'ai offert un livre au jeune homme qui a trouvé votre montre.

1. The water, of the water, to the water. 2. The tree, of the tree, to the tree. 3. The child, the pen, the knife. 4. Of the child, of the pen, of the knife. 5. To the child, to the pen, to the knife. 6. The present, the flower, the exercise. 7. Of the present, of the flower, of the exercise. 8. To the present, to the flower, to the exercise. 9. The professor, the princess, the man. 10. Of the professor, of the princess, of the man. 11. To the professor, to the princess, to the man. 12. The child's knife is bad. 13. Did you write to the man who has taken your dog? 14. When did they offer a present to the doctor's uncle? 15. Your brother has come in the omnibus. 16. I have given my kitten (little cat) to the milliner's child. 17. Did you see the tree which he has sold to my father?

16.

Before all plural nouns, use **des** for *of the* or *from the*; **aux** for *to the* or *at the.*

les frères, *the brothers.*	**les sœurs,** *the sisters.*
des frères, *of the brothers.*	**des sœurs,** *of the sisters.*
aux frères, *to the brothers.*	**aux sœurs,** *to the sisters.*

les enfants, *the children.*
des enfants, *of the children.*
aux enfants, *to the children.*

l'avocat, *the lawyer.*	**le ministre,** *the minister.*
le propriétaire, *the landlord.*	**le prêtre,** *the priest.*

1. Nous avons écrit aux sœurs du propriétaire. 2. Elles ont reçu une lettre des sœurs de l'avocat. 3. Avez-vous offert vos fleurs à la fille du ministre? 4. Le grand jardin que vous avez vu appartient aux fils de l'avocat. 5. Avez-vous donné vos plumes aux frères du prêtre? 6. A-t-elle écrit aux filles du médecin? 7. A-t-il reçu une lettre des fils du propriétaire? 8. La grande maison appartient au ministre. 9. Elle a parlé aux enfants du prince. 10. Il a écrit aux amis de son oncle.

1. The doctors, of the doctors, to the doctors. 2. The lawyer, of the lawyer, to the lawyer. 3. The lawyers, of the lawyers, to the lawyers. 4. The son, the daughter; of the son, of the daughter; to the son, to the daughter. 5. The sons, the daughters; of the sons, of the daughters; to the sons, to the daughters. 6. The tree, the trees; of the tree, of the trees; to the tree, to the trees. 7. The house, the houses; of the house, of the houses; to the house, to the houses. 8. The dog, the dogs; of the dog, of the dogs; to the dog, to the dogs. 9. The friend, the friends; of the friend, of the friends; to the

friend, to the friends. 10. The letter, the letters; of the letter, of the letters; to the letter, to the letters. 11. We have given our books and our pens to the children of the landlord. 12. They have written to the minister's sons and daughters. 13. Have you accepted a present from the maid-servant's sisters? 14. The small garden which you have seen belongs to the lawyer's brothers. 15. Did you speak to your uncle's men?

17.

(1) The comparative is formed by putting **plus,** *more*, or **moins,** *less*, before an adjective. We therefore say in French *more large*, *more small*, *more high*, etc. (instead of *larger*, *smaller*, *higher*), and *less large*, *less small*, *less high*.

(2) By exception we say **meilleur** (*better*) instead of **plus bon**.

plus, *more.*	**que**, *than, as.*
moins, *less.*	**peut-être**, *perhaps.*

1. Mon frère est plus petit que votre sœur. 2. Ma tante est plus riche que vous. 3. Votre fille est plus petite que mon fils. 4. La chambre de mon père est plus grande que leur maison. 5. Un médecin est plus utile qu'un avocat. 6. Vos filles sont très aimables, elles sont plus aimables que mes sœurs. 7. Mon crayon est peut-être meilleur que votre plume. 8. Mon frère est moins jeune que votre oncle. 9. J'ai vu vos sœurs dans le jardin, elles sont plus jolies que les filles du propriétaire. 10. Leurs arbres sont plus hauts que votre maison.

1. The dog is more useful than the cat. 2. She is younger than you. 3. The doctor's daughter is prettier

than the princess. 4. Your house is perhaps smaller than my room. 5. Their brothers are very rich, they are richer than we. 6. My daughter is taller than your sister. 7. Did you see their sisters? they are prettier than my daughter. 8. A lawyer is less useful than a doctor. 9. Your house is higher than our trees. 10. His aunt is richer than your landlord. 11. Did you offer my flowers to the minister's daughter? 12. Your children have arrived and are in the garden. 13. My sisters have become very poor. 14. Have you accepted the gift of the princesses?

18.

Pronouns, in French, must agree in gender and number with the nouns for which they stand.

In the sentence: *My pencil is larger than hers*, **mon crayon est plus grand que le sien**, the pronoun **le sien** must be masculine singular, because **crayon**, the noun which it represents, is masculine singular. In the sentence: *My watch is larger than thine*, **ma montre est plus grande que la tienne**, the pronoun **la tienne** must be feminine singular, because the noun **montre**, for which it stands, is feminine singular.

MASCULINE SINGULAR.	FEMININE SINGULAR.	
le mien,	**la mienne,**	*mine.*
le tien,	**la tienne,**	*thine.*
le sien,	**la sienne,**	*his, hers, its.*
le nôtre,	**la nôtre,**	*ours.*
le vôtre,	**la vôtre,**	*yours.*
le leur,	**la leur,**	*theirs.*

MASCULINE PLURAL.	FEMININE PLURAL.	
les miens,	**les miennes,**	*mine.*
les tiens,	**les tiennes,**	*thine.*
les siens,	**les siennes,**	*his, her, its.*
les nôtres,	**les nôtres,**	*ours.*
les vôtres,	**les vôtres,**	*yours.*
les leurs,	**les leurs,**	*theirs.*

Louis, *Louis*. **Louise**, *Louisa*.
Jean, *John*. **Jeanne**, *Jane*.

1. La chambre de mon frère est plus grande que la mienne, mais la mienne est plus jolie que la sienne. 2. Votre maison est plus haute que la leur. 3. Leur table est plus petite que la vôtre. 4. Mon frère a une fleur qui est plus jolie que la tienne. 5. Votre plume est meilleure que la mienne, mais mon crayon est meilleur que le vôtre. 6. Avez-vous vu le portrait de ma sœur? le vôtre est meilleur que le sien. 7. Louise a pris mes plumes et les tiennes. 8. Jean a perdu les siennes. 9. Les fleurs de Jeanne sont plus jolies que les vôtres. 10. Le cadeau que vous avez reçu est plus joli que le mien. 11. Vos plumes sont bonnes, mais les miennes et les siennes sont meilleures que les vôtres. 12. Votre maison est plus haute que la nôtre et que la leur.

1. Her father is richer than ours. 2. His[1] aunt is richer than mine. 3. My watch is larger than his. 4. My son has given his book to his sister, who has lost hers. 5. Did you find a dog? 6. They have lost theirs. 7. My garden is larger than yours, but your house is larger than mine. 8. The lawyer's daughters are taller than yours. 9. John has sold his watch, which is larger than mine. 10. Jane has lost hers. 11. I have lost your letters and his in the landlord's garden. 12. My books are more useful than theirs. 13. Your pencils are better than ours, but our pens are better than yours.

[1] *His* is sometimes an adjective, sometimes a pronoun. When it comes before a noun, it is an adjective and translated by **son, sa, ses**, as HIS *book* or HIS *small books*. When it is used instead of a noun, it is a pronoun and is translated by **le sien, la sienne, les siens, les siennes.**

19.

This or *that* placed before a noun (as *this* or *that book*) or before an adjective followed by its noun (as *this* or *that excellent book*) is an adjective, and must be translated by

ce, before a masculine noun or adjective beginning with a consonant;

cet, before a masculine noun or adjective beginning with a vowel or *h mute;*

cette, before any feminine noun or adjective.

ce livre, *this* or *that book.*
cet hôtel, *this* or *that hotel.*
cette table, *this* or *that table.*
cet excellent livre, *this* or *that excellent book.*
ce petit hôtel, *this* or *that little hotel.*
cette eau, *this* or *that water.*

These or *those* placed before a noun, or before an adjective followed by its noun, is an adjective, and must be translated by **ces** before all nouns or adjectives.

ces livres, *these* or *those books.*
ces hôtels, *these* or *those hotels.*
ces tables, *these* or *those tables.*
ces excellents livres, *these* or *those excellent books.*
ces petits hôtels, *these* or *those small hotels.*
ces jolies tables, *these* or *those pretty tables.*

la porte, *the door.*
la fenêtre, *the window.*
ouvert, *opened.*
fermé, *shut.*

appartiennent, *belong* (3d person plural).

1. Quand avez-vous acheté cette table? 2. Ce prince a perdu sa mère. 3. Cette eau est très bonne. 4. J'ai vendu à leur père ce jardin et cette maison. 5. Avez-vous vu la maison de cet avocat? 6. Avez-vous donné une orange à cet enfant? 7. Cette orange est plus petite

que la vôtre, mais elle est meilleure. 8. Avez-vous fermé cette porte et ces fenêtres ? 9. Où ont-ils mis ces fleurs et ces oranges ? 10. Ces arbres sont plus hauts que les nôtres. 11. J'ai offert un cadeau à ces jolis petits enfants. 12. Jeanne a acheté ces tables et ces fauteuils.

1. This child has lost his father and his mother. 2. That cat is prettier than ours. 3. When did you buy that large house ? 4. That exercise is difficult. 5. That short exercise is very difficult. 6. That man has departed. 7. That tree is higher than theirs. 8. Did you see that prince's daughter ? 9. Did you receive those books from the lawyer ? 10. That house and those gardens belong to my sister. 11. The landlord's uncle has given those trees to my brother. 12. Did you open these doors and these windows ? 13. These flowers are prettier than his.

20.

When *this* or *that*, instead of being placed *before* a noun, stands *instead* of a noun, it is a pronoun,[1] and is translated by **celui,** masculine, or **celle,** feminine.

gai, *cheerful, merry.* **encore,** *still, yet, again.*

1. Votre chambre est plus grande que celle de Louis. 2. Celle de Jean est plus gaie que la mienne. 3. Cet hôtel est plus riche que celui de mon oncle. 4. Avez-vous vu celui (*the one*) que notre propriétaire a acheté? 5. J'ai offert à Jean mon portrait et celui de Louise. 6. La montre de Jean est plus petite que la mienne, mais celle

[1] A pronoun is a word standing for a noun before mentioned, to avoid its repetition. Observe that this distinction between *this*, *that*, *these*, *those*, when adjectives and when pronouns, is of the greatest importance, and, if studied well by the pupil, will save him much trouble afterwards.

de ma sœur est encore plus petite. 7. Notre jardin est plus grand que celui de l'avocat. 8. Ce chien appartient à mon frère, mais celui que vous avez vu dans notre jardin appartient au professeur. 9. Votre fenêtre est plus haute que celle de mon frère, mais celle de mon oncle est encore plus haute. 10. Ces hommes sont restés dans la maison. 11. Les sœurs de Louis sont plus jolies que les vôtres, mais les vôtres sont plus aimables.

1. The dog which you have given to my aunt is very little, but that of John is still smaller. 2. This tree is very high, it is higher than the landlord's (*than that of the landlord*). 3. Your house is larger than my aunt's (*than that of my aunt*). 4. His watch is bad, but John's is still worse. 5. This table is pretty, but my mother's is still prettier. 6. Their son is taller than the lawyer's. 7. Jane's book is more useful than Louisa's. 8. The knife which you have found in your father's garden is better than my brother's. 9. Your brother has arrived, but Louisa's has departed. 10. These doctors have arrived and have found these pencils. 11. Did they write those letters to their children? 12. Where did you buy that book and that pen?

21.

When *these* or *those*, instead of being placed *before* a noun, stands *instead* of a noun, it is a pronoun, and is translated by the masculine **ceux**, or the feminine **celles**.

la bottine, *the boot.*	**la pomme**, *the apple.*
la robe, *the dress.*	**apportez-moi**, *bring me.*
le soulier, *the shoe.*	**donnez-moi**, *give me.*
le gant, *the glove.*	**montrez-nous**, *show us.*

1. Donnez-moi mes bottines et celles de Jean. 2. Apportez-moi aussi celles de mon frère. 3. Où avez-vous vu mes gants et ceux de Louise ? 4. J'ai vu les vôtres sur la table, et ceux de Louise dans la chambre de sa mère. 5. Montrez-nous ces petites fleurs, elles sont plus jolies que celles de ma tante. 6. Vos souliers sont plus grands que ceux de Jean. 7. Ces pommes sont plus petites que celles du propriétaire, mais elles sont meilleures. 8. Les robes de ma sœur sont plus grandes que celles de Jeanne. 9. Apportez-moi mes gants et ceux de mon frère.

1. These windows are higher than those of your hotel. 2. Did they sell your flowers and your mother's (*those of your mother*) ? 3. Bring me your boots and your father's. 4. These rooms are more cheerful than those of your house. 5. She has received that watch from the prince, and those gloves from the princess. 6. Bring me the flowers which you have, and those which are in my room. 7. Show us your portrait and your aunt's. 8. He has given to the doctor's daughter your apples, mine, and those of your sister Louisa. 9. Give me your stick and John's. 10. Your boots have fallen on this table. 11. These children have lost their father and mother and have become very poor. 12. That table is higher than mine. 13. My aunt has opened those small rooms.

22.

un, une, *one.*	**cinq,**[1] *five.*	**neuf,** *nine.*
deux, *two.*	**six,** *six.*	**dix,** *ten.*
trois, *three.*	**sept,** *seven.*	**onze,** *eleven.*
quatre, *four.*	**huit,** *eight.*	**douze,** *twelve.*

[1] In the six numbers **cinq, six, sept, huit, neuf, dix,** the final consonant is mute when the noun or adjective following them begins with a consonant

treize, *thirteen.* **seize,** *sixteen.* **dix-neuf,** *nineteen.*
quatorze, *fourteen.* **dix-sept,** *seventeen.* **vingt,** *twenty.*
quinze, *fifteen.* **dix-huit,** *eighteen.*

le franc, *the franc* (about 18 cents).
la chaise, *the chair.*
il y a, { *there is.* / *there are.* }

un an, *one year* or *a year.* **une semaine,** *one week* or *a week.*
un mois, *one month* or *a month.* **un jour,** *one day* or *a day.*
font, *make* (3d pers. plur. of the pres. indic.).

1. Il y a trois crayons et treize plumes sur cette table. 2. Cet homme a sept enfants, deux fils, et cinq filles. 3. Louise a reçu dix lettres de ses frères, de ses sœurs, et de ses oncles. 4. Nous avons trouvé dix-neuf pommes dans le jardin. 5. Il y a dans cette chambre six chaises, deux fauteuils, et une table. 6. Ses cinq frères sont revenus de Paris. 7. Douze mois font un an. 8. Donnez-moi dix-huit francs. 9. Elle a vu onze chaises et trois fauteuils dans votre chambre. 10. J'ai reçu seize lettres cette semaine. 11. Il y a quinze arbres dans ce jardin. 12. Apportez-moi les douze mouchoirs que vous avez mis sur ma table.

1. I have found three pens on your table. 2. Where did you find those eighteen francs? 3. There are six large trees in our garden. 4. They have received nine letters from their uncles, (from) their aunts, and (from) their mother. 5. Give me five francs for your brother. 6. There are in this house seven doors and sixteen windows. 7. We have in our room one arm-chair, five chairs, and one table. 8. My four brothers have gone to Paris. 9. There are eleven trees in my father's garden.

or an aspirate *h*, as in **cinq fenêtres, cinq grandes fenêtres, cinq hautes fenêtres.** In all other cases that final consonant is sounded, as in **cinq** alone or placed at the end of a clause: as **cinq enfants, cinq aimables personnes, j'en ai vu cinq qui sont très aimables.**

10. We have found fifteen pencils, seventeen pens, and thirteen books in your room. 11. Bring me nineteen francs. 12. The year has twelve months. 13. Seven days make a week.

23.

(1) The conjunction *and* is often introduced in an English number (two hundred *and* thirty-five, four hundred *and* twenty, etc.), but in French the conjunction **et** is used only in the six following numbers: 21 (**vingt-et-un**). 31, 41, 51, 61, 71.

(2) Hyphens connect the different parts of any French number from 17 to 99, either when that number is alone (**trente-sept**) or when it is part of a larger number (**deux cent trente-sept**).

(3) Neither *a* nor *one* are expressed before **cent** (a hundred) or **mille** (a thousand).

vingt, *twenty*.
vingt-et-un,[1] *twenty-one*.
vingt-deux, *twenty-two*.
vingt-trois, etc., *twenty-three*, etc.
trente, *thirty*.
trente-et-un, *thirty-one*.
trente-deux, *thirty-two*.
trente-trois, etc., *thirty-three*, etc.
quarante, *forty*.
quarante-et-un, *forty-one*.
quarante-deux, *forty-two*.
cinquante, *fifty*.
cinquante-et-un, *fifty-one*.
cinquante-deux, *fifty-two*.
soixante, *sixty*.
soixante-et-un, *sixty-one*.
soixante-deux, *sixty-two*.
soixante-trois, etc., *sixty-three*, etc.
soixante-dix, *seventy*.
soixante-et-onze, *seventy-one*.
soixante-douze, *seventy-two*.
soixante-treize, etc., *seventy-three*, etc.
quatre-vingts, *eighty*.
quatre-vingt-un, *eighty-one*.
quatre-vingt-deux, *eighty-two*.
quatre-vingt-dix, *ninety*.
quatre-vingt-onze, *ninety-one*.
quatre-vingt-douze, *ninety-two*.
cent, *one hundred*.
cent un, *one hundred and one*.
mille, *one thousand*.
un million, *one million*.

1. L'an dix-huit cent soixante-neuf. 2. J'ai reçu trois mille deux cent quatre-vingt-deux francs. 3. J'ai acheté

[1] In all numbers **un** becomes **une** before a feminine noun.

soixante-deux arbres. 4. Jeanne a perdu ses vingt-et-une lettres. 5. Cinquante-deux semaines font un an. 6. Mon oncle a vendu deux cent cinquante montres à sa sœur. 7. Il y a 44 arbres dans ce jardin. 8. Il a perdu 512 francs. 9. Nous avons vu 6,000 hommes. 10. Montrez-moi ces vingt oranges.

1. 21, 24, 27. 2. 31, 35, 38. 3. 41, 49, 52. 4. 61, 71, 73. 5. 77, 78, 79. 6. 81, 85, 88. 7. 89, 90, 93. 8. 96, 98, 99. 9. 103, 113, 123. 10. 222, 333, 444. 11. 20 and 20 make 40. 12. They have lost 58 pencils. 13. There are 555 books in that room. 14. She has lost 777 francs. 15. That house has 24 rooms. 16. There are 52 weeks in a year. 17. The year 1892 (*dix-huit cent . . . .*). 18. There are 61 men who have fallen in the garden.

24.

(1) With the exceptions only of **premier** (*first*) and **second**[1] (*second*), the ordinal number is formed by adding **-ième** to the cardinal, as **trois, troisième**.

(2) If the cardinal ends in **e**, the **e** is suppressed before adding **-ième**, as **quatre, quatrième**; **trente, trentième**.

(3) Whenever a **q** is followed by two or more vowels, the first of them must always be **u**; **cinq** will therefore make **cinquième**.

(4) For the sake of euphony, the **f** of **neuf, dix-neuf**, etc., is changed into **v** before **-ième**: **neuvième, dix-neuvième**, etc.

premier (m.), *first*, **première** (f.).	**quatrième**, *fourth*.
second or **deuxième**, *second*.	**cinquième**, *fifth*.
troisième, *third*	**sixième**, etc., *sixth*, etc.

[1] The French has two words for *second*: 1st, **second** (pronounce ce-gon); 2d, the regular ordinal number **deuxième**. Strictly speaking, **le second** is the second of only two: **le deuxième** is the second of more than two. The second floor will be called in a house two stories high **le second étage** (or simply **le second**), in a house three or four stories high **le deuxième étage** (or simply **le deuxième**).

vingtième, *twentieth.*
vingt-et-unième, *twenty-first.*
vingt-deuxième, etc., *twenty-second*, etc.
centième, *hundredth.*
millième, *thousandth.*
dernier, *last.*

dimanche (m.), *Sunday.*
lundi (m.), *Monday.*
mardi (m.), *Tuesday.*
mercredi (m.), *Wednesday.*
jeudi (m.), *Thursday.*
vendredi (m.) *Friday.*
samedi (m.), *Saturday.*

la classe, *the class.*
la partie, *the part.*
l'élève (m. or f.), *the pupil.*
je suis, *I am.*

1. Je suis la première de ma classe. 2. Jeanne est la[1] onzième. 3. Louise est la dernière. 4. Il y a vingt-cinq élèves dans cette classe. 5. Jean est le premier. 6. Mon frère est le deuxième. 7. Je suis le troisième. 8. Louis est le quatrième. 9. Charles est le dernier. 10. Six est la cinquième partie de trente. 11. Le samedi est le septième jour de la semaine. 12. Le dimanche est le premier.

1. 3, 3d. 2. 7, 7th. 3. 13, 13th. 4. 19, 19th. 5. 31, 31st. 6. 32, 32d. 7. 85, 85th. 8. 97, 97th. 9. 211, 211th. 10. 555, 555th. 11. Tuesday is the third day of the week. 12. Thursday is the fifth. 13. Saturday is the last. 14. Sunday is the first. 15. Wednesday is the fourth. 16. Monday is the second. 17. Friday is the sixth. 18. A month is the twelfth part of a year (*une année*).

25.

(1) Use the ordinal number **premier** for the first day of a month, and the cardinal numbers for the other days.

(2) The English word *on* used before days and dates is never translated in French.

[1] By exception, no letter is elided before **onze** or **onzième**.

janvier (m.), *January*.
février (m.), *February*.
mars (m.), *March*.
avril (m.), *April*.
mai (m.), *May*.
juin (m.), *June*.
juillet (m.), *July*.
août (m.), *August*.
septembre (m.), *September*.
octobre (m.), *October*.
novembre (m.), *November*.
décembre (m.), *December*.

nous sommes, *we are*. **vous êtes**, *you are*.

le cousin, la cousine, *the cousin*. **le voisin, la voisine**, *the neighbor*.
pourquoi, *why*.

1. Mes cousins sont partis[1] de Paris le 1er février. 2. Ils sont arrivés le 3. 3. Avez-vous parlé à votre cousine quand elle est venue le 13 juin? 4. Votre voisine est revenue jeudi dernier. 5. J'ai écrit à mon oncle et à ma cousine le 10 mars. 6. Quand avez-vous reçu une lettre de votre tante? 7. J'ai reçu une lettre de ma tante samedi dernier. 8. Elle a offert ce livre à votre sœur vendredi. 9. Nous sommes partis de Glasgow le 15 décembre. 10. Nous sommes arrivés le 17. 11. Pourquoi avez-vous donné votre montre à Louise mercredi? 12. Où avez-vous mis le mouchoir que vous avez trouvé mardi?

1. The 14th of[2] July, 1789. 2. The 22d of September, 1792. 3. The 24th of February, 1848. 4. They (are) arrived on Saturday. 5. She (has) found that book and those pencils on Friday. 6. Where did you go on Tuesday last? 7. We (have) departed on the 1st of June. 8. My sister (has) lost her watch on Sunday. 9. Where did you see the handkerchief which I (have) lost on Wednesday? 10. Did you speak to your aunt on Monday? 11. I saw (*have seen*) your father on

[1] The two Rules in § 40 should be studied before reading this paragraph and the next one.

[2] This *of* had better be left out in French, as it is scarcely ever used now.

Thursday. 12. Show me these fifteen letters. 13. Those four windows are higher than ours.

26.

(1) The adjective **tout** cannot, like the English *whole*, be preceded by the article **le, la, les,** or **un, une.** *The whole house*, for instance, must be turned into *all the house*, *the whole town* into *all the town*, etc.

(2) The same adjective **tout** forms the following idioms: —

SINGULAR.	PLURAL.
tout (m.), **toute** (f.),	**tous** (m.), **toutes** (f.), *all, whole, every.*

tout le monde, *everybody, every one.*	**tous les jours,** *every day.*
tous les ans, *every year.*	**tous les dimanches,** *every Sunday.*
tous les mois, *every month.*	**tous les lundis,** *every Monday,*
toutes les semaines, *every week.*	and so on for each day.

arrosé, *watered.*	**autre,** *other.*
visité, *visited.*	**même,** *same.*
il aime, *he likes.*	**la ville,** *the town.*
lu, *read.*	

1. Tous mes crayons sont mauvais. 2. Toutes les filles de l'avocat sont jeunes. 3. Avez-vous arrosé toutes mes fleurs ? 4. J'ai arrosé toutes les vôtres et toutes les miennes. 5. Elle a visité toute la ville. 6. Elle a acheté la même robe, les mêmes gants, et les mêmes fleurs que vous. 7. Tout le monde aime les enfants du médecin. 8. Avez-vous arrosé mon jardin tous les jours ? 9. Ont-ils lu les autres lettres ? 10. A-t-elle visité tout le jardin ? 11. A-t-il écrit à sa mère tous les jeudis ? 12. Donnez-moi toutes ces lettres et tous ces portraits.

1. That garden belongs to everybody. 2. She has visited my mother every week. 3. Did you see the other pupils ? 4. Jane has seen the same man as (*que*) you.

5. Everybody likes that poor man's daughters. 6. Did you visit the whole house? 7. Bring me my other boots. 8. Give me the same books and the same pens. 9. Has he watered all his flowers? 10. He has watered all yours and all his (own). 11. She has written to her sister every Friday. 12. The whole grammar is useful.

27.

Nouns of quantity and measure require the preposition **de** or **d'** (without the article) before the noun which they modify.

le mètre, *the metre* = 3 ft. $3\frac{1}{8}$ in.
le kilogramme, *the kilogramme* = 2 lbs. $3\frac{1}{2}$ oz.
la douzaine, *the dozen.*
la demi-douzaine, *the half dozen.*

le demi-kilogramme, *the half kilogramme.*
le litre, *the litre* = $1\frac{3}{4}$ pints.
une paire, *a pair.*
un panier, *a basket.*
une carafe, *a carafe* or *decanter.*
le drap, *the cloth.*
le sucre, *the sugar.*
la fraise, *the strawberry.*
le beurre, *the butter.*
la livre, *the pound.*
la demi-livre, *the half pound.*
une bouteille, *a bottle.*
un verre, *a glass.*
une tasse, *a cup.*
le thé, *the tea.*
le café, *the coffee.*
le vin, *the wine.*
la bière, *the beer, the ale.*

1. Ils ont acheté un litre de vin, un demi-kilogramme de café, et un panier de fraises. 2. Apportez-moi une tasse de café et un verre d'eau. 3. Donnez-moi une autre tasse de café. 4. Ma tante a acheté pour sa fille trois kilogrammes de beurre et deux kilogrammes de sucre. 5. Jean et son frère ont reçu de leur oncle une douzaine de bouteilles de vin. 6. Elle a offert à sa cousine cinq mètres de drap, deux paires de bottines, dix kilogrammes de sucre, et cinq kilogrammes de beurre. 7. Donnez-moi

une carafe d'eau. 8. J'ai donné deux paniers de fraises à ma sœur. 9. J'ai offert une tasse de thé à ma tante, et une tasse de café à mon oncle. 10. Ma cousine a pris un verre de vin, et mon cousin un verre de bière.

1. Did you give a glass of water to that poor woman? 2. She has taken a cup of tea. 3. We have received from our uncle six bottles of wine, two pounds of tea, one pound of coffee, three pounds of sugar, and four baskets of strawberries. 4. My sister has bought a dozen pocket-handkerchiefs. 5. He has taken a glass of beer. 6. Bring us a carafe of water. 7. She has bought one pair of boots and two pairs of shoes. 8. She has received from her aunt two pairs of pretty gloves. 9. Give me a glass of beer. 10. There are a dozen (of) pupils in his class. 11. I have given (to) my sister half a dozen handkerchiefs and three pairs of gloves. 12. Where did you buy that half dozen chairs?

28.

Adverbs of quantity require the preposition **de** (without the article) before the noun which they modify.[1]

beaucoup,	*much, a great deal, plenty.*	**beaucoup d'argent,** *much* or *a great deal of money.*
	many.	**beaucoup d'hommes,** *many men.*
peu,	*little.*	**peu d'eau,** *little water.*
	few.	**peu de livres,** *few books.*
assez,	*enough.*	**assez de viande,** *meat enough.*
	enough.	**assez de pommes,** *apples enough.*
plus,	*more.*	**plus d'argent,** *more money.*
	more.	**plus d'amis,** *more friends.*

[1] The only exception is the adverb **bien** (*a great many*); it requires the article as well as **de** before the next noun. Ex.: **beaucoup de livres, bien des livres.**

le pain, *the bread.*
la viande, *the meat.*
le lait, *the milk.*
le sel, *the salt.*
le poivre, *the pepper.*
le fromage, *the cheese.*

l'argent (m.), *the money, the silver.*
prenez, *take.*
ou, *or.*
voulez-vous? *will you have?* or, *do you wish?*

1. Voulez-vous un peu de pain et de[1] lait? 2. Prenez plus de beurre. 3. Avez-vous assez de viande? 4. Elle a peu de pain, mais elle a beaucoup de pommes. 5. Vous avez donné beaucoup de fromage à Louis. 6. Notre propriétaire a plus d'enfants que le vôtre. 7. Voulez-vous un peu plus de sel et de poivre? 8. Avez-vous assez de crayons? 9. J'ai plus de pain que vous, mais vous avez plus de lait. 10. Donnez-moi un peu de pain. 11. Prenez un peu de beurre. 12. Voulez-vous plus de sucre ou plus de café?

1. There are more flowers in your garden than in ours. 2. Have you meat enough? 3. Give me a little milk. 4. Will you have a little salt or pepper? 5. Take a little[2] of this meat, it is very good. 6. Louis has more children than you. 7. There are many omnibuses in this city. 8. You have taken many oranges. 9. My daughter has more money than yours, but your son has more books than mine. 10. Take a glass of water. 11. I have plenty of books, but I have little money. 12. Will you have a little more meat? 13. Take more wine. 14. Give me a little water. 15. I have taken a cup of milk and a little bread.

[1] Notice the repetition of **de** before every noun governed by an adverb of quantity.

[2] When **peu** is used as a noun, it is masculine.

29.

tant,	*so much.*	**tant de viande,** *so much meat.*
	so many.	**tant d'hommes,** *so many men.*
autant,	*as much.*	**autant de vin,** *as much wine.*
	as many.	**autant d'amis,** *as many friends.*
trop,	*too much, too.*	**trop d'eau,** *too much water*; **trop petit** *too little.*
	too many.	**trop d'arbres,** *too many trees.*
combien,	*how much.*	**combien d'argent,** *how much money.*
	how many.	**combien d'enfants,** *how many children.*
moins,	*less.*	**moins de beurre,** *less butter.*
	fewer.	**moins de pommes,** *fewer apples.*

ami (m.), **amie** (f.), *friend.*
mangé, *eaten.* **bu,** *drunk.*

1. Mon ami a perdu cette semaine moins d'argent que vous. 2. Combien d'argent avez-vous perdu ? 3. J'ai mangé un peu de pain et de fromage, mais j'ai bu trop de vin. 4. Combien d'enfants a-t-elle ? 5. Elle a cinq enfants, quatre fils et une fille. 6. Louise a trop d'amies. 7. Avez-vous autant d'amies qu'elle ? 8. Donnez-moi un peu de fromage. 9. Notre propriétaire a moins d'enfants que le vôtre. 10. Il y a trop de fleurs dans ce jardin. 11. Louise a autant d'argent que moi.[1] 12. Elle a moins d'oranges que lui. 13. Mes exercices sont trop difficiles. 14. Vous avez bu trop d'eau. 15. Avez-vous mangé autant de fraises que lui ?

1. Take as many apples as Louisa. 2. Will you have less butter and more cheese ? 3. How many friends have you in that town ? 4. How much money did you receive from the physician ? 5. You have fewer pencils than Jane, but you have more books. 6. He has drunk too much water. 7. There are too many doors and windows in that house. 8. Have you enough salt and pep-

[1] Translate *I* by **moi** and *he* by **lui**, when they are not placed immediately before a verb.

per? 9. She has put too many books on this table. 10. I have drunk more wine than he.[1] 11. You have eaten more meat than I. 12. How much money will you have? 13. How many baskets of strawberries did you put on my table? 14. Take as much wine as he. 15. You have taken too much milk.

30.

Exceptions to the formation of the plural of nouns and adjectives.

(1) Nouns and adjectives ending in **s**, **x**, **z**, are alike in both numbers.

SINGULAR.	PLURAL.
le fils, *the son.*	**les fils**, *the sons.*
la voix, *the voice.*	**les voix**, *the voices.*
le nez, *the nose.*	**les nez**, *the noses.*
heureux,	**heureux**, *happy, fortunate*

(2) Nouns and adjectives ending in **-au** or **-eu** take **x** in the plural.

SINGULAR.	PLURAL.
le tableau, *the picture.*	**les tableaux**, *the pictures.*
le bateau, *the boat.*	**les bateaux**, *the boats.*
le chapeau, *the hat.*	**les chapeaux**, *the hats.*
le feu, *the fire.*	**les feux**, *the fires.*
un cheveu, *a hair.*	**les cheveux**, *the hair.*
beau,	**beaux**, *beautiful, handsome, fine.*

(3) Nouns and adjectives ending in **-al** change al into **aux**: —

SINGULAR.	PLURAL.
le cheval, *the horse.*	**les chevaux**, *the horses.*
l'animal, *the animal.*	**les animaux**, *the animals.*
le général, *the general.*	**les généraux**, *the generals.*
égal,	**égaux**, *equal.*
principal,	**principaux**, *principal.*

[1] See foot-note on preceding page.

(4) Six nouns ending in **-ail** change **ail** into **aux**:[1] —

le travail, *the work, the labor.* **les travaux,** *the works, the labors.*

(5) Six nouns ending in **-ou** take **x**:[1] —

le joujou, *the toy.* **les joujoux,** *the toys.*

1. Nous avons vu beaucoup de bateaux. 2. Ces voix sont très gaies. 3. Vos cheveux sont plus beaux que les miens et que ceux de ma sœur. 4. Où avez-vous acheté ces grands chapeaux? 5. Les fils et les filles de mon oncle sont beaucoup plus aimables que les enfants de l'avocat. 6. Avez-vous vu nos tableaux? ils sont beaucoup moins jolis que ceux de votre oncle. 7. Ces enfants sont heureux, ils sont plus heureux que moi. 8. Quand avez-vous reçu ces cadeaux? 9. Louis et Jean sont égaux dans leur classe. 10. Ces animaux sont très jolis. 11. Avez-vous vu les chevaux du prince? 12. Tes joujoux sont plus jolis que les miens. 13. J'ai parlé à vos deux principaux médecins. 14. Vos travaux sont moins utiles que les leurs. 15. Nous avons autant de chevaux que de chiens. 16. Les trois généraux sont partis pour Paris.

1. My brother has bought half a dozen pictures. 2. My sister has much more hair than I. 3. These knives are for my sons. 4. They have sold all their boats to my father and my uncle. 5. Your friends are very happy,—their father has come back from Paris. 6. How many boats have you? 7. Your hats are smaller than ours. 8. Did you buy these presents for your landlord's sons? 9. Have you as many toys as I? 10. Your generals are more fortunate than ours. 11. This animal is very lit-

[1] The complete list is given in the **Appendix, p. 277.**

tle. 12. These little animals are very beautiful. 13. The works of these men are of little use (*little useful*). 14. Your brother and mine are equal. 15. Your hair is prettier than mine. 16. Your horses are finer than ours.

31.

(1) *Some* or *any*, which may be either expressed or understood before an English noun, must always be expressed in French, and is translated by —

du before a noun masculine singular beginning with a consonant; as, **du pain.**

de la before a noun feminine singular beginning with a consonant; as, **de la viande.**

de l' before a noun masculine or feminine singular beginning with a vowel or *h mute:* as, **de l'eau.**

des before nouns in the plural; as, **des pommes, des arbres.**

(2) When persons or things are spoken of in a general sense, put **le, la, les** before the noun.

(3) The English prepositions, *to*, *at*, *in*, placed before the names of towns, are translated by **à.**

la science, *science.*
l'or (m.), *gold.*
l'oiseau, *the bird.*
la vie, *life, living.*
nombreux, *numerous.*
le libraire, *the bookseller.*
le papier, *the paper.*
cher, *dear.*
rare, *rare.*
ce matin, *this morning.*
court, *short.*
Londres, *London.*
l'encre (f.), *the ink.*
il vend, *he sells.*[1]

1. Voulez-vous du pain ou de la viande? 2. Donnez-moi de l'eau. 3. La bonne a acheté du sel et du poivre. 4. Ce libraire vend de l'encre, du papier, des plumes et des crayons. 5. Nous avons reçu de Paris du café, du

[1] Observe that the 3d person singular in a French verb *never* ends with **s: il a, il est, il aime, il vend.**

vin, du fromage, des pommes et des oranges. 6. Il y a dans mon panier des plumes, des crayons et deux livres. 7. Cette femme vend du beurre et du fromage. 8. Voulez-vous de l'eau ou de la bière ce matin? 9. Il y a du pain, des fraises, de l'eau et du lait sur cette table. 10. Les sciences sont utiles aux hommes. 11. Tout le monde aime l'argent. 12. Le vin est beaucoup plus cher à Londres qu'à Paris. 13. La vie d'un oiseau est courte. 14. Les omnibus sont plus nombreux à Paris qu'à Rome. 15. Les bons princes sont rares. 16. Les chiens sont plus nombreux à Constantinople qu'à Londres.

1. Some milk, some trees. 2. Any trees, some money. 3. Any sugar, any strawberries. 4. Some men, of the men, to the men, any men. 5. The maid-servant has received some money this morning. 6. Bring me a pen and some ink. 7. John has bought dresses, gloves, and boots for his sister. 8. She has given (to) my brother some pens, pencils, books, paper, and ink. 9. There are in this basket gloves, sugar, coffee, and money. 10. Her cousin sells tables and chairs. 11. There are princes who are happy. 12. She likes dogs and cats. 13. My aunt is fond of birds (*my aunt likes birds*). 14. Everybody is fond of flowers. 15. Tea is better than coffee. 16. Horses are more useful than dogs. 17. Life is short. 18. Gold is rarer in Rome than in Paris.

32.

There is no word in English corresponding exactly to the French **on**. That word is used, —

1st, To translate the pronouns *we*, *you*, and *they*, when *we*, *you*, and *they* do not represent certain persons in particular, but anybody; as, WE *get news-*

papers, pens, paper, and ink at the bookseller's; YOU *cannot read the Bible without becoming a better man;* THEY *say that the king is dead.*

2d, To translate the word *people* used indefinitely as above; as, PEOPLE *say so, and it is thought the news is true.*

In each of these sentences the indefinite pronoun **on** must be used for the indefinite words *we, you, they,* or *people;* and being singular, requires the verb in the third person singular.

After a preposition —

translate *me*	by **moi.**	*us*	by **nous.**
thee	by **toi.**	*you*	by **vous.**
him	by **lui.**	*them*	by { **eux** (m.),
her	by **elle.**		{ **elles** (f.).

Chez (*at*, or *in*, or *to*, *the house of*), being a preposition, in French will give —

chez moi	for *at my house.*	**chez nous**	*at our house.*
chez toi	*at thy house.*	**chez vous**	*at your house.*
chez lui	*at his house.*	**chez eux** (m.)	*at their house.*
chez elle	*at her house.*	**chez elles** (f.)	

le négociant, *the merchant.*
le fer, *iron.*
le cuivre, *copper.*
le courage, *courage.*
l'ambition (f.), *ambition.*
le talent, *talent.*
la conduite, *conduct.*
l'expérience (f.), *experience.*
les manières (f.), *manners.*
le journal, *the newspaper.*
le poisson, *the fish.*
il trouve, *he finds, he gets.*
s'il vous plaît, *if you please.*

1. On trouve chez ce négociant du fer, du cuivre et de l'argent. 2. Apportez-moi, s'il vous plaît, de l'eau et du thé. 3. Cet homme a du courage et de l'ambition. 4. La vie est chère dans les grandes villes. 5. Vous avez chez vous de l'encre, du papier et des plumes. 6. Donnez-moi,

s'il vous plaît, du beurre et du fromage. 7. Votre frère est heureux, il a de l'argent et des amis. 8. On trouve chez les libraires des journaux, des crayons, du papier et de l'encre. 9. Avez-vous acheté des joujoux pour ma sœur et pour moi ? 10. J'ai acheté des gants pour elle et une petite canne pour vous. 11. Les chevaux de mon père sont plus grands et plus beaux que ceux du prince. 12. Avez-vous acheté du poisson pour elles ? 13. Il a donné du vin à sa sœur et de la bière à son frère. 14. Ils sont venus ce matin chez moi.

1. For them (*m.*), for them (*f.*). 2. Of me, of him. 3. Of you, of her. 4. At my house, at her house. 5. At his house, at our house. 6. At your house, at their house. 7. At the landlord's house. 8. At the lawyer's; at the professor's; at the prince's; at the general's. 9. We find at the bookseller's newspapers, pens, ink, and paper. 10. People find at his house wine and beer. 11. She has courage. 12. We have eaten some fish and some meat, and we have drunk water. 13. Your brother has talent and manners. 14. We find iron and copper at this merchant's. 15. Bring us, if you please, some bread and (some) knives. 16. There are trees and flowers in our garden. 17. We have spoken to the generals. 18. Fire and water are useful to man.

33.

Voici, *here is, here are.* **Voilà**, *there is, there are.*

There is and *there are* are both translated (1st) by **il y a**, when making a statement; as, *There are trees and flowers in our garden*, **Il y a des arbres et des fleurs dans notre jardin**; (2d) by **voilà**, when pointing to a thing; as, *See, there is some bread*, **Tenez, voilà du pain.**

Literally, **voici** means *see here*, and **voilà**, *see there*. **Voici** points, therefore, to nearer objects, and **voilà** to more distant ones.

la chose, *the thing.*
la dentelle, *the lace.*
une boucle d'oreille, *an ear-ring.*
la mousseline, *the muslin.*
une écharpe, *a scarf.*
le ruban, *the ribbon.*
le fil, *the thread.*
la soie, *the silk.*
une aiguille, *a needle.*
tenez ! *hold ! see !*

1. J'ai acheté beaucoup de choses pour vous, ma cousine; tenez, voilà de la dentelle, des boucles d'oreilles, de la mousseline, du fil, de la soie et des aiguilles. 2. Voici aussi une écharpe et des rubans. 3. Il y a, sur la petite table dans la chambre de ma mère, de la soie et de la dentelle. 4. Tenez, voilà un petit livre que j'ai acheté pour vous. 5. Voilà du vin pour mon frère et voici de l'eau pour moi. 6. Elle a acheté une paire de souliers et une paire de bottines. 7. Avez-vous un peu de soie et de dentelle? 8. Apportez-moi du fil et des aiguilles. 9. Voulez-vous aussi de la mousseline? 10. J'ai trouvé beaucoup de jolies choses sur ma table: trois mètres de ruban, une paire de boucles d'oreilles et cinq mètres de dentelle. 11. Votre ami a de l'ambition, mais il a aussi du talent, de l'expérience et des manières. 12. Votre sœur a beaucoup de courage. 13. Voici du pain, de la viande, du sel et du fromage. 14. Donnez-moi aussi, s'il vous plaît, une carafe d'eau et un verre. 15. Leurs chapeaux sont plus grands que les nôtres.

1. There is a little water in the carafe; bring me a glass. 2. There is the fine picture which your father has given to my brother. 3. Did you buy thread and silk for my sister and (for) me? 4. I have bought some lace, some muslin, and some ribbons for your sister, and there is a pair of ear-rings for you. 5. Give me, if you please, a little bread and a glass of wine. 6. Will you have a little meat? 7. Hold, there is some money for you. 8. Your brothers have bought two pairs of shoes

and four pairs of boots. 9. Have you as many horses as dogs? 10. How much money will you have? 11. These three animals are more useful than all yours. 12. Have you enough bread? 13. Give me less butter and more cheese. 14. There is a book which is very rare; it belongs to my uncle. 15. There is a pair of ear-rings which is very dear; it belongs to my mother. 16. You get (*on trouve*) many things at this merchant's.

34.

The Place of Adjectives.

Place after their nouns, —

1st. Adjectives of color (*black*, *red*, etc.): 2d. Adjectives of nationality (*English*, *French*, etc.): 3d. In general, adjectives having more syllables than their noun (**du drap magnifique, de l'encre excellente**, etc.): 4th. Two or more adjectives qualifying the same noun (**un général brave et habile.**)

First Exception to the rule of *some* or *any*, expressed or understood before a noun.

If the French noun is to be preceded by an adjective, *some* or *any*, expressed or understood, is translated simply by **de** (or **d'**); as:

du pain,	**de bon pain.**
de la viande,	**de bonne viande.**
de l'eau,	**de bonne eau.**
des pommes,	**de bonnes pommes.**

rouge, *red*.
blanc (m.), **blanche** (f.), *white*.
habile, *clever*.
noir, *black*.
anglais,[1] *English*.
français, *French*.

[1] An adjective never takes a capital letter in French.

chaud,[1] *hot*, or *warm*.
froid,[1] *cold*.
le roman, *the novel*.
magnifique, *magnificent*.
excellent, *excellent*.
intéressant, *interesting*.
la poire, *the pear*.

1. Jean a donné à ma mère de très jolies boucles d'oreilles. 2. Voilà de la dentelle magnifique. 3. Apportez-nous, s'il vous plaît, de meilleur vin, de l'eau chaude et du sucre. 4. Votre cousine a prêté à mon père des romans anglais qui sont très intéressants. 5. Vous avez d'habiles professeurs. 6. Nous avons acheté du drap excellent. 7. Ils ont de très mauvais sucre. 8. Apportez-moi de meilleur café. 9. Voulez-vous de l'eau chaude ou de l'eau froide ? 10. Ma sœur a acheté de jolies bottines françaises. 11. Voilà de très bon beurre, il est meilleur que celui que vous avez acheté ce matin. 12. Voilà de mauvaises aiguilles, elles sont plus mauvaises que celles de votre sœur. 13. Elle a offert à sa sœur des rubans rouges et de la soie blanche.

1. She has bought some pretty flowers and some French pears, which are very good. 2. They have excellent ink. 3. You have some fine horses. 4. How many French books have you ? 5. Louisa has given to my sister a black scarf, some English needles, and red silk. 6. Here is some pretty lace. 7. Here are pretty ear-rings. 8. Bring me some hot water, if you please. 9. Will you have some black coffee ? 10. Give me a little white bread. 11. We find interesting novels at this bookseller's. 12. My father has offered (to) my mother this morning a magnificent scarf. 13. There are some clever merchants in this town. 14. Have you good bread and good meat ? 15. Our water is bad, but we have very good beer. 16. Has he bought some presents for you ?

[1] **Chaud** and **froid** are always placed after their noun.

35.

(1) The English use the two words *this* and *that* when they have to compare two persons or two things: as, THIS *man is richer than* THAT *man;* THIS *book is smaller than* THAT *book;* THIS *watch is better than* THAT *watch.* But in French we have only one word for the adjectives *this* and *that;* namely, **ce**, **cet**, or **cette** (see § 27). In order, therefore, to mark the distinction so well expressed in English by the two contrasting words *this* and *that*, we add to the first noun **ci** (*here*), and to the second **là** (*there*); as,—

> **cet homme-ci est plus riche que cet homme-là.**
> **ce livre-ci est plus petit que ce livre-là.**
> **cette montre-ci est meilleure que cette montre-là.**

(2) The same process is used to render in French the distinction expressed in English by the plural adjectives *these* and *those;* as,—

> **ces hommes-ci sont plus riches que ces hommes-là.**
> **ces livres-ci sont plus petits que ces livres-là.**
> **ces montres-ci sont meilleures que ces montres-là.**

(3) As in each of these sentences the repetition of the same noun sounds ill, we replace the second by one of the pronouns, **celui**, **celle**, **ceux**, **celles**, according to the gender and number of that noun; as,—

> **cet homme-ci est plus riche que celui-là.**
> **ce livre-ci est plus petit que celui-là.**
> **cette montre-ci est meilleure que celle-là.**
> **ces hommes-ci sont plus riches que ceux-là.**
> **ces livres-ci sont plus petits que ceux-là.**
> **ces montres-ci sont meilleures que celles-là.**

Observe, in all these examples, that **ci**, pointing to a nearer object, **corresponds** to the English *this* and *these;* whilst **là**, pointing to a more **distant object**, corresponds with *that* and *those*.

Thérèse, *Therese.*	**Ernest,** *Ernest.*
Charles, *Charles.*	**la broche,** *the brooch.*
Henri, *Henry.*	**le parapluie,** *the umbrella.*

1. Ce livre-ci est meilleur que celui-là. 2. Cette fenêtre-ci est plus haute que celle-là. 3. Ces bouteilles-là sont plus petites que celles-ci. 4. Ces enfants-là sont plus jolis que ceux-ci. 5. Avez-vous vu ma montre et celle de ma sœur? 6. Celle-ci est la mienne, celle-là est celle de Jeanne. 7. Nous avons trouvé deux broches, et vos sœurs ont perdu les leurs. 8. Celle-ci est celle de Thérèse, et voilà celle de Louise. 9. Voici le parapluie que j'ai trouvé chez nous. 10. Ce parapluie est peut-être celui de Charles, qui a perdu le sien. 11. Celui-ci est le mien, celui-là est le vôtre. 12. Nous avons trouvé deux cannes; avez-vous perdu la vôtre, Henri? 13. J'ai perdu la mienne dans le jardin, et j'ai pris celle de mon frère. 14. Celle que vous avez est peut-être celle d'Ernest; il a perdu la sienne ce matin.

1. This house is higher than that. 2. This arm-chair is larger than that. 3. These strawberries are better than those. 4. These gloves are prettier and dearer than those. 5. That portrait is more beautiful than this. 6. That lace is prettier than this. 7. Those novels are more interesting than these. 8. Those scarfs are dearer than these. 9. Where did you see my handkerchief? 10. This one[1] is mine, that one is yours. 11. Did you also see my watch? 12. That one is your brother's, this one is yours. 13. There is your umbrella, which my brother has found. 14. That umbrella is my sister's. 15. Here is your pencil, that one is mine. 16. Those apples are better than these. 17. These pears are better than those.

[1] *One* is not translated after *this* or *that*, nor *ones* after *these* or *those*.

36.

(1) The superlative is formed by putting **le, la, les,** before the comparative.

	POSITIVE.	COMPARATIVE.	SUPERLATIVE.
Sing.	**grand** (m.), *great,*	**plus grand,** *greater,*	**le plus grand,** *the greatest.*
	grande (f.),	**plus grande,**	**la plus grande.**
Pl.	**grands** (m.),	**plus grands,**	**les plus grands.**
	grandes (f.),	**plus grandes,**	**les plus grandes.**

(2) *In,* after a superlative, is translated by **de**:—

la plus jolie fille de la ville, *the prettiest girl in the town.*

(3) *He is, she is, it is,* and *they are,* followed by a superlative, are generally translated by **c'est** before a singular, by **ce sont** before a plural: —

c'est le plus brave des hommes, *he is the bravest of men.*
ce sont les meilleures des femmes, *they are the best of women.*

le pays, *the country.* **le quartier,** *the quarter.*
la rue, *the street.* **la phrase,** *the sentence.*
le monde, *the world.* **fait,** *done, made.*

1. Prenez cette petite chambre, c'est la plus gaie de la rue. 2. Voulez-vous ces deux journaux? ce sont les meilleurs du pays. 3. Donnez-moi, s'il vous plaît, une de ces poires françaises. 4. Elles sont meilleures que les poires anglaises, ce sont peut-être les meilleures de toutes les poires. 5. Avez-vous fait votre exercice? c'est le plus difficile du livre. 6. Ces fraises sont chères, elles sont plus chères que dans mon pays. 7. Prenez cette soie blanche, c'est la plus jolie de toutes. 8. Ces souliers sont les moins beaux, mais ce sont les plus utiles. 9. Cet hôtel est excellent, c'est le meilleur de la ville et peut-être du pays. 10. Les phrases françaises de ce livre sont plus faciles que les phrases anglaises,

elles sont aussi moins utiles et moins nombreuses. 11. Thérèse est la fille la plus aimable de la ville. 12. Sa sœur est plus jolie qu'elle. 13. C'est la plus jolie fille du quartier. 14. Ce quartier est un des plus beaux de Paris.

1. This book is very useful, it is the most useful of my books. 2. Did you see my uncle's house? it is the largest in the town. 3. This needle is better than yours, it is the best of my needles. 4. Charles is very young, he is the youngest of my brothers. 5. My cousin is the merriest of all girls. 6. Your little white cat is the prettiest of all cats. 7. Our landlord is the richest man (*the man the richest*) in the town. 8. Louisa is the tallest girl in the class. 9. Your two sisters are richer than mine, but mine are more cheerful. 10. This pen is good, mine is better, but my brother's is the best. 11. The man who has bought this bottle of wine is the poorest in the town. 12. Your uncle is the best man in the world. 13. Those apples are better than these, but mine and his are the best. 14. Their house is the highest in the street. 15. Your sisters are very clever, they are cleverer than mine.

37.

The Rule of *c'est* and *ce sont* continued

He is, *she is*, *it is*, and *they are*, are translated by **c'est** or **ce sont** before a noun, or a pronoun.

c'est Henri, *it is Henry.*	**ce sont mes frères,** *it is my brothers.*
c'est un négociant, *he is a merchant.*	**ce sont des négociants,** *they are merchants*
c'est une couturière, *she is a dressmaker.*	**ce sont des couturières,** *they are dressmakers.*

c'est moi, *it is I.*	**est-ce moi?** *is it I?*
c'est toi, *it is thou.*	**est-ce toi?** *is it thou?*
c'est lui, *it is he.*	**est-ce lui?** *is it he?*
c'est elle, *it is she.*	**est-ce elle?** *is it she?*
c'est nous, *it is we.*	**est-ce nous?** *is it we?*
c'est vous, *it is you.*	**est-ce vous?** *is it you?*
ce sont eux, *it is they* (m.).	**est-ce eux?** *is it they* (m.)?
ce sont elles, *it is they* (f.).	**est-ce elles?** *is it they* (f.)?

c'est celui, **c'est celle,**	*it is that,* or *it is the one.*	**ce sont ceux,** **ce sont celles,**	*they are those.*
c'est le mien, **c'est la mienne,**	*it is mine.*	**ce sont les miens,** **ce sont les miennes,**	*they are mine.*
c'est le tien, **c'est la tienne,**	*it is thine.*	**ce sont les tiens,** **ce sont les tiennes,**	*they are thine.*
c'est le sien, **c'est la sienne,**	*it is his* or *hers.*	**ce sont les siens,** **ce sont les siennes,**	*they are his* or *hers.*
c'est le nôtre, **c'est la nôtre,**	*it is ours.*	**ce sont les nôtres,**	*they are ours.*
c'est le vôtre, **c'est la vôtre,**	*it is yours.*	**ce sont les vôtres,**	*they are yours.*
c'est le leur, **c'est la leur,**	*it is theirs.*	**ce sont les leurs,**	*they are theirs.*

Observe that **ce sont** is used before a third person plural (excepting the interrogative **est-ce eux?** and **est-ce elles?**) while **c'est** is used in all other cases.

Qui, *Who? Whom?*	**oui,** *yes.*
	la femme, *the woman, the wife.*

Notice that the interrogative pronoun *whom* is translated by **qui**; the relative pronoun *whom*, by **que**.

qui avez-vous vu? *whom have you seen?*
l'homme que vous avez vu, *the man whom you have seen.*

M. or **Monsieur,** *sir, Mr.*	**MM.** or **Messieurs,** *gentlemen, Messrs.*
Mme or **Madame,** *madam, Mrs.*	**Mmes** or **Mesdames,** *ladies, mesdames.*
Mlle or **Mademoiselle,** *miss.*	**Mlles** or **Mesdemoiselles,** *misses, the misses.*

ce monsieur, *this* or *that gentleman.*
cette dame, *this* or *that lady.*
cette demoiselle, *this* or *that young lady.*
ces messieurs, *these* or *those gentlemen.*
ces dames, *these* or *those ladies.*
ces demoiselles, *these* or *those young ladies.*

1. Qui est là? 2. Est-ce vous, Ernest? 3. Oui, c'est moi. 4. Qui sont ces messieurs? 5. Ce sont les amis du propriétaire. 6. Qui sont ces dames? 7. Ce sont les sœurs du ministre. 8. Qui est cette femme? 9. C'est la bonne de l'avocat. 10. Qui sont ces enfants? 11. Ce sont les miens, c'est mon fils et ma fille. 12. Qui avez-vous vu dans la maison? 13. J'ai vu monsieur Auguste et madame Gustave. 14. Est-ce vous, monsieur Joly? 15. De qui avez-vous reçu ces lettres? Est-ce du propriétaire ou de l'avocat? 16. C'est du propriétaire.

1. Who is that gentleman? 2. It is our landlord's brother. 3. Who is that lady? 4. It is the priest's sister. 5. Who are those men? 6. They are my cousin's friends. 7. They are[1] John, Charles, and Gustave. 8. It is[1] talent and manners that he likes. 9. It is manners and talent that he likes. 10. Is it you, Mr. Henry? 11. Yes, it is I. 12. Who is that maid-servant? 13. It is ours. 14. Who are those young ladies? 15. They are the minister's daughters. 16. Whom did you see in the garden? 17. I have seen your mother and Miss Jane. 18. She is fond of horses; they are more useful than dogs.

38.

(1) As the auxiliary verb *to do* does not exist in French (§ 6), *do* and *does* are omitted in translation:

[1] Translate by **c'est**, as the next noun is not plural.

— *To whom do these trees belong?* must, therefore, be turned into: *to whom belong these trees?*

(2) The interrogative pronoun *whose*, having no corresponding word in French, is changed into *to whom:* — *Whose garden is this?* must be changed into: *to whom belongs this garden?* or, *to whom is this garden?*

A qui appartient ce jardin? **A qui est ce jardin?**	*Whose garden is this?*
Il appartient à mon frère. **C'est celui de mon frère.** **C'est à mon frère.**	*It is my brother's.*
A qui appartiennent ces jardins? **A qui sont ces jardins?**	*Whose gardens are these?*
Ils appartiennent à ma sœur. **Ce sont ceux de ma sœur.**	*They are my sister's.*

une ombrelle, *a parasol.*
un dé, *a thimble.*
une épingle, *a pin.*
un manchon, *a muff.*

1. A qui appartient ce manchon? 2. C'est à ma sœur. 3. A qui est cette ombrelle? 4. C'est celle de Thérèse. 5. A qui appartient ce parapluie? 6. C'est celui que vous avez acheté ce matin. 7. A qui sont ces aiguilles, ces épingles, ce fil et ce dé? 8. Ils appartiennent à ma cousine. 9. A qui sont ces deux mouchoirs? 10. Ce sont les vôtres, ce sont ceux que vous avez pris ce matin. 11. Sont-ce vos cousins qui sont arrivés ce matin? 12. Oui, ce sont eux. 13. A qui sont ces épingles? Sont-ce les vôtres ou les miennes? 14. Ce sont celles de ma sœur. 15. Pour qui est ce dé? Est-ce pour vous ou pour moi? 16. C'est pour vous.

1. Whose house is this? 2. It is my uncle's. 3. To whom does this parasol belong? 4. It belongs to my sister. 5. Whose muffs are those? 6. They are The-

resa's, Jane's, and Louisa's. 7. To whom does this bread belong? 8. It is your own.[1] 9. It is the one which you have bought for your cousin. 10. To whom do these novels belong? 11. They are mine. 12. They are those which you have put this morning on my table. 13. Whose brooch is this? 14. It is Louisa's. 15. For whom have you bought these two small muffs? 16. For your two daughters. 17. Your house is very high, it is the highest in the street.

39.

PRESENT INDICATIVE.

to have, **avoir**.		*to be*, **être**.	
I have,	**j'ai.**	*I am,*	**je suis.**
thou hast,	**tu as.**	*thou art,*	**tu es.**
he has,	**il a.**	*he is,*	**il est.**
we have,	**nous avons.**	*we are,*	**nous sommes.**
you have,	**vous avez.**	*you are,*	**vous êtes.**
they have,	**ils ont.**	*they are,*	**ils sont.**

INTERROGATIVELY.

have I?	**ai-je?**	*am I?*	**suis-je?**
hast thou?	**as-tu?**	*art thou?*	**es-tu?**
has he?	**a-t-il?**	*is he?*	**est-il?**
have we?	**avons-nous?**	*are we?*	**sommes-nous?**
have you?	**avez-vous?**	*are you?*	**êtes-vous?**
have they?	**ont-ils?**	*are they?*	**sont-ils?**

triste, *sad*.
malade, *ill, unwell, sick*.
laborieux, *industrious*.
aujourd'hui, *to-day*.
parce que, *because*.
avec, *with*.

ce soir, *this evening, to-night* (till bed-time).

[1] Translate *my own, thy own, his own, her own*, etc., as if it were *mine, thine, his, hers*, etc.

1. Pourquoi êtes-vous si triste[1] aujourd'hui ? 2. Je suis triste parce que ma sœur est très malade. 3. Nous aussi, nous sommes un peu malades ce soir. 4. Vos sœurs sont plus gaies et plus aimables que les miennes. 5. Avez-vous vu votre cousine ? elle est arrivée ce soir. 6. Avec qui est-elle venue ? 7. Elle est venue avec son oncle et sa tante. 8. Etes-vous souvent dans ce jardin ? 9. Votre frère et votre cousin ont fait leurs exercices, ils sont très laborieux. 10. Elles ont acheté de très jolies boucles d'oreilles ce matin. 11. Elles sont arrivées ce soir. 12. Le ruban rouge que vous avez acheté est magnifique. 13. Combien avez-vous acheté cette écharpe ? 14. Nous avons vu aujourd'hui de très jolie dentelle. 15. Votre oncle est parti ce soir pour Londres.

1. You have, you are. 2. They have, they are. 3. She has, she is. 4. I have, I am. 5. My brothers have, my brothers are. 6. We have, we are. 7. He has, he is. 8. Thou hast, thou art. 9. My brother and my sister have. 10. My brother and my sister are. 11. Is it you who have written this letter to my mother? 12. Yes, sir, it is I. 13. Why are you sad? 14. I am sad because I am sick. 15. Are you often sad and sick? 16. I am sick every Monday. 17. They have done their exercises. 18. They have arrived. 19. Have you spoken to your uncle to-day ? 20. Yes, sir, I have seen my uncle this evening. 21. Did you sell as many things as your neighbor? 22. How much money has she lost? 23. These novels are more interesting than those. 24. English novels are very interesting. 25. They have bought three French grammars.

[1] The pronoun **vous** may stand for one as well as for several persons. When it stands for only one, the adjective referring to it must be singular.

40.

(1) [1] The past tense is the past of a verb used without *to be* or *to have*, as *I wrote*, *you saw*, *they spoke*. Translate it generally by the past participle of that verb preceded by **j'ai, tu as, il a**, etc.; as **j'ai écrit, vous avez vu, ils ont parlé.**

In other words, the French make no difference between *I wrote* and *I have written*, *I saw* and *I have seen*, *I spoke* and *I have spoken*, and, generally speaking, they use only the latter form.

(2) By exception, put **je suis, tu es, il est, nous sommes, vous êtes, ils sont** (instead of **j'ai, tu as**, etc.) before the ten past participles always used in French with *to be* (§ 13). Translate therefore in the following way: —

I went, **je suis allé.**	*I became*, **je suis devenu.**
I went out, **je suis sorti.**	*I arrived*, **je suis arrivé.**
I went away, **je suis parti.**	*I entered*, **je suis entré.**
I came, **je suis venu.**	*I remained*, **je suis resté.**
I came back, **je suis revenu.**	*I fell*, **je suis tombé.**

il y a (before a noun implying a period of time), *ago.*	**il y a quinze jours,** / **il y a une quinzaine,** } *a fortnight ago.*
il y a huit jours, / **il y a une semaine,** } *a week ago.*	**hier**, *yesterday.*
	hier soir, *last night* (till bed-time).

1. Nous avons vendu notre maison lundi dernier. 2. Ils ont perdu leur mère il y a huit jours. 3. Elle a écrit à son frère hier matin. 4. Où êtes-vous allé ce soir? 5. Je suis allé chez mon oncle. 6. Sont-ils sortis hier soir? 7. Ils sont partis il y a quinze jours. 8. Elle a vu ce matin le portrait que j'ai donné à sa

[1] Pupils are recommended to pay the greatest attention to these two rules, their application being constantly required in French conversation.

sœur il y a trois semaines. 9. Pourquoi êtes-vous restés chez vous hier? 10. Pourquoi avez-vous offert au fils du propriétaire le livre que j'ai donné l'autre jour à votre sœur? 11. Où est le couteau que vous avez trouvé jeudi dernier? 12. A-t-elle écrit à son père vendredi soir? 13. Est-elle arrivée hier matin? 14. Votre cousine est devenue très jolie.

1. He spoke; she read; we sold. 2. They lent; you received; I offered. 3. We accepted; you lost; they saw. 4. She wrote; I visited; she came back. 5. He remained; we arrived; you became. 6. They went away; they went out. 7. I went; I entered. 8. I saw your father yesterday. 9. I spoke to your sister this morning. 10. She has seen the present which I offered to her sister three or four days ago. 11. Where did he go last night? 12. When did he come back? 13. He came back on Tuesday last. 14. Show me the novel which she lent to your brother. 15. I wrote to my sister three weeks ago. 16. The bonnet which she bought at your house is very pretty. 17. Have you seen the fine picture which I received from my father last night? 18. Have you read the novel which I lent to your brother five or six months ago?

41.

Adverbs are generally placed after the verb in a simple tense, and between the auxiliary verb and the past participle in a compound tense; as —

Elle danse bien,	*She dances well.*
Ils jouent adroitement,	*They play skilfully.*
Elle a bien dansé,	*She has danced well.*
Ils ont adroitement joué,	*They have played skilfully.*
Nous avons beaucoup ri,	*We laughed much.*

EXCEPTIONS: — **Hier, aujourd'hui, demain, ici, là,** and all adverbial phrases,[1] are placed after the participle: —

Ils sont partis hier,	*They left yesterday.*
Elles sont revenues aujourd'hui,	*They came back to-day.*
Vous n'aurez pas fini demain,	*You will not have done to-morrow.*
Je suis arrivé ici hier,	*I arrived here yesterday.*
Il est tombé là,	*He fell there.*
Elle a pleuré tout à l'heure,	*She cried just now.*
Vous avez agi avec prudence,	*You have acted prudently.*

être bien mis, *to be well dressed.*	**la bague,** *the ring.*
être mal mis, *to be badly dressed.*	**le porte-monnaie,** *the purse.*
ri, *laughed.*	**la chaîne,** *the chain.*
pleuré, *wept, cried.*	**la poche,** *the pocket.*
agi, *behaved.*	**plein,** *full.*
dormi, *slept.*	**toujours,** *always.*

cette nuit, *last night* (from 12 till this morning).

1. Mon frère a beaucoup pleuré ce matin. 2. Il a perdu son porte-monnaie hier soir. 3. A-t-il beaucoup perdu? 4. Est-il venu ici? 5. Il a mal agi aujourd'hui. 6. Le fils du propriétaire est toujours bien mis. 7. Il aime beaucoup les choses qui sont chères. 8. Nous avons beaucoup ri ce soir. 9. Nous avons bien pleuré ce soir-là. 10. Votre frère est arrivé cette nuit. 11. Ses poches sont toujours pleines d'argent. 12. Vous avez mal écrit votre lettre. 13. La lettre de votre frère est très bien écrite. 14. Le pauvre enfant a pleuré toute cette nuit, il a perdu tous ses joujoux. 15. Nous sommes partis de Paris hier soir.

1. I slept well last night. 2. Your little cousin wept much this morning, her mother is ill. 3. My cousin is poor, but she is always well dressed. 4. Ernest lost

[1] An adverbial phrase is composed of two or more words: **sur-le-champ,** *at once;* **tout à fait,** *quite;* **tout à l'heure,** *just now.*

this morning his purse and his watch. 5. Did he also lose his chain and his ring? 6. Did they come here? 7. Your brother laughed much last night. 8. Did you sleep well last night? 9. He ate very little. 10. She is always badly dressed. 11. She fell there. 12. Your letter is badly written. 13. Your uncle offered some money and some books to Henry's cousin yesterday. 14. He is very fond of dogs (*he likes dogs much*).[1] 15. My mother wept very much. 16. Did she arrive Monday or Tuesday morning?

42.

(1) The negation *not* is expressed by the two words **ne** and **pas**, and the verb is placed between them.

INDICATIVE PRESENT.

I have not,	**je n'ai pas.**	*I am not,*	**je ne suis pas.**
thou hast not,	**tu n'as pas.**	*thou art not,*	**tu n'es pas.**
he has not,	**il n'a pas.**	*he is not,*	**il n'est pas.**
she has not,	**elle n'a pas.**	*she is not,*	**elle n'est pas.**
we have not,	**nous n'avons pas.**	*we are not,*	**nous ne sommes pas.**
you have not,	**vous n'avez pas.**	*you are not,*	**vous n'êtes pas.**
they have not,	**ils n'ont pas.** / **elles n'ont pas.**	*they are not,*	**ils ne sont pas.** / **elles ne sont pas.**

INTERROGATIVELY.

have I not?	**n'ai-je pas?**	*am I not?*	**ne suis-je pas?**
hast thou not?	**n'as-tu pas?**	*art thou not?*	**n'es-tu pas?**
has he not?	**n'a-t-il pas?**	*is he not?*	**n'est-il pas?**
has she not?	**n'a-t-elle pas?**	*is she not?*	**n'est-elle pas?**
have we not?	**n'avons-nous pas?**	*are we not?*	**ne sommes-nous pas?**
have you not?	**n'avez-vous pas?**	*are you not?*	**n'êtes-vous pas?**
have they not?	**n'ont-ils pas?** / **n'ont-elles pas?**	*are they not?*	**ne sont-ils pas?** / **ne sont-elles pas?**

[1] We never say **très beaucoup** for *very much*, but simply **beaucoup**.

Final exception to the rule of *some* or *any* before a noun.[1]

(2) If the verb is negative, *some* or *any*, whether expressed or understood before a noun, is translated simply by **de** (or **d'**), as: —

Je n'ai pas d'argent, *I have no money*, or *I have not any money.*
Je n'ai pas de souliers, *I have no shoes*, or *I have not any shoes.*
Je n'ai pas de livre, *I have not a book*, or *I have no book.*
Je n'ai jamais vu de lion, *I have never seen a lion.*

le diamant, *the diamond.*
la fourrure, *the fur.*
le bracelet, *the bracelet.*
le bouton, *the stud, button.*
l'habit, *the coat.*
le lion, *the lion.*
l'éléphant, *the elephant.*
le tigre, *the tiger.*
le léopard, *the leopard.*
le serpent, *the serpent.*
si, *if.*

1. Je n'ai pas de diamants, mais j'ai de la fourrure, de très beaux bracelets et de jolies boucles d'oreilles. 2. Votre frère n'a pas perdu sa chaîne, c'est un bouton qu'il a perdu dans votre jardin. 3. Son habit n'est pas meilleur que le mien. 4. Vous avez de l'expérience, vous n'êtes pas très jeune. 5. Nos maisons ne sont pas très hautes. 6. Nous ne sommes pas riches, nous n'avons pas autant d'argent que vous. 7. Je ne suis pas habile, mais j'ai du courage et de la persévérance. 8. Cette encre rouge n'est pas très bonne. 9. Vous n'avez pas encore vu de lions; moi, j'ai vu des lions, des éléphants, des tigres, des léopards et des serpents. 10. Il n'a pas encore lu de roman français. 11. Je n'ai pas de soie, mais j'ai de très beau fil blanc.

1. They have not; they are not. 2. We have not; we are not. 3. She has not; she is not. 4. I have

[1] See general rule, § 31, and 1st exception, § 34.

not; I am not. 5. You have not; you are not. 6. My brothers have not. 7. My sisters are not. 8. Have they not? 9. Are they not? 10. Has she not? 11. Is she not? 12. Have I not? 13. Am I not? 14. Have you not? 15. Are you not? 16. My pen is not better than yours. 17. My pens are not better than yours. 18. She has no books. 19. She has not an umbrella. 20. Bring us some bread, if you please, and, if you have no wine, give us some tea also. 21. We have bought wine, apples, pears, knives, paper, ink, and pens. 22. My sisters have no needles, but they have very good pins.

43.

(1) *As* followed by an adjective or an adverb is translated by **aussi**: *as beautiful*, **aussi beau**; *as well*, **aussi bien.**

(2) *So* followed by an adjective or an adverb is translated by **si**: *so beautiful*, **si beau**; *so well*, **si bien.**

aussi is used in comparisons, and is always followed by **que**; **si** is used in comparisons only when they are negative, and does not require **que** after it.

(3) *As* coming after another *as*, or after *so*, or after *same*, is translated by **que**:—

as beautiful as, **aussi beau que.** *so beautiful as*, **si beau que.**
as well as, **aussi bien que.** *so well as*, **si bien que.**
the same as, **le même que, la même que, les mêmes que.**
ne . . . point, *not*, or *not at all.*[1] **ne . . . plus,** *not again, no more, no longer.*
ne . . . jamais, *never.*

la représentation, *the representation, the picture.*
le moyen âge, *the middle ages.*
l'écrivain, *the author.*
fort, *strong.*
ordinaire, *common.*
presque, *almost.*
tout à l'heure, *just now.*

[1] The negation **ne . . . point** is more energetic than **ne . . . pas,** but is not so often used.

1. Cette mousseline est aussi belle que la mienne, mais elle n'est pas si forte. 2. Votre lettre n'est pas si bien écrite que celle de votre frère. 3. Ce papier n'est pas si beau que le vôtre, mais il est plus fort. 4. Ce roman de Dickens est aussi intéressant que beaucoup des[1] romans de Walter Scott, mais il n'est pas aussi beau qu'*Ivanhoe.* 5. Je n'ai jamais lu d'aussi beau roman. 6. *Ivanhoe* n'est pas un roman ordinaire, c'est la plus parfaite représentation du moyen âge. 7. Cet écrivain n'a pas de talent. 8. Avez-vous perdu votre porte-monnaie? 9. Je n'ai jamais de porte-monnaie. 10. Mon oncle n'est pas si riche que votre cousin. 11. Ces arbres sont presque aussi beaux que ceux de votre jardin.

1. They have not. 2. They are not. 3. We have no more. 4. We are no more. 5. My brothers have never. 6. My sisters are never. 7. Has she no more? 8. Is she no more? 9. Have you not at all? 10. Are you not at all? 11. Have they not? 12. Are they not? 13. Have we no more? 14. Are we no more? 15. Has he never? 16. Is she never? 17. The garden which you sold to my brother is not so small as ours. 18. Your brothers saw this morning two horses which are almost as high as mine. 19. The novel which you lent (to) my mother is not so interesting as this one. 20. That young man has no manners. 21. Has he not come back? 22. She has never gone away. 23. You are no longer so merry as just now; are you sick? 24. No, sir, I am never sick; but I am a little sad because I have no more money.

[1] Observe that **des**, not **de**, is used here after the adverb of quantity **beaucoup**, because it means *of the*.

44.

(1) *What* or *which* followed by a noun is an adjective and translated by —

SINGULAR. { **quel** (m.). **quelle** (f.). PLURAL. { **quels.** **quelles.**

(2) To express what o'clock it is, we name first the hour which is nearest, whether it is past or to come, and add *less so much*, if the hour has not struck yet, or *and so much*, if the hour is past.

Supposing we wish to tell what the time is every five minutes, beginning at 25 minutes to 10 till 25 minutes to 11, we shall say: —

9.35. **dix heures moins vingt-cinq minutes,** or simply, **moins vingt-cinq.**
9.40. **dix heures moins vingt minutes,** or **moins vingt.**
9.45. **dix heures moins quinze,** or **moins un quart.**
9.50. **dix heures moins dix minutes,** or **moins dix.**
9.55. **dix heures moins cinq minutes,** or **moins cinq.**
10. **dix heures.**
10.5. **dix heures et cinq minutes,** or **dix heures cinq.**
10.10. **dix heures et dix minutes,** or **dix heures dix.**
10.15. **dix heures et quart,** or **dix heures quinze.**
10.20. **dix heures et vingt minutes,** or **dix heures vingt.**
10.25. **dix heures et vingt-cinq minutes,** or **dix heures vingt-cinq.**
10.30. **dix heures et demie,** or **dix heures trente.**
10.35. **onze heures moins vingt-cinq minutes,** or **moins vingt-cinq.**

Observe that the half-hour goes with the preceding hour.

(3) *O'clock* is often dropped in English, but **heure** or **heures** must be expressed in French. It is the reverse with the word *minutes*, when the number is 5, 10, 15, etc., as: 20 *minutes to* 10, **dix heures moins vingt.**

(4) When **demi** is expressed after its noun, it is not preceded by an article, and is variable: **dix heures et demie** (not **dix heures et une demie**). — When placed before its noun, it is preceded by the article,

is invariable, and is connected with the noun by a hyphen: **une demi-heure.**

(5) To avoid a possible confusion between **douze heures** and **deux heures, douze heures** is not used in French: we say **midi** for 12 at noon, and **minuit** for 12 at night.

la minute, *the minute.*	**la station,** *the station.*
le quart, *the quarter, the fourth.*	**non,** *no.*
heure, (f.), *hour, o'clock.*	**tard,** *late.*

1. Quelle couturière a fait votre robe? 2. Dans quel quartier est votre maison? 3. De quel pays êtes-vous? 4. Sur quelle table avez-vous mis mes gants? 5. Quels souliers avez-vous pris? 6. De quelles chambres avez-vous ouvert les fenêtres? 7. Quelle heure est-il?[1] 8. Il est midi cinq ou midi dix. 9. Il n'est pas encore midi un quart. 10. Est-il parti avec elles? 11. Non, Monsieur, il est parti plus tard, à 3 heures et demie. 12. Nous avons perdu mon pauvre frère ce matin à 9 heures moins un quart.

1. We have not taken. 2. He has never taken. 3. He is never taken. 4. You have not taken. 5. You are not taken. 6. I am not taken. 7. They are never taken. 8. Have we not taken? 9. Is he never taken? 10. Have I not taken? 11. Am I not taken? 12. Have they never taken? 13. Are they never taken? 14. What French book have you read? 15. Which pen is the best? 16. Which pens are the best? 17. What handkerchiefs have you taken? 18. What hour is it? 19. It is a quarter to two. 20. It is five minutes to three. 21. It is twenty minutes past four. 22. It is half-past five. 23. It is not twenty minutes to six. 24. It is not yet a quarter past seven. 25. It is midnight. 26. It is

[1] **Est-il,** not **est-elle,** because this **il est** is an impersonal verb, and as such cannot have any other subject than the invariable **il.**

five minutes past twelve (at night). 27. At what o'clock did my sisters go away? 28. They went away from the house at five minutes of eleven, and from the station half an hour later.

45.

Which followed by *of* (expressed or understood) is a pronoun and translated by —

SINGULAR.		PLURAL.	
MASC.	FEM.	MASC.	FEM.
lequel, *which* (of),	**laquelle.**	**lesquels,**	**lesquelles.**
duquel, *of which* (of),	**de laquelle.**	**desquels,**	**desquelles.**
auquel, *to which* (of),	**à laquelle.**	**auxquels,**	**auxquelles.**

jeune personne, *young lady.*
le bagage, *the luggage.*
près de, *near.*

1. Lequel de ces messieurs est votre frère? 2. C'est celui qui est près de la table. 3. Laquelle de ces jeunes personnes est votre sœur? 4. Elle n'est pas ici, elle est sortie. 5. Duquel de ces enfants avez-vous parlé? 6. J'ai parlé de celui qui est arrivé ici il y a quinze jours. 7. De laquelle de vos sœurs avez-vous reçu ce joli cadeau? 8. De Jeanne; c'est la plus jeune de mes sœurs. 9. Auquel de nos écrivains avez-vous parlé? 10. J'ai parlé à celui qui a écrit ce beau roman. 11. A laquelle de ces dames avez-vous écrit? 12. A celle qui a tant pleuré hier. 13. Auxquelles de ces jeunes personnes avez-vous lu ma lettre? 14. J'ai lu votre lettre à toutes; elles ont beaucoup ri.

1. We (*m.*) are not found. 2. She has never found. 3. She is never found. 4. You have no more found. 5. You (*pl.*) are no more found. 6. I have not found. 7. My sons have not found. 8. My daughters

are not found. 9. Have we not found? 10. Are we not found. 11. Has she never found? 12. Is she never found? 13. Have you no more found? 14. Are you no more found? 15. Am I not found? 16. Are they (*f.*) never found? 17. Here are six hats; which (of them) is the best? 18. There are ten pens; which (of them) is the best? 19. Which of these two books did you lend to my brother? 20. Which of these chairs is the highest? 21. Which of these apples are the best? 22. To which of these young ladies did you lend your brooch? 23. To which of these gentlemen did you sell your watch? 24. Which of these rooms is the largest? 25. Which of your sisters has gone away? 26. Which of your brothers has lost his luggage?

46.

We have seen (§ 8) that the nominative *which* or *that* is translated by **qui** and the accusative by **que**.

To complete the rule, translate the pronoun *which* after a preposition by **lequel, laquelle, lesquels, lesquelles.**

Where is the pen with which I wrote this letter?	**Où est la plume avec laquelle j'ai écrit cette lettre?**
Here is the table on which I put your purse,	**Voici la table sur laquelle j'ai mis votre porte-monnaie.**

When *of which*, *of whom*, or *whose* are not interrogative, they may be expressed by **dont** for both genders and numbers, instead of the variable **duquel, de laquelle, desquels**, etc.

Bring me the book of which I spoke,	**Apportez-moi le livre dont j'ai parlé.**
The man of whom I spoke has arrived,	**L'homme dont j'ai parlé est arrivé.**

le prix, *the prize.*
le tiroir, *the drawer.*
la boîte, *the box.*
le nom, *the name.*
travaillé, *worked, wrought.*
caché, *hidden.*
coupé, *cut.*
enfin, *at last.*
demeuré, *lived.*
plusieurs, *several.*

1. Dans quelle rue avez-vous perdu votre chien? 2. Voici la rue dans laquelle j'ai perdu mon chien. 3. De quel livre avez-vous parlé à mon oncle? 4. Voilà le livre dont j'ai parlé à votre oncle. 5. Où avez-vous mis l'ardoise sur laquelle vous avez écrit votre nom et le mien? 6. Apportez-moi la table sur laquelle j'ai mis mes livres et mes papiers. 7. Dans quel journal avez-vous lu cette lettre? 8. Montrez-moi le journal dans lequel vous avez lu cette lettre. 9. Voilà ces bottines pour lesquelles vous avez tant pleuré. 10. Voici la table sur laquelle j'ai tant écrit. 11. Il a enfin reçu le prix pour lequel il a tant travaillé. 12. Apportez-moi le tiroir dans lequel vous avez mis mes gants. 13. Il n'a pas visité la chambre dans laquelle nous avons caché ses joujoux. 14. Elles ont visité la chambre dans laquelle vous avez demeuré plusieurs mois. 15. Apportez-moi le livre dont j'ai parlé à votre sœur.

1. They (*m.*) have not laughed. 2. They are not cut. 3. She has never fallen. 4. You have no more hidden. 5. You (*pl.*) are no more hidden. 6. We have never hidden. 7. We are never hidden. 8. Henry and his sister have not come. 9. Have they not hidden? 10. Are they not hidden. 11. Has she never worked? 12. Is she never hidden? 13. Are you no more hidden? 14. Have we never hidden? 15. Are we never hidden? 16. Have I not slept? 17. In which drawer did you hide my novel? 18. Did you find the drawer in which your brother has hidden your novel? 19. Where is the

brooch of which you spoke to my sister? 20. Here is the knife with which I cut bread. 21. Here is the box in which I put your letters and portrait. 22. In which room did you hide my gloves and my hat? 23. Did you find the room in which we hid your gloves and your hat? 24. Here are the two pencils with which I wrote my exercises. 25. Here are the two pens with which we wrote our letters. 26. The table upon which you have put your papers belongs to your father.

47.

Imperfect.

The termination of the imperfect, in all verbs, is: —

SINGULAR.	**-ais.** **-ais.** **-ait.**	PLURAL.	**-ions.** **-iez.** **-aient.**

Before that termination put **av-** in the imperfect of **avoir,** *to have,* and **ét-** in the imperfect of **être,** *to be:* —

I had,	**j'avais.**	*I was,*	**j'étais.**
thou hadst,	**tu avais.**	*thou wast,*	**tu étais.**
he had,	**il avait.**	*he was,*	**il était.**
she had,	**elle avait.**	*she was,*	**elle était.**
we had,	**nous avions.**	*we were,*	**nous étions.**
you had,	**vous aviez.**	*you were,*	**vous étiez.**
they had,	**ils avaient.** **elles avaient.**	*they were,*	**ils étaient.** **elles étaient.**

INTERROGATIVELY.

had I?	**avais-je?**	*was I?*	**étais-je?**
hadst thou?	**avais-tu?**	*wast thou?*	**étais-tu?**
had he?	**avait-il?**	*was he?*	**était-il?**
had she?	**avait-elle?**	*was she?*	**était-elle?**

had we?	**avions-nous?**	*were we?*	**étions-nous?**
had you?	**aviez-vous?**	*were you?*	**étiez-vous?**
had they?	**avaient-ils?** / **avaient-elles?**	*were they?*	**étaient-ils?** / **étaient-elles?**

mes parents, *my parents* or *relatives.*
la campagne, *the country* (in contradistinction to the town).
à la campagne, *in the country.*
le pays, *the country* (the whole country, the whole territory).
le bois, *the wood.*
abondant, *abundant.*
le lapin, *the rabbit.*
paresseux, *lazy, idle.*
appliqué, *diligent.*
autrefois, *formerly.*
il y a, *there is, there are.*
il y avait, *there was, there were.*

1. Quand vous étiez jeune, vous aviez de beaux joujoux. 2. Mes parents n'étaient pas si riches que les vôtres, mais j'avais aussi de jolies choses. 3. Nous avions une grande maison à la campagne. 4. Il y avait près de la maison un petit bois et de grands arbres. 5. J'avais près de ma fenêtre un petit jardin plein de fleurs rouges et blanches. 6. Mon jardin était très petit, mais mes fleurs étaient si jolies! 7. Il y avait beaucoup d'oiseaux dans le jardin et dans le bois. 8. Les oranges étaient rares, mais les fraises étaient abondantes. 9. Nous avions aussi beaucoup de poires et de pommes. 10. Nos chiens et nos chats étaient aussi heureux que nous. 11. Les chiens étaient heureux parce qu'il y avait beaucoup de lapins dans le bois, et les chats parce qu'il y avait beaucoup d'oiseaux dans le jardin. 12. Nous étions heureux parce que nous avions beaucoup de bons amis. 13. Tout le monde était heureux.

1. They had; they have. 2. They were; they are. 3. Had you? have you? 4. Were you? are you? 5. We had; we have. 6. We were; we are. 7. Had I? have I? 8. Was I? am I? 9. She had; she has; she was; she is. 10. His sisters were rich because they were very diligent. 11. My brothers were idle. 12. They

had too many horses and dogs. 13. Her father had many horses, gardens, and meadows. 14. Where were you an hour ago? 15. We were at our uncle's. 16. Our neighbor was formerly as rich as you, he had many houses. 17. John had more money than you this morning. 18. They were poor, but their children had always pretty toys. 19. There was formerly a large wood near that town.

48.

I had not,	**je n'avais pas.**	*I was not,*	**je n'étais pas.**
thou hadst not,	**tu n'avais pas.**	*thou wast not,*	**tu n'étais pas.**
he had not,	**il n'avait pas.**	*he was not,*	**il n'était pas.**
she had not,	**elle n'avait pas.**	*she was not,*	**elle n'était pas.**
we had not,	**nous n'avions pas.**	*we were not,*	**nous n'étions pas.**
you had not,	**vous n'aviez pas.**	*you were not,*	**vous n'étiez pas.**
they had not,	**ils n'avaient pas.** **elles n'avaient pas.**	*they were not,*	**ils n'étaient pas.** **elles n'étaient pas.**

INTERROGATIVELY.

had I not?	**n'avais-je pas?**	*was I not?*	**n'étais-je pas?**
	etc.		etc.

(1) **Tout** (*everything*) and **rien** (*nothing*) are placed between the auxiliary verb and the past participle: —

J'ai tout vu, *I have seen everything.*
Je n'ai rien perdu, *I have lost nothing.*

(2) **Personne** (*nobody, no one*) is placed after the past participle as in English: —

Je n'ai vu personne, *I have seen no one.*

ne . . . personne, *nobody, no one.*
ne . . . rien, *nothing.*
affaires, *business.*
eu,[1] *had.*
j'ai eu, *I have had.*
tout, *everything.*
dit, *said.*
quand, *when.*
été, *been.*
j'ai été, *I have been.*

[1] *Had* is translated by **eu** when it is a past participle, that is, when it comes after any part of the verb *to have:* I have *had,* I had *had,* etc.

il n'y a pas,	*there is not.*
il n'y avait pas,	*there was not.*
il n'y a plus,	*there is no more* (or *no longer*).
il n'y avait plus,	*there was no more* (or *no longer*).
il n'y a personne,	*there is nobody.*
il n'y avait personne,	*there was nobody.*
il n'y a rien,	*there is nothing.*
il n'y avait rien,	*there was nothing.*

1. Je suis allé chez vous hier soir à 6 heures et demie, mais il n'y avait personne. 2. N'avez-vous pas vu mes parents ou mes frères ? 3. Je n'ai vu personne. 4. N'avez-vous pas eu mon livre ce matin ? 5. Non, mon ami, je n'ai pas eu votre livre ce matin. 6. N'ont-ils pas été malades ce soir ? 7. Ils ont tous été malades. 8. Jean et Louis n'ont pas fait d'affaires aujourd'hui. 9. Ce soir, à 5 heures moins un quart, ils n'avaient encore rien vendu. 10. Je n'avais pas encore (*yet*) vu ma sœur quand vous êtes venu chez moi. 11. Donnez-moi du fil, il n'y a plus de soie. 12. Apportez-nous de l'eau, il n'y a plus de vin. 13. Il n'a rien eu, il n'a rien dit, il n'a vu personne. 14. Personne n'a vu le livre que vous avez perdu.

1. I have had nothing. 2. She has had nothing. 3. You have had nothing. 4. They have had nothing. 5. Thou hast seen nobody. 6. He has seen nobody. 7. We have seen nobody. 8. They have seen nobody. 9. I had lent everything. 10. Thou hadst lent everything. 11. She had lent everything. 12. We had lent everything. 13. You had lent everything. 14. I have not been ill. 15. He has not been ill. 16. You have not been ill. 17. They have not been ill. 18. Have you visited everything ? 19. I have visited everything and seen everything. 20. When I saw your brother, he had

written everything. 21. There was nobody at your house at 5 o'clock. 22. Have you had much business to-day? 23. I have sold nothing, everything is so dear. 24. There is no money in your purse: will you have 20 francs? 25. Did you find the thimble which you lost? 26. I found nothing. 27. There was nothing on your table.

49.

Future.

The termination of the future in all verbs is: —

SINGULAR.	**-rai.** **-ras.** **-ra.**	PLURAL.	**-rons.** **-rez.** **-ront.**

Before that termination put **au-** in the future of **avoir**, and **se-** in the future of **être**: —

I shall or *will have,*	**j'aurai.**	*I shall* or *will be,*	**je serai.**
thou shalt or *wilt have,*	**tu auras.**	*thou shalt* or *wilt be,*	**tu seras.**
he shall or *will have,*	**il aura.**	*he shall* or *will be,*	**il sera.**
she shall or *will have,*	**elle aura.**	*she shall* or *will be,*	**elle sera.**
we shall or *will have,*	**nous aurons.**	*we shall* or *will be,*	**nous serons.**
you shall or *will have,*	**vous aurez.**	*you shall* or *will be,*	**vous serez.**
they shall or *will have,*	**ils auront.** **elles auront.**	*they shall* or *will be,*	**ils seront.** **elles seront.**

INTERROGATIVELY.

shall I have? **aurai-je?**	*shall I be?* **serai-je?**
etc.	etc.

The future tense must be used after **quand, dès que, aussitôt que**, if futurity is implied, as: —

Vous aurez ce livre quand vous aurez écrit votre lettre,	*You will have that book when you have written your letter.*
Vous aurez ce livre dès que (or aussitôt que) vous aurez écrit votre lettre,	*You will have that book as soon as you have written your letter.*

dès que, } *as soon as.*
aussitôt que, }
demain, *to-morrow.*
la pantoufle, *the slipper.*
bien aise, *glad*, or *very glad.*
commandé, *ordered.*

1. Votre père sera ici demain, à 9 heures et demie du soir. 2. Serez-vous bien aise quand j'aurai fini ces jolies pantoufles pour vous? 3. Aurons-nous aujourd'hui le poisson que nous avons commandé. 4. Dès que leur mère sera ici, elles auront du fil, de la soie et des aiguilles. 5. Vous aurez aussi beaucoup de jolies choses. 6. Vous aurez une petite montre, une petite chaîne et un beau portemonnaie avec un franc. 7. Aurai-je aussi un beau cheval blanc? 8. Vous n'aurez pas de cheval blanc, ces animaux-là sont trop chers. 9. Dès qu'elle aura écrit ses exercices, elle aura une tasse de lait et des fraises. 10. Nous aurons le journal français tous les samedis. 11. Vous serez un peu plus aimable quand vous ne serez plus malade.

1. They will have; they will be. 2. We shall have; we shall be. 3. He will have; he will be. 4. You will have; you will be. 5. My cousins (*m.*) will have. 6. My cousins (*f.*) will be. 7. Will they have? 8. Will they be? 9. Shall we have? 10. Shall we be? 11. Will you have? 12. Will you be? 13. Shall I have? 14. Shall I be? 15. He shall have this stick as soon as he has done his exercise. 16. She will be prettier than her sister. 17. My exercises will not be so easy as yours. 18. They will be much more difficult. 19. As soon as they are here, they shall have some bread and some meat. 20. You will not be ill to-morrow. 21. They will be here at a quarter to six this evening. 22. We shall be very glad when you are with us.

50.

I shall or *will not have.*	*I shall* or *will not be.*
je n'aurai pas.	**je ne serai pas.**
tu n'auras pas.	**tu ne seras pas.**
il n'aura pas.	**il ne sera pas.**
elle n'aura pas.	**elle ne sera pas.**
nous n'aurons pas.	**nous ne serons pas.**
vous n'aurez pas.	**vous ne serez pas.**
ils n'auront pas.	**ils ne seront pas.**
elles n'auront pas.	**elles ne seront pas.**

INTERROGATIVELY.

shall I not have? **n'aurai-je pas?** etc. *shall I not be?* **ne serai-je pas?** etc.

il y aura, *there will be.*
la fin, *the end.*
la récompense, *the reward.*
le fruit, *the fruit.*
il n'y aura pas, *there will not be.*
libre, *free.*
préférable, *preferable.*
choisi, *chosen.*

1. Vous ne serez pas heureux si vous n'êtes pas appliqué. 2. N'aurez-vous pas de prix à la fin de cette session? 3. Laquelle de vos sœurs sera prête la première? 4. Ce ne sera pas Thérèse. 5. Ne serez-vous pas libre ce soir? 6. Ne serez-vous pas chez votre oncle à cinq heures? 7. N'aurons-nous pas de fruits? 8. Ne serez-vous pas bien aises quand vous aurez fait tout ce travail? 9. N'aurai-je pas enfin ma récompense? 10. La date choisie par mon frère ne sera pas préférable à la vôtre. 11. Vos exercices ne seront pas plus difficiles que les miens. 12. Quand serez-vous à Paris?

1. We shall not have found. 2. We shall not be found. 3. They will not have found. 4. They will not be found. 5. She will not have found. 6. She will not be found. 7. You will not have found. 8. You (*pl.*) will not be found. 9. I shall not have found. 10. I

shall not be found. 11. Shall we not have found? 12. Shall we not be found? 13. Will they not have found? 14. Will they not be found? 15. Will you not have found? 16. Will you not be found? 17. Shall I not have found? 18. Shall I not be found? 19. Shall we not have much work? 20. Shall we not be free to-morrow night? 21. Will you have much business? 22. Will you not be in a beautiful country? 23. Will they not have a reward? 24. Will they not be industrious? 25. Shall you not be at London the 23d of this month? 26. You will have a letter from your brother as soon as you are at London.

51.

Conditional.

The termination of the conditional in all verbs is: —

SINGULAR,	**-rais.**	PLURAL,	**-rions.**
	-rais.		**-riez.**
	-rait.		**-raient.**

Before that termination put **au-** in the conditional of **avoir**, and **se-** in the conditional of **être**: —

I should or *would have,*	**j'aurais.**	*I should* or *would be,*	**je serais.**
	tu aurais.		**tu serais.**
	il aurait.		**il serait.**
	elle aurait.		**elle serait.**
	nous aurions.		**nous serions.**
	vous auriez.		**vous seriez.**
	ils auraient.		**ils seraient.**
	elles auraient.		**elles seraient.**

INTERROGATIVELY.

should I have?	**aurais-je?**	*should I be?*	**serais-je?**
	etc.		etc.

Neither the future nor the conditional can be used after **si** beginning a clause. When they are so used in English, we put the present instead of the future, and the imperfect instead of the conditional, as: —

Si vous êtes chez vous à six heures, vous aurez ma visite,	*If you will be at home at six o'clock, you shall have a visit from me.*
Si vous étiez chez vous à six heures, vous auriez ma visite,	*If you would be at home at six o'clock, you would have a visit from me.*

le mot, *the word.*	**simple**, *simple.*
la réponse, *the answer.*	**malheureux**, *unhappy, unfortunate.*
l'opéra (m.), *the opera.*	**content**, *contented, pleased.*

1. Si vous étiez resté là, votre sœur ne serait pas partie. 2. Ils n'auraient pas été si contents si leur père était resté avec eux. 3. Si j'avais dit un mot, elle serait revenue. 4. Vos frères ne seraient pas si heureux s'ils[1] n'avaient pas fini leurs exercices. 5. Auriez-vous parlé à votre cousine si elle était entrée ? 6. Seriez-vous aussi gaie que votre sœur si vous étiez aussi riche qu'elle ? 7. Auraient-elles reçu une réponse si elles avaient écrit cette lettre ? 8. Aurais-je dit tant de choses aimables à votre sœur si elle avait été méchante ? 9. Il aurait acheté plusieurs paires de bottines ce jour-là si elles avaient été bien faites. 10. Elle serait allée à l'opéra si sa mère n'avait pas été malade. 11. Si j'étais allé chez eux ce soir, je n'aurais trouvé personne. 12. Rien ne serait plus utile que ce livre s'il était plus simple. 13. Nous n'aurions plus de vin si nous avions bu ces dix bouteilles.

1. They will be; they will have. 2. They would be; they would have. 3. We shall be; we shall have. 4. We should be; we should have. 5. She will be; she will have. 6. She would be; she would have. 7. Will

[1] **i** is elided in **si** only when followed by **il** or **ils** : **s'il est, s'ils sont.**

they be? 8. Will they have? 9. Would they be? 10. Would they have? 11. Shall we be? 12. Shall we have? 13. Should we be? 14. Should we have? 15. You would be very happy, if your brother were here. 16. He would always be with you. 17. They should have more prizes, if they were more industrious. 18. These ribbons would be prettier, if they were red. 19. That silk would be prettier, if it were black. 20. If that water were cold, it would be better. 21. Will you be glad when you have received that money? 22. Would you be glad, if you had received that money? 23. I should have gone to your house, if I had not been ill. 24. If I had not had any money, I should have been very unhappy. 25. They (*f.*) would have bought some lace and some silk, if they had received more money. 26. My little sister would have lost her thimble, if my brother had not been in the chamber.

52.

I should or *would not have.*	*I should* or *would not be.*
je n'aurais pas.	**je ne serais pas.**
tu n'aurais pas.	**tu ne serais pas.**
il n'aurait pas.	**il ne serait pas.**
elle n'aurait pas.	**elle ne serait pas.**
nous n'aurions pas.	**nous ne serions pas.**
vous n'auriez pas.	**vous ne seriez pas.**
ils n'auraient pas.	**ils ne seraient pas.**
elles n'auraient pas.	**elles ne seraient pas.**

INTERROGATIVELY.

should I not have? **n'aurais-je pas?** etc.

should I not be? **ne serais-je pas?** etc.

la règle, *the rule.*
l'exemple (m.), *the example.*
chagrin, *sad, vexed, sorry.*
maintenant, *now, by this time.*
sans, *without, but for.*
bien, *very.*[1]

[1] **Bien** is more emphatic than **très**; it is generally used with some feeling of admiration, surprise, desire, envy, etc.

1. N'auriez-vous pas été bien chagrin si vous n'étiez pas venu avec moi ? 2. J'aurais été très malheureux si vous étiez parti sans moi. 3. Nous étions allés à l'opéra, et la bonne était sortie. 4. Ne seraient-ils pas plus laborieux si leur père était ici ? 5. Si vous aviez mis moins d'exemples dans vos règles, ne seraient-elles pas beaucoup plus simples ? 6. Si vous étiez parti ce matin, vous seriez arrivé maintenant. 7. N'aurions-nous pas eu de réponse à notre lettre si nous avions écrit à votre père ? 8. Seriez-vous resté ici sans moi ? 9. N'auraient-ils pas été malades s'ils avaient mangé ces mauvaises poires ? 10. N'auraient-elles pas été très chagrines si elles avaient perdu leurs exercices ? 11. S'ils étaient partis à trois heures, ils ne seraient pas encore arrivés maintenant, mais ils seraient bien près de la ville. 12. Ne serais-je pas bien malheureux si vous n'étiez pas avec moi ? 13. S'il était allé dans votre chambre, n'aurait-il rien trouvé ?

1. You would not have; you would not have had. 2. You would not have been. 3. She would not have. 4. She would not have had; she would not have been. 5. They would not be; they would not have been. 6. They would not have had. 7. I should not be; I should not have been; I should not have had. 8. There is nothing; there was nothing. 9. There will be nothing; there would be nothing. 10. There is not; there was not. 11. There will not be; there would not be. 12. If you had been more diligent, your mother would not have been so sad. 13. These children would not be so unhappy, if they had not lost their mother. 14. If he had come a little later, he would not have found his father here. 15. If your brother had left three hours ago, would he not be at his house by this time ? 16. I

would have gone to the opera, if you had come with me. 17. If you had gone into my room, you would have found nothing. 18. If there were not so many words in your rules, would they not be more simple and easy? 19. I would not have written my exercises, if my mother had come back to-day. 20. Should we not have found anybody, if we had gone to your house at half past nine? 21. No, sir, you would not have found anybody.

53.

(1) In questions, if the subject is a personal pronoun (**je, tu, il, elle, nous, vous, ils, elles**), or one of the pronouns **ce, on**, it stands, as in English, after the verb:

Est-il chez nous?	*Is he at our house?*
Est-elle chez elle?	*Is she at home?*

(2) If the subject is not one of these pronouns, it begins the sentence, and is repeated after the verb under the form of a pronoun: —

Votre frère est-il heureux?	*Is your brother happy?*
Ma mère est-elle venue?	*Has my mother come?*
La vôtre est-elle partie?	*Is yours gone away?*

(3) If the question begins in English with an interrogative adverb (*why? where? when? how?* etc.), the adverb is also placed first in French, and the rest of the sentence is constructed as above: —

Pourquoi votre frère est-il si malheureux?	*Why is your brother so unhappy?*
Quand ma mère est-elle venue?	*When has my mother come?*
A quelle heure la vôtre est-elle partie?	*At what o'clock did yours go away?*

(4) When the third person singular ends with a vowel, it is followed by a euphonic **t** before **il**, **elle**, **on**, to prevent an hiatus: —

A-t-il perdu son livre?	*Has he lost his book?*
A-t-elle vu son père?	*Has she seen her father?*
Sera-t-on aimable avec vous?	*Will they be amiable towards you?*

y a-t-il?	*is there? are there?*	**n'y a-t-il pas?**	*is* or *are there not?*
y avait-il?	*was* or *were there?*	**n'y avait-il pas?**	*was* or *were there not?*

maintenant que,	*now that* or simply *now.*
la semaine prochaine,	*next week.*
le mois prochain,	*next month.*
à la campagne,	*in the country.*
fini,	*ended, finished.*

1. Votre cousin a-t-il reçu une réponse à sa lettre? 2. Votre cousine n'a-t-elle pas encore reçu de réponse à sa lettre? 3. Vos sœurs ne sont-elles pas bien aises maintenant qu'elles ont fini leur travail? 4. Votre mère n'a-t-elle pas perdu son porte-monnaie? 5. Ce vélocipède n'est-il pas bien joli? 6. Votre frère n'avait-il pas pleuré quand nous sommes entrés chez vous? 7. Ne serez-vous pas libre la semaine prochaine? 8. N'aurez-vous pas tout fini le mois prochain? 9. Pourquoi cette jeune personne est-elle si chagrine? 10. Où mon frère a-t-il caché mon porte-monnaie? 11. Où vos amis ont-ils perdu leurs bagages? 12. Quand M. Herbulot est-il parti pour la campagne? 13. A quelle heure Ernest sera-t-il à la station? 14. Combien votre oncle a-t-il vendu cette maison? 15. N'y a-t-il rien dans ce tiroir?

1. Is there? Is there not? 2. Was there? Was there not? 3. Will there be? Will there not be? 4. Would there be? Would there not be? 5. Is there never? Was there never? 6. Will there never be?

Would there never be? 7. Is there no more? Was there no more? 8. Will there no longer be? Would there no longer be? 9. Is there nobody? Was there nobody? 10. Will there be nobody? Would there be nobody? 11. Is your sister ill? 12. Are your brothers diligent? 13. Is this novel interesting? 14. Has not your mother lost her bracelets? 15. Have your parents a house in the country? 16. Which of his books has your brother lost? 17. Where has my cousin hidden my ear-rings? 18. In what box has Henry put my gloves? 19. When will Miss Louisa be in London? 20. At what o'clock will Therese have finished her exercise? 21. When did your father buy this wood?

54.

Exceptions to the formation of the feminine of Adjectives.

We have seen (§ 2) that to form the feminine of adjectives, an *e mute* is added to the masculine: **vrai**, *true*, **vraie**; **appliqué**, *diligent*, **appliquée**; **secret**, *secret*, **secrète.**[1]

Exceptions. — Adjectives ending with *e mute* in the masculine are the same in the feminine.

Adjectives ending in **-el**, **-en**, **-on**, **-et**, double the last consonant, and take an *e mute* after it: **cruel**, *cruel*, **cruelle**; **ancien**, *old*, **ancienne**; **bon**, *good*, **bonne**; **sujet**, *subject*, **sujette**. But **secret**, **complet**, and five others in **-et** form their feminine regularly.

[1] Observe that if the adjective ends in the masculine with a consonant preceded by an *e mute*, the latter takes a grave accent in the feminine: **complet, complète; premier, première; cher, chère.**

The following adjectives also double their last consonant in the feminine.

pareil,	*like, alike, such,*	**pareille.**
épais,	*thick,*	**épaisse.**
gros,	*stout, big,*	**grosse.**
gras,	*fat,*	**grasse.**
bas,	*low,*	**basse.**
gentil,	*pretty,*	**gentille.**
las,	*tired,*	**lasse.**
sot,	*foolish,*	**sotte.**

Adjectives ending in **-f** change **f** to **ve** :[1] **vif,** *lively, quick*, **vive** ; **actif,** *active*, **active** ; **neuf,** *new made*, **neuve.**

Adjectives ending in **-x** change **x** into **se** :[2] **heureux, heureuse.**

délicieux,	*delicious,*	**délicieuse.**	**jaloux,**	*jealous,*	**jalouse.**
orageux,	*stormy,*	**orageuse.**	**pluvieux,**	*rainy,*	**pluvieuse.**
studieux,	*studious,*	**studieuse.**	**généreux,**	*generous,*	**généreuse.**

nombreux, *numerous,* **nombreuse.**

garçon, *boy.*	**sauvage,** *wild.*
fille, *girl.*	**moderne,** *modern.*
histoire (f.), *history.*	**la langue,** *the language.*
la bête, *the beast.*	**italien,** *Italian.*
la géographie, *geography.*	**jamais,** *ever.*
chat (m.), **chătte** (f.), *cat.*	**appris,** *learnt.*

1. Ces dernières nuits ont été très orageuses. 2. Votre frère est paresseux, mais votre sœur est très studieuse. 3. Votre cousine n'est-elle pas un peu jalouse ? 4. Votre bonne n'est pas si active que la nôtre. 5. J'ai un chapeau neuf et aussi des bottines neuves. 6. Nos oncles sont heureux, mais nos cousines sont bien malheureuses. 7. Ces fraises ne sont-elles pas délicieuses ? 8. Vous êtes

[1] The reason is that, but for the change, there would be no difference in pronunciation between the masculine and the feminine.

[2] Were an *e mute* added to *x*, according to the general rule, the sound (**heureuxe, jalouxe**) would be too hard.

bien heureuse, Madame, vous avez des enfants laborieux. 9. Ces filles sont moins actives que ces garçons. 10. Les éléphants ne sont pas cruels, mais ces bêtes sauvages sont très cruelles. 11. L'histoire moderne n'est pas si facile que l'histoire ancienne, mais la géographie ancienne est beaucoup plus difficile que la géographie moderne. 12. La langue italienne n'est pas difficile. 13. Les grosses fraises ne sont pas si bonnes que les petites. 14. Cette viande est trop grasse, donnez-nous autre chose. 15. Cette petite fille est bien lasse. 16. Pourquoi votre frère a-t-il vendu son petit chien? il était si gentil. 17. Où votre sœur a-t-elle trouvé cette gentille petite chatte?

1. Have you ever read ancient history or learnt ancient geography? 2. Has your brother seen that pretty little beast? 3. This little boy is prettier than that little girl. 4. Yes, but in five or six years, the little girl will be prettier than the little boy. 5. Our arm-chairs are not so low as your chairs. 6. This beast is cruel. 7. Is the Italian language difficult? 8. No, sir, it is one of the easiest of languages.[1] 9. Your watch is too big. 10. That cat (*f.*) is too fat and her hairs are too thick. 11. Your brothers are very tired. 12. Omnibuses are not numerous in this town. 13. These men are generous. 14. Those women are not generous. 15. Is not your sister happy? 16. His shoes are new, but his boots are not new. 17. Aunt, your tea is delicious, but your butter is not very good. 18. We shall have a rainy night. 19. Our maid-servant is not so active as theirs.

[1] Observe that, when a superlative is placed after its noun, the article is repeated: **c'est une des langues les plus faciles.**

55.

Exceptions to the formation of the feminine of Adjectives continued.

The following adjectives form their feminine irregularly.

vieux, vieil,	*old,*	**vieille.**
beau, bel,	*beautiful, fine, handsome,*	**belle.**
nouveau, nouvel,	*new,*[1]	**nouvelle.**
fou, fol,	*mad, foolish.*	**folle.**
faux,	*false,*	**fausse.**
doux,	*sweet, gentle.*	**douce.**
blanc,	*white,*	**blanche.**
franc,	*frank,*	**franche.**
sec,	*dry,*	**sèche.**
public,	*public,*	**publique.**
grec,	*Greek,*	**grecque.**
malin,	*malignant, cunning, clever,*	**maligne.**
frais,	*fresh, cool,*	**fraîche.**
long,	*long,*	**longue.**
favori,	*favorite,*	**favorite.**

Observe that the first four adjectives of this list have each two forms for the masculine. The second form is used only before a noun beginning with a vowel or *h mute:* **un bel oiseau, le nouvel opéra, le fol enfant, mon vieil ami.**[2]

large, *broad.*	**la promenade,** *the walk.*
latin, *Latin.*	**la nouvelle,** *the news.*
régulier, *regular.*	**le bruit,** *the report.*
l'avenue (f.), *the avenue.*	**l'ouvrage** (m.), *the work, the book.*

[1] **Nouveau,** placed before its noun, means *another:* **j'ai acheté de nouveaux livres,** *I have bought some more books.*

Nouveau, placed after its noun, means *recent:* **j'ai acheté quelques livres nouveaux,** *I have bought some books which have appeared recently.*

Neuf means *new made, that has not been in use yet:* **un habit neuf, un chapeau neuf,** *a new coat, a new hat.* **Neuf** is always placed after its noun.

[2] **Vieil** is not absolutely required before a noun beginning with a vowel; we also say **mon vieux ami.**

1. Apportez-moi un verre d'eau fraîche. 2. Cette table est longue et large. 3. La langue grecque est plus riche que la langue latine : elle est aussi plus difficile. 4. Je n'ai jamais vu de petite bête plus maligne que celle-ci. 5. Cette nouvelle promenade n'est-elle pas publique ? 6. Oui, c'est maintenant ma promenade favorite. 7. Autrefois c'était cette longue avenue par laquelle nous sommes venus hier. 8. Voici des poires qui sont bien vieilles. 9. Mon nouvel ami n'est pas malin. 10. Sa sœur est la plus franche et la plus aimable des filles. 11. Mon frère avait un bel habit neuf, et ma sœur une robe blanche. 12. Sa cousine est une très belle femme. 13. Son cousin est un très bel homme. 14. Cette nouvelle est fausse. 15. Ce bruit n'est pas moins faux.

1. Did you read Dickens's new work ? 2. Is not this little girl your favorite ? 3. This wine is cool, but this water is not cool. 4. There is a fine animal. 5. My old friend (*m.*) is more cunning than you. 6. My old friend (*f.*) is more cunning than he. 7. The Italian women are more numerous in this country than the Greek women. 8. Your chain is longer than mine or (than) his. 9. We are lost if that news is true. 10. It is not true, it is false. 11. This long avenue is not public. 12. Your strawberries are not very fresh. 13. Your sister is more frank than his. 14. This muslin is as white as mine. 15. That poor woman is mad. 16. Your brother is very fond of (*likes much*) sweet ale. 17. Why is your aunt so unhappy ? Is not her daughter industrious ?

56.

VERBS.

French verbs are divided into three conjugations,[1] distinguished from each other by the termination of the infinitive.

The 1st ends in **-er**, the 2d in **-ir**, the 3d in **-re.**

The present participle is that part of a verb which ends in *-ing*. It is frequently used in English with the verb *to be*, but it is *never* so used in French. When we have to translate it from English, we turn it into the simplest form. For example, instead of *I am speaking*, we say *I speak;* instead of *I was speaking*, we say *I spoke;* instead of *I shall be speaking*, *I shall speak.*

The auxiliary verb *to do* does not exist in French, and must be suppressed in translating: *Do you speak?* is therefore turned into *speak you? Do they speak?* into *speak they?* etc.

FIRST CONJUGATION.

In the first conjugation, which contains more than four-fifths of the French verbs (3,400), the infinitive ends in **-er**, and the past participle in **-é**.

1 Most grammars divide French verbs into four conjugations; but one conjugation having only seven regular verbs and about forty irregular ones, it has been thought better to put all these among the irregular verbs.

porter, *to carry;* **porté**, *carried.*

Indicative Present.

TERMINATIONS: **-e, -es, -e, -ons, -ez, -ent.**

AFFIRMATIVE.	INTERROGATIVE.
je porte, *I carry, I am carrying, I do carry.*	**porté-je?**[1]
tu portes.	**portes-tu?**
il or **elle porte.**	**porte-t-il?**
nous portons.	**portons-nous?**
vous portez.	**portez-vous?**
ils or **elles portent.**	**portent-ils?**

NEGATIVE.	INTERROGATIVE NEGATIVE.
je ne porte pas.	**ne porté-je pas?**[1]
tu ne portes pas.	**ne portes-tu pas?**
il ne porte pas.	**ne porte-t-il pas?**
nous ne portons pas.	**ne portons-nous pas?**
vous ne portez pas.	**ne portez-vous pas?**
ils ne portent pas.	**ne portent-ils pas?**

trouver, *to find.*
donner, *to give.*
prêter, *to lend.*
accepter, *to accept.*
fermer, *to shut.*
montrer, *to show.*
arroser, *to water.*
aimer, *to like, to love.*
visiter, *to visit.*
parler, *to speak.*
pleurer, *to weep.*
travailler, *to work.*
cacher, *to hide, to conceal.*
commander, *to command.*
penser, *to think.*
admirer, *to admire.*

que, *that* (conjunction).

Imperative.[2]

porte, *carry thou.* **portons**, *let us carry.* **portez**, *carry you* or *ye.*

[1] In questions, when the 1st person singular ends in *e mute*, an acute accent is put upon it for the sake of the sound.

[2] The imperative is formed from the present indicative in all verbs.

1. Je pense que vous aimez les animaux. 2. Je trouve que votre frère travaille beaucoup. 3. N'acceptez-vous pas ce joli cadeau? 4. Ils donnent toujours de jolies choses à ma tante. 5. Si vous ne pleurez pas, vous aurez un beau ruban rouge. 6. Je ne pleure plus; montrez-moi ce beau ruban. 7. Avez-vous visité les principales villes du pays? 8. Nous n'avons rien visité, nous sommes venus par le bateau. 9. Nous ne fermons jamais cette porte. 10. Vous cachez toujours mes plumes, où sont-elles? 11. Pardon, Mademoiselle, je ne cache jamais vos plumes; je pense, au contraire, que c'est vous qui cachez toujours les miennes. 12. Vous serez malade, si vous pleurez tant. 13. Pourquoi votre frère n'arrose-t-il pas vos fleurs? 14. Il arrose les miennes tous les jours. 15. Henri n'arrose jamais les siennes. 16. Jeanne, fermez la porte.

1. He is visiting; he is visited. 2. He is not visiting; he is not visited. 3. He has visited; he has not visited. 4. He has been visited; he has not been visited. 5. He had visited; he had not been visited. 6. He will be visited; he will not be visited. 7. He will have visited; he will not have visited. 8. He would be visited; he would not be visited. 9. He would have visited; he would not have visited. 10. He would have been visited; he would not have been visited. 11. He does visit; he does not visit. 12. Does he visit (§ 53. 4)? 13. Does he not visit? 14. Are you speaking of me? 15. We are not speaking of you, we are speaking of Therese. 16. They do not accept your present, they think that you are giving too many things to your friends. 17. Did you give John the new work which I bought the other day? 18. They never shut that window. 19. Why do you not water your sister's

flowers? 20. Why are you not working? 21. I work perhaps more than you. 22. Are you fond of (*do you like*) flowers? 23. My sister is fond of birds. 24. I think that we shall have an answer to our letter nex week.

57.

The Past Participle and the Past Tense.

The past participle is the past used with *to be* or *to have*, as, I am *blamed*, I have *blamed*. It is translated literally.

The past tense (§ 40) is the past of a verb used without *to be* or *to have*, as *I blamed*. In translating an English past tense into French, first try if it can be changed into *used to* (as *I used to speak*), or into the present participle with *I was*, *thou wast*, *he* or *she was*, etc. (as *I was speaking*).

If either of these two modes can be employed, use the imperfect (**je parlais**); if neither can be employed, use the past indefinite (**j'ai parlé**), as explained in § 40.

Imperfect.

TERMINATIONS: **-ais, -ais, -ait, -ions, -iez, -aient.**

I used to carry or *I was carrying* (or *I carried*, when *I carried* means either *I used to carry* or *I was carrying*).

je portais.	**nous portions.**
tu portais.	**vous portiez.**
il or **elle portait.**	**ils** or **elles portaient.**

NEGATIVE.	INTERROGATIVE.	INTERROG. NEGATIVE.
je ne portais pas, etc.	**portais-je?** etc.	**ne portais-je pas?** etc.

flatter, *to flatter*.
tromper, *to deceive*.
le maître, *the teacher*.
le plaisir, *pleasure*.

rencontrer, *to meet.*
blâmer, *to blame.*
louer, *to praise.*
chercher, *to look (for), to seek.*
évident, *evident.*
quelquefois, *sometimes.*
partout, *everywhere.*
alors, *then, at that time.*
à présent, *now.*
ensemble, *together.*

1. Quand j'étais à Paris, je rencontrais souvent votre frère. 2. Il travaillait beaucoup alors, il n'aimait pas le vin et les plaisirs. 3. J'admirais le plan de ce jardin lorsque j'ai rencontré votre père. 4. Les maîtres louaient tous les jours nos exercices, ils trouvaient que nous travaillions beaucoup. 5. Je pense que vos maîtres flattaient un peu leurs élèves. 6. Ils blâmaient les paresseux, mais il était évident qu'ils aimaient tous leurs élèves. 7. Nous arrosions notre jardin quand votre sœur est entrée. 8. Elle a un peu travaillé avec nous. 9. Elle aimait beaucoup les fleurs autrefois, mais maintenant ce sont les livres qu'elle aime. 10. Nous parlions de vous quand vous êtes entré. 11. Où étiez-vous ce matin quand je suis allé chez vous ? 12. J'étais chez ma tante, qui est revenue hier de Paris.

1. I was not flattering; I was not flattered. 2. I am not flattering; I am not flattered. 3. I used not to flatter; I used not to be flattered. 4. I would have flattered; I would not have flattered. 5. I would have been flattered; I would not have been flattered. 6. I would be flattered; I would not be flattered. 7. I will have flattered; I will not have flattered. 8. I had flattered; I had not flattered. 9. I had been flattered; I had not been flattered. 10. I have flattered; I have not flattered. 11. I have been flattered; I have not been flattered. 12. Do I flatter? Do I not flatter? 13. We were speaking of you this morning. 14. Where were you? 15. Your father was looking everywhere

for the paper which you have lost. 16. My sister used formerly to lend her books to everybody. 17. Were not these children weeping when I came in? 18. Yes, sir, they were weeping, because they have lost their money. 19. Why were you working so much, when your father came in yesterday? 20. I was working because my father is not fond of idle children.

58.

Past Indefinite.

I have carried or *I did carry* (or *I carried*, when *I carried* does not mean either *I used to carry* or *I was carrying*).

j'ai porté.	**nous avons porté.**
tu as porté.	**vous avez porté.**
il or **elle a porté.**	**ils** or **elles ont porté.**

When a verb has several subjects of *different* persons, after enumerating them, we generally put one of the pronouns **nous** and **vous** to sum them up in one: —

Ma mère et moi, nous sommes allés chez vous,	*My mother and I went to your house.*
Mon frère et vous, vous êtes partis à cinq heures,	*My brother and you left at five.*

récompenser, *to reward.*	**la sculpture,** *sculpture.*
commencer, *to begin, to commence.*	**longtemps,** *a long time.*[1]
le mois dernier, *last month.*	**injustement,** *unjustly.*
le musée, *the museum.*	**quelque part,** *somewhere.*

1. Le maître a récompensé votre frère, parce qu'il a bien travaillé. 2. Avez-vous enfin commencé votre exercice? 3. Non, Monsieur, nous n'avons encore rien fait. 4. Mon frère et moi, nous sommes un peu malades aujourd'hui. 5. Nous sommes allés hier à la campagne,

[1] **Longtemps,** an adverb, cannot be preceded by an article.

et nous avons mangé de mauvaise viande et bu de mauvais vin. 6. Ce matin vous et votre frère, vous avez blâmé injustement votre cousin. 7. Ces dames sont-elles restées longtemps chez vous? 8. Non, Madame, elles sont arrivées à huit heures et sont parties à neuf. 9. Elles ont beaucoup admiré le tableau que mon père a acheté l'autre jour. 10. Elles ont trouvé notre vin ordinaire délicieux. 11. Henri, n'avez-vous pas caché ma montre quelque part? 12. Tenez, voici votre montre, elle était sur votre table. 13. Nous étions souvent ensemble, nous visitions les musées, qu'il admirait beaucoup. 14. Il admirait le plus, je pense, le musée de sculpture.

1. Is she praising? is she praised? 2. Was she not praising? was she not praised? 3. Has she praised? has she been praised? 4. Had she not praised? had she not been praised? 5. Will she be praised? will she have praised? 6. Would she not be praised? 7. Would she not have praised? 8. Would she not have been praised? 9. The garden which you bought last month is not so large as your uncle's. 10. I lost the book which you had lent to my mother. 11. Did you show to your landlord's wife the beautiful muff which you bought last week? 12. Did you and your sister go to the museum yesterday evening? 13. Did you see my stick anywhere? 14. Have you not worked long enough? 15. I think that the doctor has bought my uncle's house. 16. Where did your sister hide my handkerchief? 17. When did your father come back from London? 18. Why did you shut all the doors and (all) the windows? 19. When did your parents arrive? 20. My mother arrived on Thursday, my father and I arrived on Saturday, June 28th, 1889.

59.

Future.

TERMINATIONS : **-erai, -eras, -era, -erons, -erez, -eront.**

je porterai, *I shall* or *will carry.*	**nous porterons.**
tu porteras.	**vous porterez.**
il or **elle portera.**	**ils** or **elles porteront.**

Conditional.

TERMINATIONS : **-erais, -erais, -erait, -erions, -eriez, -eraient.**

je porterais, *I would* or *should carry.*	**nous porterions.**
tu porterais.	**vous porteriez.**
il or **elle porterait.**	**ils** or **elles porteraient.**

That and *which* may often be understood in English, but must always be expressed in French : —

Je pense que votre frère est malade,	*I think your brother is unwell.*
Où est le roman que vous avez acheté hier ?	*Where is the novel you bought yesterday ?*

For is translated by **pendant** when it marks the whole duration of an action or a state, from the beginning to the end ; and, in this sense, it may generally be omitted.

Je travaillerai encore pendant une heure, **Je travaillerai encore une heure,**	*I shall work yet for an hour.*
Il a été malade pendant trois jours, **Il a été malade trois jours,**	*He was unwell for three days.*

le temps, *time, weather.*	**oublier,** *to forget.*
un moment, *one moment.*	**oser,** *to dare.*

1. Mon frère a travaillé longtemps ce matin, et il travaillera encore deux ou trois heures ce soir. 2. Je commencerai mes exercices dans une heure. 3. Je

pense que nous visiterons votre mère aujourd'hui. 4. Pourquoi n'accepteriez-vous pas cette bague? 5. Ne parlez pas de cette nouvelle si vous rencontrez votre cousine. 6. Combien d'heures travaillerez-vous aujourd'hui. 7. Je travaillerai huit heures. 8. Ne visiterez-vous pas votre vieux maître quand vous serez à Londres? 9. Je n'oublierai pas l'ouvrage dont vous avez parlé. 10. Blâmeriez-vous un père qui donnerait quelquefois des mots orageux à son fils, si celui-ci était paresseux? 11. Dès qu'ils auront commencé leur travail ordinaire, je fermerai la maison et je visiterai votre père un moment. 12. Si nous avions le temps, nous visiterions cette ville, elle est pleine de tableaux magnifiques.

1. They will forget; they would forget. 2. They (*m.*) will be forgotten; they would be forgotten. 3. They will have forgotten; they would have forgotten. 4. They will have been forgotten; they would have been forgotten. 5. They used to forget; they used to be forgotten. 6. They did forget; they do forget. 7. They have been forgotten; they had been forgotten. 8. They were forgetting; they were forgotten. 9. They are forgetting; they are forgotten. 10. I think he will not work much to-day. 11. I shall be very glad if he will work for two or three hours. 12. I would accept her present if I dared. 13. But you would not dare. 14. You forget that you and your brother will have no prize this month. 15. You will not forget my ring, it is in the drawer near the door. 16. I looked for your ring and your chain for half an hour, and I found nothing. 17. If we have time, we will look together this evening. 18. She would deceive her father if she dared. 19. Your sister and you will look for the thimble I have lost.

60.

When an action or a state which began some time ago is still going on, the present tense must be used in French; and in such cases *for* is translated by **depuis.**

I have been working for three hours,	**Je travaille depuis trois heures.**
I have been here for half an hour,	**Je suis ici depuis une demi-heure.**

Observe that *for* does not mark the whole duration of the action or state in these examples, but only the beginning; it cannot, therefore, be translated by **pendant,** which expresses the whole space of time between the beginning and the end.

How long is translated: —

(1) By **depuis quand** with the present tense, if the action or state is still continuing: —

Depuis quand êtes-vous malade? *How long have you been ill?*

(2) By **combien de temps** with the past indefinite, if the action or state is past: —

Combien de temps avez-vous demeuré à Rome? *How long did you live in Rome?*

(3) By **combien de temps** with the future, if the action or state is future: —

Combien de temps resterez-vous à Jérusalem? *How long shall you stay in Jerusalem?*

rester, *to stay.*	**bientôt,** *soon.*
jouer, *to play.*	**l'après-midi** (f.), *the afternoon.*
chanter, *to sing.*	**plus tôt,** *sooner.*
à l'école, *at school.*	**gaiement,** *cheerfully.*
demeurer, *to live, to dwell.*	**donc,** *then, therefore.*
étudier, *to study.*	**ensuite,** *afterwards.*
voyager, *to travel.*	**au moins,** *at least.*

1. Je demeure à Glasgow depuis quinze ou seize ans. 2. Henri a demeuré à Glasgow pendant trois ans, de 1860 à 1863. 3. Il était trois heures quand j'ai commencé mes exercices. Il est maintenant quatre heures et demie, je travaille donc depuis une heure et demie. 4. J'étudierai encore une demi-heure, et ensuite je visiterai ma tante qui est un peu malade depuis hier. 5. Votre cousin n'est-il pas à Londres depuis longtemps? 6. Oui, Monsieur, mon cousin demeure à Londres depuis trois mois. 7. J'ai demeuré à Londres quinze jours, il y a bien longtemps. J'étais alors très jeune, et j'aimais le plaisir plus que le travail. 8. J'ai peu voyagé depuis, mais je pense que je visiterai bientôt Paris. 9. Quand êtes-vous allé à Edimbourg? 10. Il y aura trois mois à la fin de la semaine prochaine. 11. Depuis quand êtes-vous ici? 12. Je suis ici depuis deux jours. 13. Combien de temps êtes-vous restés à Paris? 14. Nous sommes restés trois jours à Marseille, deux à Lyon, deux à Dijon, et huit à Paris. 15. Combien de temps resterez-vous à Londres? 16. Quinze jours seulement.

1. I have been here for a long time, at least two hours and a half. Where were you? 2. I was at the house of the lawyer, who arrived this morning from Paris. 3. I have been looking for your brother for half an hour. Where is he? 4. He has been living at his aunt's for two days. 5. My father and my mother have been travelling for two months. They are now in Paris. 6. They have been in Paris since Wednesday. 7. They were[1] in Rome for ten days. 8. They were in Rome when they

[1] *They were*, in this sentence, cannot be translated by the imperfect **ils étaient**, as you cannot turn it either into *they used to be*, *they used to live*, or into *they were staying*, *they were living*. But, in the next sentence, *they were*, meaning *they were staying there when another event took place*, must be translated by the imperfect.

received your letter. 9. They lived in Florence for three weeks. 10. How long has he been here? 11. How long have my sisters been here? 12. How long was my brother at London? 13. How long were they (*f.*) at London? 14. How long shall I stay at Paris? 15. How long will your mother and aunt stay at Paris? 16. He would not work so much if he were rich enough. 17. When she was young, she was fond of play. 18. We used to play with your brother when we lived at your uncle's. 19. We sang together every evening. 20. You used to forget everything when you were at school. 21. If she were more diligent, she would not forget her exercises.

61.

SECOND CONJUGATION.

In verbs of the second conjugation (more than 350 in number) the infinitive ends in **-ir**, and the past participle in **-i**.

Finir, *to finish;* **fini**, *finished.*

Indicative Present.

TERMINATIONS: **-is, -is, -it, -issons, -issez, -issent.**

je finis, *I finish, I am finishing, I do finish.*	**nous finissons.**
tu finis.	**vous finissez.**
il or **elle finit.**	**ils** or **elles finissent.**

Imperative.

finis, *finish thou.* **finissons**, *let us finish.* **finissez**, *finish you* or *ye.*

obéir,[1] *to obey.*	**choisir**, *to choose.*
désobéir, *to disobey.*	**réussir**, *to succeed, to be successful.*
rougir, *to blush.*	**punir**, *to punish.*

[1] **Obéir** and **désobéir** require **à** before their object.

agir, *to act.*
remplir, *to fill, to fulfil.*
bâtir, *to build.*
le boulanger, *the baker.*
la leçon, *the lesson.*
celui qui, *he who.*
le devoir, *the duty.*
ainsi, *thus, so.*
pourtant, *yet, however.*
sévèrement, *severely.*

1. Est-ce vous qui désobéissez ainsi à votre mère ? 2. Un enfant sage obéit toujours à ses parents et à ses maîtres. 3. Est-ce votre oncle qui bâtit cette maison ? 4. Non, c'est le boulanger ; il est devenu bien riche. 5. Si vous rougissez ainsi, tout le monde pensera que vous avez mal agi. 6. Ne remplissez plus mon verre, j'ai assez bu. 7. Si vous désobéissez toujours à vos maîtres, vous serez malheureux toute votre vie. 8. Voici de bien jolis boutons ; mon frère choisit celui-ci, et ma sœur celui-là. 9. Il a du talent, des manières et de la conduite, et pourtant il ne réussit pas. 10. Punissez-vous souvent l'enfant de mon voisin ? 11. Il est moins souvent puni que votre frère. 12. Il n'a jamais désobéi à ses maîtres, et il a toujours rempli ses devoirs.

1. They are choosing ; they are chosen. 2. They do not choose. 3. Are you (*m. s.*) not choosing ? 4. Are you (*f. pl.*) not chosen ? 5. She had not chosen ; she had not been chosen. 6. She has not chosen ; she has not been chosen. 7. They do not obey their mother. 8. If he does not obey his teacher, he will be punished. 9. Does this girl obey her father ? 10. He who does not obey his parents will never be happy. 11. They are choosing the best pears, but we choose the best strawberries. 12. It is she (§ 37) who is building that beautiful museum, she is so rich ! 13. For whom is the book you are choosing ? 14. Why do you not obey your master ? 15. Why are you blushing ? 16. If you do not succeed, you will be severely punished.

17. If you had come sooner, you would have seen your cousin Jane; she arrived this morning at a quarter of eight, and went away this afternoon at half past three.

62.

Imperfect.

TERMINATIONS: **-issais, -issais, -issait, -issions, -issiez, -issaient.**

I used to finish or *I was finishing* (or *I finished*, when *I finished* means either *I used to finish* or *I was finishing*).

je finissais.	**nous finissions.**
tu finissais.	**vous finissiez.**
il or **elle finissait.**	**ils** or **elles finissaient.**

guérir, *to cure.*	**parler mal,** *to speak ill.*
trahir, *to betray.*	**grâce à,** *thanks to.*
salir, *to soil, to dirty.*	**tout à fait,** *quite.*
être enrhumé, / **avoir un rhume,** } *to have a cold.*	**l'ordre** (m.), *the order.* / **l'exactitude** (f.), *the punctuality.*
gaiement, *cheerfully.*	**le magasin,** *the shop.*

1. Ils finissaient leurs exercices quand nous sommes entrés. 2. C'est elle qui guérissait ses frères et ses sœurs quand ils étaient enrhumés. 3. Grâce à elle, nous étudiions nos leçons et nous obéissions toujours à nos parents et à nos maîtres. 4. Nous ne salissions jamais nos habits. 5. Votre frère était-il tout à fait guéri quand vous êtes parti de Liverpool? 6. Il était si bien guéri qu'il jouait du matin au soir. 7. Je choisissais une petite broche pour elle quand elle est entrée dans le magasin. 8. Elle a rougi, et je pense que j'ai rougi aussi. 9. Je n'ai jamais aimé ce monsieur. Quand nous étions à l'école chez lui, nous étions toujours punis. 10. Et pourtant nous obéissions toujours à ses ordres. Nous remplissions toujours nos devoirs avec exactitude. 11. Combien de temps ma cousine est-elle restée chez

vous ? 12. Elle est restée sept heures et demie. Elle serait partie plus gaiement, si elle avait vu son cher cousin.

1. She is not cured; she is not curing. 2. She was not curing; she was not blaming. 3. She was not cured; she was not blamed. 4. She has not been quite cured. 5. She has not been seen to-day. 6. She was choosing a red ribbon for her sister when I entered the shop. 7. She would be very naughty if she did not obey her parents and her master. 8. They used to choose the best apples, but we always chose the best strawberries. 9. I was filling her glass when your father came in. 10. It was my aunt who cured my sisters when they had a cold. 11. Why did you not (habitually) obey your mother? 12. Why were you blushing this morning when I was speaking to your mother? 13. I was thinking that you were speaking ill of me. 14. When you worked well, you always succeeded. 15. I was working well because I was never punished. 16. But were you not sometimes lazy? 17. Yes, sometimes. 18. How long were my brothers in London?

63.

Past Indefinite.

I have finished or *I did finish* (or *I finished*, when *I finished* does not mean either *I used to finish* or *I was finishing*).

j'ai fini.	**nous avons fini.**
tu as fini	**vous avez fini.**
il or **elle a fini.**	**ils** or **elles ont fini.**

We have seen (§ 60) that an action or a state which began some time ago is expressed by the present tense in French, if it is still continuing, as: —

Je travaille depuis trois heures, *I have been working for three hours.*
Depuis quand êtes-vous malade? *How long have you been ill?*

There is another and more idiomatical way to express these two ideas, namely: —

Il y a trois heures que je travaille, *It is three hours since I began to work.*
Combien y a-t-il que vous êtes malade? *How long is it that you have been ill?*

In each of these two sentences, the verb may also be put in a past tense to express a past action: —

Il y avait trois ans que j'habitais cette maison. *I had been inhabiting that house for three years.*
Combien y avait-il que votre frère était malade? } *How long was your brother sick?*

Observe that the word **depuis** cannot be expressed after **il y a** or **y a-t-il**, the conjunction **que** taking its place.

déménager, *to remove.*
parfaitement, *perfectly.*
comme, *how, as, like.*
comme à l'ordinaire, *as usual.*
un scélérat, *a scoundrel.*
violer, *to violate.*
le serment, *the oath.*
merci, *thanks.*

1. Combien y a-t-il que vous demeurez ici? 2. Il y a trois ans et demi que nous avons déménagé. 3. Combien y a-t-il que votre frère est revenu? 4. Il y a quinze jours qu'il est arrivé de Paris. 5. A-t-il réussi dans ses affaires? 6. Je pense qu'il a parfaitement réussi. 7. Combien de temps y a-t-il que vous avez commencé votre thème grec? 8. Avez-vous vu comme ma sœur a rougi? 9. Oui, Monsieur, j'ai vu qu'elle a rougi parce que vous parliez mal de votre tante. 10. Cet enfant a-t-il encore désobéi à son maître? 11. Il a désobéi aujourd'hui comme à l'ordinaire. 12. Il n'est pas assez souvent puni.

1. Does he sing? 2. Does he blush? 3. Did he play? 4. Did he succeed? 5. Is he admiring? Is he admired? 6. Is he betraying? Is he betrayed? 7. Was he in the habit of admiring? 8. Was he (usually) admired? 9. Was he in the habit of betraying? 10. Was he (usually) betrayed? 11. Was he betraying? was he betrayed? 12. Has he admired? has he been admired? 13. Has he betrayed? has he been betrayed? 14. Had he admired? had he been admired? 15. Had he betrayed? had he been betrayed? 16. Have you been here long (*translate* 16 *to* 19 *in both ways*)? 17. I have been here for an hour. 18. How long has your father been travelling? 19. He has been travelling for a month. 20. How long is it since your mother went out? 21. He is a scoundrel, he violated his oath. 22. Did you succeed in your affair? 23. I have succeeded very well, thanks? 24. Has not your sister finished her letter? 25. Where did you soil your boots thus? 26. How long did your sisters stay in Paris?

64.

Future.

TERMINATIONS: **-irai, -iras, -ira,**	**-irons, -irez, -iront.**
je finirai, *I shall* or *will finish.*	**nous finirons.**
tu finiras.	**vous finirez.**
il or **elle finira.**	**ils** or **elles finiront.**

Conditional.

TERMINATIONS: **-irais, -irais, -irait,**	**-irions, -iriez, -iraient.**
je finirais, *I would* or *should finish.*	**nous finirions.**
tu finirais.	**vous finiriez.**
il or **elle finirait.**	**ils** or **elles finiraient.**

l'entreprise (f.), *the enterprise.*	**certainement,** *certainly*
la maîtresse, *the mistress.*	**parmi,** *among.*
la gloire, *the glory.*	**le choix,** *the choice.*

1. Quand réussirez-vous dans vos entreprises ? 2. Pourquoi ne finiriez-vous pas votre thème ce soir ? 3. Obéira-t-elle à sa nouvelle maîtresse ? 4. Saliront-ils toujours leurs gants ? 5. Laquelle de ces deux robes choisiriez-vous ? 6. Je rougirais pour vous, si vous ne travailliez pas plus que votre sœur. 7. Si monsieur Ernest n'obéit pas à ses maîtres et n'étudie pas, il sera sévèrement puni. 8. Si j'étais votre maître, n'obéiriez-vous pas à mes ordres? 9. Non, certainement, je n'obéirais pas à vos ordres. 10. Je désobéirais toujours à un maître plus jeune que moi. 11. Alors le jeune maître punirait son vieil élève.

1. Will he not admire ? 2. Will he not be betrayed ? 3. Will he not have betrayed ? 4. Will he not have been admired ? 5. Would he not admire ? 6. Would he not be betrayed ? 7. Would he not have admired ? 8. Would he not have been betrayed ? 9. Would he not punish your sister if she did not work ? 10. She will punish her child if he soils his dress./ 11. Will you not fill my glass ? 12. Does she never punish her children ? 13. If he does not obey his teacher, he will be punished. 14. They would not build so many houses, if they had no money. 15. You would soil your gloves, if you carried this bottle. 16. If my sisters were here, I would finish my exercise. 17. How long is it since your brother went to Paris ? 18. He has been at Paris for two years. 19. Would you choose this book, if you had the choice among all these works ? 20. I would not choose the one which you have ; here, I think, is the most interesting of all. 21. Why would you not choose the one which I have taken ? 22. I find that it is the least interesting of the works of this writer.

65.

THIRD CONJUGATION.

In verbs of the 3d conjugation (of which there are about 240) the infinitive ends in **-re**, and the past participle in **-u**.

Rendre, *to return* (*to give back*); **rendu**, *returned.*

Indicative Present.

TERMINATIONS: **-s, -s, –, -ons, -ez, -ent.**

I give back or *return, I am giving back, I do give back.*

je rends.	**nous rendons.**
tu rends.	**vous rendez.**
il or **elle rend.**	**ils** or **elles rendent.**

Imperative.

rends, *give thou back.* **rendons,** *let us give back.* **rendez,** *give you* or *ye back.*

le voyage, *the journey.*
le tonnerre, *the thunder.*
ces gens-là, *those people.*
le beau-frère, *the brother-in-law.*
la belle-sœur, *the sister-in-law.*
le jeu, *the game, the play.*
la raison, *the reason.*
un quart d'heure, *a quarter of an hour.*
l'attention (f.), *the attention.*
attendre, *to wait, to wait for.*
entendre, *to hear* (a noise).
entendre dire, *to hear* (meaning *to hear it said, to learn*).
répondre (**à**), *to answer.*
perdre, *to lose.*
la réponse, *the answer*
exprimer, *to express.*

1. Si vous attendez un moment, nous commencerons notre voyage ensemble. 2. Avez-vous entendu le tonnerre? 3. Avez-vous entendu dire que votre frère est un peu malade? 4. Avez-vous répondu à la lettre de votre cousin? 5. Nous ne répondons jamais aux lettres de ces gens-là; nous ne perdons pas notre temps ainsi. 6. Quand vous jouez avec votre beau-frère et votre belle-sœur, n'est-ce pas toujours vous qui perdez? 7. Oui, mademoiselle, c'est toujours moi qui perds; je joue si

mal, et ma belle-sœur joue si bien ! 8. Pourquoi, Mademoiselle, ne répondez-vous jamais à mes lettres ? 9. Je ne réponds pas à vos lettres parce que. 10. Votre raison est simple et très bien exprimée, et pourtant elle n'est pas claire. 11. N'attendez pas d'autre réponse.

1. You (*m. s.*) are not losing; you are not choosing. 2. You are not lost; you are not blamed. 3. You do not lose; you do not choose. 4. You have not lost; you have not blamed. 5. You have not been lost; you have not been chosen. 6. You had not lost; you had not blamed. 7. You had not been lost; you had not been chosen. 8. You did not lose; you did not blame. 9. Have you been waiting (for) your brother-in-law long? 10. My aunt and I have been waiting for a quarter of an hour. 11. Do you hear your brother? 12. Yes, I hear my brother and yours. 13. When I play with you, I always lose. 14. You always lose because you do not play with attention. 15. If you do not answer his letter this evening or to-morrow morning, she will be very sad. 16. Are you waiting for your aunt? 17. No, sir, it is for my mother that I am waiting. 18. I hear that your sister-in-law is quite cured. 19. Was he admiring? was he admired? 20. Will he not have admired? would he not have been admired?

66.

Imperfect.

TERMINATIONS: **-ais, -ais, -ait, -ions, -iez, -aient.**

I used to return (give back) or *I was returning* (or *I returned*, when *I returned* means either *I used to return* or *I was returning*).

je rendais.	**nous rendions.**
tu rendais.	**vous rendiez.**
il or elle rendait.	**ils or elles rendaient.**

fameux, *famous.*
passer, *to pass, to spend.*
évident, *evident.*
en effet, *in effect* (or *you are right*).
déjà, *already.*
jusqu'à, *till.*
justement, *just, exactly.*
le whist, *whist.*
la somme, *the sum.*
le billet, *the note.*
descendre, *to come down.*
battre, *to beat.*
au bord de la mer, *at the coast,* or *sea-shore.*

1. Ne rendiez-vous pas cette fameuse somme à votre frère lorsqu'Henri est entré ? 2. Oui, je rendais à Louis l'argent qu'il a prêté autrefois à ma sœur. 3. Qui attendiez-vous ce matin, lorsque j'ai passé près de vous dans la rue ? 4. A quelle heure attendais-je quelqu'un dans la rue ce matin ? 5. Il était 8 heures, ou 8 heures moins dix. 6. Vous parliez avec votre cousin Ernest, mais il était évident que vous attendiez quelqu'un. 7. En effet, j'attendais l'omnibus, dans lequel je suis entré à 8 heures moins cinq. 8. Je suis allé chez votre père, qui était déjà sorti et que j'ai attendu jusqu'à 9 heures. 9. A cette heure-là je suis revenu chez moi. 10. Je répondais justement à votre billet lorsque votre père est entré. 11. Nous avons parlé du plaisir que nous avons eu au bord de la mer l'année dernière. 12. Nous passions presque tout notre temps ensemble. 13. Nous jouions au whist tous les soirs. 14. C'était lui qui perdait presque toujours. 15. Quand ce n'était pas votre mère et lui qui perdaient, c'était votre sœur et votre frère.

1. You (*m. p.*) were not lost; you were not praised. 2. You were not losing; you were not punishing. 3. You are not lost; you are not praised. 4. You are not losing; you are not punishing. 5. You used not to be lost; you used not to be praised. 6. You used not to lose; you used not to punish. 7. Do you not lose? do you not praise? 8. Did you not lose? did you not punish? 9. Why were you not waiting yesterday,

when your father was at our house? 10. I was not waiting just because my father was at your house. —11. I had not finished my exercises. 12. They have been waiting for their mother a long time (*meaning they are still waiting for her*). 13. She beats[1] this poor animal every day. 14. They used to beat these poor animals. 15. Why were you not coming down this morning? 16. She was not coming down because her mother was ill. 17. I was answering her note when you came in (40). 18. We always used to lose when we played with you. 19. We do not play so much now, we are more industrious. 20. How long have you been in Paris? 21. It is exactly two weeks since I arrived.

67.

Past Indefinite.

I have returned (*given back*) or *I did return* (or *I returned*, when *I returned* does not mean either *I used to return* or *I was returning*).

j'ai rendu.	**nous avons rendu.**
tu as rendu.	**vous avez rendu.**
il or **elle a rendu.**	**ils** or **elles ont rendu.**

In questions, when you wish to express some surprise, however little, begin the interrogative sentence by **est-ce que**: —

Est-ce qu'il n'est pas encore revenu de Paris?	*Has he not yet come back from Paris?*
Est-ce que mon frère est malade?	*Is my brother unwell?*

Est-ce que means *is it true that?* or *is it possible that?* Its use is often merely a matter of euphony.

[1] **Battre** takes only one **t** in the three persons sing. of the pres. indicative, and the second sing. of the imperative: **je bats, tu bats, il bat; ne bats pas ce chien.** In all other persons and tenses it is regular.

le coup de canon, *the cannon shot.*
la visite, *the visit.*
Crésus, *Crœsus.*
mort, -e, *dead.*
joli, *pretty-looking.*
la pluie, *the rain.*
l'empereur, *the Emperor.*
Amérique, *America.*
le louis, *the louis* (a gold coin worth 20 francs).

1. Est-ce que vous avez attendu longtemps ? 2. Est-ce que vous n'avez pas entendu ce coup de canon ? 3. Est-ce que vous n'avez pas entendu dire que votre oncle est revenu d'Amérique riche comme Crésus ? 4. Thérèse, est-ce que vous ne descendez pas ? votre mère est ici. 5. Est-ce que vous n'avez pas encore répondu à la lettre de votre père ? 6. Avez-vous enfin vendu votre maison et votre jardin ? 7. Est-ce que vous avez vendu cette jolie maison que vous aimiez tant ? 8. Pourquoi avez-vous battu ce pauvre chien ? 9. Est-ce parce qu'il est sorti sans vous ce matin ? 10. Vous êtes triste, est-ce que vous avez encore perdu votre argent ? 11. Justement, j'ai perdu mon porte-monnaie où j'avais mis six louis ce matin. 12. Est-ce que vous perdez souvent votre porte-monnaie ?

1. Were you (*f. s.*) losing ?[1] were you praising ? 2. Were you lost ? were you punished ? 3. Shall you be lost ? shall you be praised ? 4. Will you have lost ? will you have punished ? 5. Were you not losing ? were you not praising ? 6. Were you not lost ? were you not praised ? 7. Shall you not be lost ? shall you not be punished ? 8. Will you not have lost ? will you not have praised ? 9. Have you and your brother waited long for your father ? 10. Did she look for her brother ? 11. Did they lose their money ? 12. Did you not hear the rain this morning ? 13. Did you not hear

[1] Presume that each of these questions implies some surprise, and begin by **est-ce que.**

that the Emperor is dead? 14. Do you think we have sold our pretty-looking house? 15. Have you not yet returned the book which Louisa lent to your sister two years ago? 16. Has she not yet replied to your note? 17. Did they not wait for their sister? 18. Louisa, have you not lost your ear-rings? 19. My sister here? Has she already arrived from London? Why did she not wait for my visit?

68.

Future.

TERMINATIONS: **-rai, -ras, -ra, -rons, -rez, -ront.**

je rendrai, *I shall* or *will return* (*give back*).	**nous rendrons.**
tu rendras.	**vous rendrez.**
il or **elle rendra.**	**ils** or **elles rendront.**

Conditional.

TERMINATIONS: **-rais, -rais, -rait, -rions, -riez, -raient.**

je rendrais, *I would* or *should return* (*give back*).	**nous rendrions.**
tu rendrais.	**vous rendriez.**
il or **elle rendrait.**	**ils** or **elles rendraient.**

Neither . . . nor is translated by **ni** repeated, and the verb must be preceded by the usual **ne.**

Je ne blâme ni votre frère ni votre sœur,	*I blame neither your brother nor your sister.*

la terre, *the land.*	**le bruit,** *the noise.*
sembler, *to appear, to seem.*	**prêt,** *ready.*
raisonnable, *reasonable.*	

1. Rendrez-vous cette plume à votre cousin si vous trouvez la vôtre? 2. Rendriez-vous cette plume à votre cousin si vous trouviez la vôtre? 3. Combien de temps avez-vous attendu votre cousin? 4. J'aurais attendu plus longtemps, si j'avais pensé que vous attendiez aussi.

5. Avez-vous rendu à votre cousine sa bague, ses bracelets, et ses boucles d'oreilles? 6. Je ne rendrai à ma cousine ni sa bague, ni ses bracelets, ni ses boucles d'oreilles, ni ses gants, ni sa broche. 7. Est-ce que vous n'attendrez pas votre sœur? elle sera prête dans un moment. 8. Nous n'attendrons ni ma sœur ni ma cousine; elles ne sont jamais prêtes. 9. Est-ce que vous battez encore cette pauvre petite bête? elle semble si malheureuse! 10. Est-ce que vous n'entendez pas ce bruit-là?

1. Will you (*f. pl.*) not wait? will you not choose? 2. Will you not be waited for? will you not be deceived? 3. Will you not have waited? will you not have chosen? 4. Will you not have been waited for? will you not have been chosen? 5. Would you not wait? would you not deceive? 6. Would you not be waited for? would you not be chosen? 7. Would you not have waited? would you not have deceived? 8. Would you not have been waited for? would you not have been chosen? 9. They would return all the money which they received, if they were not so poor. 10. If we were playing for money, we should lose too much. 11. Will you not come down this morning? 12. Wait one minute, I am ready. 13. When will she reply to my letter? 14. I think they will sell neither their house nor their lands. 15. Why would they wait so long? 16. I shall not wait much longer. 17. If you were more reasonable, you would not beat these poor animals. 18. I never beat my cat, but I sometimes beat my dog. 19. Whom are you looking for in this long street? 20. There is the man! He is a scoundrel who has often deceived me, but he will deceive me no longer.

69.

Peculiarities in Verbs of the 1st Conjugation.

All the verbs of the 1st conjugation but two are regular, and consequently conjugated like **porter.** But a few present some peculiarities caused by pronunciation, and which may be very easily understood and remembered. These verbs are : —

1st. Those having an é before their last syllable, as **cé-lé-brer, ex-a-gé-rer, pré-fé-rer.**

2d. Those having an *e mute* before their last syllable, such as **me-ner, le-ver, ap-pe-ler, je-ter.**

3d. Those ending in **-yer.**

4th. Those ending in **-cer** or **-ger.**

Verbs having an *é* before their last Syllable.

When pronouncing the infinitive **cé-lé-brer,**[1] it will be observed that the sound is equally short on each of the three syllables, the two first ending each with an **é,** and the third ending with **er,** which in pronunciation is equivalent to **é.** But when pronouncing the singular of the present indicative, the sound, in the last two syllables, is completely changed, — the last syllable is now mute, and the preceding on that account has become much longer. **je cé-lè-bre, tu cé-lè-bres, il cé-lè-bre.** This longer sound of the second last syllable is expressed by a grave accent replacing the acute.

Therefore, all verbs of the 1st conjugation having an **é** before their last syllable in the infinitive change that **é** into an **è,** when the following syllable, in the course of the conjugation, is to be mute.[2]

[1] For the division of syllables see Introduction, page 10.

[2] The rule excepting verbs in **-éger** from the above changes in accents was abolished by the French Academy in 1878.

Cé-lé-brer, *to celebrate.*

INDICATIVE PRESENT.

je cé-lè-bre, tu cé-lè-bres, il cé-lè-bre, nous cé-lé-brons, vous cé-lé-brez, ils cé-lè-brent.

INDICATIVE IMPERFECT.

je cé-lé-brais, tu cé-lé-brais, il cé-lé-brait, etc.

INDICATIVE PAST INDEFINITE.

j'ai cé-lé-bré, tu as cé-lé-bré, il a cé-lé-bré, etc.

INDICATIVE FUTURE.

je cé-lè-bre-rai, tu cé-lè-bre-ras, il cé-lè-bre-ra, nous cé-lè-bre-rons, vous cé-lè-bre-rez, ils cé-lè-bre-ront.

CONDITIONAL.

je cé-lè-bre-rais, tu cé-lè-bre-rais, il cé-lè-bre-rait, etc.

IMPERATIVE.

cé-lè-bre, cé-lé-brons, cé-lé-brez.

Verbs having an *e* mute before their last Syllable.

Writing the singular of the present indicative of the verb **mener,** we have **je me-ne, tu me-nes, il me-ne,** in each of which there is no sound, both syllables being mute in each word. In order, therefore, to obtain a sound, we put a grave accent over the **e** of **me**; and we do so whenever **me-** is followed by a mute syllable.

Therefore, verbs of the 1st conjugation, having an *e mute* before their last syllable in the infinitive, change that *e mute* into è, when, in the course of the conjugation, the syllable following is mute.

Me-ner, *to take (to), to lead, to guide.*

INDICATIVE PRESENT.

je mè-ne, tu mè-nes, il mè-ne, nous me-nons, vous me-nez, ils mè-nent.

INDICATIVE IMPERFECT.

je me-nais, tu me-nais, il me-nait, nous me-nions, vous me-niez, ils me-naient.

INDICATIVE PAST INDEFINITE.

j'ai me-né, tu as me-né, il a me-né, etc.

INDICATIVE FUTURE.

je mè-ne-rai, tu mè-ne-ras, il mè-ne-ra, etc.

CONDITIONAL.

je mè-ne-rais, tu mè-ne-rais, il mè-ne-rait, etc.

IMPERATIVE.

mè-ne, me-nons, me-nez.

EXCEPTIONS: — In verbs ending in **-eler** as **appeler**, and **-eter**, as **jeter**, we double the **l** and the **t**, instead of putting a grave accent before a mute syllable, the effect being exactly the same.

J'appelle, tu appelles, il appelle, j'appellerai, j'appellerais, etc., **je jette, je jetterai, je jetterais**, etc.

But note that the four verbs **acheter** (*to buy*), **étiqueter** (*to label*), **geler** (*to freeze*), and **peler** (*to peel*), follow the general rule, and their **t** or **l** is never doubled: **j'achète, tu achètes, il achète, nous achetons**, etc. **Je gèle, tu gèles, il gèle, nous gelons**, etc.

espérer, *to hope, to hope for.*
préférer, *to prefer.*
posséder, *to possess.*
exagérer, *to exaggerate.*
appeler, *to call.*
jeter, *to throw, to throw away.*
acheter, *to buy.*
geler, *to freeze.*
promener, *to take out to walk.*
protéger, *to protect.*
patiner, *to skate.*
deviner, *to guess.*
vilain, *ugly, bad.*
l'habitude (f.), *the habit.*
la fortune, *fortune.*
le cas, *the case, circumstance.*
la fête, *the birthday.*
le chiffre, *the number.*
d'ailleurs, *besides.*
l'année dernière, *last year.*
avant, *before.*
fort (adv.), *much, hard.*
le coin, *the corner.*
maman, *mamma.*
l'hiver (m.), *winter.*

1. Ma sœur préfère ces bracelets-ci à ceux-là, mais je trouve ceux-là bien plus beaux que ceux-ci. 2. Est-ce que vous n'exagérez pas un peu? 3. J'exagère peut-être quelquefois, c'est une vilaine habitude, mais je n'exagère pas dans ce cas-ci. 4. Quand célèbrerez-vous

la fête de votre cousine ? 5. Je pense que sa fête tombe le 13 du mois prochain. 6. Le 13 ! c'est un bien vilain chiffre ! Je préfèrerais le 12 ou le 14. 7. D'ailleurs le 13 est un dimanche, nous célèbrerons cette fête le 12. 8. Espérons que le temps sera beau ; l'année dernière nous avons eu un temps très orageux. 9. Vous êtes bien content ce soir ; il gèle très fort, vous patinerez demain. 10. Nous n'avons pas patiné l'hiver dernier ; il n'a presque jamais gelé. 11. Où achetez-vous vos livres et vos plumes ? 12. J'achète mes livres, mes plumes et mes journaux chez le libraire qui demeure au coin de notre rue. 13. Comment appelez-vous cette enfant ? 14. Marie ! c'est un bien joli nom ; mademoiselle Marie, menez-moi près de votre maman. 15. La bonne promènera les enfants ce soir ; ils ne sont pas prêts maintenant. 16. N'est-ce pas vous qui protégez ce pauvre jeune homme ? 17. Non, monsieur, ce n'est pas moi, c'est mon frère.

1. They would not prefer these books to those. 2. Let us hope that you will always be happy. 3. Do you not exaggerate his fortune ? 4. I exaggerate nothing ; he possesses many houses and lands. 5. I hope you will not forget the book which I lent (to) your sister on Tuesday last ? 6. When will you celebrate my birthday ? 7. (On) what day does it fall ? 8. (On) a Friday. I think it is also (on) the 13th of the month. 9. Unfortunate (man), we shall never celebrate your birthday ; choose another day, if you please. 10. It is freezing a little this evening, I hope that you will skate soon. 11. When will the girls take the children out to walk ? 12. I shall buy that picture for my mother. 13. Where are you taking my brother ? 14. I am taking your brother to school. 15. Throw (away) that pear, it is very hard. 16. Guess who called your sister

at the corner of Queen Street. 17. I hope that we shall skate to-morrow. 18. I think it is freezing hard now; it has been freezing for the last twenty-four hours.

70.

Verbs ending in *-yer*.

A **y** placed between two vowels is equivalent to **iy**, the **i** uniting with the preceding vowel and the **y** beginning the next syllable. **Appuyer**, for example, is pronounced exactly as if it were written **ap-pui-yer**, the sound of both **i** and **y** being very distinct in the word.

If we write the singular of the present indicative according to the orthography of the infinitive, we shall have: **j'appuye, tu appuyes, il appuye**, or, which amounts to the same thing: — **j'ap-pui-ye, tu ap-pui-yes, il ap-pui-ye**, but this produces a very disagreeable breathing on the last syllable, to avoid which we simply change **y** into **i** before an *e mute*.

Therefore, in verbs ending in **-yer**, the **y** becomes **i** before *e mute*.

However, in verbs ending in **-ayer**, it is optional to keep the **y** throughout the whole conjugation, or to adhere to this rule strictly.

Appuyer, *to support*.

INDICATIVE PRESENT.

j'appuie, tu appuies, il appuie, nous appuyons, vous appuyez, ils appuient.

INDICATIVE IMPERFECT.

j'appuyais, tu appuyais, il appuyait, nous appuyions, etc.

INDICATIVE PAST INDEFINITE.

j'ai appuyé, tu as appuyé, il a appuyé, etc.

INDICATIVE FUTURE.

j'appuierai, tu appuieras, il appuiera, nous appuierons, etc.

CONDITIONAL.

j'appuierais, tu appuierais, il appuierait, nous appuierions, etc.

IMPERATIVE.

appuie, appuyons, appuyez.

Verbs ending in *-cer* or *-ger*.

In verbs ending in **-cer**, the **c**,[1] being soft in the infinitive, must be kept soft throughout the whole verb. When, therefore, in any tense, **c** is followed by **a** or **o**, a cedilla is placed under the **c**, to show that it must retain a soft sound: **nous commençons, je commençais**, etc.

In verbs ending in **-ger**, the **g**,[1] being soft in the infinitive, must also be kept soft throughout. When, therefore, it happens, in any tense, to be followed by **a** or **o**, a silent **e** is put after the **g**, simply to soften its sound: **nous partageons, tu corrigeais**, etc.

effrayer, *to frighten.*
essayer, *to try.*
payer, *to pay, to pay for.*
aboyer, *to bark.*
employer, *to employ.*
nettoyer, *to clean.*
envoyer, *to send.*
constamment, *constantly.*
assez (before an adjective or adverb), *pretty.*
manger, *to eat.*
déranger, *to disturb, to trouble.*
corriger, *to correct.*
obliger, *to oblige.*
annoncer, *to announce.*
menacer, *to threaten.*
sale, *dirty.*
juste, *just.*
certain, *certain.*
amener, *to bring.*
mordre, *to bite.*
casser, *to break.*
le proverbe, *the proverb.*
autrement, *otherwise.*
occupé, *busy, engaged.*
prononcer, *to pronounce.*

1. Essayez ce crayon-ci, c'est mon meilleur. 2. En effet, il est très bon, j'essaierai aussi votre plume. 3. Combien payez-vous vos plumes et vos crayons? 4. Je paie très cher les plumes et les crayons que j'achète chez le libraire du coin. 5. Nettoyez un peu cette table, elle est toujours sale. 6. Monsieur, je nettoie cette table tous les matins. 7. Ce vilain petit

[1] See Introduction, pages 6, 7.

chien que vous amenez toujours avec vous aboie constamment. 8. Tous les chiens qui aboient ne mordent pas. 9. Le proverbe est assez juste, mais votre chien a mordu le nez de Charles hier. 10. Appuyez, s'il vous plaît, ma chaise contre cette table. Merci. 11. Je mangeais, je pense, lorsque vous êtes entré. 12. Vous mangiez, en effet, avec vos frères et vos sœurs, mais je n'ai dérangé personne. 13. Nous prononçons les langues anciennes autrement que vous. 14. Si nous dérangeons votre frère, maintenant qu'il est occupé, il ne sera pas content. 15. J'achèterai une montre la semaine prochaine ; je n'ai pas assez d'argent aujourd'hui. 16. Protégeons les malheureux. 17. Si vous menacez cet enfant, il ne travaillera plus. 18. Ne menaçons personne.

1. You frightened your mother when you broke that glass. 2. They would pay their uncle this evening, if they had money enough. 3. She is very lazy ; she does not employ her time well. 4. If you do not pay my aunt before Saturday, I am certain that she will not be contented. 5. Why does he not send that book to his cousin (*m.*)? 6. Why did you not send my letter to your sister? 7. Those dogs bark all night. 8. Have you not yet cleaned my watch? 9. Do not try his pen ; it is bad. 10. My brother was correcting my exercise when my aunt came in this morning. 11. He used to correct all my letters and all my exercises formerly. 12. Let us not eat before ten o'clock. 13. Let us oblige our friends. 14. Formerly they used to pronounce very well. 15. Why do you always disturb your uncle? 16. When I was young I ate too often. 17. They were announcing sad news to their friends when your letter arrived.

THE PLACE OF PERSONAL PRONOUNS.[1]

71.

After a Preposition (*See* § 32).

moi, *me*.
toi, *thee*.
lui, *him*.
elle, *her*.
moi-même, *myself*.
toi-même, *thyself*.
lui-même, *himself*.
elle-même, *herself*.
nous, *us*.
vous, *you*.
eux, *them* (m.).
elles, *them* (f.).
nous-mêmes, *ourselves*.
vous-mêmes, *yourselves*.
eux-mêmes, *themselves* (m.).
elles-mêmes, *themselves* (f.).

Personal pronouns governed by any preposition except *to* stand in the same place as in English, and are translated as above.

après, *after*.
par, *by*.
contre, *against*.
quant à, *as for*.
sans, *but for, without*.
selon, *according to*.
malgré, *in spite of*.
tranquille, *easy*.
l'offre, (f.), *the offer*.
soyez, *be*.

1. J'ai reçu ce livre de votre frère ou de vous. 2. Nous travaillons pour lui. 3. Ils sont arrivés avant elles. 4. Soyez tranquille, je n'agirai ni contre vous ni contre eux. 5. Selon eux, nous ne réussirons pas. 6. Chez qui êtes-vous allé hier soir? 7. Je suis allé chez elles. 8. Sans vous je n'aurais pas écrit cette sotte lettre. 9. Est-ce pour elle-même qu'elle a accepté ces boucles

[1] Pupils must learn by heart the list of pronouns given in §§ 71–76, so as to be able to answer without hesitation such questions as these: "How do you translate *him* before the verb? *him* after? *them* before? *them* after? *themselves* before? *themselves* after?" etc. In this way, the rule as to the place of Personal Pronouns will become one of the easiest in the language, instead of one of serious difficulty.

d'oreilles? 10. Non, mon ami, c'est pour vous ou pour moi. 11. Elles n'agiront certainement pas contre elles-mêmes. 12. Est-ce pour eux ou pour nous-mêmes que nous travaillons maintenant? 13. C'est pour nous-mêmes. 14. Quant à eux, je suis certain qu'ils n'accepteront pas notre offre. 15. Je donnerai cette bague à Thérèse malgré vous et malgré eux. 16. Contre qui parlez-vous? 17. Nous ne parlons contre personne, nous parlons de vous et d'elle.

1. My brothers will arrive before us. 2. We went away after them. 3. We are not speaking of you, we are speaking of him and of her. 4. According to her, we shall be punished. 5. As for you, my friend, I am certain you will succeed. 6. I shall accept his present in spite of you and (in spite of) her. 7. I think you spoke this morning against me. 8. I never speak against you; on the contrary, I sometimes speak for you. 9. Why did you leave without them (*m.*)? 10. We went to her house, but she was out with you. 11. At what time did I go out with her? 12. Is it for me or for yourself that you are playing? 13. It is for myself. 14. I will play for you in half an hour. 15. They left in spite of me.

72.

Personal Pronouns before the Verb.

me, *me, to me.*	**nous**, *us, to us.*
te, *thee, to thee.*	**vous**, *you, to you.*
lui, *to him, to her.*	**leur**, *to them.*
le, *him, it.*	**les**, *them* (m.).
la, *her, it.*	**les**, *them* (f.).

Personal pronouns governed by a verb or preceded by *to* are translated as above, and must be placed immediately before the verb in simple tenses, and before the auxiliary in compound tenses; as—

Je le blâme,	*I blame him.*
Je l'ai blâmé,	*I have blamed him.*
Je ne l'ai pas blâmé,	*I have not blamed him.*
Je ne lui ai pas parlé,	*I have not spoken to him.*
garder, *to keep.*	**ingrat,** *ungrateful.*
refuser, *to refuse.*	**sûr,** *sure.*

1. Je vous parlerai dans une heure. 2. Je ne vous ai pas vu ce matin. 3. Votre cousine est arrivée, mais je ne lui ai pas parlé. 4. Si vous n'avez jamais été à ce jardin, nous le visiterons ensemble la semaine prochaine. 5. J'ai perdu ma grammaire anglaise, je la cherche partout et ne la trouve pas. 6. Votre oncle est devenu bien vieux, nous l'avons rencontré hier dans la rue. 7. Voici un nouvel ami pour vous, j'espère que vous l'aimerez bien. 8. Je l'espère aussi; s'il m'aime un peu, je suis sûr que je l'aimerai beaucoup. 9. Est-ce que vous n'admirez pas ce joli porte-monnaie? Ingrat, je l'ai acheté pour vous. 10. Si vous ne le trouvez pas beau, je le garderai pour moi. 11. Je suis sûr que votre frère ne le refusera pas. 12. Voici, je pense, le verre de votre sœur; est-ce vous qui l'avez rempli? 13. Non, monsieur, ce n'est pas moi qui l'ai rempli; je pense que c'est ma mère. 14. Votre frère m'a écrit hier, mais je ne lui ai pas encore répondu.

Models of Construction.

je ne	**lui**	**ai pas parlé.**
tu ne	**leur**	**as pas parlé.**
il ne	**nous**	**a pas parlé.**
mon frère ne	**vous**	**a pas parlé.**
nous ne	**leur**	**avons pas parlé.**
vous ne	**lui**	**avez pas parlé.**
ils ne	**vous**	**ont pas parlé.**
mes frères ne	**m'**	**ont pas parlé.**

1. I am speaking to him. 2. He is speaking to her. 3. She was speaking to them. 4. We shall speak to you no more. 5. You would not have spoken to them. 6. They had not sold it. 7. They are not praising you. 8. I will lend you my pen, if you have lost yours. 9. If you deceive him he will punish you. 10. He has offered me his book, but I have not accepted it. 11. I am looking for my pencil; I had it an hour ago, but I have lost it in this room. 12. They would not have spoken to me, if you had not been with them. 13. If you had lent me your pen, I would have written to your sister. 14. If you lend her that book, she will never return it.

73.

retrouver, *to find* (a thing lost).
réclamer à, *to claim from.*
égarer, *to mislay.*
expliquer, *to explain.*
marchander, *to bargain (for).*
supposer, *to suppose.*
tremblant, *trembling.*
promis, *promised.*
demander à, *to ask from a person.*

1. Il vous punira sévèrement si vous ne lui obéissez pas. 2. Où donc, petite méchante, avez vous caché mon dé? 3. Pardon, ma tante, je n'ai pas caché votre dé; pourquoi m'appelez-vous méchante? Voici un tiroir dans lequel je l'ai retrouvé, ce fameux dé que vous réclamez à tout le monde. 4. Qui l'avait caché dans ce tiroir? 5. Personne, je pense, ne l'avait caché; c'est vous qui l'aviez égaré. 6. Si nous arrivons avant eux, nous fermerons la porte après nous. 7. Je lui rendrai son livre quand il me rendra le mien. 8. Si vous lui portez cette somme, il la refusera. 9. Vous êtes tout tremblant, est-ce que ce chien vous a effrayé? 10. Mon frère vous a offert cette bague; l'acceptez-vous ou la refusez-vous? 11. Je ne l'accepte pas, je lui expliquerai pourquoi.

12. Je vous ai donné un journal français, l'avez-vous envoyé à votre sœur? 13. Ne lui avez-vous pas encore envoyé ces journaux? 14. Est-ce que vous m'apportez des lettres ou des journaux? 15. Il y a trop longtemps que vous marchandez ces boucles d'oreilles; les achetez-vous ou ne les achetez-vous pas?

1. I would never have lent my watch to him. 2. My sisters will not wait for you. 3. You have not given her[1] the three books which you had promised her. 4. Where did you put her ribbon? 5. I think I have put it upon the table; I suppose you have lost it. 6. Where is my book? are you not looking for it? 7. Will you lend it to your mother? 8. Will he not lend it to his mother? 9. Where are my pencils? has she taken them? 10. Were you not speaking to her? 11. Will she not lend you the book which you asked from (*to*) her? 12. Are you not working for her and for me? 13. Did he speak to you of me? 14. Did he not speak to you of me? 15. Why did she not lend you the pencil which you had asked from (*to*) her? 16. Did she not put it in your brother's pocket? 17. When shall you give her the bird which you promised her?

74.

When two personal pronouns placed before the verb are governed by the same verb, they stand in the following order:[2] —

[1] Note that the preposition *to* is often understood in English: *her* stands here for *to her*.

[2] These pronouns should be thoroughly learnt by heart in the order in which they stand. They seem complicated, but this is only in appearance, as they are perfectly regular: **me le, me la, me les: te le, te la, te les; nous le, nous la, nous les,** etc.

me le,	*him to me.* / *it to me.*	**nous le,**	*him to us.* / *it to us.*
me la	*her to me.* / *it to me.*	**nous la,**	*her to us.* / *it to us.*
me les,	*them to me.*	**nous les,**	*them to us.*
te le,	*him to thee.* / *it to thee.*	**vous le,**	*him to you.* / *it to you.*
te la,	*her to thee.* / *it to thee.*	**vous la,**	*her to you.* / *it to you.*
te les,	*them to thee.*	**vous les,**	*them to you.*
le lui,	*him to him.* / *it to him.* / *him to her.* / *it to her.*	**le leur,**	*him to them.* / *it to them.*
la lui,	*her to him.* / *it to him.* / *her to her.* / *it to her.*	**la leur,**	*her to them.* / *it to them.*
les lui,	*them to him.* / *them to her.*	**les leur,**	*them to them.*

Observe that, when two pronouns are placed before a verb, the first person precedes the second or third, the second precedes the third, **lui** and **leur** always stand last.

un article, *an article.* **défendu,** *forbidden.*
en ce moment, *at this moment.*

1. Monsieur, je vous ai demandé le *Journal des Débats* il y a une demi-heure, et vous ne me l'avez pas donné. 2. Pardon, monsieur, je finis un article très intéressant, je vous le donnerai dans un moment. 3. Quand me prêteras-tu le nouvel ouvrage de Victor Hugo? 4. Tu n'as pas oublié que tu me l'as promis? 5. Je te le prêterai samedi. 6. C'est Auguste qui l'a en ce moment, mais il me le rendra demain. 7. Je trouve que ces règles ne sont pas très faciles, mais j'espère que le professeur nous les expliquera. 8. Si vous lui demandez ces deux lettres, je suis sûr qu'il vous les refusera. 9. Si je lui demande seulement celle de Thérèse, je suppose qu'il ne me la

refusera pas. 10. Elle m'a demandé mon parapluie, mais je ne le lui ai pas donné. 11. Si mon beau-frère et ma belle-sœur vous réclamaient l'argent qu'ils vous ont prêté, est-ce que vous ne le leur rendriez pas? 12. Je le leur rendrais, si je l'avais.

1. I have asked you for it (*it to you*). 2. He would not have asked her for it (*it to her*). 3. We have forbidden it to them. 4. You had not forbidden it to us. 5. She has not returned it to me. 6. She will never return it to you. 7. I have never spoken to her of you. 8. Why do you ask me for it (*it to me*)? 9. You have not given it to me. 10. If I have promised it to her, I shall give it to her. 11. I shall have a new hat, my father has promised it to me. 12. When will he give it to you? 13. I hope he will give it to me on Thursday. 14. Mary has asked (*à*) her brother for Henry's letter, but he will refuse it to her. 15. Why did you not show him the knife which I have given you? 16. I will show it to him to-morrow, and am quite ready to give it to him if he asks me for it.

75.

poliment, *politely*.
précisément, *exactly*.
un mauvais sujet, *a bad boy, a bad fellow*.
un encrier, *an inkstand*.
le miel, *honey*.
quelqu'un, *somebody*.
quelque chose, *something*.
manquer de respect, *to be disrespectful*.
gronder, *to scold*.
conseiller, *to advise, to recommend*.
à la maison, *at home*.
demander pardon à, *to ask a person's pardon*.
reprocher à, *to reproach for*.
emprunter à, *to borrow from*
regretter, *to regret*.
pardonner, *to forgive*.
porter à, *to take to*.
apporter, *to bring here*.

une faute, *a fault committed against duty, an offence*.
un défaut, *a fault in our disposition, an imperfection, a defect*.

1. Pourquoi n'avez-vous pas prêté à Ernest le volume qu'il vous a demandé? 2. Je n'ai pas prêté ce volume à M. Ernest parce que M. Ernest ne me l'a pas demandé poliment. 3. Est-ce qu'il vous a manqué de respect? 4. Pas précisément, mais il m'a parlé comme si j'étais sa petite sœur; il a oublié qu'il parlait à sa vieille tante. 5. C'est un mauvais sujet, ma tante, mais je le gronderai, et il vous demandera pardon. 6. Très bien, ma chère, s'il regrette sa faute, je la lui pardonnerai. 7. Nous pensions qu'il avait perdu ses vilaines habitudes, mais nous les lui reprocherons tant qu'il les perdra. 8. Henri vous a demandé votre nouvel encrier, pourquoi ne le lui avez-vous pas prêté? 9. Je ne le lui ai pas prêté parce que je ne l'ai plus. 10. Quelqu'un me l'a emprunté la semaine dernière et ne me l'a pas rendu. Si je le retrouve, je le prêterai à Henri. 11. Voici le miel que je vous ai promis, la bonne vous le portera ce soir. 12. Quand je vous ai demandé ce billet, vous me l'avez refusé. 13. Vous avez supposé que je le montrerais à ma cousine, mais je ne le lui aurais certainement pas montré.

1. Why would they refuse it to us? 2. Because you would not return it to them. 3. Will you not lend it to me? 4. No, I shall not lend it to you, because you would lose it. 5. It is my mother who has asked him for it (*it to him*). 6. Have you not told it to her? 7. Does she not advise it to you? 8. We have bought a horse for our aunt, have you sent it to her? 9. She had promised me that bird, but she has not yet given it to me. 10. I should have given it to him, if he had asked me for it. 11. If he reproaches you for it (*it to you*), I shall scold him. 12. Did he borrow it from you (*it to you*)? 13. Did he ask your pardon (*did he ask pardon to you*)? 14. You are a bad boy, somebody will

scold you. 15. My sisters bought some inkstands at this bookseller's; do you think that he will send them to them? 16. I did not ask them for the book, because they would not have lent it to me. 17. If your daughter will bring it to me, this evening or to-morrow morning, I shall be at home, and shall give her something.

76.

Exception to the rule on the Place of Pronouns.

If the verb is in the imperative *affirmative*, personal pronouns are placed after it and translated thus:[1] —

donnez-le-moi,	*give him to me.* *give it to me.*	**donnez-le-nous,**	*give him to us.* *give it to us.*
donnez-la-moi,	*give her to me.* *give it to me.*	**donnez-la-nous,**	*give her to us.* *give it to us.*
donnez-les-moi,	*give them to me.*	**donnez-les-nous,**	*give them to us.*
donnez-le-lui,	*give him to him.* *give it to him.* *give him to her.* *give it to her.*	**donnez-le-leur,**	*give him to them.* *give it to them.*
donnez-la-lui,	*give her to him.* *give it to him.* *give her to her.* *give it to her.*	**donnez-la-leur,**	*give her to them.* *give it to them.*
donnez-les-lui,	*give them to him.* *give them to her.*	**donnez-les-leur,**	*give them to them.*

Observe that, when the imperative is *negative*, personal pronouns precede the verb and follow the general rule, as; —

ne me le donnez pas,	*Do not give it to me.*
ne nous le donnez pas,	*Do not give it to us.*
ne le lui donnez pas,	*Do not give it to him.*
ne le leur donnez pas.	*Do not give it to them.*

remercier, *to thank.*	**de sa part,** *from him, from her.*
raconter, *to relate, to tell.*	**rencontrer,** *to meet.*
de ma part, *from me.*	**répéter,** *to repeat.*
de ta part, *from thee.*	**comment,** *how.*

[1] Observe that their order and place are the same as in English.

l'affaire (f.), *the affair.* **le malheur,** *the misfortune.*
en un mot, *in a word.* **la permission,** *the permission.*

1. Voici deux paires de boucles d'oreilles que j'achète, envoyez-les-moi ce soir. 2. Mais ne me les envoyez pas avant cinq heures. 3. Je pense que voici mon verre, remplissez-le-moi, s'il vous plaît. 4. Je vous remercie. 5. Quand vous rencontrerez votre oncle, remerciez-le de notre part. 6. Racontez-lui comment la fameuse nouvelle nous est arrivée. 7. En un mot, expliquez-lui toute l'affaire. 8. Si vous la rencontrez aujourd'hui, racontez-lui l'affaire, mais ne lui répétez pas le mot que je vous ai dit. 9. Ces jolies fleurs appartiennent à ma tante, rendez-les-lui. 10. Ne les perdez pas. 11. Non, ne les lui rendez pas, donnez-les-nous. 12. C'est mon crayon que vous avez là près de vous; jetez-le-moi, s'il vous plaît. 13. Ce petit cadeau est pour vous, acceptez-le de moi. 14. Je vous remercie, monsieur; je l'accepterai avec la permission de mon père. 15. Dès que votre sœur sera arrivée, amenez-la-moi.

1. This pen is not very good, do not give it to him. 2. Give it to me. 3. This pencil belongs to her; give it back to her. 4. Do not give it back to her, give it to her sister. 5. She is very studious, do not punish her. 6. Lend her the book which I gave you yesterday. 7. Do not speak to me of him. 8. If you have lost your pencils, look for them. 9. You have promised me a French book, give it to me. 10. You have promised it to her, give it to her. 11. No, do not give it to her, give it to us. 12. Lend him the money (*for*) which he has asked you, but do not lend him your watch; he will never give it back to you. 13. Mary has asked you for her brother's letter; give it to her. 14. No; do not.[1]

[1] As the auxiliary verb *to do* does not exist in French, we must, in such cases, repeat the verb of the preceding sentence: *no; do not give it to her.*

PRONOMINAL VERBS.

77.

Verbs are called *pronominal* when they are conjugated with two pronouns of the same person. They follow the conjugations to which they respectively belong, the verb being preceded by the pronouns.

First Conjugation.

INDIC. PRES.	**je me cache,** *I hide myself.*
	tu te caches.
	il or **elle se cache.**
	nous nous cachons.
	vous vous cachez.
	ils or **elles se cachent.**
IMPERFECT.	**je me cachais,** etc.
FUTURE.	**je me cacherai,** etc.
CONDITIONAL.	**je me cacherais,** etc.
IMPERATIVE.	**cache-toi, cachons-nous, cachez-vous.**

Negatively.

INDIC. PRES.	**je ne me cache pas,** *I do not hide myself.*
	tu ne te caches pas.
	il or **elle ne se cache pas.**
	nous ne nous cachons pas.
	vous ne vous cachez pas.
	ils or **elles ne se cachent pas.**
IMPERFECT.	**je ne me cachais pas,** etc.
FUTURE.	**je ne me cacherai pas,** etc.
CONDITIONAL.	**je ne me cacherais pas,** etc.
IMPERATIVE.	**ne te cache pas, ne nous cachons pas, ne vous cachez pas.**

Second Conjugation.

INDIC. PRES.	**je me punis,** etc., *I punish myself,* etc.
IMPERFECT.	**je me punissais,** etc.
FUTURE.	**je me punirai,** etc.
CONDITIONAL.	**je me punirais,** etc.
IMPERATIVE.	**punis-toi, punissons-nous, punissez-vous.**

Third Conjugation.

INDIC. PRES.	**je me rends,** etc., *I surrender myself*, etc.
IMPERFECT.	**je me rendais,** etc.
FUTURE.	**je me rendrai,** etc.
CONDITIONAL.	**je me rendrais,** etc.
IMPERATIVE.	**rends-toi, rendons-nous, rendez-vous.**

The conjugation of pronominal verbs is a mere application of the rule on the place of personal pronouns in the objective case: **me,** *myself;* **te,** *thyself;* **se,** *himself* or *herself;* **nous,** *ourselves;* **vous,** *yourselves;* and **se,** *themselves,* are placed immediately before the verb; while if the verb is in the imperative affirmative, the pronoun-object is placed after: **cache-toi, cachons-nous, cachez-vous.**

se cacher, *to hide one's self.*
se flatter, *to flatter one's self.*
se montrer, *to show one's self.*
se blâmer, *to blame one's self.*
s'admirer, *to admire one's self.*
se porter, *to be.*[1]
se porter bien, *to be well.*
se porter mal, *to be unwell.*
s'appeler, *to call one's self.*
s'amuser, *to enjoy one's self.*
se punir, *to punish one's self.*
se guérir, *to cure one's self.*
se trahir, *to betray one's self.*
se rendre, *to surrender one's self.*
se perdre, *to lose one's self.*

la philosophie, *philosophy.*
la route, *the road.*
comment, *how.*
seul, *alone.*
mais, *why!*
fois, *time.*

1. Ne trouvez-vous pas que cette petite fille s'admire beaucoup? 2. Elle ne s'admirera pas tant quand elle sera plus vieille. 3. Comment vouz portez-vous? 4. Je me porte très bien, je vous remercie, et vous? 5. Je suis un peu malade ce matin. 6. Comment s'appelle ce monsieur? 7. Il s'appelle Joly, je pense, il est professeur de philosophie. 8. Et cette dame, comment s'appelle-t-elle? 9. Mais je pense que c'est madame Joly. 10. Je trouve qu'elle s'admire un peu, mais elle est si belle et si aimable! 11. Ces messieurs se flattent que nous leur raconterons notre histoire, mais nous la garderons pour d'autres. 12. Ne vous perdrez-vous pas

[1] *To be,* used with reference to health, is idiomatically rendered by **se porter,** *to carry one's self.* **Il se porte bien,** *he is well.*

si vous voyagez seul? 13. Moi, me perdre! et comment me perdrais-je? est-ce que je n'ai pas voyagé vingt fois par cette route? 14. Nous sommes battus: rendons-nous. 15. Non, ne nous rendons pas encore.

1. He is not enjoying himself. 2. He was not curing himself. 3. He will not surrender himself. 4. He would not enjoy himself. 5. She is not well. 6. She will not be well. 7. They were not well. 8. They would not be well. 9. Are you not well? 10. Were you not well? 11. Will you not be well? 12. They will show themselves here no more. 13. Are you enjoying yourself at the coast? 14. I enjoy myself everywhere. 15. What is that young man called (*how does that young man call himself*)? 16. He is called John (*he calls himself John*). 17. What is your cousin called? 18. She is called Louisa. 19. And you, sir, what are you called? 20. I am called Henry. 21. I will hide; my brother and sister would hide also, if they dared. 22. Do I not flatter myself?

78.

Pronominal verbs are divided into two classes according to their meaning. They are called *reflective* when they express action confined to the actor, like those which we have seen in the preceding section; and they are called *reciprocal* when they express action reciprocated between two or more subjects, as **nous nous aimons**, *we like each other*.

Reciprocal verbs are used only in the plural, as they express the action of more than one subject:[1] **nous nous aimons, vous vous aimez, ils s'aiment.**

[1] Except the case when **on** is used to represent several persons: **on se tuait les uns les autres.**

Supposing we have to translate *we flatter one another*, if we simply say **nous nous flattons**, a person hearing us may indeed understand *we flatter one another*, but another person may as well understand *we flatter ourselves*. To avoid that misunderstanding we add to the reciprocal verb **l'un l'autre** or **les uns les autres**: **l'un l'autre**, when the action is reciprocated between only two subjects; **les uns les autres**, if there are more than two subjects: **nous nous flattons l'un l'autre** or **nous nous flattons les uns les autres**.[1]

But this addition is unnecessary if the meaning is clearly reciprocal, as **nous nous cherchons depuis une heure**, *we have been looking for each other for an hour;* **mon frère et votre sœur s'aiment**, *my brother and your sister love each other.*

continuellement, *continually.*
personnages, *personages.*
c'est vrai, *it is true.*
en duel, *in a duel.*
faire, *to do.*
plus avancé, *better off.*
le chemin, *the way.*
se vanter, *to extol one's self* or *each other.*
se blesser, *to wound one's self* or *each other.*
se tuer, *to kill one's self* or *each other.*
se défendre, *to defend one's self* or *each other.*
se séparer, *to part from each other.*
se quereller, *to quarrel.*
s'embrasser, *to kiss each other.*
attaquer, *to attack.*
se battre, *to fight.*
recommencer, *to begin again.*
réciproquement, *reciprocally.*

1. Je pense que vous vous flattez continuellement l'un l'autre. 2. Vous vous admirez réciproquement, vous vous vantez, vous vous louez, comme si vous n'aviez jamais vu de plus grands personnages. 3. Au contraire, votre frère et votre sœur se grondent toujours. 4. C'est vrai, ils se grondent toujours, ils ne s'aiment pas. 5. Ces deux officiers se battraient en duel, si on les laissait faire. 6. Seraient-ils plus avancés s'ils se blessaient ou s'ils se tuaient? 7. Si quelqu'un vous attaque quand vous serez absent, je vous défendrai, et, si quelqu'un m'attaque quand je serai absent, vous me défendrez.

[1] Instead of **l'un l'autre, les uns les autres**, the adverb **réciproquement** is sometimes added, or **entre** is put before the verb: **Pierre et Paul se louent réciproquement**, or **Pierre et Paul s'entre-louent**. This latter form is becoming obsolete.

8. Nous nous défendrons ainsi l'un l'autre. 9. Si vous vous séparez dans le bois et si vous perdez votre chemin, vous vous appellerez les uns les autres. 10. Est-ce que deux sœurs se querellent ainsi? 11. Embrassez-vous, et ne recommencez plus. 12. Nous ne nous embrasserons pas, parce que nous ne nous embrassons jamais, mais nous ne recommencerons plus.

1. We are blaming each other (*2 persons*). 2. We were punishing each other. 3. We shall defend each other. 4. They do not defend each other (*more than 2 persons*). 5. They used not to blame each other. 6. They will not punish each other. 7. They would not defend each other. 8. Why do you not like each other? 9. Who told you that we did not like each other? 10. Nobody;[1] but you are always scolding one another. 11. Two brothers quarrel, it is true, but in spite of that they are fond of each other. 12. We always defend one another. 13. Yes, but, when you are together, you always quarrel. 14. If we lose our way in this wood, we will not part from each other; and if any one attacks us, we will defend ourselves. 15. Who will attack us? I am ready to defend myself. 16. You forget that I am no longer the young man you saw five years ago.

79.

Pronominal verbs, in all their compound tenses, take the auxiliary **être**, instead of **avoir**, as: —

PAST INDEFINITE.

je me suis caché, *I hid myself.*	**nous nous sommes cachés.**[2]
tu t'es caché.	**vous vous êtes cachés.**
il s'est caché.	**ils se sont cachés.**

[1] If there is no verb expressed, **ne** is not to be used.

[2] Past participles of pronominal verbs do not always agree, but, till the rule is explained (in § 98), only those which agree will be given.

PLUPERFECT. **je m'étais caché,** *I had hidden myself.*
FUTURE ANTERIOR. **je me serai caché,** *I shall have hidden myself.*
CONDIT. PAST. **je me serais caché,** *I should have hidden myself.*

se lever, *to rise, to get up* (to raise one's self).
se coucher, *to go to bed* (to lay one's self down).
se tromper, *to deceive one's self, to be mistaken.*

se promener, *to take a walk.* **se fâcher,** *to get angry.*
se reposer, *to rest one's self.* **simplement,** *simply.*
s'enrhumer, *to catch cold.* **sitôt,** *so soon.*

1. A quelle heure vous êtes-vous couché hier? 2. Je me suis couché hier à dix heures et demie. 3. A quelle heure vous êtes-vous levé ce matin? 4. Je me suis levé à sept heures moins un quart. 5. Votre frère s'est-il promené aujourd'hui? 6. Il s'est promené une demi-heure. 7. Votre cousine ne s'est-elle pas enrhumée hier soir? 8. Elle s'est, je pense, un peu enrhumée. 9. Est-ce que vos cousins se sont fâchés, quand vous leur avez raconté l'affaire? 10. Henri m'a dit simplement que je me trompais, mais Ernest s'est fâché. 11. Nous nous sommes promenés longtemps ce matin, si longtemps que ma sœur était fort lasse. 12. Vous êtes-vous reposés quelque part? 13. Nous nous sommes reposés un quart d'heure chez notre tante. 14. Si j'étais sorti avec vous hier soir, je me serais certainement enrhumé. 15. Nous sommes allés à l'opéra mardi dernier, nous nous sommes bien amusés.

1. We (*m.*) are not enjoying ourselves. 2. We have not enjoyed ourselves. 3. We have not surrendered ourselves. 4. We were not enjoying ourselves. 5. We had not surrendered ourselves. 6. We would not enjoy ourselves. 7. We would not punish ourselves. 8. We would not have enjoyed ourselves. 9. We would not have surrendered ourselves. 10. How long did she walk to-day? 11. She walked for three quarters of an hour. 12. When did I rise this morning? I rose at nine.

13. My brother went to bed very late last night. 14. We took cold on Wednesday night. 15. She got angry when I told her that you were gone. 16. Would you have gone to bed so soon if I had come? 17. Get up, your brother is arrived. 18. They rose this morning at 8 o'clock. 19. Have you been out this evening? 20. Yes, sir, I went out with my father at half-past seven; we walked till a quarter of nine, when we returned. 21. I enjoyed myself much, and I think he did also.

80.

EN and *Y*.

When *some* or *any* (whether expressed or understood) is not followed by its noun, it is translated by **en**, which follows the rule on the place of personal pronouns: —

Avez-vous du pain? Oui, j'en ai,	*Have you any bread? Yes, I have some*, or simply *I have.*
Non, je n'en ai pas,	*No, I have not any* or *none.*
Achetez-en,	*Buy some.*

En means also *of it*, *of them*, or *for it*.

Voulez-vous des fruits? cette caisse en est pleine,	*Will you have any fruit? this box is full of it.*

When a number (*one*, *two*, *three*, *four*, etc.), or an adverb of quantity (*much*, *many*, *little*, *few*, etc.), or noun of quantity or measure (**mètre, paire, douzaine, bouteille**, etc.). is not followed by its noun, that noun is replaced by **en**.

Avez-vous des frères? J'en ai un,	*Have you any brothers? I have one.*
Avez-vous lu des romans anglais? Oui, j'en ai beaucoup lu,	*Have you read any English novels? Yes, I have read a great many.*
Avez-vous du vin chez vous? J'en ai encore deux bouteilles,	*Have you any wine at home? I have still two bottles.*

There (expressed or understood) is translated by **là**, when pointing to a place or thing, and by **y** when referring to a place mentioned before: —

Voyez-vous cette maison-là ?	*Do you see that house?*
J'y ai demeuré trois mois,	*I lived there three months.*

Y means also *to it*, or *to them*, and follows the rule on the place of personal pronouns: —

Ces champs formeront une très belle propriété quand vous y aurez ajouté ce bois,	*These fields will form a very fine property when you have added that wood to them.*

un accès de colère, *a fit of anger.*
de temps en temps, *from time to time.*
compter, *to count.*
à l'église, *at church.*

1. Avez-vous de l'eau fraîche? 2. Oui, nous en avons. 3. Donnez-en un verre à mon frère. 4. Votre oncle n'est-il pas un peu sujet à des accès de colère? 5. Il y est beaucoup trop sujet. 6. N'êtes-vous jamais entré dans cette belle église? 7. Non, je n'y suis jamais entré. 8. Combien de sœurs avez-vous? 9. J'en ai une. 10. Il y a beaucoup de fautes dans sa lettre, mais la vôtre en est pleine. 11. J'en ai compté au moins une douzaine. 12. Voici une avenue où votre propriétaire se promène tous les soirs. 13. J'y rencontre aussi quelquefois l'avocat qui demeure près de vous. 14. N'y avez-vous jamais vu mon oncle? 15. De temps en temps, mais il n'y est jamais seul.

1. Have you any money about (*sur*) you? 2. Have I any money? my pockets are full of it. 3. If you would lend (§ 51, 3d) a little to your brother, I am sure he would be very glad of it. 4. How many French books have you at home? 5. I have ten or twelve. 6. If you have any good beer, give my brother a glass of it. 7. Has your mother been at church? 8. She has not been there.

9. Have you ever been to Paris? 10. No, I have never been. 11. Has your sister still many birds? 12. She has more than ever. 13. You have too much bread; give some to your sister. 14. But, aunt, I have not enough; it is my brother who has too much. 15. Shall I find you at church next Sunday? 16. I am sure that I shall be there, and I hope you will be there also. 17. My daughter has asked for your inkstand; why did you not lend it to her?

81.

When **y** is to be placed before the verb with one or two pronouns, it comes after them: —

Je vous les y porterai, *I shall carry them to you there.*

When **en** is to be used with any other pronoun, or with **y**, it comes last: —

Je vous y en porterai, *I shall carry some to you there.*

m'en,	*some to me.*	**nous en,**	*some to us.*
t'en,	*some to thee.*	**vous en,**	*some to you.*
lui en,	*some to him, to her.*	**leur en,**	*some to them.*

redemander,[1] *to ask again.*
de tout mon cœur, *with all my heart.*
quelques-uns, quelques-unes, *a few, some.*
une histoire, *a story.*
une chanson, *a song.*
quelque temps, *some time.*

1. Vous avez de si bon lait que je vous en demanderai encore un peu. 2. Ma sœur n'ose pas vous en redemander comme moi, mais vous lui en donnerez peut-être encore une tasse. 3. Votre sœur a eu beaucoup de bontés pour moi, je l'en remercie de tout mon cœur. 4. Votre frère a tant de jolis romans que je lui en emprunterai quelques-uns. 5. Il ne vous les prêtera pas; du moins il ne m'en a jamais prêté un seul. 6. Si vous trouvez

[1] **Re-** beginning a verb generally means *back* or *again*.

cette histoire jolie, je vous en raconterai beaucoup d'autres. 7. N'avez-vous pas reçu de livres quand vous étiez à la campagne ? 8. Mon cousin vous y en a envoyé. 9. Ces chansons sont fort jolies : chantez-nous-en encore une autre. 10. Est-ce que vous n'aimez pas notre vin ? Henri vous en a rempli un grand verre. 11. Soyez tranquilles, nous n'oublierons pas vos lettres, quand vous demeurerez chez votre tante. 12. Charles vous les y portera. 13. Et s'il les oublie, je vous les porterai moi-même. 14. Comment vous remercierai-je de vos bons soins ? 15. Ne m'en remerciez pas, et soignez-vous bien.

1. If you buy so many pretty things, I am sure your brother will ask you for some (*some to you*). 2. If he asks me for any, I will give him some; but I think he will not ask me for any. 3. I offered some to him some time ago, but he has refused me. 4. You will not forget, I hope, that you have promised me some. 5. If I have promised you any, I will give you a few. 6. Did you see any flowers in their garden ? 7. Yes, I have seen many there. 8. Were there many ladies at church ? 9. There were very few. 10. How many were there ? 11. There were fourteen or fifteen. 12. When shall you be in the country ? 13. We shall be there during the months of August and September. 14. I think I shall visit you there. 15. These rules are a little difficult, but the master has already explained some of them to us. 16. That lady flatters herself that she sings well, but she is mistaken.

SOME PECULIARITIES OF SYNTAX.

82.

This, that (see §§ 19, 20, 35), are translated by **ceci, cela,** when pointing to something without naming it, or when referring to an idea just expressed (**cela**), or about to be expressed (**ceci**); as: —

donnez-moi ceci, donnez-moi cela,	*give me this, give me that.*
le malheur dans lequel vous êtes tombé prouve bien ceci, que les plus grandes précautions sont souvent inutiles.	*the misfortune into which you fell proves indeed this, that the greatest precautions are often useless.*
cela est-il vrai ?	*is that true ?*

Such expressions as *a friend of mine, a countryman of yours, a book of hers,* must be turned, for translation, into: —

one of my friends,	**un de mes amis,** *or* **une de mes amies.**
one of your countrymen,	**un de vos compatriotes.**
one of her books,	**un de ses livres.**

As a mark of respect, the words **monsieur, madame, mademoiselle,** or their plurals, are placed before the adjective **votre** or **vos** followed by **père, mère, frère, sœur, oncle, cousin, ami,** etc., or their plurals.

J'ai rencontré monsieur votre père et madame votre mère,	*I met your father and mother.*
Comment se porte mademoiselle votre sœur ?	*How is your sister ?*

But if the person spoken to is an intimate friend or an inferior, the word **monsieur, madame,** or **mademoiselle** is left out.[1]

[1] We shall suppose this to have been the case in all the preceding exercises.

The **a** of **ma, ta, sa** is never elided; therefore, to avoid hiatus, use **mon, ton, son** before a feminine beginning with a vowel or *h mute.*

mon amitié,	*my friendship.*
ton étourderie,	*thy heedlessness.*
son aimable cousine,	*his amiable cousin.*

être à, *to belong to.*
à cause de, *on account of.*
définitivement, *positively.*
renoncer à, *to renounce.*
bien, *indeed.*
étourdi, *heedless.*
même, *even.*
l'intérêt (m.), *the interest.*
l'excuse (f.), *the excuse.*
la jeunesse, *the youth.*
s'imaginer, *to fancy.*
le wagon, *the railway carriage.*
depuis (prep. of place), *from.*
incroyable, *incredible.*
la pension, *the boarding school.*
captiver, *to captivate, to take up.*

1. Je pense que ceci appartient à monsieur votre oncle? 2. Pardon, monsieur, ceci est à moi, mais voilà quelque chose qui appartient à mon oncle. 3. Cela n'est-il pas à un de vos amis? 4. Oui, madame, cela appartient à monsieur votre fils. 5. A mon fils? est-ce que mon fils est toujours de vos amis? 6. Mais (*why*) certainement, madame, et pourquoi non? 7. Mais je pensais qu'à cause de son étourderie vous aviez définitivement renoncé à son amitié? 8. Il est bien un peu étourdi, mais cela n'annonce pas un mauvais cœur; c'est même le contraire qui est le plus souvent vrai. 9. Je vous remercie de tout mon cœur, monsieur, de l'intérêt que vous lui portez (*bear*); il a un bien grand défaut, mais son excuse est dans sa jeunesse. 10. Thérèse, n'est-ce pas une de vos petites amies qui est arrivée ce matin? 11. Oui, ma tante, c'est la petite Jeanne; imaginez-vous que cette étourdie a oublié son écharpe et son ombrelle dans le wagon, et qu'elle a perdu sa montre avec la chaîne depuis la station! 12. Cela est incroy-

able, mademoiselle Jeanne est devenue folle! 13. Son excuse est qu'elle a rencontré une de ses amies de pension dans le wagon où elle était, cela a captivé toute son attention. 14. Montrez-moi ceci.

1. When did you see that? 2. Is this for you? 3. I do not accept his excuse. 4. His sister was a friend of mine. 5. Your mother wrote to me yesterday; I shall answer her to-morrow. 6. Repeat all that to her. 7. A cousin of yours visits us from time to time. 8. He lost a son of his last week. 9. A sister of his took cold the other day. 10. I took a walk with your uncle yesterday. 11. Is not that generous? 12. Do not show all that to him. 13. How long is it since you saw your mother? 14. I met her friend, Miss Louisa, yesterday. 15. I shall visit her one of these days. 16. Give that to your brother, if you please; for a long time he has been (§ 60) a good friend of mine. He is well now, I hope?

83.

Peculiarities of Syntax continued.

(1) The passive form is not so much used in French as in English; when the agent is indefinite, the English passive sentence is in French generally changed to an active sentence with **on** (§ 32) for its subject; as: —

Some books have been given them. **On leur a donné des livres.**

On may be changed into **l'on** whenever it sounds better. For example, **on apprend facilement ce que l'on comprend,** *we learn easily what we understand,* sounds better than, **on apprend facilement ce qu'on comprend.**

If the expression is not indefinite, the noun representing the agent is put as subject instead of the indefinite **on** : —

He has been beaten by the English, **Les Anglais l'ont battu.**

(2) When the pronoun *what* means *the thing which*, it is translated by **ce qui**, if *what* is the subject; by **ce que**, if it is the object (see § 8).

Ce qui m'effraie, c'est qu'il me manque de respect, *What frightens me is, that he is disrespectful to me.*
Ce que je vous raconte est vrai, *What I tell you is true.*

un sou, *a cent.* **Prussien,** *a Prussian.*
une gravure, *an engraving.* **Autrichien,** *an Austrian.*
une bataille, *a battle.* **complètement,** *completely.*
fâcher, *to vex.* **acheter à** (p.), *to buy from.* **facilement,** *easily.*

1. Ces pauvres gens n'ont pas un sou; on leur a donné tout à l'heure du pain et de la viande. 2. Avez-vous fait ce qu'on vous a ordonné? 3. Les Prussiens ont complètement battu les Autrichiens à Sadowa. 4. Sa mère l'a puni. 5. Ne prêtez pas vos livres à ma sœur, elle perd tout ce qu'on lui prête. 6. On vous a payé, je pense, tout ce qu'on vous avait acheté. 7. On vous a cherché partout, et l'on ne vous a pas trouvé. 8. On dit qu'il a gelé très fort cette nuit. 9. On ne dit pas toujours tout ce que l'on pense. 10. Ses frères l'ont abandonné. 11. Oui, mais ses sœurs l'ont reçu chez elles et l'ont soigné. 12. Ce qui ne vous fâchera pas, ma tante, c'est que j'ai bien employé mon temps ce matin, je n'ai pas perdu une seule minute.

1. It is said (*one says*) that your brother will get (*will have*) the first prize. 2. He has been rewarded by his father (*his father has rewarded him*). 3. You do not hear (*entendre*) what you are reproached for (*what one reproaches you*). 4. I easily guess what deceives you.

5. They are very poor; some money was given them yesterday morning (*one has given them . . .*). 6. Where are these beautiful watches sold (*where does one sell . . .*)? 7. We have not yet received what we have been promised. 8. What vexes me is that he has been accepted by his uncle. 9. I will give you nothing more, you lose everything which is given to you. 10. Have any engravings been bought? 11. Yes; Jane has bought one for me and two for you. 12. Where is that sold? 13. Where is that (to be) found? 14. It is thought that you will succeed. 15. It is supposed that the Emperor will not dare to show himself in that battle. 16. Are you vexed that we do not defend one another?

84.

Peculiarities of Syntax continued.

In the following idioms **avoir** is used instead of the English *to be*: —

avoir raison, *to be right.*
avoir tort, *to be wrong.*
avoir peur, *to be afraid.*
avoir honte, *to be ashamed.*
avoir faim, *to be hungry.*
avoir soif, *to be thirsty.*
avoir chaud, *to be warm.*
avoir froid, *to be cold.*
avoir sommeil, *to be sleepy.*
avoir besoin, *to be in need.*

In all these expressions, **bien** is generally used for *very* or *quite*: **vous avez bien raison, j'ai eu bien tort, il a bien peur,** etc.

In asking or stating a person's age, the following construction is generally used: —

Quel âge avez-vous? *How old are you?*
J'ai vingt ans, *I am twenty years old.*

The adjective **âgé** may also be used, though this construction is not so frequent in conversation: —

Elle est âgée de vingt ans, *She is twenty years old.*

approuver, *to approve.*
le service, *the service.*
tout de suite, *at once.*
le morceau, *the piece.*

1. Quel âge a votre petit frère ? 2. Il a six ans et demi, il aura sept ans le 1er du mois prochain. 3. Et vous, monsieur Charles, quel âge avez-vous ? 4. Vingt-deux ans, madame. 5. Si M. votre cousin s'imagine que je lui redemanderai l'argent que je lui ai prêté, il a bien tort ; je ne le lui réclamerai jamais. 6. N'avez-vous pas trop chaud près de ce grand feu ? 7. En effet j'avais froid tout à l'heure, mais maintenant j'ai trop chaud. 8. Mon frère avait sommeil ; il s'est couché il y a une heure. 9. Il a eu raison, je l'approuve. 10. N'aurez-vous pas peur, seul dans cette grande chambre ? 11. Votre petite sœur a honte de sa conduite. 12. Vous n'aurez pas besoin de ces livres, j'espère ? 13. Mon cousin a dix-sept ans. 14. Je pensais qu'il était beaucoup plus âgé. 15. Il est moins âgé que vous.

1. If your brother repeats that, he will be wrong. 2. You are quite right; do not reply to him. 3. Speak to him a little; he is afraid of us. 4. If you are ashamed of your conduct, I will pardon you. 5. I am hungry, and you give me a glass of water! 6. Would you give me a piece of bread if I were thirsty? 7. Claim my services if ever you are in need of them. 8. We came back very late; we were cold and hungry. 9. Is your brother a little warmer? 10. I think he is very sleepy. 11. How old is he? 12. He will be ten years old in two months. 13. If he went to bed (*imperf.*) at once, he would soon be warmer. 14. You are quite right, he will take cold in this room. 15. Charles, do you hear me? go to bed at once, you are sleepy. 16. She has not done what she was bidden, and now she flatters herself that she will be happy.

THE SUBJUNCTIVE MOOD.

Preliminary Observations.

In a sentence there are as many clauses as verbs in a personal mood (that is, verbs in any other mood than the infinitive). Thus, in the sentence, *I shall send you a book if you wish,* there are two verbs in a personal mood, there are consequently two clauses.

Clauses are divided into *principal* and *secondary.*

A *principal* clause is independent, and generally expresses complete sense of itself; a *secondary* clause depends, directly or indirectly, on a principal clause, and explains or modifies it. In the sentence, *I shall send you a book if you wish, I shall send you a book* is a principal clause, *if you wish* is secondary.

The word connecting a secondary clause with the one on which it depends is either a relative pronoun or a conjunction; as —

(Relative pronoun.) — He is the only man *that* I know here.
(Conjunction.) — I fear *that* he will come.

Observe, however, that the four conjunctions, **et, ou, ni, mais,** may connect principal clauses, and they therefore announce a secondary clause *only* when they are immediately followed by another conjunction or a relative pronoun.

The subjunctive mood can *never* be used in a principal clause, and can be used *only* in a clause beginning with a conjunctive word or a relative pronoun.

The indicative mood, which may be used in either a principal or secondary clause, expresses an action or a state in a positive, certain, and absolute manner; as: —

Je crois qu'il est venu,	*I believe he is come.*
Je déclare que je lui pardonne,	*I declare that I forgive him.*

The subjunctive mood, on the contrary, always depends upon a principal clause, and is used when that principal clause implies *necessity*, *uncertainty*, or *emotion*.

Il faut qu'il soit puni,	*It is necessary that he should be punished.*
Je ne pense pas qu'il ait vu votre fils,	*I do not think he has seen your son.*
Je crains qu'il ne soit mort,	*I fear he is dead.*

Therefore, if the thought expressed in the principal clause implies *certainty*, the verb in the secondary clause must be in the *indicative*; if the thought expressed in the principal clause implies *necessity*, *uncertainty*, or *emotion*, the verb in the secondary clause must be in the *subjunctive*.

Je crois que la santé est préférable à tous les biens.	*I believe that health is preferable to all riches.*
Je ne crois pas que la santé soit préférable à tous les biens.	*I do not believe that health is preferable to all riches.*

The conjunction **que**, which is followed sometimes by the indicative, sometimes by the subjunctive, itself governs no mood. It is the *certainty* or *uncertainty in the mind of the speaker* that requires the indicative or subjunctive, as the case may be.

85.

An impersonal verb implying necessity or uncertainty requires the verb depending on it to be put in the subjunctive with the conjunction **que**; as: —

il est juste que je sois puni, *it is right that I should be punished.*
il faut qu'il soit ici ce soir, *it is necessary for him to be here this evening.*

SUBJUNCTIVE PRESENT.

que j'aie, *that I may have, that I should have, that I have.*	**que je sois,** *that I may be, that I should be, that I be.*
que tu aies.	**que tu sois.**
qu'il or **qu'elle ait.**	**qu'il** or **qu'elle soit.**
que nous ayons.	**que nous soyons.**
que vous ayez.	**que vous soyez.**
qu'ils or **qu'elles aient.**	**qu'ils** or **qu'elles soient.**

il faut,
il est nécessaire, } *it is necessary, must.*
il importe,
il est important, } *it is important, it is of consequence.*
il convient,
il est convenable, } *it is becoming,* or *proper.*
il vaut mieux,
il est préférable, } *it is better,* or *preferable.*
il se peut,
il est possible, } *it may be, it is possible.*

il est juste, *it is right,* or *just.*
il est bon, *it is good.*
il est indispensable, *it is indispensable.*
il est essentiel, *it is essential,* or *material.*
il est urgent, *it is urgent,* or *pressing.*
il est temps, *it is time.*

1. Il faut que mon frère ait ce livre aujourd'hui. 2. Il vaut mieux qu'elle soit ici ce soir. 3. Il est essentiel que vous soyez à Londres demain. 4. Est-il possible que cette histoire soit vraie? 5. Je leur ai sacrifié mon temps et mes peines, faut-il encore qu'ils aient tout mon argent? 6. Vous lui avez désobéi, il est juste que vous soyez puni. 7. Se peut-il que M. votre cousin soit encore ici après cette scandaleuse affaire! 8. Il est essentiel que j'aie cet argent ce soir: réclamez-le et envoyez-le-moi. 9. Est-il indispensable que Mme votre mère ait cette lettre cette semaine? 10. Oui, Madame, cela est urgent; il faut qu'elle ait tous les détails de l'affaire avant

mon arrivée. 11. Mais est-il nécessaire que vous soyez présent ? 12. Cela n'est pas absolument nécessaire, mais il est préférable dans mon intérêt, et peut-être aussi dans le vôtre, que je sois présent à la discussion.

1. It is possible that your father is now in Paris. 2. It is time that we should have that letter. 3. It is right that she should be punished. 4. She must have (*it is necessary that she should have*) that dress to-night. 5. They must be (*it is necessary that they should be*) here at three. 6. That letter must be sent before one. 7. My sister has given you my ring; must you have my ear-rings also? 8. Is it indispensable that you should be in Paris to-morrow? 9. It is important that they should be with us. 10. Is it proper that we should be alone? 11. Must my brother have that horse to-day? 12. Must not my brother have that horse to-day? 13. Is it right that your sister should always have the best place? 14. Is it possible that you have sacrificed so much time to that affair? 15. You are right; if my father accepts your invitation, it is possible for us to be at your house on Saturday next.

86.

Verbs used negatively or interrogatively and implying uncertainty are followed by the subjunctive with the conjunction **que**; as: —

Croyez-vous que j'aie raison? *Do you believe I am right?*
Je ne crois pas que vous ayez tort, *I do not believe you are wrong.*

Croire (an irregular verb), *to believe.*

INDIC. PRES.	**je crois.**		**nous croyons.**
	tu crois.		**vous croyez.**
	il croit.		**ils croient.**
PAST INDEF.	**j'ai cru.**	IMPERF.	**je croyais.**
FUTURE.	**je croirai.**	CONDIT.	**je croirais.**

SUBJUNCTIVE PRESENT.

1st Conjugation.	*2d Conjugation.*	*3d Conjugation.*
que je porte.	**que je finisse.**	**que je rende.**
que tu portes.	**que tu finisses.**	**que tu rendes.**
qu'il porte.	**qu'il finisse.**	**qu'il rende.**
que nous portions.	**que nous finissions.**	**que nous rendions.**
que vous portiez.	**que vous finissiez.**	**que vous rendiez.**
qu'ils portent.	**qu'ils finissent.**	**qu'ils rendent.**

1. Je crois que Mlle votre sœur espère que vous lui donnerez cette jolie broche. 2. Je ne crois pas que vous nous ayez prêté le livre que vous réclamez. 3. Supposez-vous que nous osions jamais lui parler de cela ? 4. Si vous êtes puni, ne croyez pas que j'en sois la cause : je n'ai pas parlé de vous à votre maître. 5. N'espérez pas que je trahisse mon ami pour vous faire plaisir. 6. Ils se flattent que je répondrai à leur lettre, mais ils se trompent. 7. Elle ne croit pas que vous préfériez mon livre au sien ; répétez-le-lui vous-même. 8. Je vous demande pardon, je vous assure qu'elle a écrit six lettres depuis mon arrivée. 9. Ne vous imaginez pas que nous nous amusions ici sans vous ; nous vous regrettons beaucoup ; nous parlons de vous à chaque instant. 10. Je suppose que vous me défendrez si l'on m'attaque. 11. Soyez tranquille ; je ne pense pas que personne ose vous attaquer, mais, si on le fait, je serai là et vous défendrai. 12. Je n'espère pas qu'il réussisse, mais je pense qu'il a fait de son mieux. 13. Croient-ils que je les attende ? 14. Oui, Monsieur, ils espèrent que vous les attendrez.

1. She does not think that her father is come. 2. She thinks that her father is come. 3. Does she think that her father is come? 4. It may be that he is come. 5. She must finish her exercise at once. 6. I do not pretend that he is right, but I think you are wrong.

7. Do you hope that they will lend you the money of which you have need? 8. She thinks that you have forgotten her muff. 9. She does not think that you will arrive before her father. 10. I think that her brother is ill. 11. Do you think that her brother is ill? 12. I do not think that her brother is ill. 13. Do you believe that they are in London? 14. I do not suppose you will give her all that money. 15. She does not hope that her father will answer your letter.

87.

A few impersonal verbs, implying *certainty*, are followed by the indicative. The most frequently used are: —

il résulte, *it follows, the result is.*	**il est vrai,** *it is true.*
il s'ensuit, *it follows.*	**il est évident,** *it is evident.*
il paraît, *it appears.*	**il est démontré,** *it is proved.*
il (me, te, lui . . .) semble, *it seems to me, to thee, to him. . . .*	**il est incontestable,** *it is indisputable.*
	il est clair, *it is obvious.*
il est sûr, *it is sure.*	**il est manifeste,** *it is manifest.*
il est certain, *it is certain.*	**il est décidé,** *it has been decided.*

A negative or interrogative verb is not followed by the subjunctive when there is no doubt in the mind of the speaker; as: —

Savez-vous que votre père est malade?	*Do you know that your father is unwell?*
Je ne savais pas qu'il était ici,	*I did not know that he was here.*

Hence the subjunctive is not used after **est-ce que?** **n'est-ce pas que?** nor generally after the verbs **savoir** (*to know*), **faire savoir** (*to let know*), **dire** (*to tell*), **apprendre** (*to learn, to hear, to inform*), **informer** (*to inform*), **oublier** (*to forget*), and such like, used interrogatively, or even negatively if there is no doubt whatever in the mind of the speaker.

Savoir (an irregular verb), *to know.*

INDIC. PRES.	**je sais.**		**nous savons.**
	tu sais.		**vous savez.**
	il sait.		**ils savent.**
PAST INDEF.	**j'ai su.**	IMPERF.	**je savais.**
FUTURE.	**je saurai.**	CONDIT.	**je saurais.**

1. Il paraît que mon frère est malade depuis quinze jours. 2. Il me semble que vous avez eu tort dans cette discussion ; est-ce qu'on parle ainsi à sa sœur ? 3. J'ai eu tort, c'est vrai, mais il est certain qu'elle m'a provoqué pendant une demi-heure. 4. Il est décidé que votre petit cousin n'aura pas la permission qu'il demandait. 5. Il résulte de toutes vos discussions que vous et Henri, vous avez eu tort. 6. Il est certain que ma sœur sera ici ce soir ; elle me l'a écrit ce matin. 7. Il s'ensuit que sa présence n'est pas du tout certaine. 8. Il vous semble que j'ai tort, mais je vous prouverai le contraire. 9. Il est clair que vous avez sommeil, couchez-vous vite. 10. Il est vrai que j'ai sommeil, mais j'ai tant marché aujourd'hui que je suis horriblement fatigué. 11. Oubliez-vous que je suis plus âgé que vous ? 12. Ne savez-vous pas que M. votre frère est revenu de Paris ? 13. Vous ne m'aviez pas dit que vous étiez indisposé ; j'aime à croire que vous vous portez mieux. 14. Avez-vous appris que le bateau à vapeur par lequel vous êtes venu l'année dernière a fait naufrage sur la côte d'Irlande ? 15. Est-ce que vous ne saviez pas cela ? 16. Est-ce que vous ne me croyez pas ?

1. It is certain that you are wrong. 2. It is possible that you are wrong. 3. It appears that he will be punished. 4. It is just that he should be punished.

5. It is proved that he did not buy your uncle's house. 6. It may be that he has bought your uncle's house. 7. It seems to me that you have at last completed your exercise. 8. It is essential that you should have completed your exercise before ten. 9. I must have some paper, some ink, and a better pen. 10. Did you tell them that I would thank them myself? 11. Do you not find that this water is very bad? 12. I hope you will answer your mother's letter; do you forget she is ill? 13. I do not forget that she is ill, but I shall not answer her letter yet. 14. Does she know that I have lent you some money? 15. I have not told her that you had lent me some money, but I think she knows it. 16. Do (*est-ce que*) you believe that? 17. (*Est-ce que*) Is not that true? 18. Do you know that your father and I have quarrelled? 19. Do you not think that I am right?

88.

Verbs expressing *will*, *wish*, *doubt*, *fear*, *expectation*, *prohibition*, *permission*, *complaint*, *joy*, *sorrow*, *surprise*, or *any emotion*,[1] are followed by the subjunctive with the conjunction **que**; as:—

Je désire que vous lui parliez,	*I wish you to speak to him.*
Je veux que vous m'attendiez,	*I want you to wait for me.*

After verbs expressing *wish* or *will*, the English put either the infinitive, to express a future action or state, as in the above examples; or the subjunctive to express a present or a past action or state, as *I wish I were rich*, *I wish he had been rich.*

[1] Except only **espérer**, *to hope.* **Croire** and **penser** do not express an emotion, and therefore require the indicative, unless used interrogatively or negatively.

But in French the subjunctive is *always* used after verbs expressing *wish* or *will*, except only in the case when both verbs (that is, the verb expressing *wish* or *will*, and the verb depending on it) have the same person or persons for subjects; in which case the second verb is put in the infinitive, as **je voudrais être riche,** *I should like to be rich*, or, *I wish I were rich.*

Vouloir (an irregular verb), *to wish.*

INDIC. PRES.	**je veux.**		**nous voulons.**
	tu veux.		**vous voulez.**
	il veut.		**ils veulent.**
PAST INDEF.	**j'ai voulu.**	IMPERF.	**je voulais.**
FUTURE.	**je voudrai.**	CONDIT.	**je voudrais.**

je veux,	*I command, I want.*
je veux bien,	*I consent, I am willing.*
je voudrais or **je voudrais bien,**	*I should like.*

1. Je doute qu'il réussisse. 2. Je désire que vous m'attendiez. 3. Il veut que nous lui obéissions sans réplique. 4. Vous ordonnez qu'on vous obéisse. 5. Elle exige que nous vous chassions. 6. Je défends qu'on le punisse. 7. Je suis surpris que vous lui parliez encore après ce qu'il a dit et fait contre vous. 8. Je regrette vivement que vous m'ayez attendu, mais je vous assure que ce n'est pas ma faute. 9. Adieu, Monsieur, je souhaite que vous vous portiez bien. 10. Je désire que vous m'accompagniez, mais je ne l'exige pas. 11. Voulez-vous bien permettre que ma sœur et moi nous jouions un peu? 12. Je veux que vous restiez ici l'une et l'autre, vous n'avez pas encore appris vos leçons. 13. Nous doutons fort qu'il vous attende. 14. Ma mère est bien aise que vous soyez enfin revenu.

15. Obéis, si tu veux qu'on t'obéisse un jour. — (*Voltaire.*)

1. They wish you to speak to me. 2. I am glad that you are so well. 3. Do you wish him to speak to you to-night? 4. Do you not wish her to sing that song? 5. No, I want you to sing it yourself. 6. I hope she will reply to my letter this week. 7. She forbids me to speak to you. 8. Are you not surprised that your brother has already come back? 9. Do you insist upon (*exigez-vous*) my being punished? 10. I consent (*veux bien*) that you may play a little, but you must stay here. 11. I wish I were in Paris! 12. They wish us to dine with them on Monday. 13. We regret that you have not received our letter. 14. She doubts that we shall arrive before her. 15. I want (*je veux*) you to work with me. 16. Did you not know (*imperf.*) that I had met him?

89.

The following verbs meaning *to fear*, **craindre, avoir peur**, and **trembler**, and the two verbs **prendre garde** (*to take care*), and **empêcher** (*to prevent, to keep from*) not only are followed by the subjunctive, but they also require **ne** before it.

je crains qu'il ne réussisse, *I fear that he will succeed.*

However, if they are used negatively or interrogatively, the **ne** is left out: —

n'empêchez pas qu'il réussisse, *do not prevent him from succeeding.*

Craindre (an irregular verb), *to fear.*

INDIC. PRES.	**je crains.**		**nous craignons.**
	tu crains.		**vous craignez.**
	il craint.		**ils craignent.**
PAST INDEF.	**j'ai craint.**	IMPERF.	**je craignais.**
FUTURE.	**je craindrai.**	CONDIT.	**je craindrais.**

1. Je crains bien que vous ne vous soyez trompé. 2. Je ne crains pas que vous perdiez votre belle montre, vous n'êtes plus un enfant. 3. Soyez tranquille, j'empêcherai qu'on ne vous dérange. 4. Préférez-vous que je les punisse moi-même? je le veux bien, mais je crois qu'il vaut mieux que ce soit vous. 5. Ils méritent bien que nous les corrigions, mais ne soyons pas trop sévères. 6. Quoi! vous souffrez qu'on vous batte! un grand garçon comme vous! 7. Trouvez bon que je vous punisse quand vous le méritez: vous m'en remercierez plus tard. 8. Je tremble que votre supercherie ne soit découverte. 9. Ne craignez pas que je vous afflige: je garderai tous mes chagrins pour moi seul. 10. Ne me parlez pas ainsi, j'aime mieux que vous me grondiez. 11. Est-il possible que vous souffriez qu'on vous insulte? 12. Mon père n'aime pas que vous demeuriez ici. 13. Trouvera-t-il mauvais aussi que vous voyagiez avec moi? 14. Je crains bien qu'il ne s'y oppose.

1. I fear you will lose the money which I have given you. 2. But my sister does not fear that you will lose it. 3. I am afraid you are wrong. 4. Are you afraid that I have forgotten you? 5. I shall not suffer you to insult me. 6. I shall not punish her, I much prefer that she ask my pardon. 7. We shall prevent them from succeeding. 8. Do you disapprove of her not answering your note (*trouvez-vous mauvais qu'elle . . .*)? 9. Do you approve of their disobeying you? 10. I tremble lest you should be discovered. 11. Do not fear that I shall be betrayed. 12. She requires (*exige* or *veut*) me to wait for her. 13. I hope you are better. 14. He wants us to take a walk together. 15. He does not fear that we shall lose our way. 16. Does he know that we are much better to-day?

90.

(1) A superlative (and also **le seul**, the equivalent of a superlative) is followed by the subjunctive; as: —

C'est le plus beau livre que j'aie jamais lu,	*It is the most beautiful book that I have ever read.*
C'est la plus nombreuse ménagerie qui soit jamais venue ici,	*It is the largest menagerie that has ever come here.*

(2) But the indicative should be used if the thought is positive, absolute; and it is always so when the superlative is followed by a genitive plural (that is, a noun or pronoun preceded by *of*): —

C'est le plus intéressant des romans que j'ai,	*This is the most interesting of the novels which I have.*
Voici la plus belle de toutes les ménageries que j'ai vues,	*This is the best of the menageries I have seen.*

Connaître (an irregular verb), *to know by sight, to be acquainted with.*

INDIC. PRES.	**je connais.**		**nous connaissons.**
	tu connais.		**vous connaissez.**
	il connaît.		**ils connaissent.**
PAST INDEF.	**j'ai connu.**	IMPERF.	**je connaissais.**
FUTURE.	**je connaîtrai.**	CONDIT.	**je connaîtrais.**
SUBJ. PRES.	**que je connaisse.**	SUBJ. IMP.	**que je connusse.**

(3) The following conjunctions are followed by the subjunctive: —

afin que, / **pour que,** } *in order that.*
avant que, *before.*
quoique, / **bien que,** } *although.*
jusqu'à ce que, *until.*
pourvu que, *provided that.*
sans que, *without (that).*
supposé que, *suppose that.*

(4) The three following conjunctions require not only the subjunctive, but also **ne** before it: —

à moins que, *unless.*
de crainte que, / **de peur que,** } *for fear, lest.*

1. Voilà un bel animal, c'est le plus beau cheval que j'aie jamais vu. 2. C'est, en tout cas, le plus beau des chevaux qui étaient hier sur le champ de course. 3. Votre cousine est la plus heureuse femme que je connaisse. 4. Vous avez raison; c'est bien certainement la plus aimable des femmes que je connais. 5. De ces trois officiers c'est le plus jeune que je connais. 6. Cette "Histoire de France" est la meilleure de celles que j'ai dans ma bibliothèque. 7. C'est, je crois, le seul livre sérieux que vous ayez chez vous. 8. Je suis venu moi-même afin que vous me racontiez toute l'affaire. 9. Il faut que tout soit prêt avant que M. votre père arrive. 10. Bien que vous soyez beaucoup plus âgé que moi, j'ose dire que vous avez tort et que c'est moi qui ai raison. 11. Nous travaillerons jusqu'à ce que vous arriviez. 12. Pourvu que j'aie votre approbation, je suis content. 13. Est-ce que vous croyez que vous l'insulterez sans qu'il vous punisse? 14. Supposé que votre chien me morde, est-ce que vous croyez que je ne lui donnerai pas de coups de pied? 15. Je ne vous raconterai pas l'histoire, de peur que vous ne la répétiez à votre cousin. 16. Le lion n'attaque jamais l'homme à moins qu'il ne soit provoqué. 17. La gloire est le seul bien qui me puisse tenter (*Racine*).

1. This is (*voici*) the most beautiful bird that we have ever had. 2. Do not cut this rose, it is the only one we have in our garden. 3. Give me back my French dictionary, it is the best I have ever seen. 4. Of these four ladies, it is the tallest that I know. 5. She is the happiest woman I know. 6. She is the happiest of the women that I know here. 7. I like him, although he does not always obey me. 8. You must work until I am ready. 9. I do not think he will reply to your letter

before we arrive from the country. 10. He will not give me the money he has promised me, unless I obey him. 11. I shall not punish you to-day, although you deserve it. 12. He will go away (*partira*) lest we should scold him. 13. You must be diligent, in order that your mother may be pleased with (*de*) you. 14. I shall give you a beautiful book illustrated by Gustave Doré, provided you gain (*remporter*) the first prize in (*de*) French. 15. I shall not gain that prize unless you help me a little. 16. She does not dare to come here, for fear you should scold her. 17. I shall not look for your ring until (*before*) you return me my muff. 18. He flatters us in order that we may forgive him.

The uses of the subjunctive may be shown by this short table: —

Principal clause.	*Secondary clause.*
Impersonal verbs. Negative verbs. Interrogative verbs. Emotional verbs. Superlatives. Certain conjunctions.	Subjunctive mood.

91.

The Use of the Tenses of the Subjunctive.

If the verb in the principal clause is in the present or the future tense, the subjunctive is put in the *present*; if the verb in the principal clause is in a past tense or in the conditional, the subjunctive is put in the *imperfect*;[1] as: —

[1] This rule has two exceptions, which will be explained in § 128.

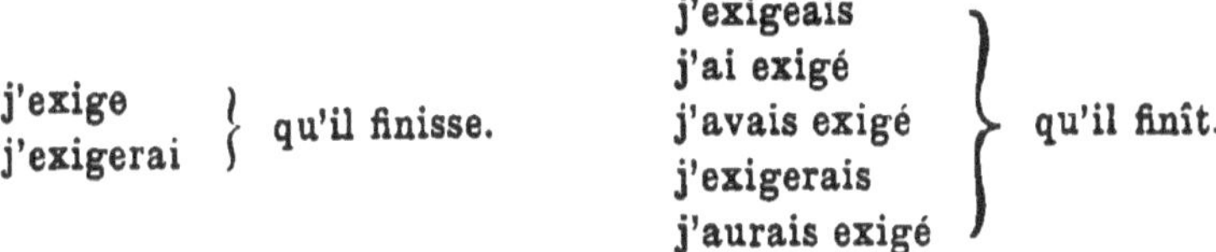

When the subjunctive is in a compound tense, the same rule applies, — that is: if the verb in the principal clause is in the present or the future tense, the auxiliary of the subjunctive is put in the *present;* if the verb in the principal clause is in a past tense or in the conditional, the auxiliary of the subjunctive is put in the *imperfect;* as: —

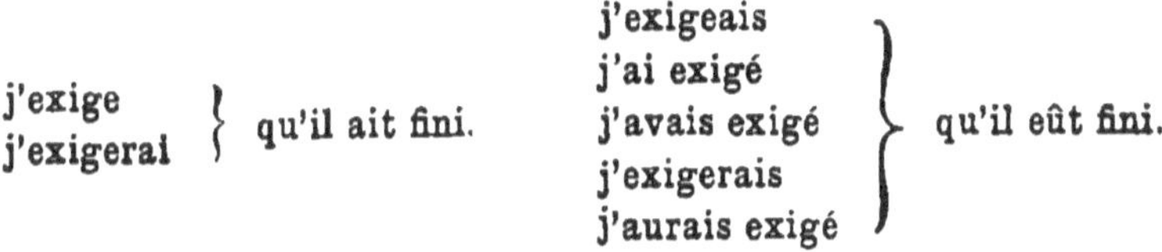

This rule for the use of the imperfect subjunctive is strictly followed in writing or in public speaking; in familiar conversation the imperfect subjunctive is rarely heard.

SUBJUNCTIVE IMPERFECT.

que j'eusse, *that I might have.*	**que je fusse,** *that I might be.*
que tu eusses.	**que tu fusses.**
qu'il eût.	**qu'il fût.**
que nous eussions.	**que nous fussions.**
que vous eussiez.	**que vous fussiez.**
qu'ils eussent.	**qu'ils fussent.**

1. Je veux que vous soyez plus attentif. 2. Je voudrais que vous fussiez plus attentif. 3. Il est indispensable qu'il ait ses livres ce soir. 4. Il était indispensable qu'il eût ses livres ce soir. 5. Elle ne croit pas que vous ayez reçu tout cet argent ce matin. 6. Elle ne croyait pas que vous eussiez reçu tout cet argent ce matin. 7. Mon père craint que vous ne soyez fatigué. 8. Mon

père craignait que vous ne fussiez fatigué. 9. C'est le plus beau morceau de musique que j'aie jamais entendu. 10. C'etait le plus beau morceau de musique que j'eusse jamais entendu. 11. Il travaille beaucoup, bien qu'il soit malade. 12. Il travaillait beaucoup, bien qu'il fût malade. 13. Je souhaite que vous ayez ma lettre à temps. 14. Je voudrais bien que vous eussiez ma lettre à temps. 15. Il n'a pas osé entrer de crainte que l'heure ne fût passée.

1. Are you thinking that he is right? 2. Were you thinking that he was right? 3. I think that he is wrong. 4. I fear that he is wrong. 5. I do not think he is wrong. 6. I did not think (*imperfect*) that he was wrong. 7. I feared (*imperfect*) he was wrong. 8. It was necessary that she should be there. 9. It is necessary that she should be there. 10. Do you believe they are guilty? 11. Did you believe they were guilty? 12. He approves of my being (*he finds it good that I am*) idle. 13. He approved of my being idle. 14. It is of importance that you should have those letters in time (*à temps*). 15. It was of importance that you should have those letters in time. 16. I will not accept your present, unless I have the permission of my father.

92.

SUBJUNCTIVE IMPERFECT.

1st Conjugation.	*2d Conjugation.*	*3d Conjugation.*
que je portasse.	**que je finisse.**	**que je rendisse.**
que tu portasses.	**que tu finisses.**	**que tu rendisses**
qu'il portât.	**qu'il finît.**	**qu'il rendît.**
que nous portassions.	**que nous finissions.**	**que nous rendissions.**
que vous portassiez.	**que vous finissiez.**	**que vous rendissiez.**
qu'ils portassent.	**qu'ils finissent.**	**qu'ils rendissent**

More is translated by **davantage** when it is not followed by *than*, or, in other words, when the second term of the comparison is understood; as:—

Il veut que je travaille davantage, *He wants me to work more* (than I do).

1. J'empêcherai qu'il ne ferme la porte. 2. J'ai empêché qu'il ne fermât la porte. 3. Il est temps qu'il finisse sa lettre et qu'il l'envoie à la poste. 4. Il était temps qu'il finît sa lettre et qu'il l'envoyât à la poste. 5. Il est préférable que vous me rendiez ce livre. 6. Il était préférable que vous me rendissiez ce livre. 7. Ne lui parlez pas de peur qu'elle ne fonde en larmes. 8. Je ne lui ai pas parlé de peur qu'elle ne fondît en larmes. 9. Je veux qu'il étudie davantage. 10. Je voudrais bien qu'il étudiât davantage. 11. Je préfère qu'elle choisisse elle-même le ruban qu'elle désire. 12. Je préférerais qu'elle choisît elle-même le ruban qu'elle désire. 13. J'ai préféré qu'elle choisît elle-même le ruban qu'elle désirait. 14. Ne commencez pas la discussion avant que votre frère arrive. 15. Vous êtes entré dans la discussion avant que votre frère arrivât.

1. Do you desire her to speak to you to-night? 2. Did you desire (*imperf.*) her to speak to you to-night? 3. Do you want my brother to help her? 4. Would you wish my brother to help her? 5. I do not think your cousin will sell his dog to that man. 6. I did not believe (*imperfect*) that your cousin would have sold his dog to that man. 7. It is time for her to choose (*that she should choose*). 8. It was time for her to choose. 9. You are the only man whom (*à qui*) she obeys. 10. You were the only man whom she obeyed. 11. It is certain that I am right. 12. It was certain that I was right. 13. I fear she will disobey you. 14. I feared she would dis-

obey you. 15. He was the best man I had ever met with. 16. I shall not speak to you, unless you stay here this evening.

The use of the tenses of the subjunctive is shown in this table: —

Verb in principal clause.	*Subjunctive.*
Present. Future.	Present.
Past. Conditional.	Imperfect.

93.

THE INFINITIVE.

When two verbs come together, the second is put in the infinitive, with or without a preposition; unless the first is one of the auxiliaries, **être** or **avoir**; as:

Je veux parler à mon frère, *I wish to speak to my brother.*
Il n'ose pas venir, *He does not dare to come.*

Of verbs requiring an infinitive after them without a preposition, there are about fifty;[1] among those most frequently used are: —

aimer mieux, *to like better.*
aller, *to go.*
compter, *to intend.*
désirer, *to desire, to wish.*
espérer, *to hope.*
oser, *to dare.*
prétendre, *to pretend.*
venir, *to come.*
voir, *to see.*
vouloir, *to wish.*

Observe, however, that *to* must be translated by **pour** whenever it may be changed into *in order to*: —

Il est venu me parler de vous une demi-heure, *He came and spoke to me of you for half an hour.*
Il est venu pour me parler de vous, mais j'étais sorti, *He came to speak to me of you, but I was out.*

[1] The list will be found in the Appendix, page 316.

1. J'aimerais mieux me battre avec vous qu'avec lui. 2. Elle est allée voir son oncle, qui est arrivé ce matin de Paris. 3. Quand comptez-vous partir? 4. N'oubliez pas de me dire quand vous partirez; je désire vous accompagner jusqu'à Londres. 5. N'espérez pas me tromper, vous n'êtes pas assez malin pour cela. 6. Est-ce que vous avez osé lui dire une pareille chose? 7. Il ne veut pas aller chez vous. 8. Je ne prétends pas dire que vous avez tort. 9. Pourquoi n'êtes-vous pas venu nous voir la semaine dernière? 10. Je vous ai vu passer sous nos fenêtres, mais je n'ai pas osé vous appeler. 11. Nous ne vivons pas pour manger, mais nous mangeons pour vivre. 12. Elles sont venues me parler. 13. Elles sont venues pour me parler, mais elles ne m'ont pas trouvé. 14. J'ai fait tout mon possible pour gagner votre amitié, mais il paraît que je n'ai pas réussi.

1. We went and saw (*we went to see*) our aunt this morning; she is much better. 2. Do you intend to leave on Friday? 3. I hope to see you[1] on Thursday. 4. She did not dare to look at me. 5. She does not wish to come to-day, unless you think that she will find her father. 6. We do not pretend to guarantee the truth of the anecdote. 7. I like better to leave to-day than to-morrow. 8. She will not be willing to accompany us. 9. They came and saw (*they came to see*) us this morning. 10. They came to (*in order to*) see us this morning, but we were out. 11. We have done our very best to receive him with honor. 12. He said that to deceive me. 13. She did it to please you. 14. They went to London in order to see you. 15. It seems to me that you are mistaken; I do not believe that I am acquainted with this lady.

[1] A pronoun is placed before the verb by which it is governed. In this sentence **vous** must be placed before **voir**, not before **espérer**.

94.

The Infinitive with the Preposition *de*.

Certain verbs require **de** before the following verb; such are:[1] —

cesser de, *to cease to.*
commander de, *to command to.*
conseiller de, *to advise to.*
craindre de, *to fear to.*
défendre de, *to forbid to.*
essayer de, *to try to.*
négliger de, *to neglect to.*
proposer de, *to propose to.*
recommander de, *to recommend to.*
refuser de, *to refuse to.*

The verb **avoir** followed by a noun requires **de** before the next verb, if that verb cannot be changed into an infinitive passive; such are: —

avoir la bonté de, *to have the kindness to.*
avoir le courage de, *to have the courage to.*
avoir l'audace de, *to have the audacity to.*
avoir le plaisir de, *to have the pleasure to.*
avoir l'occasion de, *to have an opportunity to.*
avoir l'intention de, *to intend to.*
avoir raison de, *to be right to.*
avoir tort de, *to be wrong to.*
avoir peur de, *to be afraid to.*
avoir besoin de, *to require to.*
avoir coutume de, *to be accustomed to.*
avoir envie de, *to have a mind* or *wish to.*

An adjective preceded by the impersonal verb **il est, il était,** etc., requires **de** before the next verb; as: —

Il est difficile de faire ce que vous dites, *It is difficult to do what you say.*

1. Il a cessé de me parler au mois de janvier dernier. 2. Je ne vous conseille pas de l'attendre, il n'arrive jamais à temps. 3. Est-ce que vous craignez de lui parler? c'est l'homme le plus aimable du monde. 4. Je vous défends de sortir. 5. N'essayez pas de me tromper. 6. Il a refusé de nous accompagner. 7. Elle n'a pas eu le courage d'entrer. 8. Il est plus facile de dire

[1] The complete list is given in the Appendix, page 316.

cela que de le faire. 9. J'ai eu l'occasion de faire la connaissance de Mme votre tante ; c'est une charmante vieille dame. 10. Je pense que vous avez eu tort de lui reprocher cette action, il ne vous le pardonnera jamais. 11. Où avez-vous coutume de vous promener ? 12. Avez-vous absolument besoin de les voir ? 13. Est-ce que vous avez peur de venir avec nous ? 14. Je pense qu'il serait utile de leur annoncer votre avancement.

1. He has advised me to go to London this evening. 2. I had the pleasure of meeting your uncle last night. 3. They tried to deceive me. 4. She refused to come with us. 5. Did he forbid you to speak to me ? 6. Have the kindness to ring. 7. You are right to forget that discussion. 8. We have a wish to go to the coast at the beginning of next week. 9. You will not have the audacity to ask him for some money. 10. Be so good as to shut the door. 11. It is time to set out. 12. It is absurd to speak so (*ainsi*). 13. She neglects writing to us. 14. We had the pleasure of seeing your mother this morning. 15. Do not propose to him to come with us. 16. You are the only one who has encouraged me in my labors.

95.

The Infinitive with the Preposition à.

Certain verbs require **à** before the following verb ; such are :[1] —

s'appliquer à, *to apply one's self to.*	**s'habituer à**, *to accustom one's self to.*
s'attendre à, *to expect to.*	**inviter à**, *to ask, to invite.*
consentir à, *to consent to.*	**renoncer à**, *to renounce.*
décider à, *to persuade to.*	**réussir à**, *to succeed in.*
engager à, *to induce to.*	**tarder à**, *to be late in.*

[1] The complete list is given in the Appendix, page 317.

The verb **avoir** followed by a noun requires **à** before the next verb, if that verb can be changed into an infinitive passive; as: —

J'ai une lettre à écrire,	*I have a letter to write* (meaning *to be written*).
Ils ont une maison à louer,	*They have a house to let* (meaning *to be let*).

An adjective preceded by **c'est, c'était,** . . . or **cela est, cela était,** . . . requires **à** before the next verb; as: —

C'est difficile à faire,
Cela est difficile à faire, } *that is difficult to do.*

1. Il s'est appliqué à me tourmenter hier soir et ce matin. 2. Ne vous attendez pas à le voir avant midi et demi. 3. Ils n'ont pas consenti à me laisser voyager. 4. Vous ont-ils enfin décidé à venir jouer ce soir avec nous? 5. J'ai consenti à les visiter l'un après l'autre. 6. Il ne s'est pas encore habitué à faire cinq repas par jour. 7. Mme votre mère m'a invité à dîner avec vous ce soir; j'ai accepté son invitation avec beaucoup de plaisir. 8. Il y a deux ans que j'ai renoncé à jouer et à fumer. 9. Avez-vous enfin réussi à rencontrer ce monsieur que vous avez cherché si longtemps? 10. Il me semble que vous avez beaucoup tardé à venir. 11. Avez-vous beaucoup à faire ce matin? 12. J'ai trois lettres à écrire et deux personnes à visiter. 13. C'est plus facile à dire qu'à faire.

1. They have a horse to sell. 2. I have nothing to fear. 3. Have you any money to give her? 4. I have invited him to dine with us. 5. She is late in coming. 6. He succeeded in gaining (*remporter*) the second prize. 7. Do you consent (*consentez-vous*) to see him? 8. I

expect to see you on Saturday next. 9. Who has induced you to come? 10. When will you renounce smoking? 11. Have you not a house to sell now? 12. No, sir, but we have one to let. 13. How many letters have you to write? 14. That is not easy to do. 15. That is strange to see. 16. It is possible that I am mistaken; but I fear you have forgotten me.

96.

The Subjunctive and Infinitive Moods Compared.

When the subjunctive mood can be avoided by using the infinitive in the secondary clause, as in the following cases, it must be done, because the frequent use of the subjunctive makes the style heavy.

When two verbs have the same person for subject, the second is put in the infinitive; as: —

Est-ce que vous craignez de lui parler?	*Do you fear to speak to him?*
Je voudrais bien être à votre place,	*I wish I were in your place.*

But if the first of the two verbs is **croire, penser, dire, répondre, déclarer, prétendre,** or **soutenir,** the use of the infinitive is not absolutely required; a personal tense is even often preferred. **Je crois que j'ai eu tort; je réponds que j'ai bien fait.**

If the two clauses have the same person for subject, the conjunction which joins them may often be changed to a preposition, and the verb following will in consequence be put in the infinitive:[1] —

[1] The following conjunctions may be changed into prepositions: —

CONJ.			PREP.
afin que,	*in order that,*	into	**afin de.**
pour que,	*in order that,*	"	**pour.**
avant que,	*before that,*	"	**avant de.** / **avant que de.**
sans que,	*without,*	"	**sans.**
à moins que,	*unless,*	"	**à moins de.** / **à moins que de.**
de crainte que,	*for fear that, lest,*	"	**de crainte de.**
de peur que,	*for fear that, lest,*	"	**de peur de.**
jusqu'à ce que,	*till, until,*	"	**jusque.**

Venez me voir avant de lui écrire,	*Come to see me before you write to him.*
Il ne sortira pas de peur de vous rencontrer.	*He will not go out lest he should meet you.*

Even when both clauses have not identical subjects, the second verb is put in the infinitive if its subject is clearly shown by the general sense; as: —

Elle a ordonné à l'enfant de sortir,	*She gave the child an order to go out.*

We may also say: **elle a ordonné que l'enfant sortît,** but this construction means that she gave somebody the order to take the child out; whilst, in the first case, the command, being directly given to the child, leaves no doubt as to who has to obey.

This last rule applies more particularly to impersonal verbs: —

On nous attend pour trois heures, il faut partir,	*We were expected at three, we must leave at once.*
Il est honteux de se conduire ainsi,	*It is shameful for one to behave so.*

1. Mon père a ordonné que les enfants descendissent au salon (he simply ordered). 2. Mon père a ordonné aux enfants de descendre au salon (he ordered, speaking to the children). 3. Elle a commandé que je lui achetasse un journal français. 4. Elle m'a commandé de lui acheter un journal français. 5. Je ne sortirai pas avant que j'aie obtenu votre promesse. 6. (A better way:) Je ne sortirai pas avant d'avoir obtenu votre promesse. 7. Il craint qu'il ne vous ait mécontenté. 8. Il craint de vous avoir mécontenté. 9. Il dit vous avoir écrit. 10. (Another way:) Il dit qu'il vous a écrit. 11. Il prétend avoir raison. 12. Il prétend qu'il a raison. 13. Il soutient avoir bien fait. 14. Il soutient qu'il a bien fait. 15. Je crois vous avoir écrit.

1. I fear I am wrong. 2. I feared I was wrong. 3. I am sorry I am late (*être en retard*). 4. I was sorry I

was late. 5. She has ordered me to punish you. 6. She has ordered that I should punish you. 7. I think I have seen you this morning (both ways). 8. I thought I had seen you this morning. 9. He pretends he has spoken to you (both ways). 10. He will not try it for fear (use the preposition) he should make a mistake. 11. I shall speak to him before (use the preposition) I write to you. 12. I wish I were arrived, that I might (*pour pouvoir*) rest! 13. He now believes he (*qu'il*) was wrong. 14. He says that he (*qu'il*) does not believe me. 15. It is time to leave.

97.

THE PRESENT PARTICIPLE.

	avoir, *to have.*	**ayant**, *having.*
	être, *to be.*	**étant**, *being.*
1st Conj.	**porter**, *to carry.*	**portant**, *carrying.*
2d Conj.	**finir**, *to finish.*	**finissant**, *finishing.*
3d Conj.	**rendre**, *to give back.*	**rendant**, *giving back.*

The present participle, which is an essential part of a verb, must not be confounded with the verbal adjective, — that is, an adjective derived from a verb.

Both have generally the same form, but the present participle always expresses an *action*, and is invariable; as: —

Ces hommes, prévoyant le danger, se sont mis sur leurs gardes,	*These men, foreseeing the danger, put themselves on their guard.*

The verbal adjective, on the contrary, always expresses an habitual quality, a permanent state, a manner of being, and, like all adjectives, agrees with the noun; as: —

Ces hommes prévoyants ont aperçu le danger,	*These farsighted men perceived the danger.*

The present participle in French is not of so frequent use as in English. It is much used in English with the auxiliary verb *to be* (*I am* or *was speaking*); it is never thus used in French. Again, in English it may be used after nearly all prepositions (*of*, *by*, *without*, or *before speaking*); in French **en** is the only preposition used with the present participle; all other prepositions require the infinitive; as: —

de parler, **à parler,** **sans parler,** **avant de parler,** **en parlant.**

After the following verbs the present participle is generally used in English, and the infinitive in French. Instead of the infinitive a tense of the indicative with **qui** may be used with all except **paraître** and **sembler**: —

apercevoir, *to perceive.* **regarder,** *to look at.*
écouter, *to listen.* **sentir,** *to feel.*
entendre, *to hear.* **voir,** *to see.*
observer, *to observe.* **paraître,** *to appear.*
sembler, *to seem.*

je l'entends chanter,	*I hear him singing.*	**je l'entends qui chante.**
je le vois jouer,	*I see him playing.*	**je le vois qui joue.**
je l'ai vu jouer,	*I saw him playing.*	**je l'ai vu qui jouait.**

Ne . . . que, *only, nothing but,* (**ne** is put before the verb as usual, and **que** where *but* or *only* stands in English).

1. J'ai vu courir votre frère (*or again:* J'ai vu votre frère qui courait). 2. J'entends crier ma sœur (*or:* J'entends ma sœur qui crie). 3. Regardez-le marcher, est-ce qu'il ne vous semble pas boiter? 4. Ecoutez-le rire, il me semble que ce rire est peu naturel. 5. Il travaille en chantant et en causant avec tout le monde. 6. Ces messieurs sont vraiment amusants. 7. Le champ de bataille était couvert de soldats mourants. 8. Ces photographies sont bien ressemblantes. 9. Il n'y a que les âmes aimantes qui soient propres à l'étude de la nature (*Bernardin de St. Pierre*).

1. I hear your brother speaking. 2. I heard him speaking to his friend. 3. Did you see me playing with that little girl? 4. We have looked at him eating. 5. Did they hear me singing this forenoon? 6. This lady is truly amusing. 7. Your portrait is very like. 8. I read (*lis*) while eating. 9. Appetite comes (*vient*) in eating. 10. She is an obliging person. 11. This woman appears to suffer (*the infinitive, or the verbal adjective*). 12. Your stories are not very amusing. 13. Do not call her away, she is amusing us. 14. For two hours I have been walking here and I have met only one lady. She was an old friend of mine and I was glad to see her. 15. I think I saw you walking here yesterday.

98.

THE PAST PARTICIPLE.

(1) The past participle, when used as an adjective or when conjugated with **être**, except in pronominal verbs, agrees like an adjective with the noun or pronoun to which it relates; as: —

que de remparts détruits ! que de villes forcées !	*how many ramparts destroyed! how many cities taken by storm!*
la vertu timide est souvent opprimée,	*timid virtue is often oppressed.*
ils ont été châtiés,	*they have been chastised.*

(2) The past participle, when conjugated with **avoir**, and also in all pronominal verbs (which are conjugated with **être**), agrees not with its subject but with its direct object whenever this direct object precedes it; as: —

voici une montre, mon père l'a achetée hier,	*here is a watch; my father bought it yesterday.*
les belles dames que j'ai vues,	*the beautiful women whom I saw.*

les lettres que je vous ai écrites, les avez-vous reçues ?	*the letters which I wrote you, have you received them?*
ma sœur s'est coupée,	*my sister has cut herself.*
ma sœur s'est coupé le doigt,	*my sister has cut her finger.*
elles se sont imaginé des choses fausses,	*they imagined untrue things.*
les choses fausses qu'elles se sont imaginées,	*the untrue things which they imagined.*
la dame que j'ai entendue chanter,	*the lady whom I heard sing.*
les belles chansons que j'ai entendu chanter,	*the beautiful songs which I heard sung.*
ils nous ont donné une boîte,	*they have given us a box.*
nous avons chanté,	*we have sung.*

In the first two examples the direct objects[1] **la** and **que**, referring to a feminine noun, precede the participle, which is consequently feminine.

In the third example **que** and **les**, referring to **lettres**, precede and are the direct objects of **écrites** and **reçues**, which are consequently feminine plural.

In the fourth example **coupée** is preceded by its direct object **se**, and is feminine.

In the fifth example the direct object of **coupé** is **doigt**, which follows it; **se** stands for **à elle**; **coupé** is then invariable.

In the sixth example **choses** is the direct object of **imaginé** and follows it; **se** is the indirect object and stands for **à elles.**

In the seventh example the direct object **que** precedes the participle **imaginées**, which is feminine plural.

In the eighth example **que** is the direct object of **entendue**, which then agrees with it.

In the ninth example **que** is the direct object of **chanter**, and **entendu** is invariable.

Why is the participle invariable in the last two examples ?

1. Ils sont bien reçus. 2. Elles sont venues. 3. Ils sont convaincus que j'ai eu tort de vous parler de l'affaire. 4. Ma mère est enchantée de vous revoir. 5. A peine arrivés à Paris, l'empereur de Russie et ses fils sont allés

[1] The direct object is the answer to the question *whom?* or *what?* before the verb. *What has my father bought? Whom have I seen?*

au spectacle; je les ai vus passer. 6. Nous avons lu vos deux romans français. 7. Les avez-vous finis? 8. Nous ne les avons pas encore finis, nous comptons les finir ce soir. 9. Où avez-vous mis mes pantoufles? 10. Je les ai mises sur une chaise, est-ce que vous ne les trouvez pas? 11. Ernest a vendu sa montre et sa chaîne. 12. A qui les a-t-il vendues? 13. Ils se sont bien défendus. 14. Ils se sont défendu cet amusement. 15. Elles se sont adressées à nous. 16. Elles se sont adressé des lettres.

1. Are your sisters arrived? 2. Yes, they arrived this morning. 3. Have you seen them? 4. Yes, I have seen them walking in the garden. 5. No, I have not yet seen them. 6. Did you return to them the books which they have lent you? 7. I have not yet returned them to them; I will return them (to them) to-morrow. 8. I received this morning the letter which you wrote to me. 9. I have sent it to my sister. 10. Has she not yet replied to you? 11. Yes, she has replied to me, but I think I have lost her letter. 12. I looked for it this morning, but I did not find it. 13. My sisters have amused themselves last night. 14. My cousin Louisa and your sister have written to each other. 15. I have seen both (*les deux*) letters, they are not very interesting.

99.

The Preterite or Past Definite.

j'eus, *I had.*	**je fus,** *I was.*
tu eus.	**tu fus.**
il or **elle eut.**	**il** or **elle fut.**
nous eûmes.	**nous fûmes.**
vous eûtes.	**vous fûtes.**
ils or **elles eurent.**	**ils** or **elles furent.**

je portai, *I carried.*	**je finis.**	**je rendis.**
tu portas.	**tu finis.**	**tu rendis.**
il porta.	**il finit.**	**il rendit.**
nous portâmes.	**nous finîmes.**	**nous rendîmes.**
vous portâtes.	**vous finîtes.**	**vous rendîtes.**
ils portèrent.	**ils finirent.**	**ils rendirent.**

When translating an English past tense into French, first try if it can be changed into *used to* (as *I used to speak*), or into the present participle with *I was*, etc., (as *I was speaking*).

If either of these two ways can be employed, use the imperfect (**je parlais**) ; if neither can be employed you may generally use the past indefinite (**j'ai parlé**) in conversation, and the preterite (**je parlai**) in narratives or historical style.[1]

When I was in Paris, I often went (used to go) to the opera,	**quand j'étais à Paris, j'allais souvent à l'opéra.**
I was writing while my sister played,	**j'écrivais tandis que ma sœur jouait.**
I went to see her this morning,	**je suis allé la voir ce matin.**
Prince Edward on that day did not lose sixty men,	**le prince Edouard dans cette journée ne perdit pas soixante hommes.**
The emperor alighted near the bench where I was sitting,	**l'empereur descendit auprès du banc sur lequel j'étais assis.**

[1] As in English, the *present* is sometimes used instead of the *preterite* to give more animation to a narrative.

Note on the Origin of the Preterite or historical tense. — The Latin preterite **cantavi** was transformed by the people during the Roman occupation of Gaul into **habeo cantatum** (which afterwards became **j'ai chanté**), but the authors of the time, disdaining this vulgar Latin, adhered in their Chronicles to the classical **cantavi**, which has thus remained in the *written* French under the form **je chantai, tu chantas,** etc , whilst the popular **j'ai chanté** continued to be the tense generally used *in conversation* to express the past. This remark applies, of course, not only to **chanter**, but to all French verbs.

The imperfect denotes a customary or repeated action or state, or an unfinished action, in past time.

elle chantait tous les jours,	*she used to sing every day.*

The perfect (or past indefinite) is generally used to denote a past action or state without reference to its completion or end, or a past action the effect of which still continues.

je vous ai donné dix francs,	*I have given you ten francs.*

The preterite (or past definite) is used of an action or state which was definitely completed in past time.

le roi donna dix francs au soldat et lui demanda s'il en était content,	*the king gave ten francs to the soldier, and asked him if he were satisfied with it.*

The preterite can be used to express what took place only in a time wholly past, like *yesterday, last month, last year*; as: —

je reçus hier plusieurs lettres de mon père,	*I received yesterday several letters from my father.*

But you must say, —

j'ai reçu plusieurs lettres de mon père cette semaine,	*I have received several letters from my father this week,*

because *this week* is not yet wholly past.

The past anterior, which is the compound of the preterite, expresses an action or state *immediately* anterior to the one expressed by the preterite, and is never used but after such adverbs of time as **quand, lorsque, dès que, aussitôt que, à peine**:

Calypso had scarcely uttered these words when she regretted them.	**à peine Calypso eut-elle prononcé ces paroles qu'elle s'en repentit.**
As soon as he had written that letter, he prepared to die.	**aussitôt qu'il eut écrit cette lettre, il se prépara à mourir.**

The past anterior is the compound of the preterite in the same way that the pluperfect is the compound of the imperfect.

j'eus eu, *I had had.* **j'eus été,** *I had been.*

j'eus porté, *I had carried.* **j'eus fini.** **j'eus rendu.**

j'eus été porté, *I had been carried.* **je me fus lavé,** *I had washed myself.*

1. J'eus; il fut. 2. Ils eurent; nous fûmes. 3. Il porta; ils vendirent. 4. Vous finîtes; nous vendîmes. 5. Il eut porté; il eut été porté; il fut porté. 6. Ils écoutèrent; elle regarda. 7. Le roi donna dix louis au paysan et lui pardonna sa faute. 8. Un officier anglais ayant été blessé fut transporté chez lui, où deux médecins furent appelés. 9. On demanda à un petit garçon pourquoi il prenait du sel; c'est, répondit-il, pour la viande qu'on me donnera. 10. Aussitôt qu'il eut fini son travail, il partit pour la campagne. 11. L'année dernière je visitai mon père à Londres, et je m'y amusais beaucoup. 12. C'est ici qu'on se battit, il y a trente ans.

(*Put in the Preterite every verb in italics.*)

1. He *had;* I *was.* 2. They *were;* we *had.* 3. They *had;* they *had* been; they *had* been carried. 4. She *was;* she *was* called. 5. You (*sing.*) *asked;* you (*plur.*) *asked.* 6. They *asked* her where her friends lived. 7. She *replied* that they were living at the sea-shore. 8. We *finished* our labors last week; they finished theirs this morning. 9. The king *arrived* on Thursday morning; he will leave this evening. 10. When she *had* written her letter, she *was* quite happy. 11. We *visited* the chamber in which you used to live. 12. He *asked* my pardon, and *assured* me that he had already written me six letters. 13. I *told* (*dis*) him that I had not yet received them.

100.

IRREGULAR VERBS.

Irregular verbs are those the conjugation of which differs, in some persons or tenses, from the three models of regular verbs. They are pretty numerous; the most important are conjugated here; a complete list is given in the Appendix, pages 304, 315.

The knowledge of the rules by which tenses are formed will greatly facilitate the study of irregular verbs.

Formation of Tenses.

Tenses are divided into two classes: *primitive* tenses and *derived* tenses.

Primitive tenses are those from which the others are formed. They are: 1st, The present infinitive; 2d, The present participle; 3d, The past participle; 4th, The present of the indicative; and 5th, The preterite (or past definite).

Derived tenses are those formed from the primitive tenses.

(1) From the *infinitive* are formed the *future* by changing **-r** or **-re** into **-rai**, and the *conditional* by changing **-r** or **-re** into **-rais**: —

1.	**porte-r,**	**je porte-rai,**	**je porte-rais.**
2.	**fini-r,**	**je fini-rai,**	**je fini-rais.**
3.	**rend-re,**	**je rend-rai,**	**je rend-rais.**

(2) From the *present participle* are formed two tenses, *the imperfect of the indicative* and *the present of the subjunctive,* and part of another tense, *the plural of the present indicative.*

The imperfect of the indicative is formed by changing **-ant** into **-ais**, and the present subjunctive by changing **-ant** into **-e**: —

1.	**port-ant,**	**je port-ais,**	**que je port-e.**
2.	**finiss-ant,**	**je finiss-ais,**	**que je finiss-e.**
3.	**rend-ant,**	**je rend-ais,**	**que je rend-e.**

The plural of the present of the indicative is formed by changing **-ant** into **-ons, -ez, -ent**: —

1.	**port-ant,**	**nous port-ons,**	**vous port-ez,**	**ils port-ent.**
2.	**finiss-ant,**	**nous finiss-ons,**	**vous finiss-ez,**	**ils finiss-ent.**
3.	**rend-ant,**	**nous rend-ons,**	**vous rend-ez,**	**ils rend-ent.**

(3) From the *past participle*, with **avoir** or **être**, are formed *all the compound tenses*: —

j'ai aimé, je suis aimé, j'avais fini, il était rendu, elle s'est amusée.

(4) From the *present of the indicative* are formed the corresponding persons of the *imperative*: —

INDICATIVE PRES.		IMPERATIVE.	
	je porte.		*no 1st person.*
	tu portes.		**porte.**
	il porte.		**qu'il porte.**[1]
	nous portons.		**portons.**
	vous portez.		**portez.**
	ils portent.		**qu'ils portent.**[1]

Observe that, in the first conjugation, the **s** of the second person singular of the present indicative does not appear in the imperative, unless the imperative is followed by the pronouns **en** or **y**, before which it is kept: **donnes-en la moitié à ton frère; mènes-y-moi.**

(5) From the *preterite* is formed the *imperfect of the subjunctive*, by adding **-se** to the second person singular: —

tu portas,	**que je portas-se.**
tu finis,	**que je finis-se.**
tu rendis,	**que je rendis-se.**

[1] Properly speaking, the imperative has no third person, as a command in the third person must absolutely be indirect. When an indirect command is given, the third person singular and plural of the subjunctive present are used: **(je veux) qu'il finisse** or **qu'ils finissent.**

INFIN. **aller**, *to go.* PRES. PART. **allant.** PAST PART. **allé.**

INDIC. PRES. **je vais, tu vas, il va, nous allons, vous allez, ils vont.**

IMPERF. **j'allais, tu allais, il allait, nous allions, vous alliez, ils allaient.**

PRETERITE. **j'allai, tu allas, il alla, nous allâmes, vous allâtes, ils allèrent.**

FUTURE. **j'irai, tu iras, il ira, nous irons, vous irez, ils iront.**

CONDITIONAL. **j'irais, tu irais, il irait, nous irions, vous iriez, ils iraient.**

SUBJ. PRES. **que j'aille, que tu ailles, qu'il aille, que nous allions, que vous alliez, qu'ils aillent.**

SUBJ. IMPERF. **que j'allasse.**

IMPERATIVE. **va, qu'il aille, allons, allez, qu'ils aillent.**

The parts of the verb will always be given in this order: *Infinitive; Present Participle; Past Participle; Indicative Present, Imperfect, Preterite, Future; Conditional; Subjunctive Present, Imperfect; Imperative.* The compound tenses are not given, as they are regularly formed from the past participle with the auxiliaries **avoir** or **être**. Remember that **aller** is conjugated with **être**.

Envoyer, *to send*, and **renvoyer**, *to send back*, are the only other irregular verbs in the first conjugation. Their irregularities consist in the formation of the future, which is **enverrai** and **renverrai**, and of the conditional, which is **enverrais** and **renverrais**. The change of **y** to **i** before *e mute* (as **j'envoie, tu envoies**, etc.) is explained in § 70.

The Article.

The article **le, la, les**, is used before names of continents, countries, provinces, rivers, and mountains; as, —

L'Asie, la France, l'Angleterre, les Etats-Unis, la Seine, le Mont Blanc, les Pyrénées, etc.

But the article is suppressed before the name of a country used adjectively; as, **la reine d'Angleterre, du vin de France, de l'encre de Chine**, etc.

To or *in* before Names of Places or Countries.

To or *in* is translated, —

(1) By **à** without the article before names of towns; as, —

She is going to London,	**elle va à Londres.**
He lives in Paris,	**il demeure à Paris.**[1]

(2) By **en** without the article before names of continents, countries, provinces, when they are feminine; as, —

Aller, ou résider, en Asie, en Afrique, en Chine, en Angleterre, en Ecosse, en Normandie, en Alsace.

But we say: **aller aux Indes, aux Antilles, à la Guadeloupe, à la Martinique, à la Jamaïque,** though these names are feminine.

(3) By **à** with the article (that is, by **au** or **aux**) if they are masculine; as, —

Aller, ou résider, au Japon, au Mexique, au Canada, au Brésil, au Chili, aux Etats-Unis.

But we say: **en Portugal, en Danemark,** though they are masculine.

(4) By **dans** with the article, should the name of a country be accompanied by an adjective or any attribute; as, —

Etendre son commerce dans les Indes Orientales, dans l'Amérique du Sud, dans toute la France.

From is translated by **de**, without the article, in the first two cases seen above (that is, before names of

[1] We may also say: **il demeure dans Paris,** but this means that he lives inside the town, not in the suburbs, while **à Paris** may have either sense, inside the town or in the suburbs.

A few towns are always used with the article; as, **je vais au Havre,** *I am going to Havre.*

towns or feminine names of countries), and by **du, de la, de l'**, or **des**, in the other two cases (that is, before masculine names of countries, or names of countries accompanied by an adjective); as, —

Partir ou venir de Paris, de Londres, de France, d'Angleterre, d'Italie, etc. Partir ou venir du Japon, du Mexique, du Canada, de l'Amérique du Nord, des Indes Orientales, etc.

1. J'irai en France le mois prochain. 2. Si vous étiez disposé à y aller aussi, nous partirions le 15 du mois. 3. J'ai visité plusieurs pays l'été dernier: la Belgique, la Hollande, les bords du Rhin, la Prusse, l'Autriche et l'Italie. 4. L'été prochain j'irai en Espagne et peut-être jusqu'au Maroc. 5. Dans deux ans, si je suis assez riche, j'irai au Canada, aux Etats-Unis et au Mexique. 6. Mon père m'a envoyé quelques bouteilles de vin de France; voulez-vous venir en goûter ce soir? 7. Sans l'aide de Garibaldi, Victor Emmanuel n'aurait jamais pu créer le royaume d'Italie. 8. Quand même vous me donneriez tout l'or des monts Oural, je n'irais jamais demeurer en Russie. 9. M. votre frère n'est-il pas allé passer l'hiver en Italie? 10. Non, Monsieur, il est allé dans le midi de la France, dans la petite ville de Cannes. 11. Et M. votre cousin est parti, je crois, pour le Chili? 12. Monsieur, vous vous trompez encore; il est allé aux Etats-Unis et non au Chili. 13. La laine d'Espagne est, dit-on, préférable à celle d'Angleterre et à celle de Saxe.

1. They (*m.*) are going. 2. They went (*pret.*). 3. They were going. 4. They had gone. 5. They will go. 6. They will have gone. 7. They would go. 8. They would have gone. 9. That they may go. 10. That they might go. 11. Let them go. 12. To have gone. 13. My brother lives in England. 14. He will go to Spain next month. 15. He has already visited Holland, Belgium,

Prussia, and Austria. 16. In what country does your aunt live? 17. She lived in Mexico formerly, but now she lives in (*à la*) Jamaica. 18. Have you ever been in Italy? 19. Yes, I went to Rome three years ago. 20. I saw the pope, but I did not see the king of Italy. 21. Our uncle came back from Canada last week. 22. Have you ever seen Mont Blanc? 23. They left for the south of France by this morning's train. 24. I fear they will send me to Italy next year, and I do not wish to go there.

101.

S'en aller, *to go away,* is conjugated like **aller.**

s'en allant. **s'en étant allé.**

je m'en vais, tu t'en vas, il s'en va, nous nous en allons, vous vous en allez, ils s'en vont.

IMPER. **va-t'en, qu'il s'en aille, allons-nous-en, allez-vous-en, qu'ils s'en aillent.**

je m'en suis allé,	*I have gone away.*
je m'en serai allé,	*I shall have gone away.*
je m'en étais allé,	*I had gone away.*

Idiomatical Uses of the Verb *aller.*

Instead of putting a verb in the future, the French often use the verb **aller** when the action is to be done immediately; as, —

je vais sortir,	*I shall go out immediately,* or *I am on the point of going.*
j'allais sortir,	*I was about to go.*

Aller is familiarly used instead of **se porter**: —

comment allez-vous?	*how are you?*
comment va votre frère?	*how is your brother?*
comment ça[1] **va-t-il** (very familiar)?	*how goes it with you?*

[1] **Ça** is a familiar contraction for **cela.**

Aller also means *to fit, to suit, to become:* —

votre clef ne va pas à ma montre, *your key does not fit my watch.*
ce chapeau ne vous va pas, *this hat does not fit* (or *become*) *you.*

aller à pied, *to walk* (as distinguished from other ways of locomotion).
aller à cheval, *to ride.* **aller en bateau,** *to sail.*
aller en voiture, *to drive.* **aller au-devant de,** *to go to meet.*

1. Dépêchez-vous, nous nous en allons. 2. Maintenant que j'ai écrit toutes mes lettres, je vais aller voir ma belle-sœur. 3. On m'a dit qu'elle allait partir pour Paris. 4. Comment vont vos deux frères? J'aime à croire qu'ils sont aussi bien portants et aussi gais qu'à l'ordinaire. 5. Eh bien, mon vieux camarade, comment ça va-t-il aujourd'hui? 6. Ces bottines ne me vont pas du tout, elles sont trop étroites. 7. Cette clef va à la serrure. 8. Trouvez-vous que cet habit aille bien? 9. Nous sommes allés de Stirling à Edimbourg à pied. 10. Mes sœurs y sont allées en voiture. 11. Henri, qui y est allé à cheval, est arrivé le premier. 12. Il est venu au-devant de nous. 13. Allez-vous-en tous, vous m'empêchez de travailler.

1. She is going away; she has gone away. 2. She was going away; she had gone away. 3. She will go away; she will have gone away. 4. She would have gone away. 5. That she may go away. 6. Let her go away. 7. Having gone away. 8. They will go away immediately. 9. She will go out immediately. 10. We will dine immediately. 11. How are you, my little friend? 12. I am very well, thanks; how are you (*and you*)? 13. Your coat does not fit you. 14. Your proposal suits me, I accept it. 15. If you wish, we shall go to meet my aunt. 16. She is about to arrive by the five o'clock train. 17. Shall we drive there?[1] 18. We

[1] For the sake of euphony, **y** is not used before the future and the conditional of **aller**.

shall walk, if you have no objection (*le vouloir bien*). 19. Do not go away so soon. 20. I shall go away with you. 21. Why did you go away yesterday when we came in (§ 12)? 22. I went away because it was late and (supply *que*) I was hungry.

102.

Partir, *to set out, to leave.* **partant.** **parti.**

je pars, tu pars, il part, nous partons, vous partez, ils partent.

je partais, tu partais, il partait, nous partions, vous partiez, ils partaient.

je partis, etc. **je partirai.** **je partirais.**

que je parte, que tu partes, qu'il parte, que nous partions, que vous partiez, qu'ils partent. **que je partisse.**

pars, qu'il parte, partons, partez, qu'ils partent.

je suis parti, *I have left.* **je serai parti,** *I shall have left.*

Like **partir** are conjugated: —

repartir, *to set off again;* **sortir,** *to go out;* **ressortir,** *to go out again.*

The Article continued.

The article **le, la, les,** is used instead of *a* or *an* before nouns of weight, measure, or number; but **par** is used for *a* or *an* before time; as: —

cinq francs le kilo,	*five francs a kilo.*
un franc le mètre,	*one franc a metre.*
dix centimes la douzaine,	*ten centimes a dozen.*
trois francs par jour,	*three francs a day.*

The article is omitted after **que** or **quel** used as an exclamation; as: —

quelle jolie chose! *what a pretty thing!*

1. Quand partirez-vous pour l'Ecosse ? 2. Nous partirons pour Edimbourg le 27, nous arriverons à Glasgow le 28, et nous en repartirons le 30 pour l'Irlande. 3. Si vous sortez cette après-midi, j'irai avec vous partout où vous voudrez. 4. Nous sortirons à une heure, nous irons acheter ces beaux rubans que votre cousine vend à six francs le mètre. 5. Six francs le mètre ! ne trouvez-vous pas que c'est un peu (*rather*) cher ? 6. Mlle votre sœur est sortie ce matin à dix heures, elle est rentrée à onze heures, et je crois qu'elle est ressortie à midi. 7. Elle a beaucoup d'emplettes à faire ; trois de ses amies vont venir la voir, et elle a tant de choses à préparer ! 8. Vous prétendez que ce pauvre homme gagne 75 francs par mois. 9. Eh bien ! moi je parie qu'il ne gagne pas trente sous par jour. 10. Quel magnifique chat vous avez ! 11. C'est un chat angora que M. Jones nous a donné ; voyez quelle belle queue il a ! 12. Achetez-moi (*buy from me,* see § 113 (1)) cette petite cargaison de fruits ; je vous les vendrai à trois francs la caisse. 13. Moi ! lui ai-je répondu, vous acheter ces fruits pourris à trois francs la caisse ! est-ce que vous me croyez devenu fou ?

1. I am going ; I am leaving ; I am going out. 2. He went (*imperf.*) ; he left ; he went out. 3. We had gone ; we had left ; we had gone out. 4. You will go ; you will leave ; you will go out. 5. I have gone ; I have left ; I have gone away (*s'en aller*). 6. Leave ; go out ; go away. 7. Let us leave ; let us go out ; let us go away. 8. They go out three times [1] a week. 9. This house is too dear at (*à*) fifty pounds a year. 10. He sold me that (at) two francs a dozen. 11. What a pretty piece of

[1] *Time* is translated by **fois**, when it can be numbered, *one time, two times, three times, sometimes, this time, that time ;* by **temps**, when it is the general idea of time, as, *time flies, a long time, some time, at all times, the old times ;* by **heure**, when it means *hour*, as : what *time* is it ?

ribbon you have! How much did you pay (for) it? 12. I paid (for) it seven francs a metre. 13. Did you not go out this morning? 14. No, not (*pas*) yet; I am a little indisposed. 15. I shall go out this evening, if you will (*voulez bien*) accompany me. 16. When shall you set out for London? 17. We shall set out for England on Monday next.

103.

Sentir, *to feel, to smell.* **sentant.** **senti.**

je sens, tu sens, il sent, nous sentons, vous sentez, ils sentent.

je sentais, tu sentais, il sentait, nous sentions, vous sentiez, ils sentaient.

je sentis. **je sentirai.** **je sentirais.**

que je sente, que tu sentes, qu'il sente, que nous sentions, que vous sentiez, qu'ils sentent. **que je sentisse.**

sens, qu'il sente, sentons, sentez, qu'ils sentent.

Sentir is conjugated like **partir** and **sortir**. So are:

consentir à, *to consent to.*
mentir, *to lie, to tell a lie.*
se repentir de, *to repent of.*
dormir,[1] *to sleep.*
endormir, *to lull, to send to sleep.*
s'endormir *to fall asleep.*
se rendormir, *to fall asleep again.*
servir,[1] *to serve, to serve up, to help.*
se servir de, *to help one's self to, to make use of.*

The Substantive.

(1) The preposition **de** is always put between the name of a thing and the name of the substance of which it is made; as: —

une table de marbre, *a marble table.*
un sac de papier, *a paper bag.*

[1] Just as the **t** of **sentir, sortir, partir**, disappears in the singular of the pres. ind. and the second pers. sing. of the imperative, so the **m** of **dormir** and the **v** of **servir** disappear in the same persons. But in all other persons and tenses the **t** reappears in **sentir, sortir**, and **partir**, the **m** in **dormir**, and the **v** in **servir**.

je dors, tu dors, il dort, nous dormons, vous dormez, ils dorment;
je me sers, tu te sers, il se sert, nous nous servons, vous vous servez, ils se servent.

(2) **De** is also put between two nouns, when the second is a noun of *place*, or expresses the *contents* of the object represented by the first noun :

du vin de Bourgogne,	*Burgundy wine.*
les châles de Paisley,	*Paisley shawls.*
un verre de vin, une tasse de thé,	*a glass of wine, a cup of tea.*

(3) The qualifying noun is united to the principal noun by the preposition **à** to denote the *use*, *purpose*, or *fitness* of the thing mentioned, and also the *means* by which an object is put in motion ; as : —

un couteau à papier,	*a paper knife.*
un verre à vin,	*a wine-glass.*
un pot à fleurs,	*a flower-pot.*
un bateau à vapeur,	*a steamboat.*
un moulin à vent,	*a windmill.*

1. Est-ce que vous consentez à lui donner votre joli sac de nuit ? 2. Non certainement, je ne le lui donnerai pas, je m'en sers presque toutes les semaines. 3. Ne vous repentez-vous pas d'avoir offensé votre maître de dessin ? 4. Oui, je m'en repens un peu, mais figurez-vous qu'il m'a puni parce que j'ai dormi cinq minutes pendant la classe. 5. Il a certainement bien fait : est-ce qu'on a jamais vu un élève dormir pendant sa classe de dessin ? 6. Marie, apportez-nous trois verres à vin et trois tasses à thé, nous resterons ce soir dans la salle à manger. 7. Auguste s'est endormi hier à table, et il a cassé deux verres à vin. 8. Il s'est réveillé en sursaut et ne s'est plus rendormi : maman l'a tant grondé ! 9. Remerciez Mme votre mère de m'avoir si bien servi, et priez-la d'accepter cette corbeille de fleurs. 10. Voici mes livres, mes cahiers, mon papier et mes plumes ; servez-vous-en, je vous prie. 11. Merci, Monsieur, je ne me servirai que de votre papier et de vos plumes ; je n'ai que quelques lettres à écrire.

1. He feels; he sleeps; he serves. 2. We were feeling; we were sleeping; we were serving. 3. Thou wilt feel; thou wilt sleep; thou wilt serve. 4. She had felt; she had slept; she had served. 5. They would feel; they would sleep; they would serve. 6. Sleep well, we shall meet to-morrow. 7. Let us help ourselves to a glass of water. 8. A gold watch has been given to me. 9. I shall accept a cup of tea with pleasure. 10. Mary, bring me a teacup. 11. Here is the paper knife, in case (*dans le cas où*) you should wish to read that new pamphlet. 12. Let us not fall asleep in the dining-room; everybody would mock us. 13. Where did you lose your watch-key? 14. I think I lost it in the park yesterday. 15. This paper bag will serve you as a (*de*) carpet bag. 16. Where did I put my watch? 17. I think you have put it on the little wooden table.

104.

Courir, *to run*. **courant**. **couru**.

je cours, tu cours, il court, nous courons, vous courez, ils courent.

je courais, tu courais, il courait, nous courions, vous couriez, ils couraient.

je courus. je courrai. je courrais.

que je coure, que tu coures, qu'il coure, que nous courions, que vous couriez, qu'ils courent. que je courusse.

cours, qu'il coure, courons, courez, qu'ils courent.

Notice the doubled **r** in the future and conditional, distinguishing these tenses from some forms of the present and imperfect; **nous courons, nous courrons; je courais, je courrais.**

accourir, *to hasten, to come up.*
concourir, *to compete, to concur.*
encourir, *to incur.*
parcourir, *to run, to go, over* or *through.*
secourir, *to succor, to relieve.*

Mourir, *to die.* **mourant.** **mort.**

je meurs, tu meurs, il meurt, nous mourons, vous mourez, ils meurent.

je mourais, tu mourais, il mourait, nous mourions, vous mouriez, ils mouraient.

je mourus. **je mourrai.** **je mourrais.**

que je meure, que tu meures, qu'il meure, que nous mourions, que vous mouriez, qu'ils meurent. **que je mourusse.**

meurs, qu'il meure, mourons, mourez, qu'ils meurent.

Here also notice the doubled **r** in the future and conditional.

Collective Nouns.

Some nouns, although used in the singular, represent a number of persons or things, and are called in consequence *collective nouns.* These collective nouns are *general* when they represent the whole of the persons or things mentioned, such as **l'armée, la famille, le peuple.** They are *partitive*, when they express only a part of the whole, such as **une foule, un certain nombre, une douzaine.**

Collective nouns preceded by **le** or **la** are *general*, and require their verb, adjective, and pronoun, to be put in the singular ; as : —

le comité s'est réuni, *the committee have met.*
la foule des spectateurs applaudit, *the crowd of spectators applauded.*

Collective nouns preceded by **un** or **une** are usually *partitive*, and their verb, adjective, and pronoun agree, not with the collective, but with its complement ; as :

une foule d'enfants le suivaient, *a crowd of children followed him.*
une foule d'hommes sont accourus, *a crowd of men came up.*

The collectives **la plupart de, la moitié de, peu de,** etc., are partitive and require agreement with their complement ; as, —

la plupart des enfants sont légers, *most children are thoughtless.*

1. Le clergé s'est opposé à la réforme, mais le parlement a passé outre. 2. Huit jours après la bataille, une foule de soldats étaient morts de leurs blessures. 3. La maison de ce monsieur est fermée; la famille est partie pour la campagne la semaine dernière. 4. Nous avons parcouru les plus beaux quartiers de la ville, nous avons vu une foule de choses intéressantes. 5. Bon nombre de ces messieurs ont eu recours à la protection du président, qui leur a, comme toujours, pardonné. 6. Vous n'avez pas le droit de parler mal de lui, il vous a secouru de sa bourse; vous êtes un ingrat. 7. La moitié de la classe a concouru, mais je crois que bien peu d'élèves réussiront. 8. On prétend que j'encourrai votre disgrâce si je dis la vérité; j'espère, Monsieur, qu'il n'en sera rien. 9. Le fils de notre voisine est mort ce matin. 10. C'est ce qu'on appelle mourir à la fleur de l'âge. 11. De quoi Mme votre cousine est-elle morte? 12. Elle est morte d'une haleine courte; nous avons tous admiré sa fermeté.

1. Does she sleep; does she run; does she feel? 2. Did she not run; did she not sleep; did she not die? 3. Was she not running; was she not sleeping; was she not dying? 4. Will they not sleep; will they not run; will they not die? 5. Let us not go to sleep. 6. Die, scoundrel that you are! 7. A great number of pupils have competed for that prize. 8. The crowd ran to the field of battle. 9. A crowd of children were running about in the meadow. 10. Our family has incurred your displeasure. 11. I hope you will succor them in their misery. 12. His sister died very young. 13. How old was she when she died? 14. I think she was only[1] thirteen years (of age). 15. The poor man to whom you

[1] Translate *only* by **ne . . . que**, placing **ne** before the verb and **que** before the number.

spoke last week died of hunger yesterday. 16. I do not think her uncle is dead; I saw him walking in his garden yesterday. We must (*faut*) not believe all we hear. 17. I fear that she is dead. 18. He died (*pret.*) in England.

105.

Acquérir, *to acquire*. **acquérant. acquis.**

j'acquiers, tu acquiers, il acquiert, nous acquérons, vous acquérez, ils acquièrent.

j'acquérais, tu acquérais, il acquérait, nous acquérions, etc.

j'acquis. j'acquerrai. j'acquerrais.

que j'acquière, que tu acquières, qu'il acquière, que nous acquérions, que vous acquériez, qu'ils acquièrent. que j'acquisse.

acquiers, qu'il acquière, acquérons, acquérez, qu'ils acquièrent.

conquérir, *to conquer*. **s'enquérir**, *to inquire*.

Ouvrir, *to open*. **ouvrant. ouvert.**

j'ouvre, tu ouvres, il ouvre, nous ouvrons, vous ouvrez, ils ouvrent.

j'ouvrais, tu ouvrais, il ouvrait, nous ouvrions, vous ouvriez, ils ouvraient.

j'ouvris. j'ouvrirai. j'ouvrirais.

que j'ouvre, que tu ouvres, qu'il ouvre, que nous ouvrions, que vous ouvriez, qu'ils ouvrent. que j'ouvrisse.

ouvre, qu'il ouvre, ouvrons, ouvrez, qu'ils ouvrent.

couvrir, *to cover*. **offrir**, *to offer*.
découvrir, *to uncover, to discover*. **souffrir**, *to suffer, to endure*.

The Place of Adjectives.

The following adjectives, used singly, generally precede the noun: —

joli, *pretty*.	**petit**, *little*.	**mauvais**, *bad*.
beau, *fine, beautiful*.	**jeune**, *young*.	**méchant**, *wicked*.
grand, *great, big*.	**vieux**, *old*.	**triste**, *sad*.
gros, *large, stout*.	**ancien**, *ancient*.	**vilain**, *ugly*.
bon, *good*.	**dernier**, *last*.	**premier**, *first*.

To the adjectives mentioned in § 34 as following their noun may be added: adjectives of form (*square, round*); of taste (*sweet, bitter*): and participles used adjectively.

une table carrée, *a square table.*
une orange douce, *a sweet orange.*
un prince redouté, *a dreaded prince.*
une personne séduisante, *a charming person.*

In addition, observe that, when an adjective is a mere ornament, which could be suppressed without altering the meaning of the sentence, it generally comes *before* the noun; as, **un vil scélérat.** If, on the contrary, the adjective is absolutely necessary to complete the expression and give a clear meaning to it, it is placed *after* the noun; as, **un homme vil.**[1]

The preposition *with*, placed after an adjective or a participle, is translated by **avec** when it means *along with*, and by **de** when it implies *with some of* or *with any of;* as: —

il est arrivé avec votre frère,	*he has arrived with your brother.*
elle est douée de grandes qualités,[2]	*she is gifted with great qualities.*

By after a comparative, *in* after a superlative, and *than* before a number, are translated by **de**; as: —

je suis plus grand que lui de trois centimètres,	*I am taller than he by three centimeters.*
voici le plus beau tableau de cette galerie,	*here is the finest picture in this gallery.*
nous n'étions pas plus de quinze,	*we were not more than fifteen.*

1. Ce prince a conquis des territoires vastes et nombreux, mais il est abhorré de tous les honnêtes gens.

[1] There will be found in the Appendix a list of adjectives which change their signification according as they are placed before or after the noun.

[2] *Some* is not expressed here to avoid the meeting of two **de**'s. If it were expressed, we should have, *She is gifted with (some) great qualities*, **elle est douée de (des) grandes qualités.**

2. Il a commis plus de crimes que le dernier misérable enfermé dans ses prisons. 3. Comme il est puissant et victorieux, presque tout le monde se découvre et s'incline à son passage. 4. M. votre grand-père se sert toujours d'anciennes expressions. 5. Il m'a prié de vous dire qu'il s'était "enquis de votre santé;" mon ami, on ne dit plus: "s'enquérir de la santé de quelqu'un," mais "demander des nouvelles de quelqu'un." 6. J'ai eu bien des luttes pénibles à supporter dans ma jeunesse, mais j'ai acquis de l'expérience, et, comme j'ai beaucoup souffert, je sais maintenant jouir. 7. N'ouvrez pas cette fenêtre, j'ai peur d'un courant d'air. 8. Je crains, mon bon ami, que vous n'exagériez un peu votre connaissance du français; j'ai découvert plus de dix fautes dans votre dernière lettre. 9. J'aime à croire que vous n'allez pas offrir cette rose à Mlle votre cousine, c'est la plus vilaine du jardin. 10. Je la lui ai déjà offerte, mais elle l'a refusée. 11. Elle ne veut rien accepter de moi, parce qu'elle a découvert, dit-elle, que je suis un mauvais sujet. 12. Nous avons souffert ses impertinences pendant plus de trois heures. 13. Il est si malade qu'il ne peut souffrir ni la voiture ni le cheval. 14. J'ai cruellement souffert du froid tout le temps qu'a duré l'expédition.

1. By that noble disinterestedness he conquered all hearts. 2. His father has acquired a large fortune in Spain. 3. The first French book that I read seemed to me very difficult. 4. We have bought a round table larger than the one (*celle*) which you saw. 5. Alexander conquered a great part of the known world. 6. Your brother is not a reasonable man, he is never pleased. 7. You lent my mother a very interesting book. 8. Offer this flower to your aunt, it is the most beautiful that I have found. 9. If you wish me to open this door,

aunt, you must give me the key. 10. Our dining-room is longer than yours by one metre and a half. 11. I discovered more than fifteen mistakes in her exercise. 12. She is older than her brother by three years. 13. It is by far (*de beaucoup*) the best novel I ever read. 14. This general is the oldest officer in the army. 15. We opened the door less than five minutes ago. 16. He never gives me less than ten francs a week. 17. I don't think he is by a great deal so learned as his brother. 18. She has left with her two sons. 19. Let her open the little box which her uncle has offered her; it is filled with diamonds.

106.

Cueillir, *to gather, to pluck.* **cueillant.** **cueilli.**

je cueille, tu cueilles, il cueille, nous cueillons, vous cueillez, ils cueillent.

je cueillais, tu cueillais, il cueillait, nous cueillions, vous cueilliez, ils cueillaient.

je cueillis. **je cueillerai.** **je cueillerais.**

que je cueille. **cueille, qu'il cueille, cueillons, cueillez, qu'ils cueillent.**

accueillir, *to receive, to welcome.* **recueillir,** *to harvest, to take up.*
se recueillir, *to collect one's self* or *one's thoughts.*

Assaillir, *to assail, to attack.* **assaillant.** **assailli.**

FUTURE, **j'assaillirai.** CONDITIONAL, **j'assaillirais.**

The rest as **cueillir.**

Than before a tense of the indicative is translated by **que . . . ne**; as: —

nous sommes plus riches que vous ne pensez, *we are richer than you think.*

But if the first clause of the sentence is negative or interrogative, or if there is an adverb between **que** and the verb, the **ne** is left out; as: —

n'agissez pas autrement que vous parlez,	*do not act otherwise than you speak.*
croyez-vous qu'un homme puisse être plus heureux que vous l'êtes depuis trois mois ?	*do you believe that a man can be happier than you have been for three months?*
elle est plus malheureuse que lorsqu'elle demeurait chez vous,	*she is more unhappy than when she was living with you.*

1. Nous recueillerons cette année plus de vin que nous n'en avons recueilli les deux dernières années. 2. Vous avez cueilli plus de fleurs qu'on ne vous l'avait[1] permis. 3. Ils m'ont accueilli avec plus de cordialité que je ne l'avais espéré. 4. Nous habitons un pays froid où l'on ne recueille ni blé ni vin. 5. Les poires qu'ils ont cueillies ce matin sont moins mûres qu'ils ne croyaient. 6. Il me semble que votre oncle n'est pas plus riche qu'il l'était il y a six ans. 7. Est-ce qu'il n'est pas moins malheureux qu'il l'était l'an dernier? 8. Nous avons été assaillis d'une tempête deux heures après être sortis du port. 9. Après s'être recueilli un moment, il a commencé le plus beau discours qu'il ait jamais prononcé. 10. Ne me pressez pas tant de répondre, j'ai besoin de me recueillir quelque temps.

11. Hélas! du crime affreux dont la honte me suit
Jamais mon triste cœur n'a recueilli le fruit!

1. We shall not acquire; we shall not cover. 2. Is she collecting herself; had she collected herself? 3. They would not have acquired; they would not have covered. 4. Let her collect herself; let us collect ourselves. 5. Have I acquired; have I covered; have I collected myself. 6. He acts better[2] than he speaks. 7. He is

[1] For the use of **le** in several sentences, see § 40.

[2] *Better* is sometimes an adjective, sometimes an adverb. It is an adjective and is translated by **meilleur** when it qualifies a noun or a pronoun: *your pens are better than mine*, **vos plumes sont meilleures que les miennes.** It is an adverb and is translated by **mieux** when it modifies a verb: *he reads better than you*, **il lit mieux que vous.**

richer than people think. 8. The distance is less[1] than you pretend. 9. She is less pretty than you believe. 10. They are richer than they were a year ago. 11. He is not richer than he was. 12. Is he richer than he was last year? 13. You have welcomed him with more cordiality than he deserves. 14. We shall receive these gentlemen with kindness. 15. I shall welcome your friend this time better than I did last year.

107.

Tenir, *to hold.* **tenant.** **tenu.**

je tiens, tu tiens, il tient, nous tenons, vous tenez, ils tiennent.

je tenais, tu tenais, il tenait, nous tenions, vous teniez, ils tenaient.

je tins, tu tins, il tint, nous tînmes, vous tîntes, ils tinrent.

je tiendrai. **je tiendrais.**

que je tienne, que tu tiennes, qu'il tienne, que nous tenions, que vous teniez, qu'ils tiennent. **que je tinsse.**

tiens, qu'il tienne, tenons, tenez, qu'ils tiennent.

s'abstenir de, *to abstain from.*
appartenir, *to belong.*
contenir, *to contain.*
détenir, *to detain.*
maintenir, *to maintain.*
entretenir, *to support, talk with, entertain.*
obtenir, *to obtain.*
soutenir, *to sustain, to prop up, to defend*, etc.

tenir bon, *to hold firm.*
se tenir debout, *to stand up.*
se tenir tout droit, *to stand* or *sit erect.*
tenez, *there! here! hold!*

The before a comparative is not expressed in French; as: —

plus on est riche, plus on a de soucis, *the richer a man is, the more cares he has.*

[1] When *less* is an adjective, it is translated by **moindre**, and when an adverb by **moins**.

The adverb **tout** (*quite, entirely*) varies for the sake of euphony before an adjective or participle feminine beginning with a consonant or *h* aspirated; as: —

elle est toute surprise et toute triste, *she is quite surprised and sad.*

1. Avez-vous remarqué comme il était pâle lorsqu'il s'est approché de nous en tenant son cheval par la bride? 2. Je crois qu'il serait tombé si son frère ne l'avait pas soutenu. 3. Sa mère tient pension dans une des rues les plus obscures du Quartier Latin; j'y suis allé un jour pour l'entretenir de l'affaire que vous savez. 4. Voilà deux bouquets qui sentent bien bon, à qui appartiennent-ils? 5. Je crois qu'ils appartiennent à Mlle votre sœur. 6. Elle les a oubliés tout à l'heure sur cette table, et, comme elle croit les avoir perdus, elle est maintenant toute triste. 7. Croyez-moi, plus vous vous abstiendrez de ces bruyants plaisirs, plus vous serez heureux. 8. Nous avons soutenu la guerre tant que nous avons pu; espérons qu'on va bientôt signer la paix. 9. Il faut rendre à chacun ce qui lui appartient. 10. Tenez, voici la somme que je vous avais promise; j'espère que vous allez désormais me laisser tranquille. 11. Je ne me doutais pas qu'elle pût (*was able*) crier si fort. 12. Ni moi non plus. 13. N'obtiendrons-nous jamais la vengeance ou la mort?

1. You are detaining me; they used to entertain us. 2. I was maintaining; you have been sustained. 3. That I might hold; that she may have held. 4. Do not detain me; let us not support them. 5. She will have obtained; they would maintain. 6. You must entertain me until I am ready to take a walk. 7. Do not entreat him any[1] more: the more you ask (*future*), the less you will obtain. 8. To whom do these paintings belong?

[1] *Not any more* is translated the same as *no more*, by **ne . . . plus**, or **ne . . . pas davantage**.

9. They belong to me, they cost me very dear. 10. My sisters are quite surprised that you have obtained a permission which has been refused to them (*which one has refused to them*). 11. Why did you scold Jane before (*avant*) so many people?[1] she was quite ashamed. 12. The more you attack (*future*) her cousin, the more she will defend him. 13. Hold this ladder firm till (*que with subj.*) I come down. 14. She abstained from eating and drinking for thirty-six hours. 15. I could not (*je ne pourrais pas*) abstain so long. 16. Nor I either.

108.

Venir, *to come.* **venant.** **venu.**

je viens, tu viens, il vient, nous venons, vous venez, ils viennent.

je venais, tu venais, il venait, nous venions, vous veniez, ils venaient.

je vins, tu vins, il vint, nous vînmes, vous vîntes, ils vinrent.

je viendrai. **je viendrais.**

que je vienne, etc., **que nous venions,** etc. **que je vinsse.**

viens, qu'il vienne, venons, venez, qu'ils viennent.

convenir (with **avoir**), *to suit,* (with **être**), *to agree.*
devenir, *to become.*
parvenir, *to attain, to succeed.*
prévenir, *to warn, to apprise.*
revenir, *to come back.*
se souvenir de, *to remind one's self of, to remember.*

venir, devenir, parvenir, revenir, and **se souvenir** are conjugated with **être.**

Idiomatic Use of the Verb *venir*.

Just as **aller** is used before a verb to express action which is to be done immediately, in like manner **venir de,** followed by an infinitive, expresses an action that has just taken place.

je viens de sortir, *I have just come out.*
nous venons d'arriver, *we have just arrived.*
ils venaient de partir, *they had just left.*

[1] *People* is translated by **monde** when it means *company.*

The Possessive Adjective.

(1) When a possessive adjective (*my*, *his*, *her*, *our*, *your*, *their*) is placed before a noun expressive of a part of the body, governed by a verb, it is expressed by *to me*, *to him*, *to her*, *to us*, *to you*, or *to them;* as:

He broke my finger,	**il m'a cassé le doigt.**

(2) If the possessor is clearly shown, suppress the pronoun *to me*, *to him*, etc.; as: —

He lost his right leg in the battle,	**il a perdu la jambe droite dans la bataille.**

(3) With the three words, **mal** (*pain*), **froid** (*cold*), and **chaud** (*warm*), translate by the verb **avoir**, making the person spoken of subject of the verb; as: —

Her feet are sore,	**elle a mal aux pieds.**
My hands are very cold,	**j'ai bien froid aux mains.**

1. Il est convenu avec moi que vous êtes plus instruit que lui. 2. Votre proposition lui a convenu. 3. Etes-vous parvenu à le convaincre? 4. Je viens de le rencontrer. 5. Il vient de se casser la jambe. 6. Je vous préviens que j'ai mal au pied droit et qu'il m'est impossible de marcher. 7. Je me suis souvenue que vous avez toujours froid aux pieds, et j'ai dit à la bonne de vous faire un bon feu dans votre chambre. 8. Attendez un instant, mon frère va venir. 9. Mais, Mademoiselle, j'ai vu votre frère il y a cinq minutes; il ne va pas venir, il vient de venir. 10. Cela commence à devenir fatigant. 11. Il me dit (pret. *told*) qu'il venait de Tolède et qu'il allait à Madrid; et moi je lui dis (*told*) que je venais de Burgos et que j'allais à Cordoue. 12. Devenant malheureux, il m'est devenu cher. — (*Racine.*)

1. We remember him; he remembers us; I shall remember you. 2. We were coming; he came (*pret.*); they (*fem.*) have come. 3. I fear that he will succeed; they fear that I shall not succeed. 4. You must remember this, that she did not become proud till she became rich. 5. What (§ 83) has happened does not astonish me; you remember that I warned you of it a long time ago. 6. You are right, I remember it now, but I had quite forgotten it. 7. He will come; they will have come. 8. He would remember; they (*fem.*) would have remembered. 9. She has just gone out; she had just gone out. 10. They have just arrived; they had just arrived. 11. He has just broken his leg. 12. He had just lost his left hand. 13. She has a sore foot. 14. Remember that she has a sore finger. 15. I have a headache. 16. These shoes pinch my feet.

109.

Voir, *to see.* **voyant.** **vu.**

je vois, tu vois, il voit, nous voyons, vous voyez, ils voient.

je voyais, tu voyais, il voyait, nous voyions, vous voyiez, ils voyaient.

je vis, tu vis, il vit, nous vîmes, vous vîtes, ils virent.

je verrai. **je verrais.**

que je voie, que tu voies, qu'il voie, que nous voyions, que vous voyiez, qu'ils voient. **que je visse.**

vois, qu'il voie, voyons, voyez, qu'ils voient.

prévoir, *to foresee* (FUTURE, **je prévoirai,** CONDIT., **je prévoirais**).
revoir, *to see again.*

aller voir, *to go to see, to go and see, to call on, upon, to pay a visit to.*
mériter d'être vu, *to be worth seeing.*
voyons! *let me see! let us see! come!*

Mouvoir, *to move.* **mouvant.** **mû, mue.**

je meus, tu meus, il meut, nous mouvons, vous mouvez, ils meuvent.

je mouvais, tu mouvais, il mouvait, nous mouvions, vous mouviez, ils mouvaient.

je mus. **je mouvrai.** **je mouvrais.**

que je meuve. **que je musse.**

meus, qu'il meuve, mouvons, mouvez, qu'ils meuvent.

émouvoir, *to move, to rouse.* PAST PART. **ému, émue.**
s'émouvoir, *to get excited, to be roused.*

Several tenses of **mouvoir** are scarcely ever used, except in technical language. *To move* is generally translated by **remuer, faire aller, faire marcher,** etc.

1. Si vous le voyez venir (§ 97), faites semblant (*pretend*) de ne pas l'apercevoir. 2. Allons ensemble au spectacle ce soir; on dit que la nouvelle pièce mérite d'être vue. 3. Je ne vois pas que vous vous repentiez beaucoup de la faute que vous avez commise envers moi. 4. Voyons, n'est-ce pas aujourd'hui le 1er du mois? voyez donc l'almanach. 5. Non, Monsieur, c'est aujourd'hui le 2. C'est après-demain, 4 mars, que nous verrons M. votre frère. 6. Voulez-vous me dire la date de la mort des quatre Henri qui ont été rois de France? 7. Henri Ier est mort en 1060, Henri II[1] en 1559, Henri III en 1589, et Henri IV en 1610. 8. Il vaut mieux, dit La Rochefoucauld, employer notre esprit à supporter les infortunes qui nous arrivent qu'à prévoir celles qui nous peuvent (*may*) arriver. 9. Quelle horrible histoire vous nous avez contée! j'en suis encore tout émue. 10. Je vous en prie, ne parlez plus de cela, du moins devant ces enfants; vous leur faites peur (*you frighten them*). 11. Voilà un homme qui ne s'émeut de rien. 12. Voilà une femme qui a vu la mort dans son plus terrible appareil sans en être émue.

[1] **Premier** is the only ordinal number used in naming princes, as well as for dates (§ 25).

1. Do you not see? were you not seeing? had you not seen? 2. We shall see; they will have seen; he saw (*pret.*). 3. She is getting excited; she was getting excited. 4. She will get excited; she would get excited. 5. Will you not foresee? will you not have foreseen? 6. I see him coming; I saw him coming (§ 97). 7. We went to see them on the 10th. 8. We shall go to see you on the 1st of next month. 9. She will pay you a visit to-morrow forenoon. 10. George the First, George II., George III., George IV. were kings of England. 11. The 1st of April, the 2d of March, the 3d of August, the 21st of June. 12. Come! give me what you promised me last week. 13. I am just going to give them the songs which I have promised them. 14. I have just given him his pen; has he lent it to you? (§ 74). 15. No, sir; I asked him for it, but he had already lent it to some one. 16. Do not ask him for it again.

110.

S'asseoir, *to sit down.* **s'asseyant.** **s'étant assis.**

je m'assieds, tu t'assieds, il s'assied, nous nous asseyons, vous vous asseyez, ils s'asseyent.

je m'asseyais, tu t'asseyais, il s'asseyait, nous nous asseyions, vous vous asseyiez, ils s'asseyaient.

je m'assis, tu t'assis, il s'assit, nous nous assîmes, vous vous assîtes, ils s'assirent.

je m'assiérai or **je m'asseyerai.** **je m'assiérais** or **je m'asseyerais.**

que je m'asseye, etc., **que nous nous asseyions, que vous vous asseyiez, qu'ils s'asseyent.** **que je m'assisse.**

assied-toi, qu'il s'asseye, asseyons-nous, asseyez-vous, qu'ils s'asseyent.

je me suis assis, *I sat down.* **je m'étais assis,** *I had sat down.*

Pleuvoir, *to rain.* **plu,** *rained.*

An impersonal verb, used only in the infinitive, past participle, and the third person singular of all tenses. There is no imperative.

il pleut. il pleuvait. il plut. il pleuvra. il pleuvrait.

qu'il pleuve. qu'il plût.

il a plu, *it has rained.* **il avait plu,** *it had rained.*

In the figurative sense, this verb is also used in the third person plural: **les balles pleuvaient de toutes parts,** *balls were raining* (or *pouring*) *from all sides.*

Pourvoir à, *to provide for.*

Same as **voir,** except Preterite, **je pourvus;** Future, **je pourvoirai;** Condit., **je pourvoirais;** Subj. imperf., **que je pourvusse.**

The Pronoun *le* (*so* or *it*).

In English, *I am, we are,* etc., may be used without other words in answer to a question; the French insert **le, la, les,** before the verb, to represent the word about which the question is asked.

(1) If the word is a substantive (or adjective used substantively, as **le malade,** *the patient*), use **le, la, les,** according to the gender and number of the substantive represented: —

Are you the daughter of this gentleman? Yes, I am.	**êtes-vous la fille de ce monsieur? oui, je la suis.**
Are you the sick lady who sent for me? No, I am not.	**êtes-vous la malade qui m'a fait appeler? non, je ne la suis pas.**

(2) If the word to be represented is an adjective (or a substantive used adjectively), **le** alone is used:[1] —

Are you pleased, ladies? We all are.	**êtes-vous contentes mesdames? nous le sommes toutes.**
Are you a governess? I am.	**êtes-vous gouvernante? je le suis.**

[1] Another way to express the above rules: If the predicate in the question is an adjective or a substantive with *a*, the **le** is not declined; if it is a substantive with *the*, it is declined.

Le is also used to represent a preceding adjective or participle, or even a clause, although the form of the sentence is not interrogative: —

She is more modest than she was formerly,	**elle est plus modeste qu'elle ne l'était autrefois.**
He is beloved because he deserves to be so,	**il est aimé parce qu'il est digne de l'être.**
You have made more progress than I hoped,	**vous avez fait plus de progrès que je ne l'espérais.**

1. Asseyez-vous donc. 2. Donnez-vous la peine de vous asseoir. 3. Asseyez-vous sur ce banc, je vais vous montrer quelque chose de beau. 4. Me voilà assise, et prête à voir tout ce que vous voulez me montrer. 5. Où donc voulez-vous que je m'asseye? Par terre? 6. Avez-vous pourvu ma chambre de toutes les choses nécessaires? 7. Soyez tranquille, on y pourvoira. 8. Vous savez bien que votre mère pourvoit à tout. 9. Ne m'envoyez pas ces livres s'il pleut, ils seraient tout gâtés. 10. Envoyez-les-moi plutôt demain, je serai à la maison entre quatre et cinq heures. 11. Est-ce que vous êtes le monsieur qui vient de perdre une montre? 12. Oui, monsieur, je le suis; je vous remercie de votre bonté. En effet c'est ma montre, et j'avais peur que je ne la revisse plus.

1. She sits down;[1] she sat down; she was sitting down. 2. She is seated; she was seated; she will be

[1] Observe that the reflective form is used here to express the *act* of sitting down, whilst the passive merely expresses the *state*.

It is well known that the French language was originally a development of the popular Latin spoken by the Roman soldiery, the colonists occupying Gaul, and the whole rustic population. This popular Latin showed a continuous tendency to decompose classical Latin, and among other decompositions the following two were accomplished facts in the sixth century: — 1. The present tense of the passive voice of *amare*, viz. *amor*, was transformed into *sum amatus*; 2. The preterite of the active voice, viz. *amavi*, had become *habeo amatum*. This novel use of the past participle has been so universally seated. 3. They had seated themselves; they would have seated themselves. 4. Let us sit down here; it is the only place (*lieu*) that we find where it does not rain. 5. It will rain; it will have rained; it would rain. 6. Why do you not give her the watch which you have promised her? 7. No, do not give it to her, give it to me (§ 76). 8. I am sure of it (§ 80); I am sure of him (§ 71). 9. You speak of it; you speak of her. 10. I am glad of it. 11. I shall not consent to it. 12. He has bought a great many novels, and will lend me a few. 13. Are you not a little lazy, Miss Jane? Unfortunately, I am. 14. Are you this gentleman's daughter? No, sir, I am not. 15. Are you the gentlemen who bought these horses? Yes, we are. 16. Wars are less numerous than they were. 17. He is more learned than I had thought.

constant in the French mind that the past participle no longer implies by itself any idea of *past* as it did in classical Latin, but does so when combined with **j'ai, tu as, il a**, etc. Thus the classical *cantavi* became *habeo cantatum* in popular Latin, and **j'ai chanté** in French. In the same way, used with **je suis, tu es, il est**, etc, it expresses the present: the classical *amor* became *sum amatus* in popular Latin, in French **je suis aimé.**

Bearing this in mind, and also remembering that French pronominal verbs always take **être** in their compound tenses *with the meaning of* **avoir**, one can easily understand that **je me suis blessé**, meaning **j'ai blessé moi même**, expresses a past action, whilst **je suis blessé** expresses a present state.

Observe, however, that if **je suis sorti, parti, venu**, etc., are used with a date expressed or understood, they express a *past action*, as, **il est arrivé hier**, *he arrived yesterday*, **elle est partie le 15 de ce mois**, *she left on the 15th instant*. If they are without a date expressed or understood, they express a *present state;* **je suis arrivé**, *I am arrived*, **il est sorti**, *he is out*, **elle est partie**, *she is away*.

je m'assieds, *I sit down.*	**il se lève**, *he is rising.*
je me suis assis, *I sat down.*	**il s'est levé**, *he rose.*
je suis assis, *I am seated* or *sitting.*	**il est levé**, *he is up.*
il se couche, *he goes to bed.*	**il se fâche**, *he is getting angry.*
il s'est couché, *he went to bed.*	**il s'est fâché**, *he got angry.*
il est couché, *he is in bed.*	**il est fâché**, *he is angry.*

111.

Valoir, *to be worth.* **valant.** **valu.**

je vaux, tu vaux, il vaut, nous valons, vous valez, ils valent.

je valais, tu valais, il valait, nous valions, vous valiez, ils valaient.

je valus. **je vaudrai.** **je vaudrais.**

que je vaille, que tu vailles, qu'il vaille, que nous valions, que vous valiez, qu'ils vaillent. **que je valusse.** No imperative.

The impersonal verb *to be better* is translated by **valoir mieux** : —

It is better to leave to-day than to-morrow,	**il vaut mieux partir aujourd'hui que demain.**

After **valoir mieux** and **aimer mieux**, *than* followed by an infinitive is translated by **que de** : —

It will be better to go away at once than to wait an hour,	**il vaudra mieux partir tout de suite que d'attendre une heure.**
I like better to write to him than to speak to him,	**j'aime mieux lui écrire que de lui parler.**

Savoir *to know* (by the mind). **sachant.** **su.**

je sais, tu sais, il sait, nous savons, vous savez, ils savent.

je savais, tu savais, il savait, nous savions, vous saviez, ils savaient.

je sus. **je saurai.** **je saurais.**

que je sache, que tu saches, qu'il sache, que nous sachions, que vous sachiez, qu'ils sachent. **que je susse.**

sache, qu'il sache, sachons, sachez, qu'ils sachent.

Je ne sache pas is sometimes used for the negative of the first person singular of the present indicative.

Savoir must be used instead of **pouvoir,** when *can* means *to know how, to have learned :* —

He can read and write, *He knows how to read and write,*	**il sait lire et écrire.**
Can you dance? *Do you know how to dance?*	**savez-vous danser ?**

We may say, **il peut écrire**; but the sense is, *he is able to write* (*in spite of his sore fingers or hands*). We say also, **pouvez-vous danser?** but it means, *are you able to dance* (*in spite of your sore foot*)?

Savoir is one of four verbs (§ 116) which may be used negatively without **pas** or **point**; but when *not to know* means *not to have learned*, **pas** or **point** is used: —

I know not what to say,	**je ne sais que dire.**
He does not know his lesson,	**il ne sait pas sa leçon.**
Do you not know it?	**ne la savez-vous pas?**
I do not know how to swim,	**je ne sais pas nager.**

The conditional **je ne saurais**, etc., may be used for the present **je ne puis**, etc. Only the meaning of the latter is more absolute: —

He is not able to do this, *He cannot do this,* *He does not know how to do this,*	**il ne saurait le faire.** **il ne peut le faire.**

The Use of Disjunctive Pronouns (see §§ 32, 37, 71).

Disjunctive pronouns [1] are used: —

(1) In answer to a question: —

Who is speaking? She is.	**qui parle? elle,** or **c'est elle.**
Who brought that here? I did.	**qui a apporté cela ici? moi,** or **c'est moi.**
To whom did you speak? To him.	**à qui avez-vous parlé? à lui.**

(2) After reflective verbs: —

I address myself to you,	**je m'adresse à vous.**
Do not trust (yourself) to him,	**ne vous fiez pas à lui.**

(3) When they are separated from the verb, either as subjects or objects, by some other word: —

He alone can understand you,	**lui seul peut vous comprendre.**
He is not so rich as they,	**il n'est pas si riche qu'eux.**
He loves nobody but me,	**il n'aime que moi.**

[1] They are called *disjunctive* because they are disjoined from the verb.

(4) When they are separated from their verb by a clause unnecessary to the meaning: —

lui, un homme qui pouvait parler ainsi, vous a trompé, *he, a man who could speak so, deceived you.*

But when the intervening clause is necessary to the meaning,[1] use **celui, celle, ceux, celles** for *he*, *she*, or *they*; *as*, —

celui qui vous l'a dit vous a trompé, *he who told you so deceived you.*

1. Ce drap-ci vaut dix francs cinquante centimes le mètre: j'en ai acheté quelques mètres pour vous et pour elle. 2. Et celui-là, combien vaut-il? 3. Celui-là ne vaut rien. 4. Cette affaire vaut bien la peine qu'on y pense. 5. Dans huit jours cette paire de bottines ne vaudra plus rien. 6. Les effets valent mieux que les paroles. 7. Il vaut mieux se taire que de mal parler. 8. Nous ne savons s'il viendra. 9. Je ne sais que dire ni que faire. 10. Monsieur, j'ai mal à la main droite, je n'ai pu faire mon exercice, mais je sais très bien mes leçons. 11. Je parie que lui seul sait tout. 12. Qui vous a appris tout ce que vous savez? C'est lui. 13. Qui lui? 14. Mon frère, je crois qu'il sait toute chose. 15. Il y a longtemps que j'ai dit que, pour savoir quelque chose, il le faut écrire.

1. It will be better to do it now than to wait for your father's arrival. 2. I like better to write to him than to go (and) visit him. 3. Is it not he who has lent you my Italian grammar? 4. It is not he, it is I. 5. Does she trust (herself) to him? 6. To whom did you remit

[1] Another way to express this rule: When the intervening clause *expands*, use **lui, elle, eux, elles**; when it *limits*, use **celui, celle, ceux, celles**.

A third way: If there is a comma after *he*, *she*, or *they*, use **lui, elle, eux, elles**, as the comma shows that the clause merely expands; if there is no comma, use **celui, celle, ceux, celles.**

(*remis*) the letter? To herself. 7. Who took away my glass? I did. 8. How much is this worth? 9. This is not worth five centimes. 10. Your brother is not here, that I know of (*que je sache*). 11. Do you know that your brother has arrived in America safely? 12. She is not able to tell us how the thing has passed (*s'est passée*). 13. He and your sister know the whole secret. 14. He who arrives (*future*) first (*le premier*) will get (*aura*) this engraving. 15. Your cousin's conduct is a mystery to (*pour*) me: he, who had promised us his support in this affair, has done all he could against us.

112.

Connaître, *to know by sight.* **connaissant.** **connu.**

je connais, tu connais, il connaît, nous connaissons, vous connaissez, ils connaissent.

je connaissais, tu connaissais, il connaissait, nous connaissions, vous connaissiez, ils connaissaient.

je connus. je connaîtrai. je connaîtrais.

que je connaisse. que je connusse.

connais. qu'il connaisse, connaissons, connaissez, qu'ils connaissent.

The following verbs ending in **-aître** and **-oître** are conjugated like **connaître**: —

reconnaître, *to recognize.* **disparaître,** *to disappear.*
paraître, *to appear, to seem.* **croître,** *to grow, to increase.*

In all these verbs the **i** takes a circumflex accent before **t.**

In the verb **croître,** the present **je croîs** and the preterite **je crûs** have the circumflex accent to distinguish them from **je crois,** *I believe,* **je crus,** *I believed.*

Naître, *to be born, to spring up.* **naissant.** **né.**

je nais, tu nais, il naît, nous naissons, vous naissez, ils naissent.

je naissais. je naquis. je naîtrai. je naîtrais.

que je naisse. que je naquisse.

nais, qu'il naisse, naissons, naissez, qu'ils naissent.

Distinction between *savoir* and *connaître*.

Savoir means *to know by the mind, to be sensible of, to know how to.* Therefore it never has persons for its objects, and can be followed by a conjunction or a verb: —

Do you know your lesson?	**savez-vous votre leçon?**
How many languages does he know?	**combien de langues sait-il?**
I know that she will come,	**je sais qu'elle viendra.**
He knows how to read and write,	**il sait lire et écrire.**

Connaître means *to be acquainted with, to know (by sight).* Therefore it may have persons or things for objects, but can never be followed by a conjunction or a verb: —

I know that gentleman, this lady, his house, Littré's Dictionary, etc.	**je connais ce monsieur, cette dame, sa maison, le dictionnaire de Littré,** etc.

The Use of Disjunctive Pronouns continued.

Disjunctive pronouns are used for the sake of emphasis or contradistinction: —

Would I lower myself so far!	**moi, je m'abaisserais jusque là !**
You tremble, but I am not afraid,	**vous tremblez, vous; mais moi je n'ai pas peur.**
He gave me a purse, and I presented him with my photograph,	**il m'a donné un porte-monnaie, et moi je lui ai présenté ma photographie.**

It is seen from these examples that the disjunctive pronoun comes *in addition to the conjunctive* for emphasis or contradistinction; but, in the third person singular or plural, the conjunctive **il** or **ils** is sometimes suppressed to give more rapidity to the style: —

They will not come, but he will,	**elles ne viendront pas, mais lui viendra.**
They would not do it, but you will,	**eux n'ont pas voulu le faire, mais vous, vous le ferez.**

1. Allez lui parler vous-même; vous le connaissez, vous, et moi je ne lui ai jamais dit un seul mot. 2. Ne vous trompez-vous pas? vous assurez que vous ne l'avez jamais vu, mais lui prétend vous connaître parfaitement. 3. Connaissez-vous beaucoup de monde ici? 4. Moi? je n'y connais personne. 5. Voilà un chemin que je ne reconnais pas. 6. Je l'ai vu paraître un instant et s'en aller. 7. Toute autre gloire disparaît devant la vôtre. 8. Eux vous reconnaîtront, mais lui passera sans vous parler. 9. Vous lui parlez, vous! 10. Vous la blâmez, elle! 11. Je suis né à Dinan, en Bretagne, le 12 février 1704, d'une famille honnête et ancienne. 12. Bayle naquit dans l'année 1647; la nature lui donna l'imagination, la force, la subtilité, la mémoire. 13. Qui sait comment la chose s'est passée? 14. Moi, mais je ne vous le dirai pas.

1. It is better (*valoir mieux*); it was better; it has been better.[1] 2. It will be better; it would be better; it would not have been better. 3. We do not know (*savoir*); do not let them know. 4. They did not know (imperf.); we did not know (past indef.); he did not know (pret.) 5. They will not know; they would not know; they will not have known. 6. Alfred Tennyson was born in (*en*) 1810; Macaulay was born (pret.) in (*en*) 1800 and died (pret.) in 1858. 7. They do not believe that I know him; they did not believe (imp.) that I knew him. 8. They do not believe that I know it; they did not believe that I knew it. 9. I know what I say (*dis*) when I speak of him.[2] 10. *I* have known him,

[1] Put **mieux** before the past participle.

[2] **En** and **y** apply to persons in two cases only: —

(1) To avoid the repetition of **de lui, d'elle, d'eux, d'elles**, or **à lui**, etc. Examples: *I complained of him yesterday, and I shall again (complain of him) to-day*, **je me suis plaint de lui hier, et je m'en plaindrai encore**

but *you* have never even seen him. 11. *They* will speak to you, but *he* will pass without looking at you. 12. You detest *me!* 13. You visit *her!* 14. *You* read (*lisez*) such books! 15. I see nobody[1] but her. 16. They alone know the whole story.

113.

Prendre, *to take, to catch.* **prenant.** **pris.**

je prends, tu prends, il prend, nous prenons, vous prenez, ils prennent.

je prenais. **je pris.** **je prendrai.** **je prendrais.**

que je prenne, que tu prennes, qu'il prenne, que nous prenions, que vous preniez, qu'ils prennent. **que je prisse.**

prends, qu'il prenne, prenons, prenez, qu'ils prennent.

apprendre à, *to learn.*
comprendre, *to understand.*
entreprendre de, *to undertake.*
s'éprendre, *to be smitten.*
se méprendre, *to mistake.*
surprendre, *to take by surprise.*

The letter **n** is doubled in all these verbs whenever it is followed by a mute syllable.

prendre garde, *to take care, to beware.*
prendre goût à, *to take a liking for.*
prendre part à, *to take a share in.*
prendre patience, *to be patient,* or *more patient.*
prendre plaisir à, *to take pleasure in.*

After many verbs followed by *from* in English, and marking extraction or separation, the French put the preposition **à** (it is the Latin preposition *a* or *ab* which these verbs have thus retained). Some of them are: —

aujourd'hui. *Do you trust to her? Yes, I trust to her,* **vous fiez-vous à elle? oui, je m'y fie.**

(2) When persons are spoken of vaguely: —

Example: *When a man is dead, he is no more thought of,* **quand un homme est mort, on n'y pense plus.**

But if I am speaking of a certain person, **à lui** should be used: —

When this fellow is dead, he will no longer be thought of, **quand cet individu sera mort, on ne pensera plus à lui.**

[1] *Nobody but* must be translated the same as *nothing but,* by **ne . . . que.**

acheter à.	**emprunter à.**	**ravir à.**
arracher à.	**enlever à.**	**reprendre à.**
dérober à.	**extorquer à.**	**retenir à.**
se dérober à.	**ôter à.**	**retrancher à.**
échapper à.	**prendre à.**	**se soustraire à.**
	voler à.	

C'est or *ce sont* (see §§ 36, 37).

C'est is used for *it is* when placed before an adjective not followed by the idea of the sentence: —

It is impossible,	**c'est impossible.**
It is of no use,	**c'est inutile.**

But should the idea follow the adjective, **c'est** cannot be used: —

It is impossible to do all this in a day,	**il est impossible de faire tout ceci en un jour.**
It is of no use to entreat him,	**il est inutile de le supplier.**

Observe that **ce sont** is used before a third person plural (excepting the interrogative **est-ce eux?** and **est-ce elles?**) whilst **c'est** is used in all other cases.

1. Est-ce vous qui avez pris la clef? non, c'est mon frère. 2. C'est le plus malheureux homme que je connaisse; avant-hier il a perdu une grosse somme d'argent; hier sa maison a brûlé, et aujourd'hui on lui a pris une vache dans son pré. 3. Ils ont pris le deuil pour six mois. 4. Il est inutile de le défendre: il a été pris la main dans le sac. 5. Je n'ai encore rien pris de la journée.[1] 6. Chacun prend son plaisir où il le trouve. 7. Je prends les choses comme elles viennent, et les hommes comme ils sont. 8. Où avez-vous appris ce que

[1] *All my life, the whole morning, the whole evening, the whole day*, etc., after a negation, are translated simply by **de ma vie, de la matinée, de la soirée, de la journée**, etc.

vous dites là ? 9. Apprenez ces vers par cœur. 10. Il avait appris tout ce que l'on peut apprendre, jusqu'aux danses les plus nouvelles. 11. La plupart des hommes estiment ce qu'ils ne comprennent pas. 12. Votre petit frère n'était pas le seul élève dont le maître fût content.

13. . . . Le corbeau, honteux et confus,
Jura, mais un peu tard, qu'on ne l'y prendrait plus.
(*La Fontaine.*)

1. They (fem.) are taking each other by surprise; they have taken each other by surprise; they were taking each other by surprise. 2. They took (pret.) each other by surprise; they will have taken each other by surprise. 3. They would not take each other by surprise; they would not have taken each other by surprise; let them take each other by surprise. 4. It is you who have taught me to be patient (*to take patience*). 5. Is it not your father who has undertaken the construction of a new theatre in Glasgow? 6. Yes, sir, it is my father; it will be the finest theatre in (§ 36, 2) Scotland. 7. Do you understand what (§ 83, 2) she says? *I* declare it is impossible. 8. These are pleasures for which one takes a liking easily. 9. That is easy to learn. 10. It is easier to learn this than (*que de*) to write it. 11. Take care, do not speak so freely. 12. But these people do not understand me. 13. Pardon me, they do; they are[1] all Frenchmen. 14. Since[2] they are[1] all Frenchmen, why do they not take a share in the conversation? 15. Very likely because they would not take pleasure in it.

[1] Translate by **ce sont** if you put the article **des** before **Français**, by **ils sont** if you use **français** adjectively.

[2] *Since* is translated by **puisque** when it may be changed into *as*, *seeing that*, and by **depuis** or **depuis que** when it refers to time.

114.

Mettre, *to put, to put on.* **mettant. mis.**

je mets, tu mets, il met, nous mettons, vous mettez, ils mettent.

je mettais. je mis. je mettrai. je mettrais.

que je mette. que je misse.

mets, qu'il mette, mettons, mettez, qu'ils mettent.

se mettre, *to place one's self, to sit down, to dress.*
admettre, *to admit.*
commettre, *to commit.*
permettre de, *to permit.*
promettre de, *to promise.*
remettre, *to remit.*
soumettre, *to submit.*
omettre, *to omit.*

Suivre, *to follow, to attend.* **suivant. suivi.**

je suis, tu suis, il suit, nous suivons, vous suivez, ils suivent.

je suivais. je suivis. je suivrai. je suivrais.

que je suive. que je suivisse.

suis, qu'il suive, suivons, suivez, qu'ils suivent.

s'ensuivre, *to result, to follow.*
poursuivre, *to pursue, to run after.*

The Interrogative Pronoun.

Who or *whom* used interrogatively may be rendered:

(1) By **qui** (subject or object): —

Who has just spoken to you? **qui vient de vous parler?**
Whom did you see? **qui avez-vous vu?**

(2) Or by **qui est-ce qui** when subject, and **qui est-ce que** when object: —

qui est-ce qui vient de vous parler?
qui est-ce que vous avez vu?

This second way is the more familiar of the two, but the first alone can be used before **être**: *Who is there?* **qui est là?** not: **qui est-ce qui est là?**

(3) The interrogative *whom*, governed by a preposition, is translated by **qui** alone : —

Whom do you speak to? or, *To whom do you speak?*	**à qui parlez-vous?**

In French no preposition can be placed at the end of a clause, as in the first of these two English sentences.

(4) *What*, used interrogatively, is rendered by **qu'est-ce qui** when subject, and by **qu'est-ce que** or **que** alone when object.

What prevents you from coming with us?	**qu'est-ce qui vous empêche de venir avec nous?**
What do you say?	**qu'est-ce que vous dites? or, que dites-vous?**

(5) The interrogative *what*, governed by a preposition, must be translated by **quoi**: —

What are you thinking of?	**à quoi pensez-vous?**
What do you complain of?	**de quoi vous plaignez-vous?**[1]

1. Cette chaleur est insupportable; mettez un écran devant le feu. 2. Mettez vos gants et votre chapeau, et nous irons faire un tour. 3. Qui est-ce qui vous a recommandé de mettre tous les mois un peu d'argent à la caisse d'épargne? 4. Qui est-ce qui vous a mis dans une telle colère? 5. A qui avez-vous remis le paquet que je vous avais confié? 6. Est-ce que vous n'avez pas promis à votre neveu de le mener au spectacle? 7. Qui est-ce qui vous a permis de sortir ce matin? 8. Qui est-ce qui vous permet de parler? 9. Permettez, le soleil me donne dans les yeux, je vais baisser la jalousie. 10. Qu'est-ce que vous poursuiviez si ardemment ce ma-

[1] For other ways of translating *what*, see §§ 44, 83.

tin? Il me semble vous avoir vu courir à toutes jambes. 11. Si vous cessez de les voir, que s'ensuivra-t-il? 12. Qu'est-ce que je vous répondrai? je crains qu'il ne s'ensuive de grands malheurs. 13. Allez devant, je vous suis.

1. She is permitting; she is permitted. 2. She was permitting; she was permitted. 3. She had permitted; she had been permitted. 4. She will have permitted; she will have been permitted. 5. She would have permitted; she would have been permitted. 6. Do I follow you? Do you follow me? 7. Shall we not follow? Should we not follow. 8. That they may not follow; that they might not follow. 9. What is he going to do? 10. What have you put in my carpet-bag? 11. What (§ 44) hands she has! 12. Who has permitted you to go out? 13. Who has promised you to take (*mener*) you to the theatre this evening? 14. Whom did you admit (*mettre*) into the secret? 15. Whom did they admit into their club (*cercle*) last night? 16. To whom did you submit (yourself)? 17. To whom did you promise this nosegay? 18. Guess what I have in my hand! 19. I know what it is.

115.

Vivre, *to live, to be alive.* **vivant.** **vécu.**

je vis, tu vis, il vit, nous vivons, vous vivez, ils vivent. je vivais.

je vécus, tu vécus, il vécut, nous vécûmes, vous vécûtes, ils vécurent.

je vivrai. je vivrais. que je vive. que je vécusse.

vis, qu'il vive, vivons, vivez, qu'ils vivent.

When *to live* means *to dwell*, it is expressed by **demeurer**: *Where do you live? I live in the country,* **où demeurez-vous? je demeure à la campagne.**

Craindre, *to fear.* **craignant.** **craint.**

je crains, tu crains, il craint, nous craignons, vous craignez, ils craignent.

je craignais. je craignis. je craindrai. je craindrais.

que je craigne. que je craignisse.

crains, qu'il craigne, craignons, craignez, qu'ils craignent.

For the use of **craindre** with the subjunctive and infinitive, see §§ 89, 96.

I fear he will come,	**je crains qu'il ne vienne.**
I do not fear his coming,	**je ne crains pas qu'il vienne.**
Do you fear he will come?	**craignez-vous qu'il vienne?**
I am afraid to be mistaken,	**je crains de me tromper.**

contraindre, *to compel, to constrain.*	**se joindre,** *to meet.*
éteindre, *to extinguish, to annul.*	**plaindre,** *to pity.*
joindre, *to join.*	**se plaindre,** *to complain.*

Which, whose, etc. (see §§ 45, 46).

Sometimes the relative *which* preceded by a preposition means *where* or *when*, in which case it may simply be rendered by **où, d'où, par où,** etc.; as, —

voici la boîte où j'ai mis vos lettres.
l'instant où nous naissons est un pas vers la mort.

1. De quoi vit ce monsieur? 2. Je crois qu'il vit de ses rentes, mais Auguste prétend qu'il vit de son travail. 3. Qui vivra verra. 4. Pourquoi vous décourager si vite? qu'est-ce qui vous empêche de poursuivre votre entreprise? 5. De qui ou de quoi vous plaignez-vous? 6. A qui ou à quoi pensez-vous? 7. Je ne crains pas qu'il fasse cette faute. 8. Je crains de ne pas le voir. 9. Je craignais qu'il ne vînt pas. 10. Je crains qu'il ne lui arrive quelque accident. 11. Laquelle de ces éventualités craignez-vous le plus? 12. Desquels de ses amis se plaint-il? 13. Voici la malheureuse femme dont vous

plaigniez le sort ce matin. 14. Voici l'atelier où votre oncle avait coutume de peindre. 15. Je crains Dieu, cher Abner, et n'ai point d'autre crainte. —(*Racine.*)

1. Do they not live? Are they not living? 2. Did he not live (pret.)? Did he not live (past indef.)? 3. Shall we not live? Shall we not have lived. 4. Should we not live? Should we not have lived? 5. She is not compelled to it (*y être contrainte*); she had not been compelled to it; she would not have been compelled to it. 6. She does not complain of it (*s'en plaindre*); she has not complained of it; she would not complain of it. 7. We fear he will go out; we feared he would go out. 8. We do not fear his going out; we did not fear his going out. 9. Do you fear he will go out? Did you fear he would go out? 10. I fear to see him; I feared I should see him. 11. Which of these two events does she fear most (*le plus*)? 12. Of which of these two men do you complain? 13. This is (*voici*) the house in which we lived three years ago. 14. See the state in which I am; do you not pity me? 15. What prevents you from attending this course? 16. What do you think you will do? 17. Of what do you complain. 18. What is he thinking of? 19. What impudence! 20. What a misfortune!

116.

Pouvoir, *to be able, can, may.* **pouvant. pu**

je peux (or je puis), tu peux, il peut, nous pouvons, vous pouvez, ils peuvent.

je pouvais, tu pouvais, il pouvait, nous pouvions, vous pouviez, ils pouvaient.

je pus. je pourrai. je pourrais.

que je puisse, que tu puisses, qu'il puisse, que nous puissions, que vous puissiez, qu'ils puissent. que je pusse.

The four verbs **pouvoir, oser,** *to dare,* **cesser,** *to cease,* and **savoir,** *to know,* when used negatively, do not require **pas** or **point,** but may take it: —

I cannot do this, **je ne puis (or je ne puis pas) faire ceci.**[1]

May and *might* are translated by the verb **pouvoir,** with the following verb in the infinitive: —

That may be true,	**cela peut être vrai.**
An accident might happen,	**un accident pourrait arriver.**

They can be omitted in translation if they are treated as the auxiliary of a verb in the subjunctive; but, even then, the use of **pouvoir** is more forcible: —

I wish he might come, { **je voudrais qu'il vînt.**
je voudrais qu'il pût venir.

The simplest way to express what o'clock it is (see § 44), is to name the hour which has last struck and add to it the number of minutes which have since elapsed:

12.5,	**midi cinq.**	12.30,	**midi trente.**
12.10,	**midi dix.**	12.40,	**midi quarante.**
12.15,	**midi quinze.**	12.50,	**midi cinquante.**
12.20,	**midi vingt.**	12.55,	**midi cinquante-cinq.**

1. Si je pouvais finir ce travail à 11 heures 15, je partirais par le train de midi 15. 2. Vous ne pourrez pas le finir avant midi, vous ne partirez que par le train de 1 heure 25. 3. Vous arriverez chez votre oncle à 2 heures 10, vous pourrez régler votre affaire avec lui en trois quarts d'heure et revenir par le train de 3 heures 35. 4. Je ne pourrai régler une affaire si importante que celle-ci en trois quarts d'heure. 5. Ne pouvez-vous attendre jusqu'à demain? 6. Impossible; si je ne puis

[1] The addition of **pas** to **ne pouvoir** strengthens the negation. **je ne puis** supposes obstructions and difficulties; **je ne puis pas** expresses a complete impossibility.

y aller aujourd'hui, l'affaire est manquée. 7. Je ne crois pas d'ailleurs qu'il puisse vous être très utile. 8. Pourrez-vous tenir la promesse que vous m'avez faite ? 9. Cela pourrait bien arriver. 10. Il pourra venir un meilleur temps. 11. Il pouvait être (il est probable qu'il était) dix heures ; je venais d'éteindre ma lampe et de me coucher. 12. Depuis huit jours que nous sommes à Paris, nous n'avons pu nous joindre une seule fois.

1. He can go out at 1.15, but they will not be able to go out till 3.35. 2. They were not able (imperf.) to leave; he was not able (pret.) to leave. 3. They would not have been able to arrive before 4.50. 4. That they may be able; that we might be able; that he might have been able. 5. You may go away now; it is[1] half-past three. 6. Shall we be able to leave by the quarter before four o'clock train? 7. Since you have just (§ 108) bought the whole collection of Walter Scott's novels, you might (condit.) lend me one or two. 8. I shall lend you as many (§ 80) as you (will) desire. 9. They cannot get rid of it. 10. We are going to the theatre to-night; can you not come there with us? 11. I cannot, I am engaged; I should like (*je voudrais bien*) to go (§ 80) though! 12. He may go out if his tutor allows him (*it to him*). 13. Tell him that he may come with us if his father is willing (88, 110 (2)). 14. You might give us a holiday. 15. You might show me Virginia's letter; you remember that you promised to show it to me. 16. The man whose honesty you praised (*of whom you praised the honesty*) last night has just been condemned for theft. 17. You have just spoken to a lady whose sister I am about to marry.

[1] *It is*, being here an impersonal verb, must be translated by **il est**, not **c'est**.

117.

Vouloir, *to wish, to be willing.* **voulant. voulu.**

je veux, tu veux, il veut, nous voulons, vous voulez, ils veulent.

je voulais, tu voulais, il voulait, nous voulions, vous vouliez, ils voulaient.

je voulus. je voudrai. je voudrais.

que je veuille, que tu veuilles, qu'il veuille, que nous voulions, que vous vouliez, qu'ils veuillent. que je voulusse.

veuille, qu'il veuille, veuillons, veuillez, qu'ils veuillent.

en vouloir à, *to be angry with, to bear ill will to.*
s'en vouloir, *to be angry with one's self, to reproach one's self for.*
vouloir dire, *to mean.*

(1) The verb **vouloir** is followed by the infinitive without a preposition, or the subjunctive preceded by **que**. The infinitive is used when both verbs refer to the same person; the subjunctive, when the verbs refer to different persons. See § 96.

mon frère veut s'en aller,	*My brother wishes to go away.*
ma mère veut bien que vous restiez,	*My mother wishes you to stay.*

(2) When *will* and *would* mean *to wish* or *to be willing*, they are translated by the verb **vouloir**: —

I asked him to come, but he would not,	**je lui ai demandé de venir, mais il n'a pas voulu.**
Will you come to the country with me?	**voulez-vous venir à la campagne avec moi?**

In other words, when *would* expresses the past, translate it by **vouloir** in a past tense, as in the first of the above examples. But when *would* expresses the conditional (that is, refers to a future time expressed or understood) it is an auxiliary, and the next verb is put in the conditional; as, —

He would go to the country if it were fine weather,	**il irait à la campagne s'il faisait beau temps.**

(3) *Will you* must be thus translated by **voulez-vous** when the person addressed is asked to do a thing; and the answer *I will, I am quite willing, with pleasure, I have no objection*, is rendered by **je le veux bien**: —

Will you (do you wish to) go to the country with your brother? I am quite willing.	**voulez-vous aller à la campagne avec votre frère? je le veux bien.**

But *shall* and *will*, referring to future time, are auxiliaries of the future tense: —

irez-vous demain à la campagne?	*Shall you go to the country to-morrow?*

(4) The present of **vouloir** generally means *to will, to command*: —

The law commands it,	**la loi le veut.**
Do what I command you,	**faites ce que je veux.**

But, if the word **bien** is added to it, it softens the expression and gives it the sense of a consent: —

If it is agreeable to you, we shall go at once,	**si vous le voulez bien, nous partirons tout de suite.**

(5) **Je voudrais** or **je voudrais bien** expresses a mere wish: —

I should like to see that,	**je voudrais bien voir cela.**
He would like to go to the theatre, but his mother will not allow him,	**il voudrait aller au spectacle, mais sa mère ne le veut pas.**

(6) **Vouloir,** followed by an infinitive, means sometimes *to intend:* —

He intends to do nothing,	**il ne veut rien faire.**
She intends to leave to-morrow,	**elle veut partir demain**

1. Nous comptions partir par le train de deux heures et demie, mais mon tuteur ne l'a pas voulu. 2. Voudriez-vous que je vienne vous voir, quand vous serez à la campagne? 3. Voulez-vous prendre une tasse de thé avec moi? 4. Je le veux bien. 5. Elle ne veut pas attendre une minute de plus. 6. Une fois que l'homme de cœur a dit: "je veux," il se sent bien plus maître de lui qu'il ne le croyait auparavant. 7. Je veux bien que vous alliez patiner cette après-midi, mais je veux que vous soyez de retour avant cinq heures. 8. Je voudrais vous parler un moment en particulier. 9. Je voudrais bien être riche, je voyagerais six mois de l'année. 10. C'est l'homme le plus irrésolu que je connaisse, il ne sait jamais ce qu'il veut. 11. Celui-ci, au contraire, est un modèle de fermeté: il veut ce qu'il veut. 12. Que voulez-vous dire? 13. Je veux dire que j'ai raison, et que c'est vous qui avez tort.

14\. . . . . Veuillez être discret,
Et n'allez pas, de grâce, éventer mon secret.

— (*Molière.*)

1. I wish to go away. 2. I want him to go away. 3. I wished to pay him, but he would not receive my money. 4. They are ready to depart, they will not wait one minute longer (*de plus*). 5. They were wishing to send me to Germany, but I would not go. 6. Will you come to take a walk with me? With pleasure. 7. I wonder (*je m'étonne*) if you will receive (*recevrez*) your money to-day. 8. I am quite willing to receive it, but I know they will not give it to me. 9. I want him to come, he must obey me. 10. I consent that he may come. 11. If it is agreeable to you, we shall pay (*ferons*) a visit to your sister-in-law. 12. I wish I were rich! 13. I should like to see him beating you! 14. I

think she intends to write to you. 15. What does that mean? 16. When I am in the country (§ 49), would you like to come to see me? 17. Will you tell me, please, the name of the lady whom we heard sing (§ 98), last evening? 18. It is impossible for me to lend you this novel; I have promised to lend it to him.

118.

Devoir, *to owe, to have to, must, ought.* **devant.** **dû,**[1] **due.**

je dois, tu dois, il doit, nous devons, vous devez, ils doivent.

je devais. **je dus.** **je devrai.** **je devrais.**

que je doive, que tu doives, qu'il doive, que nous devions, que vous deviez, qu'ils doivent. **que je dusse.**

dois, qu'il doive, devons, devez, qu'ils doivent.

apercevoir, *to perceive, to see* (with the eyes).
s'apercevoir, *to be aware of, to notice* (by the mind).
recevoir, *to receive.* **décevoir,** *to deceive.*

Different Meanings of the Verb *devoir*.

(1) The original meaning of **devoir** is *to owe, to be owing:* —

He owes me money,	**il me doit de l'argent.**
He owes more than he possesses,	**il doit plus qu'il ne possède.**

Its figurative meaning is *to be one's duty*, as in most of the following cases: —

(2) When *should* can be changed into *ought*, translate it by **je devrais,** etc.; when *should have* can be changed into *ought to have*, translate it by **j'aurais dû,** etc., with the next verb in the present infinitive; as —

You should come with me,	**vous devriez venir avec moi.**
You should have come with me,	**vous auriez dû venir avec moi.**

[1] The circumflex accent is put upon the past participle **dû** merely to distinguish it from the article **du,** *of the.*

(3) When *to be* is followed by an infinitive, translate it by the verb **devoir**: —

He is to (intends to, shall) dine with us,	**il doit dîner avec nous.**
He was to (intended to) dine with us,	**il devait dîner avec nous.**

(4) When *to have* is followed by an infinitive, translate it either by **devoir** or by **avoir à**: —

She has to go out this morning,	**elle doit sortir ce matin.**
She is obliged to go out this morning,	**elle a à sortir ce matin.**

(5) When *must* implies supposition, translate it by **je dois**, etc., and *must have* by **j'ai dû**, etc., with the next verb in the infinitive present: —

You must be ill after so much fatigue,	**vous devez être malade après tant de fatigues.**
You must have been well pleased,	**vous avez dû être bien content.**
You must have been very glad to hear that your father arrived safely,	**vous avez dû être bien aise d'apprendre que M. votre père est arrivé sans accident.**

(6) The imperfect of the subjunctive (**dussé-je, dusses-tu, dût-il**, etc.), placed at the beginning of a clause, means *even though*: —

Even though I should be blamed, I shall support you,	**dussé-je être blâmé, je vous soutiendrai.**

1. Il me devait dix mille francs, il y a trois mois, mais aujourd'hui il ne m'en doit plus que cinq mille. 2. Vous lui devez tout. 3. C'est à elle qu'il doit la place qu'il occupe. 4. Je ne dois compte de mes actions à personne. 5. On devrait planter des arbres le long de cette route. 6. Vous auriez dû me prévenir. 7. Vous n'auriez pas dû sortir sans ma permission. 8. Je dois aller demain

à la campagne. 9. Il doit partir après-demain. 10. Il devait sortir hier. 11. Nous devons chanter ce soir. 12. Il doit y avoir cette semaine une assemblée de soldats. 13. C'est lui qui doit avoir fait cela.[1] 14. Des actes d'une nature si sublime doivent être rares. 15. Il a dû partir ce matin par le train de 9 heures 40. 16. Dussé-je être blâmé, je lui donnerai mon appui. 17. Dussions-nous échouer, nous essayerons.

18. Je dois quatre cents francs à mon marchand de vin,
Un fripon qui demeure au cabaret voisin.

— (*Regnard.*)

1. He does not receive; she is not received. 2. We have not received; she has not been received. 3. You were not receiving; she was not received. 4. I will not receive; she will not be received. 5. He will not have received; she will not have been received. 6. Thou wouldst not have received; she would not have been received. 7. That she may receive; that she might receive; that she may not have been received; that she might not have been received. 8. I owe her still fifty-one francs. 9. You should pay her at once. 10. You should have paid her when she was at my father's house last month. 11. I think I should not go out with you. 12. Should they not have sent me that parcel long ago? 13. We are to spend (*passer*) two months in the country this summer. 14. She was to pay (*rendre*) us a visit this morning, but we have not yet seen her. 15. I have to go to the market, come along (*venez*) with me. 16. You must be very hungry. 17. He must have left[1] last night or this morning. 18. You must have been

[1] It is seen by this sentence that *must have* is not invariably rendered by **j'ai du**, etc., as is said in the 5th Rule of this chapter. It is translated by **je dois avoir**, etc., when the action or its consequences are still lasting.

very sorry (*peiné*) to hear that your cousin was dead. 19. Even though he should scold me, I shall take a holiday. 20. What am I to bring (*apporter*) you? Would you like a glass of fresh water?

119.

Faire, *to do, to make.* **faisant.** **fait.**

je fais, tu fais, il fait, nous faisons, vous faites, ils font.

je faisais, tu faisais, il faisait, nous faisions, vous faisiez, ils faisaient.

je fis, tu fis, il fit, nous fîmes, vous fîtes, ils firent.

je ferai. **je ferais.** **que je fasse.** **que je fisse.**

fais, qu'il fasse, faisons, faites, qu'ils fassent.

In **faisant** and its derivatives (**faisons, faisais,** etc.) **ai** has the sound of *e mute.*

se faire à, *to accustom one's self to.*
défaire, *to undo, to overthrow.*
se défaire de, *to get rid of, to come undone.*
refaire, *to do over again.*
se refaire, *to recruit one's strength.*

faire une faute, *to make a mistake.*
faire une bévue, *to make a blunder.*
faire bon accueil, bonne mine, bon visage à, *to welcome.*
faire peur à, *to frighten.*
faire pitié, *to excite pity.* **faire plaisir,** *to afford pleasure.*

faire place à, *to make room for.* **faire faillite,** *to fail.*
faire naufrage, *to be shipwrecked.*

faire un voyage, *to take a journey.* **faire un pas,** *to take a step.*
faire un kilomètre, un mille, *to walk a kilometer, a mile.*
faire une promenade, un tour, un tour de promenade, *to take a walk.*
faire une course, *to go out on business.*
faire un tour de jardin, *to take a turn in the garden.*

faire, *to act, to pretend to be.*
faire le sourd, *to counterfeit deafness.*
faire le mort, *to feign death, to keep still.*
faire le difficile, *to be particular, hard to please.*
faire l'enfant, *to be childish.*
faire le magnanime, *to affect magnanimity.*

1. La description que vous venez de nous faire est très intéressante. 2. Quelles bévues j'ai faites dans cet exercice! 3. Je craignais qu'on ne nous fît pas bon accueil, mais on nous a reçus avec la plus franche cordialité. 4. Vous nous faites peur avec vos histoires de revenants; allez-vous-en, vilain homme! 5. Ce pauvre enfant nous faisait vraiment pitié; il avait les pieds nus et grelottait de froid. 6. Nous avons fait ce matin une petite promenade qui nous a fait beaucoup de plaisir. 7. Si vous me faites place près de vous, je vous conterai une petite histoire qui vous intéressera beaucoup. 8. Ce monsieur fait argent de tout. 9. Laissez-moi sortir, j'ai deux ou trois courses à faire avant le dîner. 10. Allez faire un tour de jardin, cela vous donnera de l'appétit. 11. Ne faites donc pas l'enfant, dites oui tout de suite, et partons. 12. Je crois, mon petit bonhomme, que tu fais le difficile; avant peu tu seras corrigé de ce défaut-là. 13. Tu me braves, Cinna, tu fais le magnanime!

1. We accustom ourselves to it (*se faire à*); they were accustoming themselves to it. 2. They accustomed themselves (pret.) to it; we had accustomed ourselves to it. 3. He will accustom himself to it; we shall have accustomed ourselves to it. 4. I should accustom myself to it; you would have accustomed yourselves to it. 5. That he may accustom himself to it; that you (sing.) may have accustomed yourself to it. 6. We are accustomed to it; we were accustomed to it (§110, note). 7. You make too many mistakes in your exercises, you are not attentive enough. 8. You frighten these children with your faces (*grimaces*). 9. We have enjoyed that walk: (*that walk caused great pleasure to us.*) 10. We were shipwrecked (pret.) on the 2d of April, 1870. 11. I heard your uncle had failed lately, I hope

that it is not true. 12. What a grand voyage I took that summer! I shall never forget it. 13. How many kilometres did you walk[1] this morning? 14. I walked only seven or eight. 15. Come (and) take a turn in the garden, you will see what beautiful roses and (what) dahlias we have. 16. Don't be childish, put on your hat and go take a walk with your cousin. 17. He pretends to be deaf, but he hears all that we say. 18. Were you not rather particular when you were young?

120.

(1) Used impersonally, the verb **faire** expresses the state of the weather: —

il fait jour, *it is daylight.*
il fait nuit, *it is night.*
il fait sombre, *it is dark.*
il fait beau temps, or simply **beau**, *it is fine weather.*
il fait mauvais temps, or simply **mauvais**, *it is bad weather.*
il fait chaud, *it is warm.*
il fait froid, *it is cold.*
il fait soleil, *it is sunny.*
il fait clair de lune, *it is moonlight.*
il fait du vent, *it is windy.*
il fait de la pluie, or **il pleut**, *it rains.*
il fait du brouillard, *it is foggy.*
il fait de la neige, or **il neige**, *it snows.*
il fait de la grêle, or **il grêle**, *it hails.*
il fait bon, *it is pleasant.*
il fait doux, *it is mild.*
il fait humide, *it is damp.*
il fait glissant, *it is slippery.*
il fait sec, *it is dry.*
il fait des éclairs, *there is lightning.*
il fait de la poussière, *it is dusty.*
il fait de l'orage, *it is stormy.*
il fait du tonnerre, or **il tonne**, *it is thundering.*
il fait sale, *it is dirty.*

If the word **temps, air, route, rue**, etc., is made the subject of the verb, **être**, not **faire**, must be used: —

le temps est beau,	*the weather is fine.*
le temps est froid,	*the weather is cold.*
l'air est doux,	*the air is mild.*
le pavé est glissant,	*the pavement is slippery.*
les rues sont sales,	*the streets are dirty.*

[1] The past participle **fait** is invariable when it is used intransitively.

(2) **Année, journée, matinée,** and **soirée** are used: (*a*) to express the whole duration of the *year, day, morning,* and *evening;* (*b*) in speaking of the weather.

In all other cases use **an, jour, matin,** and **soir**: —

on travaille toute l'année, toute la journée, toute la matinée, toute la soirée. — on paye à un ouvrier sa journée. — on souhaite une bonne et heureuse année. — des années de sècheresse, d'abondance. — l'année, la journée, etc., **sont belles, pluvieuses.**	*People work the whole year, the whole day, the whole morning, the whole evening. — A workman is paid for his day's work. — People wish a happy new year. — Years of drought, of abundance. — The year, the day,* etc., *are fine, wet.*
un événement a eu lieu l'an 1870, tel jour, un matin, un soir. — le soleil se lève le matin et se couche le soir. — mon frère a vingt ans. — il y a trois ans que nous ne l'avons vu. — il gagne cinq mille francs par an.	*Such an event took place in the year* 1870, *on such a day, in the morning, in the evening. — The sun rises in the morning and sets in the evening. — My brother is twenty years old. — We have not seen him for three years. — He makes five thousand francs a year.*

1. Il fait un temps charmant ce matin: quelle belle promenade nous allons faire! 2. L'air est un peu froid, mais il fait un soleil magnifique. 3. Ne trouvez-vous pas qu'il fait un peu trop de vent? 4. Peut-être, mais c'est un vent nord-ouest qui nous rafraîchera. 5. Vous souvenez-vous du temps qu'il faisait samedi dernier? 6. Le matin il a fait du brouillard, à midi il pleuvait, et le soir la neige tombait à gros flocons. 7. Quelle journée désagréable nous avons eue là, et quelle triste promenade nous avons faite! 8. Oui, mais le lendemain quelle agréable soirée nous avons passée au parc! 9. Il faisait un beau clair de lune, et l'air était doux quoiqu'un peu humide. 10. Quel beau jour! 11. Quelle belle journée!
12. Pendant ces derniers temps, combien en a-t-on vus
Qui du soir au matin sont pauvres devenus
Pour vouloir trop tôt être riches! — (*La Fontaine.*)

1. I am getting rid of them (*s'en défaire*); thou hast got rid of them. 2. He got rid of them (pret.); we were getting rid of them. 3. You will get rid of them; they shall have got rid of them. 4. That he may get rid of us; that they might have got rid of her. 5. Let us get rid of him; let them not get rid of us. 6. What a fine morning! 7. What a splendid evening! 8. If the weather is dry to-morrow, we shall go to the country. 9. The weather will be dry and warm, I think, but it will be dusty. 10. I have just received a letter from London; they tell me it has been foggy there for the last ten days.[1] 11. Take an umbrella if you go out, it will be wet in less than (*before*) an hour. 12. The streets are always dirty in that quarter of the town. 13. The air is very cold, but it is very pleasant in your parlor. 14. Is it daylight at five o'clock? 15. No, not yet; the sun rose at six o'clock this morning. 16. What a fine day we have had! 17. Who is that gentleman to whom you were just speaking? 18. Why, don't you know? That is the President (*Monsieur le Président*) of the French Republic, a man whom everybody respects.

121.

In a great number of cases, **faire** is immediately followed by an infinitive; it then means *to cause* or *to get* or *to have something done*, and becomes in many of its constructions an auxiliary verb.

je fais bâtir une maison,	*I am building a house.*
j'ai fait bâtir une maison,	*I have built a house.*

[1] *Last* is not rendered here, as the verb being in the present and the preposition **depuis** show that the fog is still continuing.

il m'a fait sortir, *He made me go out.*
elle a fait relier sa grammaire, *She has had her grammar bound.*
je vous ferai nommer capitaine, *I shall get you made a captain.*
nous ferons venir le médecin, *We shall send for the doctor.*
je ferai bâtir ma maison à or par cet architecte, *I shall have my house built by this architect.*
j'ai fait dire par un messager au médecin de venir, *I sent word by a messenger to the doctor to come.*
vous faites dire à Cicéron une chose qu'il n'a jamais dite, *You make Cicero say a thing which he never said.*
il a fait faire un nouvel habit, *He has had a new coat made.*
faites repasser mon chapeau, *Have my hat ironed.*

If the infinitive following **faire** is a pronominal verb, its pronoun-object is generally omitted: —

je l'en ferai repentir,
instead of } *I shall make him repent.*
je l'en ferai se repentir,

In the auxiliary uses of **faire** with the infinitive, the pronoun-objects precede **faire** in all forms except the imperative affirmative, where they follow it.[1]

faites-le bien garder, *Have him well kept.*
je le ferai partir, *I shall make him set out.*
non, ne le faites pas partir, *No, don't make him set out.*

Faire followed by an infinitive has no passive. If, therefore, you translate *to put to death* by **faire mourir,** do not say, **il a été fait mourir,** but **on l'a fait mourir.**

ne faire que sortir, *to do nothing but go out.*
ne faire que de sortir, *to have but just gone out.*
faire savoir, *to let know.* **faire faire,** *to get made* or *done.*
faire venir, *to send for.* **faire dire,** *to send word.*

[1] The same rule applies to **laisser** with the infinitive: —
laissez-le sortir, *let him go out.*
ne le laissez pas sortir, *do not let him go out.*
je le laisserai sortir, *I shall let him go out.*

1. Mon oncle a fait bâtir une maison à la campagne cet été. 2. Vous m'avez fait faire une bévue. 3. Je me ferai couper les cheveux cette semaine. 4. Faites porter cette lettre à la poste. 5. Faites venir le médecin. 6. Non, ne le faites pas venir, elle va beaucoup mieux. 7. Le travail fait dormir. 8. Faites entrer cette dame, mais ne la faites pas monter au salon. 9. Cette pauvre bête souffrait tant qu'on l'a fait[1] mourir. 10. Votre visite a détruit les soupçons qu'un malentendu avait fait naître. 11. On vous fera savoir tout ce qui s'est passé. 12. Faites-le asseoir sur cette chaise. 13. Faites-moi donc voir la photographie de votre frère. 14. Vous ne faites que jouer toute la journée. 15. Nous ne faisons que d'arriver. 16. Mon frère ne fait que de sortir. 17. Vous ne faisiez que d'entrer.

1. You make me laugh. 2. Get your coat mended. 3. I shall have him punished by his master. 4. Did you get my parcel carried to the bookseller's? 5. If you like, I will send for your brother-in-law. 6. I shall make him rise at half-past six. 7. They make us go to bed at half-past eight every evening. 8. Make him work ten hours a day. 9. I cannot make him work two hours; I never saw a (§ 42, 2) more lazy boy. 10. They did not let me know your arrival in (*à*) time. 11. I shall get a little bridge made over that stream. 12. He has been put out of the room (*one has made him go out. . . .*). 13. He does nothing but play the whole evening. 14. They do nothing but go and come. 15. She has (pres. of *faire*) but just arrived. 16. I ought to have my hair (plural) cut; don't you think it is too long? 17. I wish to have a new coat made: would you please send to my house the best tailor that you know?

[1] The participle **fait** followed by an infinitive is always invariable, because it is considered as forming a single word with the infinitive.

122.

Plaire, *to please.* **plaisant.** **plu.**

je plais, tu plais, il plaît, nous plaisons, vous plaisez, ils plaisent.

je plaisais. **je plus.** **je plairai.** **je plairais.**

que je plaise. **que je plusse.**

plais, qu'il plaise, plaisons, plaisez, qu'ils plaisent.

The **i** of the root of **plaire, complaire,** etc., takes a circumflex accent before **t.** The participle **plu** is always invariable.

se plaire à, *to like* (a place).
complaire, *to humor.*
se complaire, *to delight in.*
déplaire, *to displease.*
se déplaire à, *to dislike* (a place).
taire, *to pass over in silence.*
se taire, *to remain silent, to hold one's tongue.*

Conduire, *to conduct, to lead.* **conduisant.** **conduit.**

je conduis, tu conduis, il conduit, nous conduisons, vous conduisez, ils conduisent.

je conduisais. **je conduisis.** **je conduirai.** **je conduirais.**

que je conduise. **que je conduisisse.**

conduis, qu'il conduise, conduisons, conduisez, qu'ils conduisent.

se conduire, *to behave.*
construire, *to construct, to build.*
se construire, *to construe.*
cuire, *to cook, to bake.*
détruire, *to destroy.*
instruire, *to instruct.*
produire, *to produce.*
réduire, *to reduce.*
traduire, *to translate.*

The Passive Form.

For translation of the English passive, see § 83, 1.

I was scolded this morning, **on m'a grondé ce matin.**
He has been punished by his father, **son père l'a puni.**

The passive voice is also elegantly rendered in French by the pronominal form, in speaking of inanimate objects: —

This sells (is sold) *very well,* **ceci se vend très bien.**

1. Elle a le don de plaire. 2. Ce qui lui a plu lui plaira toujours. 3. Cela ne plaît pas à tout le monde. 4. Vous plairait-il de venir dîner avec moi à la campagne ? 5. Je ne me déplais pas ici. 6. Il paraît que vous vous plaisiez à Paris. 7. La vigne se plaît dans les terrains pierreux. 8. On a bien mal traduit cette phrase ; le sens qu'on en a donné est tout différent du vrai sens. 9. Tous vos arguments se réduisent à démontrer que vous n'avez pas eu tout à fait tort. 10. Une foule de fautes se sont trouvées dans votre première édition. 11. Les adjectifs *sur* et *certain* se construisent avec *de*. 12. Il nous a tû les détails. 13. Faites taire votre chien. 14. Voulez-vous vous taire, impertinente ; vous venez toujours mêler vos extravagances à toutes choses.

15. Messieurs les courtisans, cessez de vous détruire ;
Faites, si vous pouvez, votre cour sans vous nuire.

1. I like the place (*s'y plaire*) ; she has liked the place. 2. We used to like the place ; he liked the place (pret.). 3. You will like the place ; they would have liked the place. 4. He is behaving better ; they used to behave better. 5. She has behaved better ; she had behaved better. 6. We should behave better ; we should have behaved better. 7. Show her, if you please, the letter which I addressed to you on Wednesday. 8. This house has been very badly constructed, there are draughts in every room. 9. I confess that I was wrong to write you that letter, I had been led into error (lead into error, *faire égarer*). 10. Has this letter been translated ? 11. Yes, sir, it has been translated by your brother. 12. I was told that you had behaved badly last Sunday (*dimanche dernier*). 13. Take me to your father's office, I wish to speak to him on (*pour*) business. 14. Sir, I am told (*dit*) that your brother has failed ; do you know

anything (*quelque chose*) about it (*en*)? 15. I was told the same thing an hour ago. 16. His books sell very well. 17. Wood is sold very dear in this country. 18. That is worn no longer. 19. Advise him to hold his tongue. 20. Do hold your tongue!

123.

Dire, *to tell, to say.* **disant.** **dit.**

je dis, tu dis, il dit, nous disons, vous dites, ils disent.

je disais, tu disais, il disait, nous disions, vous disiez, ils disaient.

je dis, tu dis, il dit, nous dîmes, vous dîtes, ils dirent.

je dirai. **je dirais.** **que je dise.** **que je disse.**

dis, qu'il dise, disons, dites, qu'ils disent.

redire, *to say again,* is conjugated in all tenses and persons like **dire**.

se dédire, *to retract one's word,*
contredire, *to contradict,*
interdire, *to forbid,*
médire, *to speak ill of, to slander,*
prédire, *to predict,*
} make in the second person plural of the present indicative and in the imperative: **dédisez, contredisez, interdisez, médisez,** and **prédisez.**

maudire, *to curse,* doubles the **s** in the plural of the pres. indic. and imper., in the imperf. indic., the pres. part., and the subjunctive.

For the use of **ne** without **pas** or **point** see §§ 89, 90 (4), 106, 116.

Ne is also commonly used without **pas** or **point**: —

(1) After **si** used negatively and meaning *unless*: —

j'irai le trouver, si vous n'y allez vous-même,	*I will go to him if you yourself do not go.*

(2) After **que** beginning a negative sentence and meaning *why*: —

que ne lui dites-vous tout ce qui s'est passé?	*Why do you not tell him all that has taken place?*

This form of speaking is used only to hint a reproach, a regret, or a wish. For a real interrogation **pourquoi** must be used.

(3) After **depuis que**, **il y a . . . que**, followed by the past indefinite, with a negative meaning; as —

il y a dix jours que je ne l'ai vu, *It is ten days since I saw him.*

If the verb is not in the past indefinite, **pas** or **point** must be used: —

il y a dix jours que nous ne nous parlons point,	*We have not spoken to each other for ten days.*
il y avait dix jours que nous ne nous parlions point,	*We had not spoken to each other for ten days.*

See also § 126 (3).

I say! **dites donc** (the **c** of **donc** is not sounded here).
To tell the truth, **à dire vrai,** or **à vrai dire.**
All is said, **voilà qui est dit, tout est dit.**
That is a matter of course, **cela va sans dire.**
Without uttering a word, **sans mot dire.**
So to say, so to speak, **pour ainsi dire.** *That is to say,* **c'est-à-dire.**

1. Vous lui direz bien des choses honnêtes de ma part. 2. Je me le suis dit vingt fois. 3. Il est parti sans mot dire. 4. Il paraît qu'on vous a reçu autrement que vous ne l'espériez; je vous l'avais bien dit (*I told you so before, you were warned*). 5. Il a, m'a-t-on dit, l'intention de parler. 6. Je crains qu'il ne m'interdise cette démarche. 7. Prenez garde qu'il ne se dédise. 8. Elle dira la chose mieux que vous ne pensez. 9. Il ne sait que dire. 10. Voilà qui est dit (la chose est convenue). 11. Dites donc, mon ami, qu'est-ce que vous faites là? 12. Ils sont, pour ainsi dire, morts à toutes les joies. 13. Vous avez bien raison, mon cher maître; on veut toujours dire mieux qu'on ne doit dire; c'est le défaut de presque tous nos écrivains. 14. Que ne vous est-il permis de m'accompagner! 15. Que n'est-il à cent lieues de nous! 16. Je ne sortirai point si vous ne venez me prendre en voiture. 17. Prince, si tu n'as des vertus, on te rendra des hom-

mages, et on te haïra. 18. Bien des choses se sont passées depuis que je ne vous ai vu. 19. Il y a six mois que je ne lui parle plus.

1. You say so;[1] they were saying so. 2. They have not said so; he said (pret.) so. 3. We shall say so; we shall have said so. 4. That you may say so; that you might say so; that you might have said so. 5. I do not know why you always contradict me. 6. I do not know if the day will be fine to-morrow, I cannot predict the weather. 7. She will repeat the story better than people think. 8. I say, take care lest[2] they (*on*) forbid you to come here. 9. I fear that she will contradict you. 10. I say, why did you not send the letter which you wrote yesterday? 11. To tell the truth, I am too idle to write. 12. What does he mean? 13. All is said, we shall leave together at nine. 14. I am always wrong, and you are always right, that's a matter of course. 15. If you don't come at once, I am off. 16. If you are cold, why (*que*) do you not put on your great-coat? 17. Tell me, why did you never visit your aunt? 18. I have not spoken to him for a long time [*it is* (*a*) *long time since* (*que*) *I have spoken* (neg.) *to him*]. 19. *Turn the same sentence into,* It is a long time since I no longer speak to him. 20. Since I saw you (neg.), things have changed much (*bien changé*). 21. Now that (*depuis que*) I no longer see you, I am sad and ill. 22. How have you been since I saw you (neg.)?

[1] *So* is translated after transitive verbs by **le**, after intransitive verbs by **ainsi**: —

To think so, **le penser.**	*To speak so,* **parler ainsi.**
To believe so, **le croire.**	*To act so,* **agir ainsi.**
To say so, **le dire.**	*To behave so,* **se conduire ainsi.**
To do so, **le faire,** etc.	

[2] *Lest,* after the verbs *to fear, to be afraid, to tremble, to take care,* is translated simply by **que.**

124.

Lire, *to read.* **lisant.** **lu.**

je lis, tu lis, il lit, nous lisons, vous lisez, ils lisent.

je lisais. **je lus.** **je lirai.** **je lirais.**

que je lise. **que je lusse.**

lis, qu'il lise, lisons, lisez, qu'ils lisent.

Ecrire, *to write.* **écrivant.** **écrit.**

j'écris, tu écris, il écrit, nous écrivons, vous écrivez, ils écrivent.

j'écrivais. **j'écrivis.** **j'écrirai.** **j'écrirais.**

que j'écrive. **que j'écrivisse.**

écris, qu'il écrive, écrivons, écrivez, qu'ils écrivent.

décrire, *to describe.* **souscrire,** *to subscribe.*
prescrire, *to prescribe.* **transcrire,** *to transcribe.*

The Adverb.

Mieux, bien, mal, jamais, toujours, pas, plus, and **trop,** generally precede the infinitive: —

mieux écrire, bien parler, mal prononcer, ne jamais se tromper, ne pas rire, ne plus manger, trop courir.

For the position of adverbs and adverbial phrases in simple and compound tenses, see § 41.

These words and phrases require the preposition **de** before a following adjective or participle: —

quelque chose, *something* or *anything.*
rien, *nothing* or *not anything.*
quelqu'un, *somebody* or *anybody.*
personne, *nobody.*
que (interrogative), *what.*
quoi (admirative), *what.*
tout ce que, *all that.*

quelque chose de nouveau, *something new.*
rien de bon, *nothing good.*
quelqu'un de malade, *somebody ill.*
personne de blessé, *nobody wounded.*

qu'y a-t-il de nouveau ?	*what is there new ?*
quoi de plus charmant que ce poème ?	*what is more charming than this poem ?*
tout ce qu'il y a de beau.	*all that is beautiful.*

1. Ne me parlez pas, je lis en ce moment quelque chose de très intéressant. 2. Il n'y a rien de nouveau dans les journaux que j'ai lus ce matin. 3. Les voici, je crois, ce sont eux que votre frère vient de jeter sur le fauteuil. 4. Ne lisez pas si haut, il y a quelqu'un de malade dans la chambre voisine. 5. Qu'on est heureux d'aimer à lire ! a dit Mme de Sévigné. 6. Oui, mais qu'a dit Rollin, ce bon et modeste Rollin que Montesquieu a appelé *l'abeille de la France :* "On songe plus à lire beaucoup qu'à lire utilement." 7. Il n'y a de[1] bon que ce qu'on peut relire sans dégoût (*Voltaire*). 8. Avec quelque attention que j'aie lu cet écrivain, sa pensée m'a échappé (*Condillac*). 9. On s'accoutume à bien parler en lisant les auteurs qui ont bien écrit (*Voltaire*). 10. Ecrivez-moi votre nom au bas de ce petit papier. 11. Il vous a écrit que son frère était impatient de recevoir de vos nouvelles ;[2] pourquoi ne lui avez-vous pas répondu ? 12. Je vous ai écrit que j'étais malade, mais vous n'en avez pas tenu compte. 13. Je ne vous ai pas écrit que je fusse rétabli. 14. Ces deux personnes s'écrivent. 15. Tout ce qui se dit ne s'écrit pas.

16. Son visage était triste et beau ;
A la lueur de mon flambeau,
Dans mon livre ouvert il vint lire.
— (*A. de Musset.*)

1. Are you reading ? Were they writing ? 2. He reads better than he writes, but that is not saying (*vouloir*

[1] The **de** is required by **rien** understood.
[2] *To hear of* or *from* (p.) is **recevoir des nouvelles de** (p.).

dire) much. 3. He wrote and read very well; he was the best pupil that I ever had. 4. You should (118) try to read better. 5. You ought to read better books. 6. Doctor (*le docteur*) Robinson has advised me to read no more at night (*le soir*). 7. Get away now, you will not have anything more. 8. Is there anybody ill in your house? 9. No, madam, there is nobody seriously ill, but we are all somewhat (*un peu*) indisposed. 10. Have you anything good to eat? 11. Here is, sir, all that is (*tout ce qu'il y a de*) good in the house. 12. What[1] (can be) more fortunate than what happens to you? 13. I entreat you not to show him my letter? 14. I recommend you not to speak to him any more. 15. She consented not to go away. 16. I wrote you to come at once; why did you not obey me? 17. She will not have the boldness to write me after such a scandal (*a such scandal*). 18. Have you no remedy to prescribe for my headache? 19. It is not so easy as you think to prescribe remedies for an imaginary illness. 20. This is pleasant to read. 21. Where is your father? I have come here to speak to him. 22. I did my very best to persuade him.

125.

Rire, *to laugh.* **riant.** **ri.**

je ris, tu ris, il rit, nous rions, vous riez, ils rient.

je riais. **je ris.** **je rirai.** **je rirais.**

que je rie. **que je risse.**

ris, qu'il rie, rions, riez, qu'ils rient.

se rire de, } *to laugh at.*
rire au nez de, }

sourire, *to smile.*
se moquer de, *to make fun of.*

Nuire, *to injure,* **nuisant, nui,** and **luire,** *to shine,* **luisant, lui,** are conjugated like **conduire,** § 122; the past participles **nui** and **lui** are always invariable; **luire** has no preterite and no imperfect subjunctive.

[1] *What,* followed by an adjective, is translated by **quoi de.**

***For* translated by depuis, pendant, or pour.**[1]

Depuis marks the beginning of a period of time; **pendant** marks the whole duration from beginning to end, and is often omitted; see §§ 59, 60.

He has been unwell for a week,	**il est malade depuis huit jours.**
He was unwell only for three days,	**il n'a été malade que pendant trois jours,** *or simply*, **que trois jours.**

Pour denotes the end: —

He has gone for three weeks,	**il est parti pour trois semaines.**
We have provisions for the whole winter,	**nous avons des provisions pour tout l'hiver.**

Avant, auparavant, devant (*before*).

(1) **Avant** denotes time, and, being a preposition, requires an object. It is used in opposition to **après**, *after*: —

il est arrivé une heure avant moi,	*He arrived an hour before me.*

(2) **Auparavant** also denotes time, but, being an adverb, it cannot have an object: —

je partirai avec vous, mais je veux finir cette lettre auparavant,	*I shall leave with you, but I want to finish this letter before.*

(3) **Devant** marks a situation, and its contrary is **derrière** (*behind*). **Devant** may mean also *in presence of.*

ne vous placez pas devant cette dame,	*Do not place yourself before that lady.*
ne répétez pas cela devant elle,	*Do not repeat that in her presence.*

[1] The following diagram may help pupils to remember the distinction between **depuis, pendant,** and **pour**: —

beginning.	**depuis**	**pour**	end.		beginning.	**pendant**	end.

Dans and *en* used to express Time.

Dans marks the end of an action, and **en** the time of performing it: —

il fera cela dans trois jours,	*He will do that in three days* (after three days have elapsed).
il fera cela en trois jours,	*He will finish that in three days* (it will not take him more than three days to finish that).

1. Vous riez; qu'y a-t-il donc de si comique dans ce que je dis là? 2. Je riais des menaces que vous me faites. 3. Vous voulez rire; il n'est pas possible qu'on soit si bête! 4. Il se rit de tout ce que vous pouvez dire et faire contre lui. 5. Je crois qu'il a cherché à vous nuire quand nous voyagions en Ecosse. 6. On me l'a dit à Edimbourg, mais je m'en suis moqué. 7. Longtemps (*or* pendant longtemps) j'ai craint l'effet de ses propos, mais depuis trois ans je ne m'en inquiète plus. 8. Vous savez sans doute que, depuis que j'ai hérité de mon oncle, j'ai de quoi vivre pour toute ma vie. 9. Madame, vos bons offices n'ont pas nui à mon succès; je vous suis fort obligé. 10. Ils se sont nui l'un à l'autre. 11. On voyait de loin luire les épées, les casques et les cuirasses. 12. Le soleil luit pour tout le monde. 13. Tout ce qui reluit n'est pas or. 14. Allez devant moi, je vous en prie. 15. Voilà ce que je faisais auparavant, mais maintenant je n'en ferai rien; c'est à vous d'aller le premier. 16. Avant de partir il m'a dit qu'il serait de retour dans huit jours.

1. I am not laughing; you are not reading; they are not writing. 2. We were not laughing; he was not reading; thou wast not writing. 3. I did not laugh (pret.);

he did not read; they did not write. 4. We shall not laugh; you would not read; they would not have written. 5. That I may not laugh; that he might not read; that you might not have written. 6. She has been very well all this winter. 7. Only she has had (*she has*) a bad (*gros*) cold for the (last) ten days. 8. I have been studying French for the (last) six months; I take a lesson every second day (*tous les deux jours*). 9. My father has left for three months; he is travelling on the Continent. 10. Have you (got) enough pocket money for a whole week? 11. Do not wait for me; I have to write for two hours. 12. I think they have been in England for the last three years, but, before, they lived long in North America. 13. We walked from Rheims to Paris in three days, and arrived a few hours before your father. 14. In a week I shall resume my work, and I will study nothing but French for two months and a half. 15. I wish you would repeat that before your cousin; she studies much less than she ought. 16. She is learning to write; she is only nine years old. 17. She wrote to us to tell us of her arrival. 18. That is not easy to describe.

126.

Croire, *to believe.* **croyant. cru.** (See § 86.)

je crois. je croyais. je crus. je croirai. je croirais.

que je croie, etc., que nous croyions, que vous croyiez, qu'ils croient.

que je crusse. crois, qu'il croie, croyons, croyez, qu'ils croient.

Used affirmatively, **croire** (as well as **penser**) is followed by the indicative; used negatively or interrogatively, it requires the subjunctive if there is a doubt in the speaker's mind as to the fact mentioned in the question: —

je crois qu'elle viendra,	*I believe she will come.*
je ne crois pas qu'elle vienne,	*I do not believe she will come.*
croyez-vous qu'elle vienne ?	*Do you believe she will come ?*
est-ce que vous croyez qu'elle viendra ?	*You don't believe she will come, do you ?*

Vaincre, *to conquer, overcome.* **vainquant.** **vaincu.**

je vaincs, tu vaincs, il vainc, nous vainquons, vous vainquez, ils vainquent.

je vainquais. je vainquis. je vaincrai. je vaincrais.

que je vainque. que je vainquisse.

vaincs, qu'il vainque, vainquons, vainquez, qu'ils vainquent.

convaincre, *to convince.*

Observe that the letter **c** is changed into **qu** before **a, e, i, o.**

The present and imperfect indicative and the singular of the present subjunctive are seldom used. **Etre victorieux** or **vainqueur** are employed instead.

conquérir, *to conquer, to gain possession of.*

The Conjunction *que.*

(1) **Que** may be used to avoid the repetition of any conjunction: —

comme je n'ai pas beaucoup d'argent et que je suis un peu malade, je ne ferai pas ce voyage,	*As I have not much money, and as I am rather unwell, I shall not take that journey.*

(2) **Que** requires the subjunctive ONLY when it stands for a conjunction requiring the subjunctive, or for **si**: —

venez que nous vous grondions,	*Come that we may scold you.*
s'il vient, et que je ne sois pas à la maison, faites venir mon frère,	*If he comes, and I should not be at home, send for my brother.*

(3) **Ne** is required before the following verb when **que** stands for **à moins que, avant que, sans que, jusqu'à**

ce que, de peur que, de crainte que, and **depuis que** (or **il y a . . . que**): —

je ne partirai pas d'ici que vous ne m'ayez tout confessé,	*I shall not go from this place till you have confessed everything to me.*
je ne partirai pas que vous n'arriviez,	*I shall not leave before* (or *till*) *you arrive.*
je ne puis travailler qu'aussitôt je ne sois malade,	*I cannot work without being immediately ill.*
je ne leur donnai point de repos qu'ils ne m'eussent fait venir un fripier,	*I gave them no rest till they had sent for an old clothesman.*
prenez garde (de peur *or* **de crainte) qu'il ne vous voie,**	*Take care lest he see you.*
Il y a deux mois que je ne l'ai vu,	*I have not seen him for two months.*
il s'est passé bien des choses depuis que nous ne nous sommes vus,	*Many things have taken place since we have seen each other.*

Observe that, when **que** stands for any of the four conjunctions, **à moins que, avant que, sans que,** and **jusqu'à ce que,** the first clause of the sentence must be negative.[1]

(4) **Que** is also used for the adverbs *how*, *how much*, *how many*, and expresses wonder, irony, indignation. The adjective following it must be translated without **très, bien,** or **fort**: —

qu'il a l'air maladroit!	*How very awkward he looks!*

The adjective or adverb following **que** is generally put after the verb in French, as in the preceding example. If, instead of an adjective or an adverb, a noun is modified by **que**, the noun may also be placed after the verb, but is more commonly placed after **que.**

que la révolution française a détruit de préjugés! or, **que de préjugés la révolution française a détruits!**	*How many prejudices has the French Revolution destroyed!*

[1] However, **que** may stand for **jusqu'à ce que** after **attendre** used without a negation: *Wait till I come down,* **attendez que je descende.**

The conjunction *and*, sometimes used after the verbs *to go, to come, to run*, is omitted in French: as, —

Go and take that letter to your uncle.	**allez porter cette lettre à votre oncle.**
Will you come and take a walk with me?	**voulez-vous venir faire un tour avec moi?**

1. Si vous croyez ce qu'elle vous dit, et que, malgré cela, vous agissiez contre ses intérêts, je ne vous pardonnerais de ma vie. (*See* § 113, *note* 1.) 2. Je ne saurais faire un pas que je ne l'aie aussitôt à mes trousses. 3. Il ne peut faire un seul mouvement du bras que la douleur ne lui arrache un cri. 4. Puisqu'ils vous ont désobéi, je ne leur permettrai pas de sortir qu'ils ne vous demandent pardon. 5. A quelles ruses hypocrites ces gens-là ont dû descendre, que de mensonges savamment élaborés ils ont débités, que de crimes ils ont commis, pour arriver au rang qu'ils occupent! 6. Qu'étiez-vous donc devenu, mon petit ami? il y a bien (*full*) quinze jours que nous ne vous avons vu. Nous vous croyions malade? 7. Ce qui se dit souvent finit par se croire. 8. Je croyais à cet homme plus de droiture qu'il n'en a. 9. Sapor, roi des Perses, vainquit et fit prisonnier l'empereur Valérien l'an 260 après J. C. 10. Il faut tâcher de vaincre cette difficulté. 11. Je suis parvenu à vaincre son indifférence et sa froideur. 12. Miltiade, après s'être rendu maître de la Chersonèse, après avoir conquis Lemnos et les Cyclades, après avoir vaincu à Marathon, fut accusé de trahison et mourut dans les fers. 13. Je ne pouvais faire autrement; je me suis laissé vaincre par ses prières et par ses larmes. 14. J'ai fait ce que j'ai pu pour le convaincre. 15. Cela doit suffire pour vous convaincre que je n'ai pas voulu mal faire. 16. Qui veut vaincre est déja bien près de la victoire.

1. I can hardly (*avoir de la peine à*) believe that; an you, Miss, do you believe it? 2. No, sir, I do not believe that the affair took place (*se passer*) so. 3. Is it believed (active with *on*)? was it believed? has it been believed? 4. Will it be believed? would it be believed? would it have been believed? 5. If they go to my house, and if I be not there, they will certainly come here. 6. Wait till he comes. 7. We shall not leave till we have seen him. 8. Do not send your letter till you have showed it to me. 9. He cannot walk (*faire*) a mile without being tired. 10. How often (*how many times*) I have come here! 11. How many services he has rendered me! 12. How very pleasant that remembrance must (§ 118) be to you! 13. How long that night seemed to me! 14. I came, I saw, I conquered. 15. We were unable to conquer his resistance; I never saw a (§ 42, 2) more obstinate fellow. 16. Try, and you will conquer all these difficulties. 17. He conquered an enemy worthy of himself (*lui*). 18. Run and tell him that we have arrived. 19. Come and pay (*faire* or *rendre*) a visit to my mother.

127.

Falloir, impersonal verb, *must, to be necessary, want.*

No present participle. **fallu.**

il faut. **il fallait.** **il fallut.** **il faudra.** **il faudrait.**

qu'il faille. **qu'il fallût.**

We have seen (§ 118) that *must* implying supposition is translated by **je dois, tu dois,** etc., and *must have* by **j'ai dû, tu as dû,** etc.; as, —

You must be hungry,	**vous devez avoir faim.**

In all other cases *must* is translated by **falloir** in one of the four following ways: —

(1) When it is clear who *must* or *must not* do a thing, the pronoun-subject of *must* is not translated, and the next verb is put in the infinitive; as,—

We must always speak the truth,	**il faut toujours dire la vérité,**
You must not[1] *break this glass,*	**il ne faut pas casser ce verre.**

(2) If the subject of *must* (whether a noun or a pronoun) has to be expressed, *must* is translated by **il faut que**, and the next verb is put in the subjunctive:—

She must go out,	**il faut qu'elle sorte.**
The servant must not come,	**il ne faut pas que la bonne vienne.**

(3) Or, again, if the subject of *must* is a pronoun and has to be expressed for the sake of clearness, we may translate by **il faut** and an infinitive, putting one of the objective pronouns **me, te, lui, nous, vous, leur,** before **faut**:—

I must go out,	**il me faut sortir.**
He or *she must go out,*	**il lui faut sortir.**
You must go out,	**il vous faut sortir.**
They must go out,	**il leur faut sortir.**

(4) Lastly, the same form, but without an infinitive, is used to express a *want;* as—

I want, or *must have, a coat,*	**il me faut un habit.**
He or *she wants a dictionary,*	**il lui faut un dictionnaire.**
We want, or *must have, pens and ink,*	**il nous faut des plumes et de l'encre.**
They want, or *must have, money,*	**il leur faut de l'argent.**

Or, again, if the subject is a noun instead of a pronoun:—

My brother wants a coat,	**il faut un habit à mon frère.**

[1] The negation generally goes with **falloir**, not with the following verb.

un homme comme il faut, *a man as one ought to be, a gentleman.*
une personne comme il faut, *a ladylike person.*
par le froid qu'il fait, *with* or *in this cold weather.*

1. Nous voici au 15 avril; la campagne doit être déjà belle. 2. Vous devez mourir de faim après une si longue abstinence. 3. Il va falloir[1] partir. 4. Attendons encore un peu, il faut voir ce que cela deviendra. 5. Il dit qu'il m'empêchera de passer, c'est ce qu'il faudra voir. 6. Il ne faut pas[2] croire tout ce qu'on dit. 7. Il vous faudra faire ce voyage. 8. Il faudra que nous partions demain par le train de 7 heures. 9. Aristote disait qu'on doit examiner dans un livre si l'auteur dit tout ce qu'il faut, s'il ne dit que ce qu'il faut, s'il le dit comme il faut. 10. Voilà précisément ce qu'il me faut. 11. Quelle somme vous faut-il? 12. Vous faut-il beaucoup d'argent? 13. Qu'il m'a fallu de force pour cacher à tous les yeux les tourments que j'éprouvais! 14. Voilà un homme comme il faut. 15. C'est une femme tout-à-fait comme il faut. 16. Rien ne va comme il faut. 17. Allez-vous-en, je le veux, il le faut.

1. You must have been glad to hear that I have succeeded in getting (*à obtenir*) this situation. 2. They must be very sorry to know that you are ill. 3. We must learn our lessons well to-day, the professor will perhaps give us a holiday; this is (*c'est aujourd'hui*) his birthday. 4. You must not repeat to him what I have told you. 5. You must not go out in this cold weather, you would catch cold. 6. We must write to them. 7. Your brother must leave the door open. 8. She must

[1] When an impersonal verb is in the infinitive, the verb which governs it must be used impersonally.

[2] **il ne faut pas** always means *must not*, never *it is not necessary*, which we translate into French by **il n'est pas nécessaire.**

not go out alone. 9. You will be obliged to write all this before you go. 10. They must have patience (*prendre patience*). 11. We shall be obliged to go and visit your uncle this evening. 12. He wants another French grammar. 13. I want another watch. 14. My sister wants another book. 15. They need a good punishment. 16. You will need some courage. 17. How long do you take (*combien*, or *combien de temps vous faut-il*) to write your exercises? 18. I take (*il me faut*, or *j'y mets*) about an hour.

128.

Exceptions to the Rule on the Use of the Tenses of the Subjunctive.

FIRST EXCEPTION. — Although the verb in the principal clause is in the present or the future, the subjunctive is put in the *imperfect* or *pluperfect* if it is accompanied by some condition expressed or understood,[1] as —

je ne crois pas qu'il vînt, si on ne l'y forçait, — *I do not believe that he would come, if he were not obliged.*

je ne crois pas qu'il fût venu, si on ne l'y avait forcé, — *I do not believe that he would have come, if he had not been obliged.*

je ne pense pas que votre frère vous eût fait ce cadeau s'il avait su ce qui s'est passé, — *I do not think your brother would have given you that present if he had known what has taken place.*

je ne crois pas que vous eussiez agi autrement que moi (*understood:* si vous aviez été à ma place), — *I do not believe that you would have acted differently from me (if you had been in my place.*

[1] However, if the condition be expressed by the present indicative, the present subjunctive must be used: —

je crains qu'il ne tombe si vous ne le soutenez, — *I fear he will fall unless you support him.*

je ne crois pas qu'il réussisse sans vous (*that is,* si vous ne le protégez pas), — *I do not think that he will succeed without your support.*

SECOND EXCEPTION. — After a *past indefinite* followed by one of the conjunctions **afin que** or **pour que, de crainte que** or **de peur que, quoique** or **bien que**, the subjunctive is put in the *present* to express a present or future time: —

je ne lui ai pas dit tout ce qui s'était passé, quoiqu'il soit mon frère (pres.),	*I did not tell him all that had taken place, although he is my brother.*
je vous ai écrit la semaine dernière, pour que vous ayez tout le temps de songer à ma proposition et que vous puissiez me répondre avant la fin de cette semaine (future),	*I wrote to you last week in order that you may have plenty of time to think of my proposal, and that you may answer me before the end of this week.*

1. Je n'espère pas qu'il réussisse. 2. Je ne crois pas, je ne croirai jamais, qu'il réussît si vous ne le protégiez. 3. Je ne suppose pas qu'il eût réussi sans votre protection. 4. Croyez-vous qu'elle se rétablît si elle allait à Bath? 5. Je ne croirai jamais qu'il se fût rendu coupable de cette faute s'il eût tant soit peu réfléchi. 6. Votre frère s'est trop mal conduit pour que je prenne sur moi de l'excuser. 7. On m'a dit qu'il n'avait pas été admis dans votre régiment, quoiqu'il soit plus grand que vous. 8. J'ai préparé vos deux malles afin que vous ne vous fassiez pas attendre. 9. Il m'a trahi quoiqu'il soit mon ami. 10. Je n'ai osé lui répéter ce que vous m'aviez dit de peur qu'il ne vous en veuille ainsi qu'à moi. 11. Bien qu'il soit beaucoup plus jeune que moi, il a prétendu que je lui cédasse le pas. 12. Dieu a voulu, dit Pascal, que les vérités divines entrent du cœur dans l'esprit, et non de l'esprit dans le cœur.

1. I do not think that he will come. 2. I do not think that he is come. 3. I do not think that he would come if he knew that you were (present tense) here. 4. I

do not think that he would have come if he had known that you were here. 5. We fear that he shall deceive you. 6. We fear that he would deceive you if he dared. 7. We fear that he has deceived you. 8. We fear that he would have deceived you if he had dared. 9. I do not wish him to know all my business, although he is my uncle. 10. I did not wish him to know all my business, although he is my uncle. 11. They doubt that I shall succeed. 12. They doubt that I have succeeded. 13. They doubt that I would succeed but for your support. 14. They doubt that I would have succeeded but for your support.

129.

The Second Form of the Conditional Past.

The *pluperfect of the subjunctive* of any verb is sometimes used (without **que**) as a second form of the conditional past: —

j'eusse eu, *I would have had.*	**je fusse allé,** *I would have gone.*
tu eusses eu.	**tu fusses allé.**
il eût eu.	**il fût allé.**
nous eussions eu.	**nous fussions allés.**
vous eussiez eu.	**vous fussiez allés.**
ils eussent eu.	**ils fussent allés.**

Like the preterite and the past anterior, this second form of the conditional past is kept for elevated style, while the first form is used in conversation: —

O Fabricius, qu'eût pensé votre grande âme, si, pour votre malheur, rappelé à la vie, vous eussiez vu la face pompeuse de cette Rome sauvée par votre bras. — (*J. J. Rousseau.*)	*O Fabricius, what would your great soul have thought, if, unhappily for yourself, recalled to life, you had seen the gorgeous appearance of this Rome, saved by your arm!*

j'aurais fini ma besogne si ce monsieur n'était pas venu.	*I would have finished my work if that gentleman had not come.*

Although the conjunction **si** beginning a clause cannot be followed by the conditional (§ 51), yet, by exception, this second form of the conditional past may be elegantly used after **si** in elevated style: —

il est vrai, s'il m'eût cru, qu'il n'eût point fait de vers. — (*Boileau.*)	*It is true, if he had believed me, he would have made no verses.*
si le sombre empire de Pluton se fût entr'ouvert, je n'aurais pas été saisi, je l'avoue, d'une plus grande horreur. — (*Fénélon.*)	*If the dark empire of Pluto had half-opened before me, I should not have been seized, I confess, with greater horror.*

INSECTES HABITANT UN FRAISIER.

Quelque petits que fussent ces objets, ils étaient dignes de mon attention, puisqu'ils avaient mérité celle de la nature. Je n'eusse pu leur refuser une place dans son histoire générale, lorsqu'elle leur en avait donné une dans l'univers. A plus forte raison, si j'eusse écrit l'histoire de mon fraisier, il eût fallu en tenir compte. Les plantes sont les habitations des insectes, et on ne fait point l'histoire d'une ville sans parler de ses habitants. D'ailleurs mon fraisier n'était point dans son lieu naturel, en pleine campagne, sur la lisière d'un bois ou sur le bord d'un ruisseau, où il eût été fréquenté par bien d'autres espèces d'animaux. Il était dans un pot de terre, au milieu des fumées de Paris. Je ne l'observais qu'à des moments perdus; je ne connaissais point les insectes qui le visitaient dans le cours de la journée, encore moins ceux qui n'y venaient que la nuit attirés par de simples émanations, ou peut-être par des lumières phosphoriques qui nous échappent. — BERNARDIN DE ST. PIERRE.

(Put in the second form of the conditional past the verbs printed in italics.)

Napoleon I. was gifted with[1] ambition as wonderful as his genius, and it was his misfortune and that of France. Sprung[2] from the Revolution, of which he defended (*pluperfect*) the principles at the beginning of his career,[3] he turned aside,[4] for the advantage[5] of himself and of his family, the great movement of the nations which were demanding[6] liberty and equality. His glory, which will perhaps equal[7] that of Alexander and of Cæsar,[8] *would have been* much greater if he *had labored* for humanity instead of pursuing his selfish views,[9] and his name, cursed to-day by several contemporary[10] historians, *would have been* surrounded by[11] the unanimous[12] love of posterity. If *he had remained* faithful to law and to honor, he *would not have destroyed*[13] without warrant,[14] and by force and craft,[15] the established government; he *would not have assassinated* the Duke[16] of Enghien; Paris *would not have* twice[17] *seen* within her walls,[18] what she[19] had not seen since the reign[20] of an insane[21] king, Charles VI., an army of foreigners[22] mistress of her gates,[23] of her streets, and of her palaces.

[1] *gifted with*, doué d'une.
[2] *sprung*, sorti.
[3] *career*, carrière (f.).
[4] *he turned aside*, il détourna.
[5] *for the advantage*, au profit.
[6] *to demand*, vouloir.
[7] *to equal*, égaler.
[8] *Cæsar*, César.
[9] *selfish views*, vues égoïstes.
[10] *contemporary*, contemporain.
[11] *surrounded by*, entouré de.
[12] *unanimous*, unanime.
[13] *to destroy*, détruire.
[14] *warrant*, mandat.
[15] *craft*, la ruse.
[16] *the Duke*, le duc.
[17] *twice*, deux fois.
[18] *within her walls*, dans ses murs.
[19] *she*, il.
[20] *the reign*, le règne.
[21] *insane*, en démence.
[22] *foreigner*, étranger.
[23] *mistress of her gates*, maîtresse de ses portes.

EXTRACTS FOR READING.

1. UN DRÔLE DE PRISONNIER.

"A moi,[1] à moi! mon capitaine, criait un soldat, à moi! je tiens un prisonnier. — Eh bien, lui dit le capitaine, amène-le. — Je ne demande pas mieux;[2] mais il ne veut pas me laisser aller."

2. COMMENT ON DEVIENT MARÉCHAL DE FRANCE.

Le maréchal Lefebvre avait un camarade de régiment qui vint le voir un jour et qui admirait, non sans un sentiment d'envie, son bel hôtel, ses belles voitures, sa nombreuse livrée,[3] ses magnifiques appartements, tout le train enfin d'un grand dignitaire de l'empire: "Parbleu, lui dit-il, il faut avouer que tu es bien heureux, et que le ciel t'a bien traité! — Veux-tu, lui répondit le maréchal, avoir tout cela? — Oui, certainement. — La chose est très-simple: tu vas descendre dans la cour de mon hôtel; je mettrai à chaque fenêtre deux soldats qui tireront sur toi. Si tu échappes aux balles, je te donnerai tout ce que tu m'envies. C'est comme cela que je l'ai obtenu."

1 *Help!*
2 *I ask nothing better*, or, *I wish I could.*
3 *His numerous retinue.*

3. L'OPÉRATION INUTILE.

Un officier anglais ayant reçu une balle dans la jambe, fut transporté chez lui, où deux médecins furent appelés. Pendant huit jours ils ne firent que [1] sonder et fouiller la plaie. L'officier, qui souffrait beaucoup, leur demanda ce qu'ils cherchaient: "Nous cherchons la balle qui vous a blessé. — C'est trop fort! [2] s'écria le patient, pourquoi ne le disiez-vous pas plus tôt? je l'ai dans ma poche."

4. A QUOI SERT [3] LA VACCINE?

Un homme très-crédule disait qu'il n'avait pas de confiance dans la vaccine. "A quoi sert-elle, ajoute-t-il; je connais un enfant beau comme le jour, que sa famille avait fait vacciner... eh bien! il est mort deux jours après... — Comment! deux jours après?... — Oui... il est tombé du haut d'un arbre, et s'est tué raide... Faites donc vacciner vos enfants après cela!"

5. SCÈNE D'OMNIBUS.

La scène se passe [4] dans un omnibus, à Paris. Deux vieilles dames sont assises l'une à côté de l'autre. L'une veut que la portière soit fermée, l'autre la veut ouverte. On appelle le conducteur pour décider la question. "Monsieur, dit la première, si cette fenêtre reste ouverte, je suis sûre d'attraper un rhume qui m'emportera. — Monsieur, si on la ferme, je suis certaine de mourir d'un coup d'apoplexie." Le conducteur ne savait que faire, [5] lorsqu'un vieux monsieur, qui jusque là s'était

[1] *They did nothing but.*
[2] *That is too much!*
[3] *Of what use is.*
[4] *Takes place.*
[5] *Did not know what to do.*

tenu tranquille dans un coin de la voiture, le tira d'embarras. "Ouvrez donc la portière, mon cher ami, cela fera mourir l'une; puis vous la fermerez, cela nous débarrassera de l'autre, et nous aurons la paix."

6. LE BON CHASSEUR.

Un ministre protestant établi à Smyrne, M. Kuhn, homme très grave, se détermina un jour à suivre à la chasse quelques personnes de sa connaissance; il s'était fait accompagner d'un petit garçon [1] pour porter et charger son fusil. On lui assigna son poste; il s'y plaça, s'assit, mit ses lunettes, et tirant un livre de sa poche, il commença sa lecture, après avoir recommandé au petit garçon de l'avertir lorsqu'il verrait une pièce de gibier. Chaque fois que le petit drôle en apercevait une, il disait au ministre: "Monsieur, en voilà une." Mais avant que celui-ci eût posé son livre, ôté ses lunettes, pris son fusil, ce qu'il faisait toujours très flegmatiquement, la bête disparaissait, et le petit garçon désolé lui disait: "Eh! mais, monsieur, elle est partie. — Mon ami, répondait gravement le pasteur, j'en aurais fait autant [2] à sa place."

7. LA CORRESPONDANCE DU ROI DE PRUSSE ET DU SACRISTAIN.

Le sacristain de l'église cathédrale de Berlin écrivit un jour à Frédéric II: "Sire, j'avertis Votre Majesté, 1. qu'il manque des livres de cantique [3] pour la famille royale; j'avertis Votre Majesté, 2. qu'il n'y a pas assez de bois pour chauffer comme il faut la tribune royale; j'avertis

1 *He had taken with him a small boy.*
2 *I should have done the same.*
3 *Hymn-books.*

Votre Majesté, 3. que la balustrade qui est sur la rivière, derrière l'église, menace ruine.

Signé SCHMIDT,
Sacristain de la cathédrale."

Le roi de Prusse s'amusa beaucoup de cette lettre, et fit la réponse suivante :

"J'avertis M. le sacristain Schmidt, 1. que ceux qui veulent chanter peuvent acheter des livres ; j'avertis M. le sacristain Schmidt, 2. que ceux qui veulent se chauffer peuvent acheter du bois ; j'avertis M. le sacristain Schmidt, 3. que la balustrade qui est sur la rivière ne le regarde point ;[1] enfin j'avertis M. le sacristain Schmidt, 4. que je ne veux plus avoir de correspondance avec lui."

8. LE DOCTEUR ABERNETHY.

Le docteur Abernethy était bien connu par son laconisme. Il détestait les longues consultations et les détails inutiles. Une dame, connaissant cette particularité, se présente chez lui pour le consulter sur une grave blessure qu'un chien lui avait faite au bras. Elle entre sans rien dire, découvre la partie blessée, et la place sous les yeux du docteur. M. Abernethy regarde un instant, puis il dit : "Egratignure ? — Morsure. — Chat ? — Chien. — Aujourd'hui ? — Hier. — Douloureux ? — Non."

Le docteur fut si enthousiasmé de cette conversation, qu'il aurait presque embrassé la dame.

Il n'aimait pas non plus qu'on vînt le déranger la nuit. Une fois, qu'il se couchait à une heure du matin de fort mauvaise humeur, parce qu'on était venu le faire lever[2] à minuit, il entendit la sonnette retentir. "Qu'y a-t-il ?

[1] *Is no business of his.*

[2] *Some one had come to call him up.*

s'écria-t-il avec colère. — Docteur... vite! vite!... Mon fils vient d'avaler une souris. — Eh bien, dites-lui d'avaler un chat et laissez-moi tranquille!" fit[1] le docteur, en se recouchant.

9. SWIFT ET LE DOMESTIQUE.

Un jour un ami de Swift lui envoya un magnifique turbot. Le groom chargé de la commission s'était déjà maintes fois acquitté de pareils messages sans avoir jamais rien reçu de Swift. Fatigué d'une besogne aussi peu lucrative, il déposa brusquement le poisson sur une table en s'écriant: "Voici un turbot que vous envoie mon maître. — Plaît-il?[2] repartit aussitôt Swift. Est-ce ainsi que tu remplis tes fonctions? Tiens, prends ce siège; nous allons changer de rôle, et tâche, une autre fois, de mettre à profit ce que je vais t'enseigner." Swift alors s'avance respectueusement vers le domestique, qui s'était assis dans un large fauteuil, et lui dit, en lui présentant le turbot: "Monsieur, je suis chargé par mon maître de vous prier de bien vouloir accepter ce petit cadeau. — Vraiment? reprit effrontément le valet, c'est très-aimable à lui; et tiens, mon brave garçon, voici trois francs pour ta peine."

Swift s'empressa de congédier le groom.

10. LE DÉSERTEUR.

Quelque temps avant la bataille de Rosbach, époque à laquelle les affaires du grand Frédéric allaient de mal en pis, ce prince était couché et dormait sur la paille entouré de ses grenadiers. Au milieu de la nuit, l'un d'eux le réveilla, en lui criant: "Frédéric, voilà un de tes grena-

[1] *Said.* [2] *What do you say?*

diers qui avait déserté, et qu'on te ramène. — Fais-le avancer, dit le roi... Pourquoi m'as-tu abandonné ? continua-t-il, quand le déserteur fut en sa présence. — Parce que tes affaires sont dans un tel état, qu'il m'a fallu aller chercher fortune ailleurs. — Tu as raison, répondit Frédéric ; mais je te demande de rester encore avec moi cette campagne ; et si les choses ne vont pas mieux, je te promets de déserter avec toi."

11. LE CHEVAL TROP COURT.

Lalande, musicien de la chapelle de Versailles, était connu comme un homme jovial et qui aimait beaucoup le plaisir. Jeune, il lui prit envie, pendant la semaine sainte, d'aller figurer à Longchamps.[1] Il va trouver Mousset, loueur de chevaux, retient un cheval richement caparaçonné, et donne neuf francs à compte sur dix-huit,[2] le prix convenu. Sorti de l'écurie, il rencontre un ami qui lui parle d'une partie de Longchamps, dans sa voiture avec deux amis. "Si seulement, dit Lalande, je pouvais retirer les neuf francs que je viens de donner ! En tout cas, allons chez Mousset, et nous verrons... M. Mousset, montrez-moi encore une fois le cheval que je vous ai loué. — Monsieur, le voici. — Savez-vous, monsieur Mousset, que ce cheval-là est bien court ? — Comment, Monsieur, bien court ? — Mais certainement..." Puis s'adressant à son ami : " Voilà bien ma place, voilà la tienne, voilà celle de Daigremont... Mais où donc se placera Mondonville, et cependant il vient avec nous ? — Comment, Monsieur, vous montez à quatre ? [3] — Mais oui. — Tenez, voilà votre argent ; allez chercher un cheval ailleurs ; je ne loue pas le mien pour qu'on l'éreinte."

1 *To go and cut a figure at Longchamps*, a race-course outside of Paris.
2 *Nine francs on account, out of eighteen.*
3 *You mean to ride four together?*

12. JUNOT ET BONAPARTE.

Un jour, pendant le siège de Toulon, un commandant d'artillerie, venu de Paris depuis peu de jours pour diriger les opérations du siège, demanda au lieutenant du poste un jeune sous-officier qui eût en même temps de l'audace et de l'intelligence. Le lieutenant appelle aussitôt *La Tempête*,[1] et Junot se présente. Le commandant fixe sur lui cet œil qui semblait déjà connaître les hommes. "Tu vas quitter ton habit,[2] dit le commandant, et tu iras là, porter ces ordres." Il lui indiquait de la main un point plus éloigné de la côte, et lui expliqua ce qu'il voulait de lui. Le jeune sergent devint rouge comme une grenade, ses yeux étincelèrent. "Je ne suis pas un espion, répondit-il au commandant; cherchez un autre que moi pour exécuter ces ordres." Et il se retirait. "Tu refuses d'obéir ? lui dit l'officier supérieur d'un ton sévère ; sais-tu bien à quoi tu t'exposes ? — Je suis prêt à obéir, dit Junot, mais j'irai là où vous m'envoyez avec mon uniforme, ou je n'irai pas." Le commandant sourit, en le regardant attentivement. "Mais ils te tueront! reprit-il. — Que vous importe ?[3] Vous ne me connaissez pas assez pour que cela vous fasse de la peine, et quant à moi, ça m'est égal... Allons, je pars comme je suis, n'est-ce pas ?" Alors il mit la main dans sa giberne. "Bien ! avec mon fusil et ces dragées-là,[4] du moins la conversation ne languira pas, si ces messieurs veulent causer."

Et il partit en chantant. Après son départ: "Comment s'appelle ce jeune homme ? demanda l'officier

[1] *The Tempest*, a nickname given to Junot.
[2] *You are to change your clothes.*
[3] *What is that to you?*
[4] *These sugar-plums;* that is, the cartridges.

supérieur. — Junot. — Il fera son chemin." Alors le commandant inscrivit son nom sur ses tablettes. On a facilement deviné que l'officier d'artillerie était Napoléon.

Peu de jours après, se retrouvant à cette même batterie, Bonaparte demanda quelqu'un qui eût une belle écriture; Junot sortit des rangs et se présenta. Bonaparte le reconnut pour le sergent qui déjà avait fixé son attention. Il lui témoigna de l'intérêt, et lui dit de se placer pour écrire sa lettre sous sa dictée. Junot se mit sur l'épaulement même de la batterie.[1] A peine avait-il terminé sa lettre, qu'une bombe lancée par les Anglais éclate à dix pas, et le couvre de terre ainsi que la lettre. "Bien, dit en riant Junot, nous n'avions pas de sable pour sécher l'encre." Bonaparte arrêta son regard sur le jeune sergent; il était calme et n'avait pas même tressailli. Cette circonstance décida de sa fortune.

13. LA PLUS GRANDE GANACHE DE L'EMPIRE.

Un jour Napoléon, fort mécontent à la lecture d'une dépêche de Vienne, dit à Marie-Louise, "Votre père est une *ganache*." Marie-Louise, qui ignorait beaucoup de termes français, s'adressa au premier chambellan: "L'empereur dit que mon père est une *ganache*, que veut dire cela?"[2] A cette demande inattendue, le courtisan balbutia que cela voulait dire un homme sage, de poids, de bon conseil. A quelques jours de là,[3] et la mémoire encore toute fraîche de sa nouvelle acquisition, Marie-Louise présidait le conseil de famille. Voyant la discussion plus animée qu'elle ne voulait, elle interpella, pour

[1] *The very crest of the fort.* [2] *What does that mean?*
[3] *A few days afterwards.*

y mettre fin, M. R..., qui, à ses côtés,[1] bayait aux corneilles.[2] "C'est à vous à nous mettre d'accord dans cette occasion importante, lui dit-elle; vous serez notre oracle, car je vous tiens pour la plus grande *ganache* de l'empire."

14. JOSEPH II ET LE SERGENT.

L'empereur Joseph II n'aimait ni la représentation ni l'appareil. Un jour, revêtu d'une simple redingote boutonnée,[3] accompagné d'un seul domestique à cheval[4] et sans livrée, il était allé, dans une calèche à deux places qu'il conduisait lui-même, faire une promenade du matin dans les environs de Vienne. Comme il reprenait le chemin de la ville, il fut surpris par la pluie.

Il en était encore éloigné, lorsqu'un piéton, qui regagnait aussi la capitale, fait signe au conducteur d'arrêter, ce que Joseph II fait aussitôt. "Monsieur, lui dit le militaire (car c'était un sergent), y aurait-il de l'indiscrétion à vous demander une place à côté de vous? cela ne vous gênerait pas prodigieusement, puisque vous êtes seul dans votre calèche, et ménagerait mon uniforme que je mets aujourd'hui pour la première fois. — Ménageons votre uniforme, mon brave, lui dit Joseph, et mettez-vous là. D'où venez-vous? — Ah! dit le sergent, je viens de chez un garde-chasse de mes amis,[5] où j'ai fait un fier déjeuner. — Qu'avez-vous donc mangé de si bon? — Devinez. — Que sais-je,[6] moi; une soupe à la bière? — Ah! bien, oui, une soupe; mieux que ça. — De la choucroute? — Mieux que ça. — Une longe de veau?[7] — Mieux

[1] *For his part.*
[2] *Was gaping at the crows*, that is, was staring in the air.
[3] *Dressed in a plain frock-coat, buttoned up close.*
[4] *On horseback.*
[5] *A game-keeper, a friend of mine.*
[6] *How do I know?*
[7] *A loin of veal.*

que ça, vous dit-on. — Oh ! ma foi, je ne puis plus deviner, dit Joseph. — Un faisan, mon digne homme, un faisan tiré sur les plaisirs[1] de Sa Majesté, dit le camarade en lui frappant sur le genou. — Tiré sur les plaisirs de Sa Majesté, il n'en devait être que meilleur.[2] — Je vous en réponds."

Comme on approchait de la ville, et que la pluie tombait toujours, Joseph demanda à son compagnon dans quel quartier il logeait, et où il voulait qu'on le descendît. "Monsieur, c'est trop de bonté, je craindrais d'abuser de... — Non, non, dit Joseph, votre rue ? " — Le sergent, indiquant sa demeure, demanda à connaître celui dont il recevait tant d'honnêtetés. "A votre tour, dit Joseph, devinez. — Monsieur est militaire, sans doute ? — Comme dit monsieur. — Lieutenant ? — Ah ! bien oui, lieutenant; mieux que ça. — Capitaine ? — Mieux que ça. — Colonel, peut-être ? — Mieux que ça, vous dit-on. — Comment ! s'écrie le sergent, en se rencognant aussitôt dans la calèche, seriez-vous feld-maréchal ? — Mieux que ça. — Ah ! mon Dieu, c'est l'empereur ! — Lui-même, dit Joseph, se déboutonnant pour montrer ses décorations." Il n'y avait pas moyen de tomber à genoux dans la voiture; l'invalide[3] se confond en excuses et supplie l'empereur d'arrêter pour qu'il puisse descendre. "Non pas, lui dit Joseph; après avoir mangé mon faisan, vous seriez trop heureux de vous débarrasser de moi aussi promptement; j'entends bien que vous ne me quittiez qu'à votre porte." Et il l'y descendit.

1 *The pleasure grounds, the preserves.*
2 *There ought to be nothing better.*
3 *The veteran.*

APPENDIX OF FORMS AND RULES.

I. THE ARTICLE.

	SINGULAR.			PLURAL.
	Before a consonant or *h* aspirate.		Before a vowel or *h* mute.	Before all nouns.
	Masculine.	*Feminine.*	*Masc. or Fem.*	
the	le	la	l'	les
of the *or* from the,	du	de la	de l'	des
to the, at the,	au	à la	à l'	aux

THE NOUN.

II. The gender of inanimate objects.

The shortest and most satisfactory rule yet given for the gender of French nouns is as follows: —

Nouns having the following terminations are feminine: —

ale, ole, ule ; ure, ère, eur ;
rre, lle, ie, ié ; ée, ue, ion ;
be, ce, de ; fe, ne, pe ;
se, te, té ; ve, he, aison.

As **cathédrale, école, nature, faveur, terre, conversation, clémence, beauté, marche, maison.**

Nouns not having these terminations are masculine.

As **port, cheval, café, crime, village.**

There are, of course, exceptions to this rule; but according to its author, it holds good in 99 cases out of 100.

Observe that the rule does not apply to nouns evidently denoting males, as **prince, homme**; nor to nouns evidently denoting females, as **princesse, dame**, etc.

III. Formation of the feminine in nouns representing animate beings.

Nouns representing animate beings usually have a particular form for each sex, and their feminine, like the feminine of adjectives, is more or less regularly formed: —

un Français,	*a Frenchman,*	**une Française.**
un Prussien,	*a Prussian,*	**une Prussienne.**
un jardinier,	*a gardener,*	**une jardinière.**
un baron,	*a baron,*	**une baronne.**
un jumeau,	*a twin,*	**une jumelle.**
un époux,	*a husband,*	**une épouse.**
un compagnon,	*a companion,*	**une compagne.**

(1) Those ending with an *e mute* are the same for both genders: —

un Russe,	*a Russian,*	**une Russe.**
un esclave,	*a slave,*	**une esclave.**
un artiste,	*an artist,*	**une artiste.**

PRINCIPAL EXCEPTIONS.

un âne,	*an ass,*	**une ânesse.**
un chanoine,	*a canon,*	**une chanoinesse.**
un comte,	*a count,*	**une comtesse.**
un hôte,	*a host,*	**une hôtesse.**
un maître,	*a master,*	**une maîtresse**
un nègre,	*a negro,*	**une négresse.**
un prêtre,	*a priest,*	**une prêtresse.**
un Suisse,	*a Swiss,*	**une Suissesse.**
un tigre,	*a tiger,*	**une tigresse.**
un traître,	*a traitor,*	**une traîtresse.**

(2) Substantives ending in **-eur**, and which are derived from a present participle, change **-eur** into **-euse**: —

le danseur (from **dansant**),	*the dancer,*	**la danseuse.**
le plaideur (from **plaidant**),	*the suitor,*	**la plaideuse.**
le buveur (from **buvant**),	*the drinker,*	**la buveuse.**

(3) Substantives ending in **-teur**, and which are not derived from a present participle, change **-teur** into **-trice**: —

l'accusateur,	*the accuser,*	**l'accusatrice.**
l'acteur,	*the actor,*	**l'actrice.**
l'instituteur,	*the teacher,*	**l'institutrice.**

Add to these: **le débiteur,** *debtor;* **l'inspecteur,** *the inspector;* **l'exécuteur,** *the executor;* **l'inventeur,** *the inventor;* **le persécuteur,** *the persecutor.*

(4) Some in **-eur** change it into **-eresse** for the feminine, such as: **l'enchanteur,** *the enchanter,* **l'enchanteresse; le pécheur,** *the sinner,* **la pécheresse; le vengeur,** *the avenger,* **la vengeresse; le défendeur,** *the defendant,* **la défenderesse; le chasseur,** *the hunter,* **la chasseresse.** — **Chanteur** has two feminines, **chanteuse** and **cantatrice**: the latter is said only of professional singers. **Empereur** makes **impératrice; gouverneur** makes **gouvernante, serviteur** makes **servante. Témoin** is used for both genders, and also **auteur, poète, philosophe, peintre, juge, guide,** etc., and even **possesseur** and **successeur.**

(5) Some nouns originally feminine keep that gender, even when applied to man: **la dupe,** *the dupe;* **la sentinelle,** *the sentry;* **la recrue,** *the recruit;* **la caution,** *the bail;* **la victime,** *the victim,* etc.

(6) The names of animals form their feminine irregularly: —

le bélier,	*the ram,*	**la brebis.**
le bouc,	*the he-goat,*	**la chèvre.**
le cheval,	*the horse,*	**la jument.**
le mouton,	*the sheep,*	**la brebis.**
le sanglier,	*the wild boar,*	**la laie.**
le singe,	*the monkey,*	**la guenon.**
le canard,	*the duck,*	**la cane.**
le chat,	*the cat,*	**la chatte.**
le lapin,	*the rabbit,*	**la lapine.**
le mulet,	*the mule,*	**la mule.**
l'ours,	*the bear,*	**l'ourse.**
le perroquet,	*the parrot,*	**la perruche.**
le loup,	*the wolf,*	**la louve.**
le dindon,	*the turkey,*	**la dinde.**

(7) Most of the names of animals have only one **form for both** genders; such are:—

ALL MASCULINE.

le castor, *the beaver.*	**le cigne**, *the swan.*
le chameau, *the camel.*	**le hibou**, *the owl.*
l'écureuil, *the squirrel.*	**le vautour**, *the vulture.*
l'éléphant, *the elephant.*	**le merle**, *the blackbird.*
le léopard, *the leopard.*	**le saumon**, *the salmon.*

ALL FEMININE.

la baleine, *the whale.*	**l'alouette**, *the lark.*
la girafe, *the giraffe.*	**l'hirondelle**, *the swallow.*
la panthère, *the panther.*	**la perdrix**, *the partridge*
l'hyène, *the hyena.*	**la pie**, *the magpie.*
la souris, *the mouse.*	**la tortue**, *the tortoise.*

To all these nouns, when we want to determine the **sex**, we add **mâle** or **femelle: la panthère mâle, la panthère femelle; l'éléphant mâle, l'éléphant femelle.**

IV. Formation of the plural.

Nouns and adjectives form their plural by adding **s** to the singular; §§ 9, 10.

EXCEPTIONS.—(1) Nouns and adjectives ending in **s, x, z,** in the singular, are the same in the plural; § 30.

(2) Nouns and adjectives ending in **-au** or **-eu** take **x** in the plural; § 30.

But the noun **landau**, *a landau* (sort of carriage), and the adjective **bleu**, *blue*, take **s** in the plural.

(3) Nouns and adjectives in **-al** change **al** into **aux**; § 30.

But **s** is added in the plural to the nouns **bal, carnaval, chacal, régal**, and to the adjectives **amical, fatal, final, glacial, initial, matinal, naval, pénal, théâtral**, and a few others seldom used.

(4) Six nouns ending in **-ail** change **ail** into **aux**:—

le bail,	*the lease,*	**les baux.**
le corail,	*the coral,*	**les coraux.**
l'émail,	*the enamel,*	**les émaux.**

le soupirail,	*the air hole,*	**les soupiraux.**
le travail,	*the work, the labor,*	**les travaux.**
le vitrail,	*the glass windows,*	**les vitraux.**

(5) Six nouns ending in **-ou** take **x** : —

le bijou,	*the jewel,*	**les bijoux.**
le caillou,	*the flint,*	**les cailloux.**
le chou,	*the cabbage,*	**les choux.**
le genou,	*the knee,*	**les genoux.**
le hibou,	*the owl,*	**les hiboux.**
le joujou,	*the toy,*	**les joujoux.**

(6) **Aïeul, ciel,** and **œil,** generally make **aïeux,** *ancestors ;* **cieux,** *heavens ;* **yeux,** *eyes.* But **aïeul** makes **aïeuls** when it means the paternal and maternal grandfathers ; **ciel** makes **ciels** when it means the testers of beds, the roofs of quarries, or " skies " in painting ; and in the cases when **œil** does not mean properly *eye,* it makes **œils,** as, **des œils-de-bœuf,** *oval windows.*

(7) Foreign words, which have not yet been naturalized in France by custom, remain invariable, such as : **des alibi, des errata, des in-folio, des in-quarto, des post-scriptum, des fac-simile,** etc.

But the following take the mark of the plural : **des bravos, des duos, des trios, des numéros, des opéras, des zéros, des impromptus, des échos, des déficits,** etc.

THE ADJECTIVE.

V. Formation of the feminine of adjectives.

General Rule. — To form the feminine of adjectives, add *e mute* to the masculine (§ 2).

Exceptions. — (1) Adjectives ending with *e mute* in the masculine are the same in the feminine (§ 2).

(2) Adjectives ending in **-el, -en, -on, -et,** double the last consonant, and take an *e mute* after it (§ 54).

(3) Eight other adjectives also double their last consonant in the feminine (§ 54).

(4) Adjectives ending in **-f** change **f** into **ve** (§ 54).

(5) Adjectives ending in **-x** change **x** into **se** (§ 54).

(6) Adjectives ending in **-eur,** and which are derived from a present participle, change **eur** into **euse.**

Flatteur (from **flattant**), **flatteuse**; **grondeur** (from **grondant**), **grondeuse**.

(7) Adjectives ending in **-teur**, and which are not derived from a present participle, change **teur** into **trice**.

Profanateur, profanatrice; corrupteur, corruptrice.

Adjectives ending in **-érieur**, not belonging to either of the above exceptions, follow the general rule: **inférieur, inférieure; ultérieur, ultérieure.** Add to them **meilleur, majeur,** and **mineur.**

(8) Some adjectives form their feminines irregularly (§ 55).

The plural of adjectives is formed in the same way as that of nouns (see page 276).

For the comparison of adjectives see §§ 24, 48.

VI. Possessive adjectives.

	SINGULAR.		PLURAL.
	Masculine.	*Feminine.*	*Both genders.*
My,	**mon.**	**ma.**	**mes.**
Thy,	**ton.**	**ta.**	**tes.**
His, her, its,	**son.**	**sa.**	**ses.**
Our,	**notre.**		**nos.**
Your,	**votre.**		**vos.**
Their,	**leur.**		**leurs.**

OBSERVE. — Possessive adjectives are compared with possessive pronouns in § x.

VII. Demonstrative adjectives.

	MASCULINE.		FEMININE.
SINGULAR.	Before a consonant,	Before a vowel.	Before any letter.
This or that,	**ce.**	**cet.**	**cette.**
PLURAL. *These or those,*	**ces.**		

NUMERAL ADJECTIVES.

VIII. Cardinal Numbers.

1, **un, une.**
2, **deux.**
3, **trois.**
4, **quatre.**
5, **cinq.**
6, **six** (*siss*).
7, **sept** (*sett*).
8, **huit** (*weet*, short).
9, **neuf.**
10, **dix** (*diss*).
11, **onze.**
12, **douze.**
13, **treize.**
14, **quatorze.**
15, **quinze.**
16, **seize.**
17, **dix-sept** (*diz-sett*).
18, **dix-huit** (*diz-huite*).
19, **dix-neuf** (*diz-neufe*).
20, **vingt** (*vin*).
21, **vingt-et-un** (*vinté-un*).
22, **vingt-deux** (*vinte*).
23, **vingt-trois** (*vinte*).
24, **vingt-quatre** (*vinte*).
25, **vingt-cinq** (*vinte*).
26, **vingt-six** (*vinte*).
27, **vingt-sept** (*vinte*).
28, **vingt-huit** (*vinte*).
29, **vingt-neuf** (*vinte*).
30, **trente.**
31, **trente-et-un.**
32, **trente-deux**, etc.
40, **quarante.**
41, **quarante-et-un.**
42, **quarante-deux**, etc.
50, **cinquante.**
51, **cinquante-et-un.**
52, **cinquante-deux.**
60, **soixante.**
61, **soixante-et-un.**
62, **soixante-deux.**
70, **soixante-dix.**
71, **soixante-et-onze.**
72, **soixante-douze.**
73, **soixante-treize.**
74, **soixante-quatorze.**
75, **soixante-quinze.**
76, **soixante-seize.**
77, **soixante-dix-sept.**
78, **soixante-dix-huit.**
79, **soixante-dix-neuf.**
80, **quatre-vingts** (*vin*).
81, **quatre-vingt-un.**
82, **quatre-vingt-deux.**
90, **quatre-vingt-dix.**
91, **quatre-vingt-onze.**
92, **quatre-vingt-douze.**
93, **quatre-vingt-treize.**
94, **quatre-vingt-quatorze.**
95, **quatre-vingt-quinze.**
96, **quatre-vingt-seize.**
97, **quatre-vingt-dix-sept.**
98, **quatre-vingt-dix-huit.**
99, **quatre-vingt-dix-neuf.**
100, **cent.**
150, **cent cinquante.**
200, **deux cents.**
230, **deux cent trente.**
300, **trois cents.**
1000, **mille.**
1203, **mille deux cent trois.**
2000, **deux mille.**
2100, **deux mille cent.**
1,000,000, **un million.**

IX. Ordinal Numbers.

1st,	**premier, première.**	17th,	**dix-septième.**
2nd,	**deuxième,** *or* **second, e.**	18th,	**dix-huitième.**
3rd,	**troisième.**	19th,	**dix-neuvième.**
4th,	**quatrième.**	20th,	**vingtième.**
5th,	**cinquième.**	21st,	**vingt-et-unième.**
6th,	**sixième.**	22nd,	**vingt-deuxième.**
7th,	**septième.**	30th,	**trentième.**
8th,	**huitième.**	40th,	**quarantième.**
9th,	**neuvième.**	50th,	**cinquantième.**
10th,	**dixième.**	60th,	**soixantième.**
11th,	**onzième.**	70th,	**soixante-dixième.**
12th,	**douzième.**	80th,	**quatre-vingtième.**
13th,	**treizième.**	90th,	**quatre-vingt-dixième.**
14th,	**quatorzième.**	100th,	**centième.**
15th,	**quinzième.**	1,000th,	**millième.**
16th,	**seizième.**	1,000,000th,	**millionième.**

THE PRONOUN.

Definition.

A pronoun is a short word standing instead of a noun to avoid its repetition, while an adjective always accompanies a noun to qualify it or determine it.

In the sentence **ma plume est bonne, la tienne est bonne aussi, ma** is an adjective determining the noun **plume,** that is to say, expressing whose pen it is; **la tienne,** on the contrary, is a pronoun standing for **ta plume** and is used to avoid the repetition of that noun, which would be disagreeable to the ear.

X. Possessive pronouns.

	SINGULAR.		PLURAL.	
	Masculine.	*Feminine.*	*Masculine.*	*Feminine.*
Mine,	**le mien.**	**la mienne.**	**les miens.**	**les miennes.**
Thine,	**le tien.**	**la tienne.**	**les tiens.**	**les tiennes.**
His, hers, its,	**le sien.**	**la sienne.**	**les siens.**	**les siennes.**
Ours,	**le** or **la nôtre.**		**les nôtres.**	
Yours,	**le** or **la vôtre.**		**les vôtres.**	
Theirs,	**le** or **la leur.**		**les leurs.**	

Comparing possessive adjectives with possessive pronouns, observe: —

(1) The o of the possessive pronouns **le nôtre, le vôtre, les nôtres, les vôtres,** has a circumflex accent, while that o is short in the adjectives **notre** and **votre.**

(2) The same pronouns take s in the plural, **les nôtres, les vôtres,** while the adjectives change their form entirely and become **nos, vos.**

THE VERB.

Auxiliary Verbs.

There are only two auxiliary verbs in French, **avoir** (*to have*) and **être** (*to be*). They are the most frequently used and the most important of all verbs.

XI. Avoir.

INFINITIVE PRESENT.	INFINITIVE PAST.
avoir, *to have.*	**avoir eu,** *to have had.*

PARTICIPLE PRESENT.	PARTICIPLE PAST.
ayant, *having.*	**eu,** *had.*

INDICATIVE PRESENT.	PAST INDEFINITE.
j'ai, *I have.*	**j'ai eu,** *I have had, I had.*
tu as.	**tu as eu.**
il or **elle a.**	**il** or **elle a eu.**
nous avons.	**nous avons eu.**
vous avez.	**vous avez eu.**
ils or **elles ont.**	**ils** or **elles ont eu.**

IMPERFECT.	PLUPERFECT.
j'avais, *I had.*	**j'avais eu,** *I had had.*
tu avais.	**tu avais eu.**
il or **elle avait.**	**il** or **elle avait eu.**
nous avions.	**nous avions eu.**
vous aviez.	**vous aviez eu.**
ils or **elles avaient.**	**ils** or **elles avaient eu.**

PRETERITE.

j'eus, *I had.*
tu eus.
il or **elle eut.**
nous eûmes.
vous eûtes.
ils or **elles eurent.**

PAST ANTERIOR.

j'eus eu, *I had had.*
tu eus eu.
il or **elle eut eu.**
nous eûmes eu.
vous eûtes eu.
ils or **elles eurent eu.**

FUTURE.

j'aurai, *I shall* or *will have.*
tu auras.
il or **elle aura.**
nous aurons.
vous aurez.
ils or **elles auront.**

FUTURE ANTERIOR.

j'aurai eu, *I shall have had.*
tu auras eu.
il or **elle aura eu.**
nous aurons eu.
vous aurez eu.
ils or **elles auront eu.**

CONDITIONAL PRESENT.

I would or *should have.*
j'aurais.
tu aurais.
il or **elle aurait.**
nous aurions.
vous auriez.
ils or **elles auraient.**

CONDITIONAL PAST.

I would or *should have had.*
j'aurais eu.
tu aurais eu.
il or **elle aurait eu.**
nous aurions eu.
vous auriez eu.
ils or **elles auraient eu.**

SUBJUNCTIVE PRESENT.

that I may have, that I have.
que j'aie.
que tu aies.
qu'il or **qu'elle ait.**
que nous ayons.
que vous ayez.
qu'ils (elles) aient.

SUBJUNCTIVE PAST.

that I may have had.
que j'aie eu.
que tu aies eu.
qu'il or **qu'elle ait eu.**
que nous ayons eu.
que vous ayez eu.
qu'ils (elles) aient eu.

SUBJUNCTIVE IMPERFECT.

that I might have, that I had.
que j'eusse.
que tu eusses.
qu'il or **qu'elle eût.**
que nous eussions.
que vous eussiez.
qu'ils (elles) eussent.

SUBJUNCTIVE PLUPERFECT.

that I might have had.
que j'eusse eu.
que tu eusses eu.
qu'il or **qu'elle eût eu.**
que nous eussions eu.
que vous eussiez eu.
qu'ils (elles) eussent eu.

IMPERATIVE.

aie, *have (thou).* **ayons,** *let us have.* **ayez,** *have (you).*

XII. Etre.

INFINITIVE PRESENT.

être, *to be.*

INFINITIVE PAST.

avoir été, *to have been.*

PARTICIPLE PRESENT.

étant, *being.*

PARTICIPLE PAST.

été, *been.*

INDICATIVE PRESENT.

je suis, *I am.*
tu es.
il or **elle est.**
nous sommes.
vous êtes.
ils or **elles sont.**

PAST INDEFINITE.

j'ai été, *I have been, I was.*
tu as été.
il or **elle a été.**
nous avons été.
vous avez été.
ils or **elles ont été.**

IMPERFECT.

j'étais, *I was.*
tu étais.
il or **elle était.**
nous étions.
vous étiez.
ils or **elles étaient.**

PLUPERFECT.

j'avais été, *I had been.*
tu avais été.
il or **elle avait été.**
nous avions été.
vous aviez été.
ils or **elles avaient été.**

PRETERITE.

je fus, *I was.*
tu fus.
il or **elle fut.**
nous fûmes.
vous fûtes.
ils or **elles furent.**

PAST ANTERIOR.

j'eus été, *I had been.*
tu eus été.
il or **elle eut été.**
nous eûmes été.
vous eûtes été.
ils or **elles eurent été.**

FUTURE.

je serai, *I shall* or *will be.*
tu seras.
il or **elle sera.**
nous serons.
vous serez.
ils or **elles seront.**

FUTURE ANTERIOR.

j'aurai été, *I shall have been.*
tu auras été.
il or **elle aura été.**
nous aurons été.
vous aurez été.
ils or **elles auront été.**

CONDITIONAL PRESENT.

je serais, *I would* or *should be.*
tu serais.
il or **elle serait.**
nous serions.
vous seriez
ils or **elles seraient.**

CONDITIONAL PAST.

j'aurais été, *I would* or *should have been.*
tu aurais été.
il or **elle aurait été.**
nous aurions été.
vous auriez été.
ils or **elles auraient été.**

SUBJUNCTIVE PRESENT.

que je sois, *that I may be, that I be.*
que tu sois.
qu'il or **qu'elle soit.**
que nous soyons.
que vous soyez.
qu'ils (elles) soient.

SUBJUNCTIVE PAST.

que j'aie été, *that I may have been.*
que tu aies été.
qu'il or **qu'elle ait été.**
que nous ayons été.
que vous ayez été.
qu'ils (elles) aient été.

SUBJUNCTIVE IMPERFECT.

that I might be.

que je fusse.
que tu fusses.
qu'il or **qu'elle fût.**
que nous fussions.
que vous fussiez.
qu'ils or **qu'elles fussent.**

SUBJUNCTIVE PLUPERFECT.

that I might have been.

que j'eusse été.
que tu eusses été.
qu'il or **qu'elle eût été.**
que nous eussions été.
que vous eussiez été.
qu'ils or **qu'elles eussent été.**

IMPERATIVE.

sois, *be (thou).* **soyons,** *let us be.* **soyez,** *be (you).*

XIII. Avoir used interrogatively.

INDICATIVE PRESENT.

ai-je? *have I?*
as-tu?
a-t-il? a-t-elle?
avons-nous?
avez-vous?
ont-ils? ont-elles?

PAST INDEFINITE.

ai-je eu? *have I had? had I?*
as-tu eu?
a-t-il eu? a-t-elle eu?
avons-nous eu?
avez-vous eu?
ont-ils eu? ont-elles eu?

IMPERFECT.

avais-je? *had I?*
avais-tu?
avait-il? avait-elle?
avions-nous?
aviez-vous?
avaient-ils? avaient-elles?

PLUPERFECT.

avais-je eu? *had I had?*
avais-tu eu?
avait-il eu? avait-elle eu?
avions-nous eu?
aviez-vous eu?
avaient-ils (elles) eu?

PRETERITE.

eus-je? *had I?*
eus-tu?
eut-il? eut-elle?
eûmes-nous?
eûtes-vous?
eurent-ils? eurent-elles?

PAST ANTERIOR.

eus-je eu? *had I had?*
eus-tu eu?
eut-il eu? eut-elle eu?
eûmes-nous eu?
eûtes-vous eu?
eurent-ils (elles) eu?

FUTURE.

aurai-je? *shall I have?*
auras-tu?
aura-t-il? aura-t-elle?
aurons-nous?
aurez-vous?
auront-ils? auront-elles?

FUTURE ANTERIOR.

aurai-je eu? *shall I have had?*
auras-tu eu?
aura-t-il eu? aura-t-elle eu?
aurons-nous eu?
aurez-vous eu?
auront-ils (elles) eu?

CONDITIONAL PRESENT.

aurais-je? *should I have?*
aurais-tu?
aurait-il? aurait-elle?
aurions-nous?
auriez-vous?
auraient-ils (elles)?

CONDITIONAL PAST.

aurais-je eu? *should I have had?*
aurais-tu eu?
aurait-il eu? aurait-elle eu?
aurions-nous eu?
auriez-vous eu?
auraient-ils (elles) eu?

XIV. Etre used interrogatively.

INDICATIVE.

suis je? *am I?*
es-tu?
est-il? est-elle?
sommes-nous?
êtes-vous?
sont-ils? sont-elles?

PAST INDEFINITE.

ai-je été? *have I been? was I?*
as-tu été?
a-t-il été? a-t-elle été?
avons-nous été?
avez-vous été?
ont-ils été? ont-elles été?

IMPERFECT.

étais-je? *was I?*
étais-tu?
était-il? était-elle?
étions-nous?
étiez-vous?
étaient-ils? étaient-elles?

PLUPERFECT.

avais-je été? *had I been?*
avais-tu été?
avait-il été? avait-elle été?
avions-nous été?
aviez-vous été?
avaient-ils (elles) été?

PRETERITE.	PAST ANTERIOR.
fus-je ? *was I ?*	**eus-je été ?** *had I been ?*
fus-tu ?	**eus-tu été ?**
fut-il ? fut elle ?	**eut-il été ? eut-elle été ?**
fûmes-nous ?	**eûmes-nous été ?**
fûtes-vous ?	**eûtes-vous été ?**
furent-ils ? furent-elles ?	**eurent-ils (elles) été ?**

FUTURE.	FUTURE ANTERIOR.
serai-je ? *shall I be?*	**aurai-je été ?** *shall I have been ?*
seras-tu ?	**auras-tu été ?**
sera-t-il ? sera-t-elle ?	**aura-t-il été ? aura-t-elle été ?**
serons-nous ?	**aurons-nous été ?**
serez-vous ?	**aurez-vous été ?**
seront-ils ? seront-elles ?	**auront-ils (elles) été ?**

CONDITIONAL PRESENT.	CONDITIONAL PAST.
serais-je ? *should I be ?*	**aurais-je été ?** *should I have been ?*
serais-tu ?	**aurais-tu été ?**
serait-il ? serait-elle ?	**aurait-il-été ? aurait elle été ?**
serions-nous ?	**aurions-nous été ?**
seriez-vous ?	**auriez-vous été ?**
seraient-ils ? seraient-elles ?	**auraient-ils (elles) été ?**

XV. Avoir used negatively.

INDICATIVE PRESENT.	PAST INDEFINITE.
I have not.	*I have not had, I had not had.*
je n'ai pas.	**je n'ai pas eu.**
tu n'as pas.	**tu n'as pas eu.**
il or **elle n'a pas.**	**il** or **elle n'a pas eu.**
nous n'avons pas.	**nous n'avons pas eu.**
vous n'avez pas.	**vous n'avez pas eu.**
ils or **elles n'ont pas.**	**ils** or **elles n'ont pas eu.**

IMPERFECT.	PLUPERFECT.
je n'avais pas, *I had not.*	**je n'avais pas eu,** *I had not had.*
tu n'avais pas.	**tu n'avais pas eu.**
il or **elle n'avait pas.**	**il** or **elle n'avait pas eu.**
nous n'avions pas.	**nous n'avions pas eu.**
vous n'aviez pas.	**vous n'aviez pas eu.**
ils or **elles n'avaient pas.**	**ils** or **elles n'avaient pas eu.**

PRETERITE.

je n'eus pas, *I had not.*
tu n'eus pas.
il or elle n'eut pas.
nous n'eûmes pas.
vous n'eûtes pas.
ils or elles n'eurent pas.

PAST ANTERIOR.

je n'eus pas eu, *I had not had.*
tu n'eus pas eu.
il or elle n'eut pas eu.
nous n'eûmes pas eu.
vous n'eûtes pas eu.
ils or elles n'eurent pas eu.

FUTURE.

I shall not have.

je n'aurai pas.
tu n'auras pas.
il or elle n'aura pas.
nous n'aurons pas.
vous n'aurez pas.
ils or elles n'auront pas.

FUTURE ANTERIOR.

I shall not have had.

je n'aurai pas eu.
tu n'auras pas eu.
il or elle n'aura pas eu.
nous n'aurons pas eu.
vous n'aurez pas eu.
ils or elles n'auront pas eu.

CONDITIONAL PRESENT.

I should not have.

je n'aurais pas.
tu n'aurais pas.
il or elle n'aurait pas.
nous n'aurions pas.
vous n'auriez pas.
ils or elles n'auraient pas.

CONDITIONAL PAST.

I should not have had.

je n'aurais pas eu.
tu n'aurais pas eu.
il or elle n'aurait pas eu.
nous n'aurions pas eu.
vous n'auriez pas eu.
ils or elles n'auraient pas eu.

SUBJUNCTIVE PRESENT.

that I may not have.

que je n'aie pas.
que tu n'aies pas.
qu'il or qu'elle n'ait pas.
que nous n'ayons pas.
que vous n'ayez pas.
qu'ils (elles) n'aient pas.

SUBJUNCTIVE PAST.

that I may not have had.

que je n'aie pas eu.
que tu n'aies pas eu.
qu'il or qu'elle n'ait pas eu.
que nous n'ayons pas eu.
que vous n'ayez pas eu.
qu'ils (elles) n'aient pas eu.

SUBJUNCTIVE IMPERFECT.

that I might not have.

que je n'eusse pas.
que tu n'eusses pas.
qu'il or qu'elle n'eût pas.
que nous n'eussions pas.
que vous n'eussiez pas.
qu'ils (elles) n'eussent pas.

SUBJUNCTIVE PLUPERFECT.

that I might not have had.

que je n'eusse pas eu.
que tu n'eusses pas eu.
qu'il or qu'elle n'eût pas eu.
que nous n'eussions pas eu.
que vous n'eussiez pas eu.
qu'ils (elles) n'eussent pas eu.

IMPERATIVE.

n'aie pas, *have not (thou).*
n'ayons pas, *let us not have.*
n'ayez pas, *have not (you).*

XVI. Etre used negatively.

INDICATIVE PRESENT.

I am not.

je ne suis pas.
tu n'es pas.
il or elle n'est pas.
nous ne sommes pas.
vous n'êtes pas.
ils or elles ne sont pas.

IMPERFECT.

je n'étais pas, *I was not.*
tu n'étais pas.
il or elle n'était pas.
nous n'étions pas.
vous n'étiez pas.
ils or elles n'étaient pas.

PRETERITE.

je ne fus pas, *I was not.*
tu ne fus pas.
il or elle ne fut pas.
nous ne fûmes pas.
vous ne fûtes pas.
ils or elles ne furent pas.

FUTURE.

I shall not be.

je ne serai pas.
tu ne seras pas.
il or elle ne sera pas.
nous ne serons pas.
vous ne serez pas.
ils or elles ne seront pas.

PAST INDEFINITE.

I have not been, I was not.

je n'ai pas été.
tu n'as pas été.
il or elle n'a pas été.
nous n'avons pas été.
vous n'avez pas été.
ils or elles n'ont pas été.

PLUPERFECT.

je n'avais pas été, *I had not been.*
tu n'avais pas été.
il or elle n'avait pas été.
nous n'avions pas été.
vous n'aviez pas été.
ils or elles n'avaient pas été.

PAST ANTERIOR.

je n'eus pas été, *I had not been.*
tu n'eus pas été.
il or elle n'eut pas été.
nous n'eûmes pas été.
vous n'eûtes pas été.
ils or elles n'eurent pas été.

FUTURE ANTERIOR.

I shall not have been.

je n'aurai pas été.
tu n'auras pas été.
il or elle n'aura pas été.
nous n'aurons pas été.
vous n'aurez pas été.
ils or elles n'auront pas été.

CONDITIONAL PRESENT.

I should not be.

je ne serais pas.
tu ne serais pas.
il or **elle ne serait pas.**
nous ne serions pas.
vous ne seriez pas.
ils or **elles ne seraient pas.**

CONDITIONAL PAST.

I should not have been.

je n'aurais pas été.
tu n'aurais pas été.
il or **elle n'aurait pas été.**
nous n'aurions pas été.
vous n'auriez pas été.
ils or **elles n'auraient pas été.**

SUBJUNCTIVE PRESENT.

that I may not be.

que je ne sois pas.
que tu ne sois pas.
qu'il (elle) ne soit pas.
que nous ne soyons pas.
que vous ne soyez pas.
qu'ils (elles) ne soient pas.

SUBJUNCTIVE PAST.

that I may not have been.

que je n'aie pas été.
que tu n'aies pas été.
qu'il (elle) n'ait pas été.
que nous n'ayons pas été.
que vous n'ayez pas été.
qu'ils (elles) n'aient pas été.

SUBJUNCTIVE IMPERFECT.

that I might not be.

que je ne fusse pas.
que tu ne fusses pas.
qu'il or **qu'elle ne fût pas.**
que nous ne fussions pas.
que vous ne fussiez pas.
qu'ils (elles) ne fussent pas.

SUBJUNCTIVE PLUPERFECT.

that I might not have been.

que je n'eusse pas été.
que tu n'eusses pas été.
qu'il or **qu'elle n'eût pas été.**
que nous n'eussions pas été.
que vous n'eussiez pas été.
qu'ils (elles) n'eussent pas été.

IMPERATIVE.

ne sois pas, *be not (thou).* **ne soyons pas,** *let us not be.*
ne soyez pas, *be not (you).*

OBSERVATION FOR ALL VERBS USED NEGATIVELY. — Instead of **pas**, put **point** for a stronger negation, **jamais** for *never*, and **plus** for *no more* or *no longer.*

XVII. Avoir used negatively and interrogatively.

INDICATIVE PRESENT.

n'ai-je pas ? *have I not ?*
n'as-tu pas ?
n'a-t-il (elle) pas ?
n'avons-nous pas ?
n'avez-vous pas ?
n'ont-ils (elles) pas ?

PAST INDEFINITE.

n'ai-je pas eu ? *have I not had ?*
n'as-tu pas eu ?
n'a-t-il (elle) pas eu ?
n'avons-nous pas eu ?
n'avez-vous pas eu ?
n'ont-ils (elles) pas eu ?

IMPERFECT.

'avais-je pas ? *had I not?*
etc.

PLUPERFECT.

n'avais-je pas eu ? *had I not had?*
etc.

PRETERITE.

n'eus-je pas ? *had I not?*
etc.

PAST ANTERIOR.

n'eus-je pas eu ? *had I not had?*
etc.

FUTURE.

shall I not have?
n'aurai-je pas ?
etc.

FUTURE ANTERIOR.

shall I not have had?
n'aurai-je pas eu ?
etc.

CONDITIONAL PRESENT.

should I not have?
n'aurais-je pas ?
etc.

CONDITIONAL PAST.

should I not have had?
n'aurais-je pas eu ?
etc.

XVIII. Etre used negatively and interrogatively.

INDICATIVE PRESENT.

am I not?
ne suis-je pas ?
n'es-tu pas ?
n'est-il pas ? n'est-elle pas ?
ne sommes-nous pas ?
n'êtes-vous pas ?
ne sont-ils (elles) pas ?

PAST INDEFINITE.

have I not been? was I not?
n'ai-je pas été ?
n'as-tu pas été ?
n'a-t-il pas été ? n'a-t-elle pas été ?
n'avons-nous pas été ?
n'avez-vous pas été ?
n'ont-ils (elles) pas été ?

IMPERFECT.

was I not?
n'étais-je pas ?
etc.

PLUPERFECT.

had I not been?
n'avais-je pas été ?
etc.

PRETERITE.

was I not?
ne fus-je pas ?
etc.

PAST ANTERIOR.

had I not been?
n'eus je pas été ?
etc.

FUTURE.

shall I not be?
ne serai-je pas ?
etc.

FUTURE ANTERIOR.

shall I not have been?
n'aurai-je pas été ?
etc.

CONDITIONAL PRESENT.	CONDITIONAL PAST.
should I not be ?	*should I not have been ?*
ne serais-je pas ?	**n'aurais-je pas été ?**
etc.	etc.

XIX. Terminations of the three regular conjugations.

CONJUGATION.	*Infinitive.*	*Present participle.*	*Past participle.*	*Present Indicative.*	*Imperfect.*	*Preterite.*	*Future.*	*Conditional.*	*Imperative.*	*Subjunctive Present.*	*Subjunctive Imperfect.*
1.	er.	ant.	é.	e. es. e. ons. ez. ent.	ais. ais. ait. ions. iez. aient.	ai. as. a. âmes. âtes. èrent.	erai. eras. era. erons. erez. eront.	erais. erais. erait. erions. eriez. eraient.	e. e. ons. ez. ent.	e. es. e. ions. iez. ent.	asse. asses. ât. assions. assiez. assent.
2.	ir.	issant.	i.	is. is. it. issons. issez. issent.	issais. issais. issait. issions. issiez. issaient.	is. is. it. îmes. îtes. irent.	irai. iras. ira. irons. irez. iront.	irais. irais. irait. irions. iriez. iraient.	is. isse. issons. issez. issent.	isse. isses. isse. issions. issiez. issent.	isse. isses. ît. issions. issiez. issent.
3.	re.	ant.	u.	s. s. — ons. ez. ent.	ais. ais. ait. ions. iez. aient.	is. is. it. îmes. îtes. irent.	rai. ras. ra. rons. rez. ront.	rais. rais. rait. rions. riez. raient.	s. e. ons. ez. ent.	e. es. e. ions. iez. ent.	isse. isses. ît. issions. issiez. issent.

Observations on these terminations.

(1) All verbs in the French language terminate in the same way in three of their tenses:—

The imperfect in **-ais, -ais, -ait, -ions, -iez, -aient.**
The future in **-rai, -ras, -ra, -rons, -rez, -ront.**
The conditional in **-rais, -rais, -rait, -rions, -riez, -raient.**

(2) The termination of the past participle is the most important to be remembered, as all compound tenses are formed by that participle preceded by **avoir** or **être.**

(3) The imperative is exactly like the present indicative. It must, however, be remarked that the **s** of the second person singular of the present indicative in verbs of the 1st conjugation does not appear in the imperative.

XX. The Three Conjugations.

Verbs in **-er.**	Verbs in **-ir.**	Verbs in **-re.**
	INFINITIVE PRESENT.	
porter, *to carry.*	**finir,** *to finish.*	**rendre,** *to give back.*
	INFINITIVE PAST.	
avoir porté.	**avoir fini.**	**avoir rendu.**
	PARTICIPLE PRESENT.	
portant.	**finissant.**	**rendant.**
	PARTICIPLE PAST.	
porté.	**fini.**	**rendu.**
	INDICATIVE PRESENT.	
	(I *come back*, I *am coming back*, I *do come back.*)	
je porte.	**je finis.**	**je rends.**
tu portes.	**tu finis.**	**tu rends.**
il porte.	**il finit.**	**il rend.**
nous portons.	**nous finissons.**	**nous rendons.**
vous portez.	**vous finissez.**	**vous rendez.**
ils portent.	**ils finissent.**	**ils rendent.**

PAST INDEFINITE.

(I *came back* last year or this year, last month or this month, last week or this week, yesterday, to-day, this morning, an hour ago.)

j'ai porté.	**j'ai fini.**	**j'ai rendu.**
tu as porté.	**tu as fini.**	**tu as rendu.**
il a porté.	**il a fini.**	**il a rendu.**
nous avons porté.	**nous avons fini.**	**nous avons rendu.**
vous avez porté.	**vous avez fini.**	**vous avez rendu.**
ils ont porté.	**ils ont fini.**	**ils ont rendu.**

IMPERFECT.

(I *came back* — meaning *used to come back* — every day for dinner; I *was coming back* from the town when I met your brother.)

je portais.	**je finissais.**	**je rendais.**
tu portais.	**tu finissais.**	**tu rendais.**
il portait.	**il finissait.**	**il rendait.**
nous portions.	**nous finissions.**	**nous rendions.**
vous portiez.	**vous finissiez.**	**vous rendiez.**
ils portaient.	**ils finissaient.**	**ils rendaient.**

PLUPERFECT.

(I *had come back* already when the Emperor died; he *had died* before I came in.)

j'avais porté.	**j'avais fini.**	**j'avais rendu.**
tu avais porté.	**tu avais fini.**	**tu avais rendu.**
il avait porté.	**il avait fini.**	**il avait rendu.**
nous avions porté.	**nous avions fini.**	**nous avions rendu.**
vous aviez porté	**vous aviez fini.**	**vous aviez rendu.**
ils avaient porté.	**ils avaient fini.**	**ils avaient rendu.**

PRETERITE

(I *came back*, in narratives or historical style.)

je portai.	**je finis.**	**je rendis.**
tu portas.	**tu finis.**	**tu rendis.**
il porta.	**il finit.**	**il rendit.**
nous portâmes.	**nous finîmes.**	**nous rendîmes.**
vous portâtes.	**vous finîtes.**	**vous rendîtes.**
ils portèrent.	**ils finirent.**	**ils rendirent.**

PAST ANTERIOR.

(Scarcely *had* Cæsar *entered* the Senate when he was slaughtered: historical style.)

j'eus porté.	**j'eus fini.**	**j'eus rendu.**
tu eus porté.	**tu eus fini.**	**tu eus rendu.**
il eut porté.	**il eut fini.**	**il eut rendu.**
nous eûmes porté.	**nous eûmes fini.**	**nous eûmes rendu.**
vous eûtes porté.	**vous eûtes fini.**	**vous eûtes rendu.**
ils eurent porté.	**ils eurent fini.**	**ils eurent rendu.**

FUTURE.

(I *shall* or *will come back*.)

je porterai.	**je finirai.**	**je rendrai.**
tu porteras.	**tu finiras.**	**tu rendras.**
il portera.	**il finira.**	**il rendra.**
nous porterons.	**nous finirons.**	**nous rendrons.**
vous porterez.	**vous finirez.**	**vous rendrez.**
ils porteront.	**ils finiront.**	**ils rendront.**

FUTURE ANTERIOR.

(I *shall have come back* — or *shall be back* — before you go.)

j'aurai porté.	**j'aurai fini.**	**j'aurai rendu.**
tu auras porté.	**tu auras fini.**	**tu auras rendu.**
il aura porté.	**il aura fini.**	**il aura rendu.**
nous aurons porté.	**nous aurons fini.**	**nous aurons rendu.**
vous aurez porté.	**vous aurez fini.**	**vous aurez rendu.**
ils auront porté.	**ils auront fini.**	**ils auront rendu.**

CONDITIONAL PRESENT.

(I *should* or *would come back if* . . .)

je porterais.	**je finirais.**	**je rendrais.**
tu porterais.	**tu finirais.**	**tu rendrais.**
il porterait.	**il finirait.**	**il rendrait.**
nous porterions.	**nous finirions.**	**nous rendrions.**
vous porteriez.	**vous finiriez.**	**vous rendriez.**
ils porteraient.	**ils finiraient.**	**ils rendraient.**

CONDITIONAL PAST.

(I *should have come back* but for your brother.)

j'aurais porté.	j'aurais fini.	j'aurais rendu.
tu aurais porté.	tu aurais fini.	tu aurais rendu.
il aurait porté.	il aurait fini.	il aurait rendu.
nous aurions porté.	nous aurions fini.	nous aurions rendu.
vous auriez porté.	vous auriez fini.	vous auriez rendu.
ils auraient porté.	ils auraient fini.	ils auraient rendu.

SUBJUNCTIVE PRESENT.

(Is it necessary, *or* do you think, *or* do you wish that he *should come back?*)

que je porte.	que je finisse.	que je rende.
que tu portes.	que tu finisses.	que tu rendes.
qu'il porte.	qu'il finisse.	qu'il rende.
que nous portions.	que nous finissions.	que nous rendions.
que vous portiez.	que vous finissiez.	que vous rendiez.
qu'ils portent.	qu'ils finissent.	qu'ils rendent.

SUBJUNCTIVE PAST.

(Is it necessary, *or* do you think, *or* do you wish that he *should have come back* before my departure?)

que j'aie porté.	que j'aie fini.	que j'aie rendu.
que tu aies porté.	que tu aies fini.	que tu aies rendu.
qu'il ait porté.	qu'il ait fini.	qu'il ait rendu.
que nous ayons porté.	que nous ayons fini.	que nous ayons rendu.
que vous ayez porté.	que vous ayez fini.	que vous ayez rendu.
qu'ils aient porté.	qu'ils aient fini.	qu'ils aient rendu.

SUBJUNCTIVE IMPERFECT.

(Was it necessary, *or* did you think, *or* did you wish that he *should come back?*)

que je portasse.	que je finisse.	que je rendisse.
que tu portasses.	que tu finisses.	que tu rendisses.
qu'il portât.	qu'il finît.	qu'il rendît.
que nous portassions.	que nous finissions.	que nous rendissions.
que vous portassiez.	que vous finissiez.	que vous rendissiez.
qu'ils portassent.	qu'ils finissent.	qu'ils rendissent.

SUBJUNCTIVE PLUPERFECT.

(Was it necessary, *or* did you think, *or* did you wish that he *should have come back* before my departure?)

que j'eusse porté.	**que j'eusse fini.**	**que j'eusse rendu.**
que tu eusses porté.	**que tu eusses fini.**	**que tu eusses rendu.**
qu'il eût porté.	**qu'il eût fini.**	**qu'il eût rendu.**
que nous eussions porté.	**que nous eussions fini.**	**que nous eussions rendu.**
que vous eussiez porté.	**que vous eussiez fini.**	**que vous eussiez rendu.**
qu'ils eussent porté.	**qu'ils eussent fini.**	**qu'ils eussent rendu.**

IMPERATIVE.

(*Come back* at once.)

porte.	**finis.**	**rends.**
portons.	**finissons.**	**rendons.**
portez.	**finissez.**	**rendez.**

XXI. Peculiarities in verbs of the first conjugation.

All the verbs of the 1st conjugation, but two, are regular, and consequently conjugated like **porter**. But a few, besides those which have been seen in §§ 69–70, present some peculiarities.

(1) Verbs in **-ier**, such as **prier**, **crier**, have two consecutive **i**'s in the 1st and 2nd persons plural of the imperfect indicative and present subjunctive: **priions**, **priiez**, **criions**, **criiez**; the first **i** belongs to the root, the second to the termination.

(2) In verbs in **-yer**, after the **y** of the root, there is an **i** belonging to the termination in the same parts of the verb: **employions**, **employiez**.

XXII. Peculiarity in the second conjugation.

The verb **haïr**, *to hate*, loses the diæresis in the singular of the present indicative: **je hais**, **tu hais**, **il hait**; and the second singular of the imperative: **hais**.

XXIII. Peculiarity in the third conjugation.

Battre, and all verbs formed with it (**abattre**, **combattre**, etc.) take only one **t** in the singular of the present indicative, and the second singular of the imperative: **je bats**, **tu bats**, **il bat**, **ne bats pas**. In all other tenses they are regular.

XXIV. Verbs in -evoir.

Seven verbs ending **-evoir** form a whole conjugation in most grammars, according to which the 1st ends in **-er**, the 2nd in **-ir**, the 3rd in **-evoir**, and the 4th in **-re**.

INFINITIVE PRESENT.	INFINITIVE PAST.
recevoir, *to receive.*	**avoir reçu,** *to have received.*
PARTICIPLE PRESENT.	PARTICIPLE PAST.
recevant, *receiving.*	**reçu,** *received.*
INDICATIVE PRESENT.	PAST INDEFINITE.
je reçois, *I receive.*	**j'ai reçu,** *I received.*
tu reçois.	**tu as reçu.**
il, elle reçoit.	**il, elle a reçu.**
nous recevons.	**nous avons reçu.**
vous recevez.	**vous avez reçu.**
ils, elles reçoivent.	**ils, elles ont reçu.**
IMPERFECT.	PLUPERFECT.
je recevais, *I was receiving.*	**j'avais reçu,** *I had received.*
tu recevais.	**tu avais reçu.**
il, elle recevait.	**il, elle avait reçu.**
nous recevions.	**nous avions reçu.**
vous receviez.	**vous aviez reçu.**
ils, elles recevaient.	**ils, elles avaient reçu.**
PRETERITE.	PAST ANTERIOR.
je reçus, *I received.*	**j'eus reçu,** *I had received.*
tu reçus.	**tu eus reçu.**
il, elle reçut.	**il, elle eut reçu.**
nous reçûmes.	**nous eûmes reçu.**
vous reçûtes.	**vous eûtes reçu.**
ils, elles reçurent.	**ils, elles eurent reçu.**
FUTURE.	FUTURE ANTERIOR.
je recevrai, *I shall receive.*	**j'aurai reçu,** *I shall have received.*
tu recevras.	**tu auras reçu.**
il, elle recevra.	**il, elle aura reçu.**
nous recevrons.	**nous aurons reçu.**
vous recevrez.	**vous aurez reçu.**
ils, elles recevront.	**ils, elles auront reçu.**

CONDITIONAL PRESENT.	CONDITIONAL PAST.
je recevrais, *I should receive.*	**j'aurais reçu,** *I should have received.*
tu recevrais.	**tu aurais reçu.**
il, elle recevrait.	**il, elle aurait reçu.**
nous recevrions.	**nous aurions reçu.**
vous recevriez.	**vous auriez reçu.**
ils, elles recevraient.	**ils, elles auraient reçu.**

SUBJUNCTIVE PRESENT.	SUBJUNCTIVE PAST.
that I may receive.	*that I may have received.*
que je reçoive.	**que j'aie reçu.**
que tu reçoives.	**que tu aies reçu.**
qu'il, qu'elle reçoive.	**qu'il, qu'elle ait reçu.**
que nous recevions.	**que nous ayons reçu.**
que vous receviez.	**que vous ayez reçu.**
qu'ils, qu'elles reçoivent.	**qu'ils, qu'elles aient reçu.**

SUBJUNCTIVE IMPERFECT.	SUBJUNCTIVE PLUPERFECT.
that I might receive.	*that I might have received.*
que je reçusse.	**que j'eusse reçu.**
que tu reçusses.	**que tu eusses reçu.**
qu'il, qu'elle reçût.	**qu'il, qu'elle eût reçu.**
que nous reçussions.	**que nous eussions reçu.**
que vous reçussiez.	**que vous eussiez reçu.**
qu'ils, qu'elles reçussent.	**qu'ils, qu'elles eussent reçu.**

IMPERATIVE.

reçois, *receive (thou).* **recevons,** *let us receive.* **recevez,** *receive (ye).*

XXV. The Passive Form.

Verbs have two Voices, namely: —

The Active Voice, when the subject does something, as, —

> **mon père me punit,** *my father punishes me.*
> **mon père m'a puni,** *my father has punished me.*

The Passive Voice,[1] when the subject has something done to it, as, —

> **je suis puni par mon père,** *I am punished by my father.*
> **j'ai été puni par mon père,** *I was punished by my father.*

[1] Only transitive verbs have a passive voice.

Conjugation of the passive verb **être frappé.**

INFINITIVE PRESENT.

être frappé, *to be struck.*

INFINITIVE PAST.

avoir été frappé, *to have been struck*

PARTICIPLE PRESENT.

étant frappé, *being struck.*

PARTICIPLE PAST.

ayant été frappé, *having been struck*

INDICATIVE PRESENT.

I am struck.

je suis frappé (ée).
tu es frappé (ée).
il est frappé (ée).
nous sommes frappés (ées).
vous êtes frappés (ées).
ils sont frappés (ées).

PAST INDEFINITE.

I have been struck, I was struck.

j'ai été frappé (ée).
tu as été frappé (ée).
il a été frappé (ée).
nous avons été frappés (ées).
vous avez été frappés (ées).
ils ont été frappés (ées).

IMPERFECT.

I was struck.

j'étais frappé (ée).
tu étais frappé (ée).
il était frappé (ée).
nous étions frappés (ées).
vous étiez frappés (ées).
ils étaient frappés (ées).

PLUPERFECT.

I had been struck.

j'avais été frappé (ée).
tu avais été frappé (ée).
il avait été frappé (ée).
nous avions été frappés (ées).
vous aviez été frappés (ées).
ils avaient été frappés (ées).

PRETERITE.

I was struck.

je fus frappé (ée).
tu fus frappé (ée).
il fut frappé (ée).
nous fûmes frappés (ées).
vous fûtes frappés (ées).
ils furent frappés (ées).

PAST ANTERIOR.

I had been struck.

j'eus été frappé (ée).
tu eus été frappé (ée).
il eut été frappé (ée).
nous eûmes été frappés (ées).
vous eûtes été frappés (ées).
ils eurent été frappés (ées).

FUTURE.

I shall be struck.

je serai frappé (ée).
tu seras frappé (ée).
il sera frappé (ée).
nous serons frappés (ées).
vous serez frappés (ées).
ils seront frappés (ées).

FUTURE ANTERIOR.

I shall have been struck.

j'aurai été frappé (ée).
tu auras été frappé (ée).
il aura été frappé (ée).
nous aurons été frappés (ées).
vous aurez été frappé (ées).
ils auront été frappés (ées).

CONDITIONAL PRESENT.

I should be struck.

je serais frappé (ée).
tu serais frappé (ée).
il serait frappé (ée).
nous serions frappés (ées).
vous seriez frappés (ées).
ils seraient frappés (ées).

CONDITIONAL PAST.

I should have been struck.

j'aurais été frappé (ée).
tu aurais été frappé (ée).
il aurait été frappé (ée).
nous aurions été frappés (ées).
vous auriez été frappés (ées).
ils auraient été frappés (ées).

SUBJUNCTIVE PRESENT.

that I may be struck.

que je sois frappé (ée).
que tu sois frappé (ée).
qu'il soit frappé (ée).
que nous soyons frappés (ées).
que vous soyez frappés (ées).
qu'ils soient frappés (ées).

SUBJUNCTIVE PAST.

that I may have been struck.

que j'aie été frappé (ée).
que tu aies été frappé (ée).
qu'il ait été frappé (ée).
que nous ayons été frappés (ées).
que vous ayez été frappés (ées).
qu'ils aient été frappés (ées).

SUBJUNCTIVE IMPERFECT.

that I might be struck.

que je fusse frappé (ée).
que tu fusses frappé (ée).
qu'il fût frappé (ée).
que nous fussions frappés (ées).
que vous fussiez frappés (ées).
qu'ils fussent frappés (ées).

SUBJUNCTIVE PLUPERFECT.

that I might have been struck.

que j'eusse été frappé (ée).
que tu eusses été frappé (ée).
qu'il eût été frappé (ée).
que nous eussions été frappés (ées).
que vous eussiez été frappés (ées).
qu'ils eussent été frappés (ées).

IMPERATIVE.

sois frappé (ée), *be struck.* **soyons frappés (ées),** *let us be struck.*
soyez frappés (ées), *be you* or *ye struck.*

XXVI. Conjugation of a reflective verb.

INFINITIVE PRESENT.

se laver, *to wash one's self.*

INFINITIVE PAST.

s'être lavé, *to have washed one's self.*

PARTICIPLE PRESENT.

se lavant, *washing one's self.*

PARTICIPLE PAST.

s'étant lavé, *having washed one's self.*

INDICATIVE PRESENT.

I wash myself.

je me lave.
tu te laves.
il se lave.

nous nous lavons.
vous vous lavez.
ils se lavent.

PAST INDEFINITE.

I have washed myself.

je me suis lavé (ée).
tu t'es lavé (ée).
il s'est lavé (ée).
nous nous sommes lavés (ées).
vous vous êtes lavés (ées).
ils se sont lavés (ées).

IMPERFECT.

I was washing myself.

je me lavais.
tu te lavais.
il se lavait.
nous nous lavions.
vous vous laviez.
ils se lavaient.

PLUPERFECT.

I had washed myself.

je m'étais lavé (ée).
tu t'étais lavé (ée).
il s'était lavé (ée).
nous nous étions lavés (ées).
vous vous étiez lavés (ées).
ils s'étaient lavés (ées).

PRETERITE.

I washed myself.

je me lavai.
tu te lavas.
il se lava.
nous nous lavâmes.
vous vous lavâtes.
ils se lavèrent.

PAST ANTERIOR.

I had washed myself.

je me fus lavé (ée).
tu te fus lavé (ée).
il se fut lavé (ée).
nous nous fûmes lavés (ées).
vous vous fûtes lavés (ées).
ils se furent lavés (ées).

FUTURE.

I shall wash myself.

je me laverai.
tu te laveras.
il se lavera.
nous nous laverons.
vous vous laverez.
ils se laveront.

FUTURE ANTERIOR.

I shall have washed myself.

je me serai lavé (ée).
tu te seras lavé (ée).
il se sera lavé (ée).
nous nous serons lavés (ées).
vous vous serez lavés (ées).
ils se seront lavés (ées).

CONDITIONAL PRESENT.

I should wash myself.

je me laverais.
tu te laverais.
il se laverait.
nous nous laverions.
vous vous laveriez.
ils se laveraient.

CONDITIONAL PAST.

I should have washed myself.

je me serais lavé (ée).
tu te serais lavé (ée).
il se serait lavé (ée).
nous nous serions lavés (ées).
vous vous seriez lavés (ées).
ils se seraient lavés (ées).

SUBJUNCTIVE PRESENT.	SUBJUNCTIVE PAST.
that I may wash myself.	*that I may have washed myself.*
que je me lave.	**que je me sois lavé (ée).**
que tu te laves.	**que tu te sois lavé (ée).**
qu'il se lave.	**qu'il se soit lavé (ée).**
que nous nous lavions.	**que nous nous soyons lavés (ées).**
que vous vous laviez.	**que vous vous soyez lavés (ées).**
qu'ils se lavent.	**qu'ils se soient lavés (ées).**

SUBJUNCTIVE IMPERFECT.	SUBJUNCTIVE PLUPERFECT.
that I might wash myself.	*that I might have washed myself.*
que je me lavasse.	**que je me fusse lavé (ée).**
que tu te lavasses.	**que tu te fusses lavé (ée).**
qu'il se lavât.	**qu'il se fût lavé (ée).**
que nous nous lavassions.	**que nous nous fussions lavés (ées).**
que vous vous lavassiez.	**que vous vous fussiez lavés (ées).**
qu'ils se lavassent.	**qu'ils se fussent lavés (ées).**

IMPERATIVE.

lave-toi, *wash thyself.* **lavons-nous,** *let us wash ourselves.*
lavez-vous, *wash yourselves.*

Observe that the pronoun object is placed after the imperative. See § 94. If the imperative is negative, the pronoun is placed before, according to the general rule, as: —

ne te lave pas,	*do not wash thyself.*
ne nous lavons pas,	*let us not wash ourselves.*
ne vous lavez pas,	*do not wash yourselves.*

XXVII. Conjugation of a reciprocal verb.

INDICATIVE PRESENT.

	Speaking of two persons only.	Speaking of more than two.
nous nous flattons	**l'un[1] l'autre,**	**les uns[1] les autres.**
vous vous flattez	**l'un l'autre,**	**les uns les autres.**
ils se flattent	**l'un l'autre,**	**les uns les autres.**

[1] All through the conjugation, put **l'une l'autre** if speaking of ***two feminine*** subjects, and **les unes les autres** if speaking of more than two.

PAST INDEFINITE.

nous nous sommes flattés	**l'un l'autre,**	**les uns les autres.**
vous vous êtes flattés	**l'un l'autre,**	**les uns les autres.**
ils se sont flattés	**l'un l'autre,**	**les uns les autres.**

IMPERFECT.

nous nous flattions	**l'un l'autre,**	**les uns les autres.**
vous vous flattiez	**l'un l'autre,**	**les uns les autres.**
ils se flattaient	**l'un l'autre,**	**les uns les autres.**

and so on till the

IMPERATIVE AFFIRMATIVE.

flattons-nous	**l'un l'autre,**	**les uns les autres.**
flattez-vous	**l'un l'autre,**	**les uns les autres.**

IMPERATIVE NEGATIVE.

ne nous flattons pas	**l'un l'autre,**	**les uns les autres.**
ne vous flattez pas	**l'un l'autre,**	**les uns les autres.**

If the reciprocal verb requires the preposition **à** before its object, it is conjugated in this way: —

INDICATIVE PRESENT.

We speak to each other.

nous nous parlons	**l'un à l'autre,**	**les uns aux autres.**
vous vous parlez	**l'un à l'autre,**	**les uns aux autres.**
ils se parlent	**l'un à l'autre,**	**les uns aux autres.**

If the reciprocal verb requires any other preposition before its object, the preposition is likewise placed between **l'un** and **l'autre**, or **les uns** and **les autres**, as: —

PAST INDEFINITE.

We fought against each other.

nous nous sommes battus	**l'un contre l'autre,**	**les uns contre les autres.**
vous vous êtes battus	**l'un contre l'autre,**	**les uns contre les autres.**
ils se sont battus	**l'un contre l'autre,**	**les uns contre les autres.**

XXVIII. Formation of Tenses.

For the formation of tenses, see pages 183, 184.

INFINITIVE.	PARTICIPLES.	PRESENT INDICATIVE.	
Absoudre, *to absolve.*	absolvant, absous, absoute.	j'absous, tu absous, il absout,	nous absolvons, vous absolvez, ils absolvent.
Acquérir, *to acquire.*	acquérant, acquis, -e.	j'acquiers, tu acquiers, il acquiert,	nous acquérons, vous acquérez, ils acquièrent.
Aller, *to go.*	allant, allé, -e.	je vais, tu vas, il va,	nous allons, vous allez, ils vont.
Assaillir, *to assail.*	assaillant, assailli, -e.	j'assaille, tu assailles, il assaille,	nous assaillons, vous assaillez, ils assaillent.
Asseoir, *to seat.*	asseyant, assis, -e.	j'assieds, tu assieds, il assied,	nous asseyons, vous asseyez, ils asseyent.
Battre, *to beat.*		*all regular except* je bats, tu bats, il bat.	
Boire, *to drink.*	buvant, bu, -e.	je bois, tu bois, il boit,	nous buvons, vous buvez, ils boivent.
Bouillir, *to boil.*	bouillant, bouilli, -e.	je bous, tu bous, il bout,	nous bouillons, vous bouillez, ils bouillent.
Clore, *to close.*	*no pres. part.* clos, -e.	je clos, tu clos, il clôt.	*no plural.*
Conclure, *to conclude.*	concluant, conclu, -e.	je conclus, tu conclus, il conclut,	nous concluons, vous concluez, ils concluent.
Conduire, *to conduct.*	conduisant, conduit, -e.	je conduis, tu conduis, il conduit,	nous conduisons, vous conduisez, ils conduisent.
Confire, *to preserve.*	confisant, confit, -e.	*In all other parts like* suffire.	

FUTURE.	IMPF. & PRET.	PRES. SUBJUNCTIVE.	IMPERATIVE.
j'absoudrai.	j'absolvais. *no preterite.*	que j'absolve.	absous, absolvons, absolvez
j'acquerrai.	j'acquérais. j'acquis.	que j'acquière.	acquiers, acquérons, acquérez.
j'irai.	j'allais. j'allai.	que j'aille, que nous allions, qu'ils aillent.	va, allons, allez.
j'assaillirai.	j'assaillais. j'assaillis.	que j'assaille.	assaille, assaillons, assaillez.
j'assiérai *or* j'asseyerai.	j'asseyais. j'assis.	que j'asseye.	assieds, asseyons, asseyez.
je boirai.	je buvais. je bus.	que je boive, que nous buvions, qu'ils boivent.	bois, buvons, buvez.
je bouillirai.	je bouillais. je bouillis.	que je bouille.	bous, bouillons, bouillez.
je clorai.	*wanting.*	que je close.	clos.
je conclurai.	je concluais. je conclus.	que je conclue.	conclus.
je conduirai.	je conduisais. je conduisis.	que je conduise.	conduis, conduisons, conduisez

INFINITIVE.	PARTICIPLES.	PRESENT INDICATIVE.	
Connaître, *to know.*	connaissant, connu, -e.	je connais, tu connais, il connaît,	nous connaissons, vous connaissez, ils connaissent.
Construire, *to*	*construct, is*	*conjugated like* conduire.	
Coudre, *to sew.*	cousant, cousu, -e.	je couds, tu couds, il coud,	nous cousons, vous cousez, ils cousent.
Courir, *to run.*	courant, couru.	je cours, tu cours, il court,	nous courons, vous courez, ils courent.
Craindre, *to fear.*	craignant, craint, -e.	je crains, tu crains, il craint,	nous craignons, vous craignez, ils craignent.
Croire, *to believe.*	croyant, cru, -e.	je crois, tu crois, il croit,	nous croyons, vous croyez, ils croient.
Croître, *to grow.*	croissant, crû, crue.	je crois, tu crois il croît,	nous croissons, vous croissez, ils croissent.
Cueillir, *to gather.*	cueillant, cueilli, -e.	je cueille, tu cueilles, il cueille,	nous cueillons, vous cueillez, ils cueillent.
Cuire, *to cook.*	cuisant, cuit, -e.	*is conjugated like* conduire.	
Déchoir, *to fall.*	*wanting.* déchu, -e.	je déchois, tu déchois, il déchoit,	nous déchoyons. vous déchoyez, ils déchoient.
Devoir, *to owe, must.*	devant, dû, due.	je dois, tu dois, il doit,	nous devons, vous devez, ils doivent.
Dire, *to say.* *For compounds of*	disant, dit, -e. dire *see p.* 243.	je dis, tu dis, il dit,	nous disons, vous dites, ils disent.

FUTURE.	IMPF. & PRET.	PRES. SUBJUNCTIVE.	IMPERATIVE.
je connaîtrai.	je connaissais. je connus.	que je connaisse.	connais, connaissons, connaissez.
je coudrai.	je cousais. je cousis.	que je couse.	couds, cousons, cousez.
je courrai	je courais. je courus.	que je coure.	cours, courons, courez.
je craindrai.	je craignais. je craignis.	que je craigne.	crains. craignons, craignez.
je croirai.	je croyais. je crus.	que je croie, que nous croyions.	crois, croyons, croyez.
je croîtrai.	je croissais. je crûs.	que je croisse.	croîs, croissons, croissez.
je cueillerai.	je cueillais. je cueillis.	que je cueille.	cueille, cueillons, cueillez.
Or it may with faire	*be used in as an*	*the infinitive auxiliary.*	
je décherrai.	je déchoyais. je déchus.	que je déchoie.	déchois, déchoyons, déchoyez.
je devrai.	je devais. je dus.	que je doive, que nous devions.	dois, devons, devez.
je dirai.	je disais. je dis.	que je dise.	dis, disons, dites.

INFINITIVE.	PARTICIPLES.	PRESENT INDICATIVE.	
Dormir, *to sleep.*	dormant, dormi.	je dors, tu dors, il dort,	nous dormons, vous dormez, ils dorment.
Ecrire, *to write.*	écrivant, écrit, -e.	j'écris, tu écris, il écrit,	nous écrivons, vous écrivez, ils écrivent.
Envoyer, *to send.*	envoyant, envoyé, -e.	j'envoie, tu envoies, il envoie,	nous envoyons, vous envoyez, ils envoient.
Faillir, *to fail.*	*wanting.* failli.	il faut,	ils faillent.
Faire, *to do.*	faisant, fait, -e.	je fais, tu fais, il fait,	nous faisons, vous faites, ils font.
Falloir, *to be necessary.*	*wanting.* fallu.	il faut.	
Fuir, *to flee.*	fuyant, fui.	i *becomes* y *before a vowel, except before* -e, -es, -ent.	
Gésir, *to lie.*	gisant.	il gît,	nous gisons, vous gisez, ils gisent.
Joindre, *to join.*	joignant, joint, -e.	*is conjugated like* craindre, *substituting* oi *for* ai.	
Lire, *to read.*	lisant, lu, -e.	je lis, tu lis, il lit,	nous lisons, vous lisez, ils lisent.
Luire, *to shine.*	luisant, lui.	*is conjugated like* conduire.	
Mettre, *to put.*	mettant, mis, -e.	je mets, tu mets, il met,	nous mettons, vous mettez, ils mettent.
Moudre, *to grind.*	moulant, moulu, -e.	je mouds, tu mouds, il moud,	nous moulons. vous moulez, ils moulent.

FUTURE.	IMPF. & PRET.	PRES. SUBJUNCTIVE.	IMPERATIVE.
je dormirai.	je dormais. je dormis.	que je dorme.	dors, dormons, dormez.
j'écrirai.	j'écrivais. j'écrivis.	que j'écrive.	écris, écrivons, écrivez.
j'enverrai.	j'envoyais. j'envoyai.	que j'envoie.	envoie, envoyons, envoyez.
je faudrai.	je faillis.		
je ferai.	je faisais. je fis.	que je fasse.	fais, faisons, faites.
il faudra.	il fallait. il fallut.	qu'il faille.	
	je gisais.		
je lirai.	je lisais. je lus.	que je lise.	lis, lisons, lisez.
	no preterite.		
je mettrai.	je mettais. je mis.	que je mette.	mets, mettons, mettez.
je moudrai.	je moulais. je moulus.	que je moule.	mouds, moulons, moulez.

INFINITIVE.	PARTICIPLES.	PRESENT INDICATIVE.	
Mourir, *to die.*	mourant, mort, -e.	je meurs, tu meurs, il meurt,	nous mourons, vous mourez, ils meurent.
Mouvoir, *to move.*	mouvant, mû, mue.	je meus, tu meus, il meut,	nous mouvons, vous mouvez, ils meuvent.
Naître, *to be born.*	naissant, né, -e.	*is conjugated like* connaître *except preterite.*	
Nuire, *to injure.*	nuisant, nui.	*is conjugated like* conduire.	
Offrir, *to offer.*	offrant, offert, -e.	*is conjugated like* ouvrir.	
Ouïr, *to hear.*	ouï, -e.	*is conjugated only in the infinitive and compound tenses.*	
Ouvrir, *to open.*	ouvrant, ouvert, -e.	j'ouvre, tu ouvres, il ouvre,	nous ouvrons, vous ouvrez, ils ouvrent.
Paître, *to graze.*	paissant. *no past part.*	*is conjugated like* connaître.	
Partir, *to set out.*	partant, parti, -e.	je pars, tu pars, il part,	nous partons, vous partez, ils partent.
Peindre, *to paint.*	peignant, peint, -e.	*is conjugated like* craindre, *substituting* ei *for* ai.	
Plaire, *to please.*	plaisant, plu.	je plais, tu plais, il plaît,	nous plaisons, vous plaisez, ils plaisent.
Pleuvoir, *to rain.*	pleuvant, plu.	il pleut.	
Pourvoir, *to provide.*	pourvoyant, pourvu, -e.	je pourvois, tu pourvois, il pourvoit,	nous pourvoyons, vous pourvoyez, ils pourvoient.

FUTURE.	IMPF. & PRET.	PRES. SUBJUNCTIVE.	IMPERATIVE.
je mourrai.	je mourais. je mourus.	que je meure, que nous mourions, qu'ils meurent.	meurs, mourons, mourez.
je mouvrai.	je mouvais. je mus.	que je meuve, que nous mouvions. qu'ils meuvent.	meus, mouvons, mouvez.
	je nacquis.		
j'ouvrirai.	j'ouvrais. j'ouvris.	que j'ouvre.	ouvre, ouvrons, ouvrez.
	no preterite.		
je partirai.	je partais. je partis.	que je parte	pars, partons, partez.
je plairai.	je plaisais. je plus.	que je plaise.	plais, plaisons, plaisez.
il pleuvra.	il pleuvait. il plut.	qu'il pleuve.	
je pourvoirai.	je pourvoyais. je pourvus.	que je pourvoie.	pourvois, pourvoyons, pourvoyez.

INFINITIVE.	PARTICIPLES.	PRESENT INDICATIVE.	
Pouvoir, *to be able.*	pouvant, pu.	je peux (puis), tu peux, il peut,	nous pouvons, vous pouvez, ils peuvent.
Prendre, *to take.*	prenant, pris, -e.	je prends, tu prends, il prend,	nous prenons, vous prenez, ils prennent.
Se repentir, *to repent.*	repentant, repenti, -e.	*is conjugated like* partir.	
Résoudre, *to resolve.*	résolvant, résolu, -e, résous.	je résous, tu résous, il résout,	nous résolvons, vous résolvez, ils résolvent.
Rire, *to laugh.*	riant, ri.	je ris, tu ris, il rit,	nous rions, vous riez, ils rient.
Rompre, *to break.*	rompant, rompu, -e.	*the third person singular is* il rompt.	
Saillir, *to project,* *to gush forth,*	 *is conjugated* *is regular*	 *like* assaillir. *like* finir.	
Savoir, *to know.*	sachant, su, -e.	je sais, tu sais, il sait,	nous savons, vous savez, ils savent.
Sentir, *to feel.*	sentant, senti, -e.	*is conjugated like* partir.	
Servir, *to serve.*	servant, servi, -e.	je sers, tu sers, il sert,	nous servons, vous servez, ils servent.
Sortir, *to go out.*	sortant, sorti, -e.	*is conjugated like* partir.	
Souffrir, *to suffer.*	souffrant, souffert, -e.	*is conjugated like* ouvrir.	
Suffire, *to suffice.*	suffisant, suffi.	je suffis, tu suffis, il suffit,	nous suffisons, vous suffisez, ils suffisent.

FUTURE.	IMPF. & PRET.	PRES. SUBJUNCTIVE.	IMPERATIVE.
je pourrai.	je pouvais. je pus.	que je puisse.	*wanting.*
je prendrai.	je prenais. je pris.	que je prenne, que nous prenions, qu'ils prennent.	prends, prenons, prenez.
je résoudrai.	je résolvais. je résolus.	que je résolve.	résous, résolvons, résolvez.
je rirai.	je riais. je ris.	que je rie.	ris, rions, riez.
All the rest	*of the verb is*	*regular.*	
je saurai.	je savais. je sus.	que je sache.	sache, sachons, sachez.
je servirai.	je servais. je servis.	que je serve.	sers, servons, servez.
je suffirai.	je suffisais. je suffis.	que je suffise.	suffis, suffisons, suffisez.

INFINITIVE.	PARTICIPLES.	PRESENT INDICATIVE.	
Suivre, *to follow.*	suivant, suivi, -e.	je suis, tu suis, il suit,	nous suivons, vous suivez, ils suivent.
Taire, *to keep silent.*	taisant, tu, -e.	*is conjugated like* plaire.	
Tenir, *to hold.*	tenant, tenu, -e.	je tiens, tu tiens, il tient,	nous tenons, vous tenez, ils tiennent.
Traire, *to milk.*	trayant, trait, -e.	je trais, tu trais, il trait,	nous trayons, vous trayez, ils traient.
Tressaillir, *to start.*	tressaillant, tressailli, -e.	*is conjugated like* assaillir.	
Vaincre, *to overcome.*	vainquant, vaincu, -e.	je vaincs, tu vaincs, il vainc,	nous vainquons, vous vainquez, ils vainquent.
Valoir, *to be worth.*	valant, valu.	je vaux, tu vaux, il vaut,	nous valons, vous valez, ils valent.
Venir, *to come.*	venant, venu, -e.	*is conjugated like* tenir.	
Vêtir, *to clothe.*	vêtant, vêtu, -e.	je vêts, tu vêts, il vêt,	nous vêtons. vous vêtez. ils vêtent.
Vivre, *to live.*	vivant, vécu.	je vis, tu vis, il vit,	nous vivons, vous vivez. ils vivent.
Voir, *to see.*	voyant, vu, -e.	je vois, tu vois, il voit,	nous voyons, vous voyez, ils voient.
Vouloir, *to be willing.*	voulant. voulu, -e.	je veux, tu veux, il veut,	nous voulons. vous voulez. ils veulent.

FUTURE.	IMPF. & PRET.	PRES. SUBJUNCTIVE.	IMPERATIVE.
je suivrai.	je suivais. je suivis.	que je suive.	suis, suivons, suivez.
je tiendrai.	je tenais. je tins.	que je tienne, que nous tenions, que vous teniez.	tiens, tenons, tenez.
je trairai.	je trayais. *no preterite.*	que je traie, que nous trayions, que vous trayiez.	trais, trayons, trayez.
je vaincrai.	je vainquais. je vainquis.	que je vainque.	vaincs, vainquons, vainquez.
je vaudrai.	je valais. je valus.	que je vaille, que nous valions, que vous valiez.	*wanting.*
je vêtirai.	je vêtais. je vêtis.	que je vête.	vêts, vêtons, vêtez.
je vivrai.	je vivais. je vécus.	que je vive.	vis, vivons, vivez.
je verrai.	je voyais. je vis.	que je voie, que nous voyions, que vous voyiez.	vois, voyons, voyez.
je voudrai.	je voulais. je voulus.	que je veuille, que nous voulions, que vous vouliez.	veuille, veuillons, veuillez.

XXIX. List of verbs governing the infinitive without a preposition.

aimer mieux, *to prefer.*
aller, *to go, to be about to.*
affirmer, *to affirm.*
apercevoir, *to perceive.*
assurer, *to assert.*
avouer, *to confess.*
compter, *to expect.*
concevoir, *to conceive, to represent to one's self.*
confesser, *to confess.*
croire, *to believe.*
daigner, *to deign.*
déclarer, *to declare.*
déposer, *to depose* (as a witness).
désirer, *to desire.*
devoir, *to be to, to have to, must.*
écouter, *to listen.*
entendre, *to hear.*
envoyer, *to send.*
espérer, *to hope.*
faillir, *to have like to, to be near...*
faire, *to cause, to get, to have.*
falloir, *to be necessary.*
s'imaginer, *to fancy.*
laisser, *to allow, to let.*
mener, *to take.*
nier, *to deny.*
observer, *to observe.*
oser, *to dare.*
ouïr, *to hear.*
paraître, *to appear.*
penser, *to be like to, to be near...*
pouvoir, *to be able.*
préférer, *to prefer.*
prétendre, *to pretend.*
rapporter, *to relate.*
reconnaître, *to acknowledge.*
regarder, *to look at.*
retourner, *to go back.*
revenir, *to come back.*
savoir, *to know.*
sembler, *to seem.*
sentir, *to feel.*
souhaiter, *to wish.*
soutenir, *to maintain.*
témoigner, *to testify.*
valoir mieux, *to be better.*
venir, *to come.*
voir, *to see.*
vouloir, *to be willing.*

XXX. List of verbs requiring *de* before an infinitive.

accepter, *to accept.*
accorder, *to permit.*
achever, *to finish.*
affecter, *to affect.*
ambitionner, *to be ambitious to.*
appréhender, *to apprehend.*
s'aviser, *to bethink one's self.*
blâmer, *to blame.*
brûler, *to be impatient.*
cesser, *to cease.*
choisir, *to choose.*
commander, *to command.*
conjurer, *to entreat.*
conseiller, *to advise.*
se contenter, *to be satisfied.*
craindre, *to fear.*
crier, *to cry out.*
dédaigner, *to disdain.*
défendre, *to forbid.*
se dépêcher, *to hasten.*
détester, *to detest.*
différer, *to differ.*
dire, *to say, to tell.*
discontinuer, *to discontinue.*
écrire, *to write.*
s'efforcer, *to exert one's self.*
éluder, *to elude.*
empêcher, *to hinder.*
entreprendre, *to undertake.*
essayer, *to try.*
s'étonner, *to wonder.*
éviter, *to shun.*
s'excuser, *to excuse one's self.*
feindre, *to pretend.*
finir, *to finish.*
se flatter, *to flatter one's self, to hope.*
frémir, *to shudder.*
gager, *to wager.*
se garder, *to take care not.*
gémir, *to groan.*
se hâter, *to make haste.*
imaginer, *to take into one's head.*
s'indigner, *to be indignant.*
inspirer, *to inspire.*
interdire, *to forbid.*
jurer, *to swear.*
louer, *to praise.*

mander, *to write word.*
manquer, *to fail to.*
méditer, *to contemplate.*
se mêler, *to interfere.*
menacer, *to threaten.*
mériter, *to deserve.*
négliger, *to neglect.*
obliger, *to oblige, to do a service.*
obtenir, *to obtain.*
offrir, *to offer.*
omettre, *to omit.*
ordonner, *to prescribe.*
pardonner, *to forgive.*
permettre, *to permit.*
persuader, *to persuade.*
se plaindre, *to complain.*
prier, *to request, to ask.*
projeter, *to project.*
promettre, *to promise.*
proposer, *to propose.*
se proposer, *to purpose.*
protester, *to protest.*
recommander, *to recommend.*
redouter, *to fear.*
refuser, *to refuse.*
regretter, *to regret.*
se réjouir, *to rejoice.*
remercier, *to thank.*
se repentir, *to repent.*
reprocher, *to reproach.*
se réserver, *to reserve to one's self a right.*
résoudre, *to resolve.*
risquer, *to risk.*
rougir, *to blush.*
sommer, *to summon.*
se soucier, *to mind, to care.*
soupçonner, *to suspect.*
se souvenir, *to remember.*
suggérer, *to suggest.*
tenter, *to attempt.*
tâcher, *to endeavor.*
trembler, *to fear.*
se vanter, *to boast.*

XXXI. List of verbs requiring à before an infinitive.

s'abaisser, *to stoop to.*
aboutir, *to end in.*
s'accorder, *to agree in.*
s'accoutumer, *to accustom one's self.*
s'acharner, *to be eager at.*
admettre, *to admit.*
aguerrir, *to inure.*
s'aguerrir, *to inure one's self.*
aider, *to help.*
aimer, *to like.*
s'amuser, *to amuse one's self.*
s'appliquer, *to apply.*
apprendre, *to learn.*
s'apprêter, *to prepare one's self.*
aspirer, *to aspire.*
assigner, *to summon.*
assujettir, *to compel.*
s'assujettir, *to submit.*
s'attacher, *to make it one's study.*
s'attendre, *to expect.*
autoriser, *to authorize.*
s'avilir, *to demean one's self.*
avoir, *to have.*
balancer, *to hesitate.*
se borner, *to confine one's self.*
chercher, *to seek.*
commencer, *to begin.*
se complaire, *to delight.*
concourir, *to concur.*
condamner, *to condemn.*
se condamner, *to condemn one's self.*
condescendre, *to condescend.*
consentir, *to consent.*
consister, *to consist.*
conspirer, *to conspire.*
se consumer, *to ruin one's health.*
contribuer, *to contribute.*
convier, *to invite.*
coûter, *to cost.*
décider, *to persuade.*
se décider, *to decide.*
destiner, *to destine, to design.*
déterminer, *to persuade, to induce.*
se déterminer, *to determine.*
se dévouer, *to devote one's self.*
disposer, *to prepare, to fit.*
se disposer, *to prepare.*
dresser, *to train.*
employer, *to employ, to occupy.*
s'employer, *to employ, to occupy one's self.*
encourager, *to encourage.*
s'encourager, *to incite one's self.*
engager, *to induce.*
s'engager, *to bind one's self.*

s'enhardir, *to make bold.*
enseigner, *to teach.*
s'entendre, *to know how.*
s'étudier, *to make it one's study.*
exceller, *to excel.*
exciter, *to urge.*
s'exciter, *to stimulate one's self.*
s'exercer, *to exercise one's self.*
exhorter, *to exhort.*
s'exposer, *to expose one's self.*
se fatiguer, *to fatigue one's self.*
gagner, *to gain.*
s'habituer, *to accustom one's self.*
se hasarder, *to venture.*
hésiter, *to hesitate.*
instruire, *to instruct.*
s'instruire, *to instruct one's self.*
inviter, *to invite, to ask.*
se mettre, *to set about, to begin.*
s'obstiner, *to be obstinate.*
occuper, *to occupy, to employ.*
s'occuper, *to be engaged.*
s'offrir, *to offer, to stand forth.*
s'opiniâtrer, *to be obstinate.*
parvenir, *to succeed.*
pencher, *to lean.*
penser, *to think, to have some thoughts.*
persévérer, *to persevere.*
persister, *to persist.*
se plaire, *to delight.*
plier, *to bend.*
se plier, *to bend, to stoop.*
porter, *to induce, to prompt.*
préparer, *to prepare.*
se préparer, *to prepare one's self.*
prétendre, *to aspire.*
provoquer, *to provoke.*
réduire, *to reduce.*
se refuser, *to refuse one's self, not to admit.*
renoncer, *to renounce.*
répugner, *to be repugnant.*
se résigner, *to resign, to submit one's self.*
se résoudre, *to resolve.*
réussir, *to succeed.*
servir, *to serve.*
songer, *to think.*
suffire, *to be sufficient.*
tarder, *to delay, to be long.*
travailler, *to study, to endeavor.*
se tuer, *to kill one's self, to take much trouble.*
viser, *to aim, to aspire.*
vouer, *to devote.*
se vouer, *to devote, to apply, one's self.*

XXXII. Adjectives which change their signification according as they are placed before or after the noun.

Bon. Un homme bon, *a good man:* un bon homme, *a simple man:* un bon mot, *a pun:* une bonne parole, *a good word.*

Brave. Un homme brave, *a brave man:* un brave homme, *a worthy man.*

Certain. Une chose certaine, *a positive thing;* une certaine chose, *a particular thing.*

Commun. Une voix commune, *a common voice;* d'une commune voix, *unanimously.*

Dernier. Le mois dernier, *last month:* le dernier mois, *the last month* (of the year, of my stay in London, etc.).

Faux. Une fausse clef, *a skeleton key:* une clef fausse, *a wrong key:* une fausse porte, *a secret door;* une porte fausse, *a false door.*

Furieux. Un furieux menteur, *a terrible liar;* un homme furieux, *an enraged man.*

Galant. Un galant homme, *a well-bred man;* un homme galant, *a man polite to ladies.*

Gentil. Un gentilhomme, *a nobleman;* un homme gentil, *a gay, polite man.*

Grand. Un grand homme, *a great man;* un homme grand, *a tall man.* But if, after *grand homme*, some other external qualities are added, it means *tall: C'est un grand homme blond, bien fait.* In like manner if, after *un homme grand*, some moral qualification is added, *grand* does not refer to the size: *Un homme grand dans ses desseins.* Le grand air, *noble manners;* l'air grand, *a noble look.*

Haut. Le haut ton, *an arrogant manner;* le ton haut, *a loud voice.*

Honnête. Un honnête homme, *an honest man;* un homme honnête, *a polite man.*

Mauvais. Le mauvais air, *vulgar appearance;* l'air mauvais, *ill-natured look.*

Méchant. Une méchante épigramme, *a poor epigram;* une épigramme méchante, *a wicked epigram.*

Mortel. Un mortel ennemi, *a deadly enemy:* l'homme mortel, *mortal man.*

Neuf. Un habit neuf, *a new-made coat;* un habit nouveau, *a coat of new fashion;* un nouvel habit, *another coat.*

Nouveau. Le nouveau vin, *wine different from that which was drunk before, newly broached wine;* du vin nouveau, *wine newly made.*

Pauvre. When placed before the noun, it has the various significations which the word *poor* has in English: *assister un pauvre vieillard, une pauvre veuve, un pauvre homme,* means to assist one in poverty; *le pauvre enfant, les pauvres innocents, le pauvre animal,* are terms of endearment; *un pauvre orateur, de pauvre vin,* are terms of contempt. When placed after the noun it always signifies poverty: un homme pauvre, *a needy man.*

Petit. Un petit homme, *a little man;* un homme petit, *a mean man.* Observe that *petit* has its natural meaning when placed before the noun, its figurative when placed after. It is the reverse with *grand.*

Plaisant. Un plaisant conte, *an unlikely, absurd tale;* un conte plaisant, *an amusing story.* Un plaisant homme, *a ridiculous man;* un homme plaisant, *a humorous man.*

Propre. Mon propre habit, *my own coat;* un habit propre, *a clean coat.*

Seul. Un seul homme, *a single man;* un homme seul, *a man alone.*

Triste. Un triste homme, *a poor kind of a man;* un homme triste, *a sorrowful man.*

Vilain. Un vilain homme, *a disagreeable man;* un homme fort vilain, *an ugly man.*

THE ADVERB.

Formation of qualificative adverbs.

(1) Qualificative adverbs are formed either from the masculine of adjectives, or from the feminine.

(2) If the masculine ends with a vowel, the termination **-ment** is added: **poli, poliment; sage, sagement.**

Exceptions. — **Impuni** makes **impunément**; **prodigue, prodigalement**; **traître, traîtreusement. Aveugle, conforme, énorme, incommode, opiniâtre,** and **uniforme,** change *e mute* into **é**; **aveuglément.**

(3) If the masculine ends with a consonant, it is to the feminine that the termination **-ment** is added.

Pur, purement; franc, franchement; sec, sèchement; complet, complètement; heureux, heureusement; actif, activement.

Exceptions. — **Gentil** makes **gentiment. Commun, confus, diffus, exprès, importun, obscur, précis, profond,** end in **-ément** instead of **-ement: communément, confusément,** etc.

The adjectives **beau, nouveau, fou, mou,** being derived from **bel, nouvel, fol, mol,** are considered as ending with a consonant, and make **bellement, nouvellement, follement, mollement.**

(4) If the masculine ends in **-nt, nt** is changed into **-mment,** and the last two syllables are pronounced **amant: méchant, méchamment; prudent, prudemment.**

Exceptions. — The three adjectives **lent, présent, véhément,** make **lentement, présentement, véhémentement.**

VOCABULARY.

I. — FRENCH-ENGLISH.

A, *has.*
il y a, *there is, there are, ago.*
à, *to, at, in, by.*
abandonner, *to abandon.*
abeille, *bee.*
abhorré de, *abhorred by.*
abondant, *abundant.*
d'abord, *at first.*
aboyer, *to bark.*
absolument, *entirely, absolutely.*
s'abstenir, *to abstain.*
abstinence, *abstinence.*
abuser, *to abuse.*
accepté, *accepted.*
accepter, *to accept.*
accès, *fit.*
accident, *accident.*
accompagner, *to accompany.*
accord, *agreement.*
accoutumer, *to accustom.*
accueil, *reception, welcome.*
accueillir, *to receive.*
accuser, *to accuse.*
acheté, *bought.*
acheter, (à), *to buy from.*
acquérir, *to acquire.*
s'acquitter, *to perform.*
acte, *act.*
actif, *active.*
action, *engagement, action.*
adjectif, *adjective.*
admettre, *to admit.*
admirer, *to admire.*
adresser, *to apply to.*
s'adresser (à), *to address.*
affaire, *affair, matter.*
affliger, *to afflict, to distress.*
affreux, *sombre, frightful.*
afin de, *in order to.*
afin que, *so that.*
âge, *age.*
moyen âge, *Middle Ages.*
âgé, *old.*
agi, *behaved.*
agir, *to act, to behave.*
agréable, *pleasant, agreeable.*
aide, *help.*
aiguille, *needle.*
ailleurs, *elsewhere.*
d'ailleurs, *besides.*
aimable, *amiable, kind.*
aimer, *to like, to love.*
ainsi, *thus, so.*
aise, bien aise, *glad.*
allé, *gone.*
aller, *to go.*
allons! *come!*
almanach, *almanac.*
alors, *then, at that time.*
ambition, *ambition.*
amener, *to bring.*
Amérique, *America.*
ami, *friend.*
amitié, *friendship.*
amusant, *amusing.*
amuser, *to amuse.*
s'amuser, *to enjoy one's self.*
an, *year.*
ancien, *old, ancient.*
anglais, *English.*
Angleterre, *England.*
angora, *angora.*
animal, *animal.*
animé, *animated.*
année, *year.*
l'année dernière, *last year.*
annoncer, *to announce.*
août, *August.*
apercevoir, *to perceive.*
apoplexie, *apoplexy.*
appareil, *form, display.*
appartement, *room.*

appartenir, *to belong.*
appeler, *to call, summon.*
s'appeler, *to call one's self, to be called.*
appétit, *appetite.*
appliqué, *diligent.*
s'appliquer, *to apply one's self.*
apporter, *to bring (here).*
apportez-moi, *bring me.*
apprendre, *to learn.*
appris, *learnt.*
approbation, *approbation.*
s'approcher de, *to go up to, to come near.*
approuver, *to approve.*
appui, *support.*
appuyer, *to support.*
après, *after, afterwards.*
après-demain, *the day after to-morrow.*
après-midi, *afternoon.*
arbre, *tree.*
ardemment, *eagerly.*
ardoise, *slate.*
argent, *money, silver.*
argument, *argument.*
Aristote, *Aristotle.*
arracher, *to take out, to extort.*
arrêter, *to stop ; to fix.*
arrivé, *arrived.*
arrivée, *arrival.*
arriver, *to arrive, to happen.*
arrosé, *watered.*
arroser, *to water.*
article, *article.*
artillerie, *artillery.*
assemblée, *assembly, meeting.*
asseoir, *to seat.*
s'asseoir, *to sit down.*
assez, *enough ;* (bef. adj. or adv.), *pretty.*
assigner, *to assign.*
assurer, *to affirm, to maintain.*
atelier, *workshop, studio.*
attaquer, *to attack.*
attendre, *to wait (for).*
attentif, *attentive.*
attention, *attention, notice.*
attentivement, *attentively.*
attirer, *to attract, to drag.*
attraper, *to catch.*
au, *to the, at the.*
aucun, *any.*
audace, *audacity.*
au-devant, *before.*
aujourd'hui, *to-day.*
au moins, *at the least.*
auparavant, *before.*
auquel, à laquelle, auxquels, auxquelles, *to which.*
aussi, *also, as, therefore.*
aussitôt, *immediately, at once.*
aussitôt que, *as soon as.*
autant, *as much, as many.*
auteur, *author.*
autre, *other.*
autrefois, *formerly.*
autrement, *otherwise.*
Autriche, *Austria.*
Autrichien, *Austrian.*
aux, *to the, at the.*
il y avait, *there was, there were.*
avaler, *to swallow.*
plus avancé, *better off.*
avancement, *promotion.*
avancer, *to advance.*
avant, *before.*
avant-hier, *the day before yesterday.*
avec, *with.*
avenue, *avenue.*
avertir, *to warn, to notify.*
avocat, *lawyer.*
avoir, *to have.*
avouer, *to confess.*
avril, *April.*
ayant, *having.*

Bagage, *luggage.*
bague, *ring.*
baisser, *to stoop, to lower down.*
balbutier, *to stammer.*
balle, *ball, bullet.*
balustrade, *railing.*
banc, *bench.*
bas, *low.*
au bas, *at the foot.*
bataille, *battle.*
bateau, *boat.*
bateau à vapeur, *steamer.*
bâtir, *to build.*
bâton, *stick.*
batterie, *battery.*
battre, *to beat, to flap.*
se battre, *to fight.*
battu, *beaten.*
beau, bel, belle, *beautiful, fine, handsome.*
beau frère, *brother-in-law.*
beaucoup, *much, many, a great deal, plenty.*
Belgique, *Belgium.*
belle-sœur, *sister-in-law.*
besogne, *task, job.*

besoin (avoir), *to be in need, to need.*
bête, *beast, animal.*
bête (adj.), *stupid.*
beurre, *butter.*
bévue, *blunder.*
bibliothèque, *bookcase.*
bien, *well, very, a great many, most; indeed.*
eh bien! *well!*
bientôt, *soon.*
bière, *beer.*
billet, *note.*
blâmer, *to blame.*
blanc, blanche, *white.*
blé, *wheat.*
blessé, *wounded.*
blesser, *to wound.*
blessure, *wound.*
bleu, *blue.*
boire, *to drink.*
bois, *wood, grove.*
boite, *box.*
boiter, *to halt.*
bombe, *bomb.*
bon, bonne, *good.*
bonheur, *happiness, pleasure.*
bonhomme, *fellow, 'little man.'*
bonne, *maid-servant, nursemaid.*
bonté, *goodness.*
bord, *edge, bank, shore.*
au bord de la mer, *at the coast.*
bottine, *boot.*
boucle d'oreille, *earring.*
boulanger, *baker.*
bouquet, *nosegay.*
bourse, *purse; exchange.*
bouteille, *bottle.*
bouton, *stud.*
bracelet, *bracelet.*
bras, *arm.*
brave, *brave; honest.*
braver, *to brave.*
Bretagne, *Brittany.*
bride, *bridle.*
broche, *brooch.*
brouillard, *fog.*
bruit, *noise, report.*
brûler, *to burn.*
brusquement, *rudely.*
bruyant, *noisy.*
bu, *drunk.*

Ça (a familiar contraction for *cela*), *that.*
ça et là, *here and there.*
cabaret, *tavern.*
caché, *hidden.*
cacher, *to hide, to conceal.*
cadeau, *present.*
café, *coffee.*
cahier, *copy-book.*
caisse, *box.*
caisse d'épargne, *savings bank.*
calèche, *carriage.*
calme, *calm.*
camarade, *comrade.*
campagne, *country; campaign.*
à la campagne, *in the country.*
canne, *cane.*
caparaçonné, *caparisoned.*
capitaine, *captain.*
capitale, *capital.*
captiver, *to captivate, to take up.*
car, *for, as.*
carafe, *carafe, decanter.*
cargaison, *cargo.*
cas, *case, circumstance.*
en tous cas, *at any rate.*
casque, *helmet.*
casser, *to break.*
cathédrale, *cathedral.*
cause, *cause.*
à cause de, *on account of.*
causer, *to talk, to chat.*
ce, cet, cette, *this, that.*
ce qui, ce que, *what.*
ce que c'est que (voilà), *see what . . . is.*
ce sont, *they are.*
ceci, *this thing.*
céder, *to yield, to give way* or *place.*
céder le pas, *to give precedence.*
cela, *that thing.*
célébrer, *to celebrate.*
celle, *that, this.*
celle-ci, *this, this one.*
celle-là, *that, that one.*
celles, *those, these.*
celles-ci, *these, these ones.*
celles-là, *those, those ones.*
celui, *that, this.*
celui qui, *he who.*
celui-ci, *the latter, this, this one.*
celui-là, *that, that one.*
cent, *hundred.*
centime, *centime,* $=\frac{1}{5}$ of a cent.
cependant, *however, meanwhile.*
certain, *certain.*
certainement, *certainly.*
ces, *these, those.*
cesser, *to cease.*
c'est, *he is, she is, it is, they are.*

cet, cette, *this, that.*
ceux, *those, these.*
ceux-ci, *these, these ones.*
ceux-là, *those, those ones.*
chacun, *each, every one.*
chagrin, *sad, vexed, sorry.*
chaîne, *chain.*
chaise, *chair.*
chaleur, *warmth, heat.*
chambellan, *chamberlain.*
chambre, *room.*
champ de course, *race-ground.*
changement, *change.*
changer, *to change.*
chanson, *song.*
chanter, *to sing.*
chapeau, *hat.*
chapelle, *chapel.*
chaque, *each, every.*
charger, *to load, to charge.*
Charles, *Charles.*
charmant, *charming.*
charmé, *delighted.*
chasse, *hunt.*
chasser, *to drive, to hunt.*
chasseur, *huntsman.*
chat, chatte, *cat.*
chaud, *hot, warm.*
chaud (avoir), *to be warm.*
chauffer, *to warm.*
chemin, *way.*
cher, *dear.*
cherché, *looked for, sought.*
chercher, *to look for, to seek, to bring, to try.*
Chersonèse, *Chersonese.*
cheval, *horse.*
cheveu, *hair.*
chez, *at, in,* or *to the house of.*
chien, *dog.*
chiffre, *number.*
Chili, *Chili.*
choisi, *chosen.*
choisir, *to choose.*
choix, *choice.*
chose, *thing.*
chose (autre), *something else.*
choucroute, *sour-crout.*
ci, *here.*
ciel, *heaven, sky.*
cinq, *five.*
cinquante, *fifty.*
cinquième, *fifth.*
circonstance, *circumstance.*
clair, *clear, obvious.*
clair de lune, *moonlight.*
clameur, *noise.*
classe, *class.*
clé, *key.*
clergé, *clergy.*
cœur, *heart.*
de tout mon cœur, *with all my heart.*
coin, *corner.*
colère, *anger, passion.*
colonel, *colonel.*
combattre, *to fight.*
combien, *how much, how many.*
combien de temps, *how long.*
comique, *comical.*
commandant, *commander.*
commandé, ordered.
commander, *to order, to command.*
comme, *as, like, how.*
comme à l'ordinaire, *as usual.*
commencer, *to begin, to commence.*
comment, *how, what.*
commettre, *to commit.*
commission, *errand.*
compagnon, *companion.*
complet, *complete.*
complètement, *completely.*
composé, *composed.*
comprendre, *to understand.*
compte, *account.*
compter, *to count, to intend.*
concourir, *to take part.*
conducteur, *conductor, driver.*
conduire, *to take to; to drive.*
se conduire, *to behave.*
conduite, *conduct.*
confiance, *confidence.*
confier, *to trust, to intrust.*
se confondre, *to be lost in*
confus, *confused.*
congédier, *to dismiss.*
connaissance, *acquaintance, knowledge.*
connaître, *to know.*
conquérir, *to conquer.*
conseil, *advice; council.*
conseiller, *to advise, to recommend.*
consentir, *to consent.*
constamment, *constantly.*
consulter, *to consult.*
content, *satisfied, pleased.*

conter, *to relate.*
continuellement, *continually.*
continuer, *to continue.*
contraindre, *to compel.*
contraire, *contrary, reverse.*
au contraire, *on the contrary.*
contre, *against.*
convaincre, *to convince.*
convaincu, *convinced.*
convenable, *becoming.*
convenablement, *properly.*
convenir, *to agree.*
convenu, *appointed, agreed upon.*
conversation, *conversation.*
il convient, *it is proper.*
corbeau, *crow.*
corbeille, *basket.*
cordialité, *cordiality.*
Cordoue, *Cordova.*
corps, *body.*
correspondance, *correspondence.*
corriger, *to correct.*
côte, *coast.*
côté, *side; à . . . , to the side; de l'autre . . . , on the other side.*
cou, *neck.*
se coucher, *to go to bed, to lie down.*
coup, *shot, blow, stroke.*
coup de canon, *cannon-shot.*
coup de pied, *kick.*
tout à coup, *suddenly.*
coupable, *guilty.*
coupé, *cut.*
couper, *to cut, to cut off.*
cour, *court, court-yard.*
courage, *courage.*
courant d'air, *current of air.*
courir, *to run.*
cours, *course.*
course, *errand.*
court, *short.*
courtisan, *courtier.*
cousin, *cousin.*
couteau, *knife.*
coûter, *to cost.*
coutume, *habit.*
avoir coutume, *to be accustomed.*
couturière, *dressmaker.*
couvert (de), *covered (with).*
couvrir, *to cover.*
craindre, *to fear.*
crainte, *fear.*
crayon, *pencil.*
créer, *to create.*
crédule, *credulous.*
crême, *cream.*
Crésus, *Crœsus.*
cri, *cry.*
crier, *to cry, to cry out, to exclaim, to call out.*
crime, *crime.*
croire, *to believe.*
cruel, *cruel.*
cruellement, *cruelly.*
cueillir, *to gather, to harvest.*
cuirasse, *cuirass.*
cuisinière, *cook.*
cuivre, *copper.*
curieux, *curious.*

Dame, *lady.*
dans, *in.*
danse, *dance.*
date, *date.*
davantage, *more.*
de, *of, from, any, in, with, by.*
dé, *thimble.*
débarrasser, *to rid.*
se débattre, *to struggle.*
débiter, *to recite.*
debout, *standing up.*
déboutonner, *to unbutton.*
décembre, *December.*
décider, *to decide.*
décoration, *decoration.*
décourager, *to discourage.*
découvert, *discovered.*
découvrir, *to uncover.*
se découvrir, *to take off one's hat.*
dédire, *to contradict.*
défaut, *fault, defect.*
défendre, *to forbid.*
se défendre, *to defend one's self or each other.*
défendu, *forbidden.*
définitivement, *positively.*
dégoût, *dislike.*
déjà, *already.*
déjeuner (n.), *breakfast.*
déjeuner (v.), *to breakfast.*
de l', de la, *of the, some, any.*
délicieux, *delicious, delightful.*
demain, *to-morrow.*
demande, *inquiry.*
demander, *to ask (for); se ..., to ask one's self, to wonder.*

démarche, *step.*
déménager, *to remove.*
demeure, *dwelling.*
demeuré, *lived.*
demeurer, *to remain, to live.*
demi, à demi, *half.*
demi-douzaine, *half-dozen.*
demi-livre, *half pound.*
demoiselle, *young lady, unmarried lady.*
démontrer, *to prove.*
dent, *tooth.*
dentelle, *lace.*
départ, *departure.*
dépêche, *despatch.*
dépêcher, *to hasten.*
déplaire, *to displease.*
déposer, *to lay down.*
depuis, *since, for, from.*
depuis quand, *how long.*
déranger, *to disturb.*
dernier, *last.*
derrière, *behind.*
des, *of the, from the, some, any.*
dès que, *as soon as.*
désagréable, *disagreeable.*
descendre, *to come down, to let out, get out.*
déserter, *to desert.*
déserteur, *deserter.*
désirer, *to wish.*
désobéir, *to disobey.*
désolé, *grieved.*
désormais, *in future, henceforth.*
dessin, *design, drawing.*
dessus, *upon, above.*
détail, *detail.*
determiner, *to determine.*
détester, *to detest.*
détruire, *to destroy.*
deuil, *mourning.*
deux, *two.*
deuxième, *second.*
devant, *before, in front.*
devenir, *to become.*
devenu, *become.*
deviner, *to guess.*
devoir (n.), *duty.*
devoir (v.), *to owe, must.*
diamant, *diamond.*
dictée, *dictation.*
Dieu, *God.*
différent, *different.*
difficile, *difficult.*
difficulté, *difficulty.*
digne, *worthy.*
dignitaire, *dignitary.*
dimanche, *Sunday.*
dîner (n.), *dinner.*
dîner (v.), *to dine.*
dire, *to say.*
diriger, *to direct.*
discret, *discreet.*
discussion, *discussion.*
disgrâce, *displeasure.*
disparaître, *to disappear.*
disparu, *disappeared.*
disposé, *inclined.*
dit, *said.*
divin, *divine.*
dix, *ten.*
dix-huit, *eighteen.*
dixième, *tenth.*
dix-neuf, *nineteen.*
dix-sept, *seventeen.*
docteur, *doctor.*
doigt, *finger.*
domestique, *servant.*
don, *gift.*
donc, *then, so.*
donné, *given.*
donner, *to give, to ascribe.*
donner dans, *to come into, to strike.*
donnez, *give.*
dont, *of which, of whom, whose, with which.*
dormi, *slept.*
dormir, *to sleep.*
doué, *gifted.*
douleur, *grief, pain.*
douloureux, *painful.*
sans doute, *doubtless, of course.*
douter, *to doubt.*
doux, douce, *sweet, gentle.*
douzaine, *dozen.*
douze, *twelve.*
douzième, *twelfth.*
drap, *cloth.*
droit, *right ; straight.*
droite (à), *to the right.*
droiture, *uprightness.*
drôle, *strange, queer*. n., *rascal.*
du, *of the, from the ; some, any.*
dû, due, *due, must.*
duel, *duel.*
duquel, de laquelle, desquels, desquelles, *of which.*
dur, *hard.*
durer, *to last.*

Eau, *water.*
échapper, *to escape.*
écharpe, *scarf.*
échouer, *to fail.*
éclat, *brightness, lustre.*
éclater, *to burst.*
à l'école, *at school.*

écossais, *Scotch, Scotchman.*
Ecosse, *Scotland.*
écouter, *to listen.*
écran, *screen.*
s'écrier, *to exclaim.*
écrire, *to write.*
écrit, *written.*
écriture, *handwriting.*
écrivain, *writer.*
écurie, *stable.*
Edimbourg, *Edinburgh.*
édition, *edition.*
effet, *effect, fact, deed.*
en effet, *truly, so it is.*
effrayer, *to frighten.*
s'effrayer, *to be frightened.*
effrontément, *impudently.*
égal, *equal.*
cela m'est égal, *it is all the same to me.*
égarer, *to mislay.*
s'égarer, *to lose one's way.*
église, *church.*
égratignure, *scratch.*
eh bien ! *well !*
élaboré, *contrived.*
éléphant, *elephant.*
élève, *pupil.*
elle, *she, her, it.*
elle-même, *herself.*
elles, *they, them.*
elles-mêmes, *themselves.*
éloigné, *distant.*
émanation, *emanation.*
embarras, *embarrassment.*
embrasser, *to embrace.*
s'émouvoir, *to be moved.*
empêcher, *to hinder, to prevent.*
empereur, *emperor.*
empire, *empire.*
emplette, *purchase.*
employer, *to employ.*
emporter, *to carry off.*
s'empresser, *to hasten.*
emprunter (à), *to borrow (from).*
ému, *moved.*
en (pr.), *some, any, of it, of him, of her, of them, for it, hence, thence.*
en (prep.), *while, in, at.*
enchanté, *delighted.*
encore, *still, as yet, again.*
encourir, *to incur.*
encre, *ink.*
encrier, *inkstand.*
enfant, *child.*
enfermer, *to shut up.*
enfin, *at last.*
enlever, *to carry off.*
s'enlever, *to rise.*
ennemi, *enemy.*
s'enquérir, *to inquire.*
être enrhumé, *to have a cold.*
s'enrhumer, *to catch cold.*
enseigner, *to teach.*
ensemble, *together.*
il s'ensuit, *it follows.*
ensuite, *afterwards.*
s'ensuivre, *to follow, to result.*
entendre, *to hear ; to mean.*
entendre dire, *to hear, to learn.*
enthousiasmé, *carried away.*
entourer, *to surround.*
entre, *between.*
entré, *entered, come in.*
entreprise, *undertaking.*
entrer, *to go in, to enter.*
entretenir, *to converse with.*
envers, *towards.*
envie, *desire, fancy ; envy.*
environs, *neighborhood.*
envoyer, *to send.*
épais, *thick.*
épée, *sword.*
épingle, *pin.*
époque, *period.*
éprouver, *to feel, to experience.*
épuisé, *exhausted.*
éreinter, *to break the back.*
Ernest, *Ernest.*
erreur, *mistake.*
es, *art.*
espace, *space.*
Espagne, *Spain.*
espèce, *kind.*
espérer, *to hope (for).*
espion, *spy.*
esprit, *spirit, wit.*
essayer, *to try.*
essentiel, *essential, material.*
est, *is, belongs.*
n'est-ce pas ? *is it not ?*
estimer, *to esteem, to set a value on.*
et, *and.*
établir, *to establish, to secure.*
étant, *being.*
état, *condition.*
Etats-Unis, *United States.*
été (n.), *summer.*
été (partic.), *been.*

éteindre, *to put out.*
étinceler, *to flash.*
étonner, *to astonish.*
étourdi, *heedless.*
étrange, *strange.*
être (n.), *being.*
être (v.), *to be.*
être à, *to belong to.*
étroit, *narrow.*
étude, *study.*
étudier, *to study.*
eu, *had.*
Europe, *Europe.*
eux, *they, them.*
eux-mêmes, *themselves.*
éventer, *to divulge, to let out.*
éventualité, *event.*
évident, *evident.*
exactitude, *punctuality.*
exagérer, *to exaggerate.*
examiner, *to examine.*
excellent, *excellent.*
excepté, *except.*
excuse, *excuse.*
excuser, *to excuse.*
exécuter, *to execute.*
exemple, *example.*
exercice, *exercise, drill.*
exiger, *to demand, to require, to insist upon.*
expédition, *expedition.*
expérience, *experience.*
expliquer, *to explain.*
s'exposer, *to expose one's self.*
expression, *expression.*
exprimer, *to express.*
extravagance, *extravagance.*
extrême, *extreme.*

Face, *face, surface.*
en face de, *opposite.*

fâcher, *to vex.*
se fâcher, *to get angry.*
facile, *easy.*
facilement, *easily.*
faim, *hunger.*
faire, *to do, to make.*
faisan, *pheasant.*
fait, *does, makes; done, made, shaped; fact.*
falloir, *to be necessary, must, want.*
fameux, *famous.*
famille, *family.*
fatigant, *tiresome.*
fatigué, *tired, fatigued.*
il faut, *it is necessary, must.*
faute, *fault, offence.*
fauteuil, *arm-chair.*
faux, fausse, *false, artificial, adulterated.*
favori, favorite, *favorite.*
feld-maréchal, *field-marshal.*
femme, *woman, wife.*
fenêtre, *window.*
fer, *iron;* fers, *fetters.*
fermé, *shut.*
fermer, *to shut, to close.*
fermeté, *firmness.*
féroce, *fierce, ferocious.*
fête, *birthday.*
feu, *fire.*
février, *February.*
fidèle, *faithful.*
fier, *proud.*
se figurer, *to fancy.*
fil, *thread.*
fille, *daughter, girl.*
fils, *son.*
fin, *end.*
à la fin, *after all.*
fini, *ended, finished.*

finir, *to finish.*
fixer, *to fix.*
flambeau, *torch.*
flatter, *to flatter.*
se flatter, *to hope.*
flegmatiquement, *calmly.*
fleur, *flower.*
fleuve, *river.*
flocon, *flake.*
fois, *time.*
fonction, *function.*
fondre en larmes, *to burst into tears.*
font, *make.*
force, *strength, power.*
forêt, *forest.*
fort (adj.), *strong, hard,* (adv.), *much, very.*
fortune, *fortune.*
fou, fol, folle, *mad, foolish.*
foudre, *lightning.*
fouiller, *to ransack.*
foule, *crowd.*
fourrure, *fur.*
frais, fraîche, *fresh, cool.*
fraise, *strawberry.*
fraisier, *strawberry-bush.*
franc, *franc.*
franc, franche, *straightforward, frank.*
français, *French.*
France, *France.*
frapper, *to strike.*
fréquenter, *to frequent.*
frère, *brother.*
fripon, *rogue.*
froid, *cold.*
avoir froid, *to be cold.*
froideur, *coldness.*
fromage, *cheese.*

fruit, *fruit*.
fumée, *smoke*.
fumer, *to smoke*.
fureur, *fury*; en . . . , *wild*.
furieux, *furious*.
fusil, *gun*.

Gagner, *to reach, to gain*.
gai, *cheerful, merry*.
gaiement, *cheerfully*.
ganache, *blockhead*.
gant, *glove*.
garçon, *boy*.
garde, *notice*; *keeper, guard*.
prendre garde, *to look out, to take care*.
garder, *to keep*.
gâter, *to spoil*.
gauche (à), *to the left*.
geler, *to freeze*.
gêner, *to inconvenience*.
général, *general*.
généreux, *generous*.
genou, *knee*.
gens, *people*.
gentil, *pretty*.
géographie, *geography*.
giberne, *cartridge-pouch*.
gibier, *game*.
gloire, *glory*.
goût, *taste*.
goûter, *to taste, to lunch*.
grâce à, *thanks to*.
de grâce, *pray, I pray you*.
gracieux, *graceful*.
grammaire, *grammar*.
grand, *large, tall, great*.
grand-père, *grandfather*.
gras, *fat*.
grave, *grave, severe*.
gravement, *gravely*.
gravure, *engraving*.
grec, grecque, *Greek*.
grêle, *hail*.
grelotter, *to shiver*.
grenade, *pomegranate*.
grenadier, *grenadier*.
gronder, *to growl, to scold*.
groom, *lackey*.
gros, *stout, big, large, rough*.
guérir, *to cure*.
guerre, *war*.

Habile, *clever*.
habilement, *skilfully*.
habit, *coat*.
habitant, *inhabitant*.
habitation, *habitation*.
habiter, *to dwell in*.
habitude, *habit*.
habitué, *accustomed*, n., *frequenter*.
haïr, *to hate*.
haleine, *breath*.
haricots, *beans*.
hasard, *chance*; par. . .; *perchance*.
haut (adv.), *loud*; (adj.), *high, tall*; (subst.), *height*.
Henri, *Henry*.
hériter, *to inherit*.
heure, *hour, o'clock*.
heureusement, *happily*.
heureux, *happy, fortunate*.
hier, *yesterday*.
hier soir, *last night*.
histoire, *history, story*.
hiver, *winter*.
hommage, *homage*.
homme, *man*.
honnête, *honest, polite, civil*.
honnêteté, *kindness*.
honte, *shame*.
honteux, *shameful*.
horrible, *horrible*.
horriblement, *dreadfully*.
hôtel, *hotel, mansion*.
huit, *eight*.
huitième, *eighth*.
humeur, *temper*.
humide, *damp, moist*.
hypocrite, *hypocritical*.

Ici, *here*.
ignorer, *to be ignorant of*.
il, *he, it*.
île, *island*.
ils, *they*.
s'imaginer, *to fancy*.
imiter, *to imitate*.
immense, *immense*.
impatient, *impatient*.
impertinence, *impertinence*.
impertinent, *impertinent fellow*.
impitoyable, *pitiless*.
important, *important*.
il importe, *it is important*.
impossible, *impossible*.
inattendu, *unexpected*.
incliner, *to bend*.
s'incliner, *to bow*.
incroyable, *incredible*.
indiquer, *to indicate*.
indiscrétion, *indiscretion*.

indispensable, *indispensable.*
indisposé, *indisposed.*
infâme, *infamous.*
inférieur, *lower.*
infiniment, *infinitely.*
infortune, *misfortune.*
ingrat, *ungrateful.*
injustement, *unjustly.*
inquiéter, *to annoy.*
s'inquiéter, *to trouble one's self.*
inscrire, *to write down.*
insecte, *insect.*
instant, *moment.*
instruit, *wise.*
s'instruire, *to acquire information.*
insulter, *to insult.*
intelligence, *intelligence.*
interdire, *to forbid.*
intéressant, *interesting.*
intéresser, *to interest.*
intérêt, *interest.*
interpeller, *to speak to.*
inutile, *useless.*
invitation, *invitation.*
inviter, *to invite.*
Irlande, *Ireland.*
irrésolu, *irresolute.*
Italie, *Italy.*
italien, *Italian.*

J' stands for *je.*
J. C., *Christ.*
jalousie, *jealousy; blind.*
jaloux, *jealous.*
jamais, *ever.*
ne. . . jamais, *never.*
jambe, *leg.*
à toutes jambes, *at full speed.*
janvier, *January*
jardin, *garden.*
jaune, *yellow.*
je, *I.*
Jean, *John.*
Jeanne, *Jane.*
jeter, *to cast, to throw.*
jeu, *game, play.*
jeudi, *Thursday.*
jeune, *young.*
jeûner, *to fast.*
jeunesse, *youth.*
joie, *joy.*
joindre, *to join.*
se joindre, *to meet.*
joli, *pretty.*
jouer, *to play.*
jouir de, *to enjoy.*
joujou, *toy.*
jour, *day.*
journal, journaux, *newspaper.*
journée, *day.*
jovial, *jovial.*
joyeux, *cheerful.*
juillet, *July.*
juin, *June.*
jurer, *to swear.*
jusqu'à, *as far as, till.*
juste, *just.*
tout juste, *exactly.*
justement, *just, exactly.*

Kilogramme, *kilogramme.*

L' stands for *le* or *la.*
la, *the, her, it.*
là, *there.*
laborieux, *industrious.*
lâche, *cowardly.*
laconisme, *laconism.*
laid, *ugly.*
laine, *wool.*
laisser, *to let, to allow, to leave.*
laisser tranquille, *to let alone.*
lait, *milk.*
lampe, *lamp.*
lancer, *to throw.*
langue, *tongue, language*
languir, *to languish.*
lapin, *rabbit.*
laquelle, *which.*
large, *broad.*
larme, *tear.*
las, *tired.*
latin, *Latin.*
le, la, *the, him, it.*
leçon, *lesson.*
lecture, *reading.*
lendemain, *next day.*
lentement, *slowly.*
léopard, *leopard.*
lequel, laquelle, lesquels, lesquelles, *which.*
les, *the, them.*
lest, *ballast.*
lettre, *letter.*
leur, leurs, *their, to them.*
le leur, la leur, les leurs, *theirs.*
lever, *to raise.*
se lever, *to rise, to get up.*
lèvre, *lip.*
libraire, *bookseller.*
libre, *free.*
lieu, *place.*
au lieu de, *instead of.*
lieue, *league.*
lieutenant, *lieutenant.*
ligne, *line.*

lion, *lion.*
lionne, *lioness*
lire, *to read.*
lisière, *verge.*
lit, *bed.*
litre, *litre.*
livre (m.), *book.*
livre (f.), *pound.*
livrée, *livery.*
loger, *to lodge.*
l'on *stands for* on, *one, people, they.*
loin, *far.*
loin de, *far from.*
de loin, *from afar.*
Londres, *London.*
long, longue, *long.*
le long de, *through, along.*
longtemps, *a long time, long.*
lorsque, *when.*
louer, *to praise.*
louer, *to hire, to rent.*
loueur, *one who lets out.*
Louis, *Louis.*
louis, *louis* (a coin)
Louise, *Louisa.*
lourd, *heavy.*
lu, *read.*
lucratif, *lucrative.*
lueur, *gleam, flash, light.*
lui, *he, to him, to her.*
lui-même, *himself.*
de lui-même, *of his own accord.*
luire, *to shine, to glitter.*
lumière, *light.*
lundi, *Monday.*
lune, *moon.*
lunettes, *spectacles.*
lutte, *struggle*
lutter, *to struggle, to fight.*

M' stands for me
M. stands for Monsieur, *Sir, Mr.*
ma, *my.*
Madame, *Madam, Mrs.*
Mademoiselle, *Miss.*
magasin, *shop.*
magnanime, *magnanimous.*
magnifique, *magnificent.*
mai, *May.*
main, *hand.*
maint, *many, many a.*
maintenant, *now, by this time.*
maintenant que, *now that.*
mais, *but, why!*
maison. *house.*
à la maison, *at home.*
maître, *teacher, master.*
maîtresse, *mistress.*
majesté, *majesty.*
mal (n.), *harm, evil.*
mal (adv.), *ill, badly.*
de mal en pis, *from bad to worse.*
se porter mal, *to be unwell.*
malade, *ill, unwell, sick.*
maladie, *illness.*
malentendu, *misunderstanding.*
malgré, *in spite of.*
malheur, *misfortune.*
malheureusement, *unfortunately.*
malheureux. *unhappy, unfortunate.*
malin, maligne, *malignant, cunning, clever.*
malle, *trunk.*

maman, *mamma.*
manchon, *muff.*
mangé, *eaten.*
manger, *to eat.*
manière, *way, manner.*
manquer, *to miss, to fail.*
manquer de, *to lack, to be in need of.*
marchand, *dealer, merchant.*
marchander, *to bargain for.*
marche, *step.*
marcher, *to walk, to march, to go to work.*
mardi, *Tuesday.*
maréchal, *marshal.*
Maroc, *Morocco.*
mars, *March.*
matin, *morning.*
mauvais, *bad.*
mauvais sujet, *bad boy, bad fellow.*
me, *me, to me, myself, to myself.*
méchant, *naughty.*
mécontent, *displeased.*
mécontenter, *to displease.*
médecin, *doctor.*
meilleur, *better* (adj.).
mêler, *to mix.*
même, *same, even.*
de même, *likewise.*
mémoire, *remembrance, memory.*
menace, *threat.*
menacer, *to threaten.*
ménager, *to save.*
mener, *to take to, to lead.*
mensonge, *deceit, lie.*
mer, *sea.*
merci, *thanks.*

mercredi, *Wednesday*
mère, *mother.*
mériter, *to merit.*
mes, *my.*
Mesdames, *ladies, Mesdames.*
Mesdemoiselles, *Misses, the Misses.*
message, *message.*
Messieurs, *gentlemen, Messrs.*
mesure, *measure.*
mètre, *metre.*
mettre, *to put, to put on.*
le Mexique, *Mexico.*
midi, *noon; south.*
miel, *honey.*
le mien, la mienne, les miennes, les miens, *mine.*
mieux, *better* (adv.).
faire de son mieux, *to do one's best.*
milieu, *middle.*
au milieu de, *in the middle of, among.*
militaire, *soldier.*
mille, *thousand.*
million, *million.*
Miltiade, *Miltiades.*
ministre, *minister.*
minute, *minute.*
mis, *put, dressed.*
misérable, *miserable.*
misère, *misery.*
Mlle. stands for Mademoiselle, *Miss.*
Mlles. stands for Mesdemoiselles, *Misses, the Misses*
MM. stands for Messieurs, *gentlemen, Messrs.*
Mme. stands for Madame, *Madam, Mrs.*
Mmes. stands for Mesdames, *ladies, Mesdames.*
modèle, *model.*
moderne, *modern.*
modiste, *milliner.*
moi, *I, me, to me, as for me*; à moi! *help!*
moi-même, *myself.*
moins, *less, fewer.*
à moins de, *unless.*
au moins, *at the least.*
du moins, *at least.*
mois, *month.*
le mois dernier, *last month.*
moitié, à moitié, *half.*
moment, *moment.*
moments perdus, *spare moments.*
mon, ma, mes, *my.*
monde, *world.*
beaucoup de monde, *many people.*
personne au monde, *nobody in the world.*
tout le monde, *everybody.*
Monsieur, *Sir, Mr., gentleman.*
mont, *hill.*
monter, *to go up.*
montre, *watch.*
montrer, *to show, to point to.*
se moquer de, *to sneer at, laugh at.*
morceau, *piece.*
mordre, *to bite.*
morsure, *bite.*
mort (n.), *death.*
mort (part.), *dead.*
mot, *word.*
mouche, *fly.*
mouchoir, *handkerchief.*
mourant, *dying.*
mourir, *to die.*
mousseline, *muslin.*
moutarde, *mustard.*
mouvement, *movement.*
moyen, *means, way.*
moyen âge, *Middle Ages.*
mur, *wall.*
mûr, *ripe.*
musée, *museum.*
musicien, *musician.*
musique, *music.*

Naître, *to be born.*
faire naître, *to produce, to give rise to.*
nature, *nature.*
naturel, *natural.*
naufrage, *wreck.*
faire naufrage, *to be wrecked.*
ne . . . pas, *not.*
ne . . . que, *only, nothing but.*
né, *born.*
nécessaire, *necessary.*
négociant, *merchant.*
neige, *snow.*
nettoyer, *to clean.*
neuf, *nine.*
neuf, neuve, *new-made.*
neuvième, *ninth.*
neveu, *nephew.*
nez, *nose.*
ni . . . ni, *neither . . . nor.*
noir, *black.*
nom, *name.*
nombre, *number.*
nombreux, *numerous.*

non, *no.*
non plus, *either.*
nord-ouest, *north-west.*
nos, *our.*
notre, *ours.*
le nôtre, la nôtre, les nôtres, *ours.*
nous, *we, us, to us; ourselves, to ourselves.*
nous-mêmes, *ourselves.*
nouveau, nouvel, nouvelle, *new.*
de nouveau, *again.*
nouvelle, *report, news.*
novembre, *November.*
nu, *bare.*
nuire, *to injure.*
nuit, *night.*
cette nuit, *last night* (from 12 till this morning).

Obéir, to obey.
objet, *object.*
obligé, *obliged.*
obliger, *to oblige.*
obscur, *obscure, dark.*
observer, *to observe, to keep.*
obtenir, *to obtain.*
occasion, *opportunity.*
occupé, *busy, engaged.*
occuper, *to occupy.*
octobre, *October.*
œil, *eye.*
offenser, *to offend.*
offert, *offered.*
office, *office.*
bons offices, *kind offices.*
officier, *officer.*
offre, *offer.*
offrir, *to offer.*
oiseau, *bird.*
ombrelle, *parasol.*
omnibus, *omnibus.*
on, *one, people, we, you, they.*
oncle, *uncle.*
ont, *have.*
onze, *eleven.*
onzième, *eleventh.*
opéra, *opera.*
opération, *operation.*
s'opposer (à), *to oppose, to object.*
or, *gold.*
oracle, *oracle.*
orageux, *stormy.*
orange, *orange.*
ordinaire, *common.*
à l'ordinaire, *as usual.*
ordonner, *to order.*
ordre, *order.*
oreille, *ear.*
boucle d'oreille, *earring.*
oser, *to dare.*
ôter, *to take off* or *away.*
ou, *or.*
où, *where.*
oublier, *to forget.*
oui, *yes.*
les monts Oural, *Ural Mountains.*
outre, *beyond, besides.*
ouvert (adj.), *open;* (part.), *opened.*
ouverture, *opening.*
ouvrage, *work, book.*
ouvrir, *to open.*

Page, *page.*
paille, *straw.*
pain, *bread.*
paire, *pair.*
paix, *peace.*
palais, *palace.*
pâle, *pale.*
panier, *basket.*
pantoufle, *slipper.*
papier, *paper.*
paquet, *parcel.*
par, *by, through;* before words expressing time, *a* or *an.*
il paraît, *it appears.*
paraître, *to appear.*
parapluie, *umbrella.*
parbleu! *upon my word!*
parc, *park.*
parce que, *because.*
parcourir, *to perambulate.*
par-dessus, *over.*
demander pardon à, *to ask a person's pardon.*
pardonner, *to forgive.*
pareil, *like, alike, such.*
parents, *parents, relatives.*
paresseux, *lazy, idle.*
parfaitement, *perfectly, quite.*
parier, *to wager.*
parlé, *spoken.*
parlement, *parliament.*
parler, *to speak.*
parmi, *among.*
parole, *word.*
de ma (ta, sa) part, *from me, (thee, him, her).*
quelque part, *somewhere.*
parti, *gone away, departed, set out, left.*
en particulier, *privately.*
particularité, *peculiarity.*

partie, *part, party, excursion.*
partir, *to set out, to leave.*
partout, *everywhere.*
parvenir, *to reach, succeed.*
pas (noun), *step.*
passage, *passage.*
passer, *to spend, to hand, to escape, to go, to pass.*
se passer, *to take place, occur.*
pasteur, *pastor.*
patiner, *to skate.*
pauvre, *poor.*
payer, *to pay (for).*
pays, *country.*
paysan, *peasant.*
peine, *trouble, labor, grief*
à peine, *scarcely.*
pendant, *during, for.*
pendant que, *during, while.*
pénible, *painful.*
pensée, *thought.*
penser, *to think.*
pension, *boarding-school.*
perdre, *to lose.*
perdu, *lost.*
père, *father.*
permettre, *to permit.*
permission, *permission.*
Perses, *Persians.*
personnages, *personages.*
personne, *person, people, any one.*
jeune personne, *young lady.*
personne au monde, *nobody in the world.*
ne . . . personne, *nobody, no one.*
persuader, *to persuade.*
petit (adj.), *little, small, short.*
peu, *little, few.*
peu à peu, *by degrees.*
peuple, *people, nation.*
peur (avoir), *to be afraid.*
de peur de, *for fear of.*
peut-être, *perhaps.*
philosophie, *philosophy.*
phosphorique, *phosphorescent.*
photographie, *photograph.*
phrase, *sentence.*
pièce, *piece,* (theat.) *play.*
pied, *foot.*
à pied, *on foot.*
pierre, *stone.*
pierreux, *stony.*
piéton, *pedestrian.*
pis, *worse.*
pitié, *pity.*
place, *place, situation.*
placer, *to place.*
plaie, *wound.*
plaindre, *to pity.*
se plaindre, *to complain.*
plaire, *to please.*
plaisir, *pleasure.*
s'il vous plaît, *if you please.*
plante, *plant.*
planter, *to plant.*
plein, *full; open.*
pleuré, *wept, cried.*
pleurer, *to weep.*
pleuvoir, *to rain.*
pluie, *rain.*
plume, *feather, pen.*
la plupart, *most.*
plus, *more.*
ne . . . plus, *not again, no more, no longer.*
de plus en plus, *more and more.*
plus tôt, *sooner.*
plusieurs, *several.*
plutôt, *rather.*
pluvieux, *rainy.*
poche, *pocket.*
poids, *weight.*
point, *point.*
ne . . . point, *not, not at all.*
poire, *pear.*
poisson, *fish.*
poivre, *pepper.*
poliment, *politely.*
politesse, *politeness.*
pomme, *apple.*
pont, *bridge.*
bien portant, *well.*
porte, *door.*
porte-monnaie, *purse.*
porter, *to carry, to bear, to wear, to put.*
porter à, *to take to.*
se porter, *to be.*
portière, *door.*
portrait, *portrait.*
poser, *to place, to put down.*
posséder, *to possess.*
possible, *possible.*
poste, *post: post-office.*
pot de terre, *earthen pot.*
pour, *for, to, in order to.*
pourquoi, *why.*
poursuivre, *to pursue.*
pourtant, *yet, however.*
pourvoir, *to provide.*

pourvu que, *provided.*
pousser, *to carry, to utter.*
poussière, *dust.*
pouvoir, *to be able.*
pré, *meadow.*
précieux, *precious.*
précisément, *exactly.*
préférable, *preferable.*
préférer, *to prefer.*
premier, *first, former.*
prendre, *to take, catch.*
prendre garde, *to beware.*
prenez, *take.*
préparer, *to prepare.*
près de, *near, beside, closely, on the point of.*
présence, *presence.*
présent, *present.*
à présent, *now.*
présenter, *to show, to present.*
présider, *to preside over.*
presque, *almost.*
prêt, *ready.*
prêté, *lent.*
prétendre, *to pretend.*
prêter, *to lend.*
prêtre, *priest.*
prévenir, *to warn.*
prévenu, *warned.*
prévoir, *to foresee.*
prier, *to pray, to beg.*
prière, *prayer, entreaty.*
prince, *prince.*
princesse, *princess.*
principal, principaux, *principal.*
printemps, *spring.*
pris, *taken.*
prison, *prison.*
prisonnier, *prisoner.*
prix, *prize.*

prochain, *next.*
le mois prochain, *next month.*
prodigieusement, *greatly.*
professeur, *professor.*
profit, *benefit.*
proie, *prey.*
promenade, *walk; ride.*
promener, *to take out to walk.*
se promener, *to take a walk.*
promesse, *promise.*
promettre, *to promise.*
promis, *promised.*
promptement, *quickly.*
prononcer, *to pronounce, to utter.*
propos, *talk.*
proposition, *proposal.*
propre à, *fit for.*
propriétaire, *landlord.*
propriété, *property.*
protection, *patronage.*
protéger, *to protect.*
prouver, *to prove.*
proverbe, *proverb.*
provoquer, *to provoke.*
prudence, *prudence.*
Prusse, *Prussia.*
Prussien, *Prussian.*
pu, *been able.*
public, publique, *public.*
puis, *then.*
puisque, *since, as.*
puissant, *mighty.*
punir, *to punish.*

Qu' stands for *que.*
quand, *when.*
depuis quand, *how long.*
quant à, *as for.*

quarante, *forty.*
quart, *quarter, fourth.*
quart d'heure, *quarter of an hour.*
quartier, *quarter.*
Quartier Latin, *the Latin Quarter,* a part of Paris in which many colleges and schools are situated.
quatorze, *fourteen.*
quatre, *four.*
quatre-vingts, *eighty.*
quatre-vingt-dix, *ninety.*
quatrième, *fourth.*
que, *whom, which, that; than, as, how, let, since;* (interr.) *what.*
quel, quels, quelle, quelles, *what, which.*
quelque chose, *something.*
quelque part, *somewhere.*
quelque . . . que, *however, whatever.*
quelque temps, *sometime.*
quelqu'un, *somebody.*
quelquefois, *sometimes.*
quelques-uns, *a few.*
se quereller, *to quarrel.*
qu'est-ce que . . .? *what?*
question, *question.*
queue, *tail.*
qui, *who, which, that.*
qui (interr. or after prepos.), *whom.*
quinzaine, *fortnight.*
quinze, *fifteen.*
quitter, *to leave.*
quoi, *which, what.*
de quoi, *wherewith.*
quoique, *although.*

Raconter, *to relate, to tell.*
rafraichir, *to refresh.*
rageur, *angry.*
raide, *stiff.*
raison, *reason.*
avoir raison, *to be right.*
raisonnable, *reasonable, sensible.*
ramener, *to bring back.*
rang, *rank.*
rapidement, *quickly.*
rappeler, *to remind, to recall.*
rare, *rare.*
recevoir, *to receive.*
recherché, *sought after.*
réciproquement, *reciprocally.*
réclamer, *to claim.*
recogner, *to draw back.*
recommander, *to recommend, to order.*
recommencer, *to begin again.*
recompense, *reward.*
récompenser, *to reward.*
reconnaissant, *grateful*
reconnaitre, *to recognize.*
se recoucher, *to go to bed again.*
recueillir, *to harvest.*
reçu, *received.*
reculer, *to go back.*
redemander, *to ask back* or *again.*
reduire, *to reduce.*
réfléchir, *to reflect.*
réforme, *reform.*
refuser, *to refuse.*
regagner, *to get back to.*
regard, *look ; eyes.*
regarder, *to look at ; to concern.*
régiment, *regiment.*
règle, *rule.*
régler, *to settle.*
regretter, *to regret.*
régulier, *regular.*
réjouir, *to rejoice.*
relever, *to lift up, to push up.*
relire, *to read again.*
reluire, *to shine, glitter.*
remarquable, *remarkable.*
remarquer, *to notice.*
remercier, *to thank.*
remettre, *to put on again ; to send.*
remplir, *to fill, to fulfil.*
remuer, *to move.*
rencontrer, *to meet.*
rendre, *to render, to make, to return, to restore, to yield.*
rendre visite, *to pay a visit.*
se rendre, *to surrender one's self.*
renoncer, *to renounce*
rentes, *income, property.*
rentrer, *to enter, to return, to come home again.*
répandre, *to spread.*
repartir, *to set off again ; to answer.*
repas, *meal.*
se repentir, *to repent.*
répéter, *to repeat.*
sans réplique, *without replying, at once.*
répondre, *to answer.*
réponse, *answer.*
se reposer, *to rest one's self.*
reprendre, *to resume ; to reply.*
representation, *representation, show.*
reprocher, *to reproach.*
république, *republic.*
respect, *respect.*
manquer de respect, *to be disrespectful.*
respectueusement, *respectfully.*
ressembler, *to resemble.*
ressortir, *to go out again.*
du reste, *however.*
resté, *remained, stayed.*
rester, *to remain, to stay.*
résulter, *to follow.*
rétabli, *recovered.*
se rétablir, *to be restored to health.*
retenir, *to engage, to keep.*
retentir, *to resound.*
retirer, *to withdraw, draw back.*
retour, *return.*
de retour, *returned.*
retourner, *to return.*
retrouver, *to find, to find again.*
reussir, *to succeed, to be successful.*
réveiller, *to awaken.*
revenant, *ghost.*
revenir, *to come back.*
revenu, *come back, returned.*
revoir, *to see again.*
Rhin, *the Rhine.*
rhume, *cold.*
ri, *laughed.*

riant, *laughing.*
riche, *rich*
richement, *richly.*
ne . . . rien, *nothing.*
rire (n.), *laughter.*
rire (v.), *to laugh.*
rive, *bank, shore.*
rivière, *river.*
robe, *dress, robe.*
roi, *king.*
rôle, *character, part.*
roman, *novel.*
rompre, *to break.*
rose, *rose.*
rouge, *red.*
rougir, *to blush.*
rouler, *to roll.*
route, *road, way.*
royal, *royal.*
royaume, *kingdom.*
ruban, *ribbon.*
rue, *street.*
ruine, *ruin.*
ruisseau, *stream.*
ruse, *cunning, trick.*
Russie, *Russia.*

S' stands for *se*; before *il* or *ils*, for *si*.
sa, *his, her, its.*
sable, *sand.*
sac, *bag.*
sac de nuit, *carpet-bag.*
sacrifier, *to sacrifice.*
sacristain, *sexton.*
sage, *wise, good.*
saint, *holy.*
saisir, *to seize.*
saison, *season.*
sale, *dirty.*
salir, *to soil.*
salle à manger, *dining-room.*
salon, *drawing-room.*
samedi, *Saturday.*
sang, *blood.*
sans, *without, but for.*
santé, *health.*
sauf, *except.*
sauvage, *wild.*
sauver, *to save.*
savamment, *cunningly.*
savant, *learned.*
savoir, *to know.*
Saxe, *Saxony.*
scandaleux, *scandalous.*
scélerat, *scoundrel.*
scène, *scene.*
science, *science.*
sculpture, *sculpture.*
se, *himself, to himself, herself, to herself; one's self, to one's self; themselves, to themselves.*
sec, sèche, *dry.*
sécher, *to dry up*
second (adj.), *second.*
secouer, *to shake.*
secourir, *to assist*
secret, *secret.*
secrètement, *secretly.*
seize, *sixteen.*
sel, *salt.*
selon, *according to.*
semaine, *week.*
faire semblant, *to pretend.*
ce me semble, *it seems to me.*
sembler, *to appear, to seem.*
s'en repentir, *to repent it.*
sens, *sense, meaning.*
sentier, *path.*
sentiment, *feeling.*
sentir, *to feel, to smell.*
séparer, *to separate.*
se separer, *to part.*
sept, *seven.*
septembre, *September.*
septième, *seventh.*
sergent, *sergeant.*
sérieux, *serious.*
serment, *oath.*
serpent, *serpent.*
serrure, *lock.*
service, *service.*
servir, *to serve.*
se servir (de), *to use.*
ses, *his, her, its.*
seul, *alone.*
seulement, *only.*
sevère, *severe.*
sevèrement, *severely.*
si, *if, so.*
siège, *seat; siege.*
le sien, les siens, la sienne, les siennes, *his, hers, its.*
signe, *sign, signal.*
signer, *to sign.*
simple, *simple, foolish.*
simplement, *simply, merely.*
sire, *sire.*
sitôt, *so soon.*
six, *six.*
sixième, *sixth.*
sœur, *sister.*
soi, *one's self, himself.*
soie, *silk.*
soif, *thirst.*
avoir soif, *to be thirsty.*
soigner, *to nurse.*
ce soir, *this evening, to-night.*
hier soir, *last night.*
soirée, *evening, night.*
soixante, *sixty.*

soixante-dix, *seventy.*
soldat, *soldier.*
soleil, *sun.*
somme, *sum.*
sommeil, *sleep.*
avoir sommeil, *to be sleepy.*
son (n.), *sound.*
son, sa, ses, *his, her, its.*
sonder, *to probe.*
songer, *to think.*
sonnette, *bell.*
sont, *are, belong.*
sort, *fate.*
sortant, *going out.*
sortir, *to go out, to issue.*
sot, sotte, *foolish.*
sou, *cent.*
soudain, *suddenly.*
souffler, *to blow.*
souffrir, *to suffer.*
souhaiter, *to wish.*
soulier, *shoe.*
soupçon, *suspicion.*
soupe, *soup.*
souper (v.), *to sup.*
souper (n.), *supper.*
sourire (n.), *smile.*
sourire (v.), *to smile.*
souris, *mouse.*
sous, *under, below, beneath.*
sous-officier, *non-commissioned officer.*
soutenir, *to bear, to maintain.*
se souvenir, *to remember.*
souvent, *often.*
spectacle, *sight, play.*
splendeur, *splendor.*
station, *station.*
studieux, *studious.*
stupide, *stupid.*
subitement, *suddenly.*
subtilite, *subtlety.*
succès, *success.*
sucre, *sugar.*
suffire, *to suffice.*
tout de suite, *at once.*
suivant, *following.*
suivre, *to follow.*
sujet, sujette, *subject.*
supercherie, *deceit.*
supérieur, *superior.*
supplier, *to implore.*
supporter, *to support.*
supposer, *to suppose.*
sur, *on, upon.*
sûr, *sure, certain.*
surpris, *surprised.*
en sursaut, *in a start.*
surtout, *above all.*

T' stands for *te.*
ta, *thy.*
table, *table.*
tableau, *picture.*
tablette, *tablet.*
tâcher, *to try.*
taire, *to say nothing about, to be silent.*
se taire, *to hold one's tongue.*
talent, *talent.*
tandis que, *while.*
tant, *so much, so many.*
tant soit peu, *however little.*
tante, *aunt.*
tantôt, *sometimes.*
tard, *late.*
tarder à, *to be long in, to delay.*
tasse, *cup.*
te, *thee, to thee, thyself, to thyself.*
tel, *such.*
tellement, *so much so.*
temoigner, *to show, to express.*
tempête, *tempest, storm.*
temps, *time; weather.*
à temps, *in time.*
combien de temps, *how long.*
de temps en temps, *now and then.*
tendre (v.), *to hold out.*
tenez, *hold, see here.*
tenir, *to hold, to keep.*
tenir compte, *to take into consideration.*
tenter, *to attempt; to tempt.*
termes, *terms.*
terminer, *to end.*
terrain, *soil, ground.*
terre, *land, earth.*
territoire, *territory.*
tes, *thy.*
tête, *head.*
thé, *tea.*
théâtre, *scene, theatre.*
Thérèse, *Theresa.*
thème, *exercise.*
le tien, la tienne, les tiens, les tiennes, *thine.*
tiens! *there! I say!*
tigre, *tiger.*
tiré, *drawn: shot.*
tirer, *to draw: to fire.*
se tirer, *to get out.*
tiroir, *drawer.*
Tolède, *Toledo.*
toi, *thou, thee, to thee.*
toi-même, *thyself.*
toit, *roof.*
tombé, *fallen.*
tomber, *to fall.*

ton, ta, tes, *thy.*
ton (n.), *tone.*
tonnerre, *thunder.*
avoir tort, *to be wrong.*
plus tôt, *sooner.*
toujours, *always, still.*
tour, *turn ; tower.*
faire un tour, *to take a turn.*
tourment, *torment.*
tourmenter, *to tease.*
tourner, *to turn round.*
tous, *all, every.*
tousser, *to cough.*
tout, *all, whole, every, everything.*
tout (adv.), *quite.*
tout à coup, *suddenly.*
tout à fait, *quite.*
tout à l'heure, *a little ago, just now.*
tout au moins, *at the very least.*
tout de suite, *at once.*
tout en, *while.*
tout juste, *exactly.*
traduire, *to translate.*
tragédie, *tragedy.*
tragique, *tragic.*
trahir, *to betray.*
trahison, *treason, treachery.*
train, *train, style.*
traîneau, *sledge.*
traîner, *to drag.*
se traîner, *to run along.*
traiter, *to use ;* (de), *to treat as.*
tranquille, *easy ; in peace.*
transporter, *to carry, to take.*
travail, travaux, *work.*
travaillé, *worked.*
travailler, *to work.*
à travers, *through.*
treize, *thirteen.*
tremblant, *trembling.*
trembler, *to shake.*
trente, *thirty.*
très, *very.*
tressaillir, *to tremble.*
tribune, *gallery.*
triste, *sad, sorry.*
trois, *three.*
troisième, *third.*
trompé, *mistaken, deceived.*
tromper, *to deceive.*
se tromper, *to be mistaken.*
trop, *too much, too many.*
à mes trousses, *at my heels.*
trouvé, *found.*
trouver, *to find ; to think.*
se trouver, *to happen to be.*
tu, *thou.*
tuer, *to kill.*
se tuer, *to kill one's self* or *each other.*
turbot, *turbot.*
tuteur, *guardian.*

Un, une, *a, an, one.*
l'un et l'autre, *both.*
uniforme, *uniform.*
univers, *universe.*
urgent, *urgent, pressing.*
utile, *useful.*
utilement, *usefully.*

Vaccine, *vaccination.*
vache, *cow.*
vague, *wave.*
en vain, *in vain.*
vaincre, *to overcome.*
vaincu, *vanquished.*
vainqueur, *conqueror.*
Valérien, *Valerian.*
valet, *valet.*
valoir, *to be worth.*
valoir mieux, *to be better.*
se vanter, *to extol one's self* or *each other.*
vaste, *vast.*
veiller, *to watch.*
vend, *sells.*
vendre, *to sell.*
vendredi, *Friday.*
vendu, *sold.*
vengeance, *vengeance.*
venir, *to come.*
vent, *wind.*
venu, *come.*
vérité, *truth.*
verre, *glass.*
vers (prep.), *towards.*
vers (n.), *verse.*
vert, *green.*
vertu, *virtue.*
veuve, *widow.*
viande, *meat.*
victoire, *victory.*
victorieux, *victorious.*
vider, *to empty.*
vie, *life, living.*
Vienne, *Vienna.*
vieux, vieil, vieille, *old.*
vif, vive, *lively, quick, keen, alive.*
vigne, *vine.*
village, *village.*
vilain, *ugly, bad.*
ville, *town, city.*
vin, *wine.*
vingt, *twenty.*
vingtième, *twentieth.*

violer, *to violate.*
visage, *face, look.*
viser, *to aim.*
visite, *visit.*
visité, *visited.*
visiter, *to visit.*
vite, *quickly, quick.*
vivement, *greatly.*
vivre, *to live.*
voici, *here is, here are.*
voilà, *there is, there are.*
voir, *to see.*
voisin (n.), *neighbor.*
voisin (adj.), *next, near.*
voiture, *carriage.*
voix, *voice.*
voler, *to fly.*
votre, vos, *your.*
le vôtre, la vôtre, les vôtres, *yours.*
voulez-vous, *will you have? do you wish?*
vouloir, *to wish, to will.*
vouloir bien, *to consent, to permit.*
en vouloir à, *to be angry.*
vous, *you, to you; yourself, to yourself; yourselves, to yourselves.*
vous-même, *yourself.*
vous-mêmes, *yourselves.*
voyage, *voyage, journey.*
vogager, *to travel.*
voyageur, *traveller.*
vrai, *true.*
c'est vrai, *it is true.*
vraiment, *truly, really.*
vu, *seen.*
vue, *sight.*

Wagon, *railway carriage.*
whist, *whist.*

Y, *there; to it, to them; to him, to her; in it, in them.*
yeux, *eyes.*

II. — ENGLISH-FRENCH.

A, *un, une.*
about, *environ, près de.*
absent, *absent.*
absolutely, *absolument.*
to abstain, *s'abstenir.*
absurd, *absurde.*
abundant, *abondant.*
to accept, *accepter.*
to accompany, *accompagner.*
according to, *selon.*
on account of, *à cause de.*
to accuse, *accuser.*
to act, *agir.*
active, *actif, active.*
to address, *adresser, s'adresser à.*
to admire, *admirer.*
to admire one's self *or* each other, *s'admirer.*
to admit, *admettre.*
to advise, *conseiller.*
affair, *affaire* (f).
to affirm, *affirmer.*
to be afraid, *avoir peur, craindre.*
after, *après.*
afternoon, *après-midi* (f).
afterwards, *ensuite.*
again, *encore, de nouveau.*
against, *contre.*
age, *âge* (m).
aged, *âgé.*
ago, *il y a.*
ale, *bière* (f).
all, *tout, -e, tous, toutes.*
not at all, *pas du tout.*
to allow, *permettre.*
almost, *presque.*
alone, *seul, -e.*
already, *déjà.*
also, *aussi.*
always, *toujours.*
ambition, *ambition* (f).
America, *Amérique* (f).
amiable, *aimable.*
among, *parmi.*
amusing, *amusant.*
an, *un, une.*
ancient, *ancien, -ne.*
and, *et.*
anecdote, *anecdote* (f)
anger, *colère* (f).
angry, *rageur.*

to get angry, *se fâcher.*
animal, *animal* (m).
to announce, *annoncer.*
answer, *réponse* (f).
to answer, *répondre.*
any, *du, de la, de l', des, en.*
to appeal, *en appeler* (à).
to appear, *sembler, paraître.*
appetite, *appétit* (m).
apple, *pomme* (f).
to approve, *approuver, trouver bon.*
April, *avril.*
architecture, *architecture* (f).
arm, *bras* (m).
armchair, *fauteuil* (m).
army, *armée* (f).
arrival, *arrivée* (f).
to arrive, *arriver.*
arrived, *arrivé.*
article, *article* (m).
artist, *artiste* (m *or* f).
as, *aussi, que.*
as for, *quant à.*
as many, *autant.*
as much, *autant.*
as soon, *dès que, aussitôt que.*
as usual, *comme à l'ordinaire.*
ashamed, *honteux, -se.*
to be ashamed, *avoir honte.*
Asia, *Asie* (f).
to ask, to ask for, *demander.*
to ask back, *redemander.*
to ask pardon, *demander pardon à.*
to assassinate, *assassiner.*
astonishing, *étonnant.*
at, *à.*
at last, *enfin.*
at once, *tout de suite.*
at present, *à présent.*
to be attached to, *tenir à.*
to attack, *attaquer.*
to attend to, *soigner.*
attention, good care, *bons soins* (m).
attention, *attention* (f).
attentive, *attentif, -ve.*
audacity, *audace* (f).
August, *août.*
aunt, *tante.*
Austria, *Autriche* (f).
Austrian, *Autrichien.*
author, *écrivain* (m).
avenue, *avenue* (f).

Bad, *mauvais, vilain.*
bad boy, *mauvais sujet.*
badly, *mal.*
bag, *sac* (m).
carpet bag, *sac* (m) *de nuit.*
baker, *boulanger.*
to bark, *aboyer.*
to bargain for, *marchander.*
basket, *panier* (m).
battle, *bataille* (f).
to be, *être.*
to be (health), *se porter.*
" well, *se porter bien.*
" ill, *se porter mal.*
" afraid, *avoir peur.*
" ashamed, *avoir honte.*
" cold, *avoir froid.*
" hungry, *avoir faim.*
to be off, *s'en aller, se sauver.*
" right, *avoir raison.*
" sleepy, *avoir sommeil.*
" thirsty, *avoir soif.*
" in want, *avoir besoin.*
" warm, *avoir chaud.*
" wrong, *avoir tort.*
to bear, *porter.*
beast, *bête* (f).
to beat, *battre.*
beautiful, *beau, belle.*
because, *parce que.*
to become, *devenir.*
become, *devenu.*
to go to bed, *se coucher.*
been, *été.*
beer, *bière* (f).
before (followed by an infin.), *avant de, avant que de.*
" (conj.), *avant que.*
" (prep. of time), *avant.*
" (prep. of place), *devant, en présence de.*
" (adv. of time), *auparavant.*
to begin, *commencer.*
beginning, *commencement* (m).
to behave, *agir.*
Belgium, *Belgique* (f).
to belong, *appartenir, être à.*
besides, *d'ailleurs.*
to betray, *trahir.*
to betray one's self *or* each other, *se trahir.*
better off, *plus avancé.*

to be better (health), *se porter mieux*, *aller mieux*.
to be better worth, *valoir mieux*.
to bid, *commander*, *dire*.
bill, *billet* (m).
bird, *oiseau* (m).
birthday, *fête* (f).
to bite, *mordre*.
black, *noir*.
to blame, *blâmer*.
" one's self or each other, *se blâmer*.
to blush, *rougir*.
boarding-school, *pension* (f).
boat, *bateau* (m).
boldness, *audace* (f).
bonnet, *chapeau* (m).
book, *livre* (m)
bookseller, *libraire* (m).
boot, *bottine* (f).
to borrow, *emprunter à*.
bottle, *bouteille* (f).
bought, *acheté*.
box, *boîte* (f)
boy, *garçon*.
bracelet, *bracelet* (m).
bread, *pain* (m).
to break, *casser*.
bridge, *pont* (m).
to bring, *amener*, *apporter*.
bring me, *apportez-moi*.
broad, *large*.
brooch, *broche* (f).
brother, *frère*.
brother-in-law, *beau-frère*.
to build, *bâtir*.
business, *affaires* (f).
busy, *occupé*.
but, *mais*.
but for, *sans*.
butter, *beurre* (m).
button, *bouton* (m).
to buy, *acheter*.
by, *par*.
by far, *de beaucoup*.
by that road, *par cette route*.

Cabbage, *choux* (m).
to call, *appeler*.
to call one's self, *s'appeler*.
Canada, *Canada* (m).
cane, *canne* (f).
cannon shot, *coup* (m) *de canon*.
to captivate, *captiver*.
carafe, *carafe* (f).
good care, *bons soins* (m).
carpet bag, *sac de nuit*.
to carry, *porter*.
case, *cas* (m).
the cat, *le chat*, *la chatte*.
to catch cold, *s'enrhumer*.
to celebrate, *célébrer*.
cent, *sou* (m).
certain, *certain*.
certainly, *certainement*.
chain, *chaîne* (f).
chair, *chaise* (f)
to change, *changer*.
to charge, *accuser de*.
Charles, *Charles*.
cheerful, *gai*, *-e*.
cheerfully, *gaiement*.
cheese, *fromage* (m).
child, *enfant* (m or f).
China, *Chine* (f)
choice, *choix* (m).
to choose, *choisir*.
chosen, *choisi*.
Christmas, *Noël* (m).
church, *église* (f).
city, *ville* (f).
to claim, *réclamer*.
class, *classe* (f).
to clean, *nettoyer*.
clever, *habile*, *malin*.
cloth, *drap* (m).
coast, *bord* (m) *de la mer*.
coat, *habit* (m).
coffee, *café* (m).
cold, *froid*.
to have a cold, *être enrhumé*.
to be cold, *avoir froid*.
collection, *collection* (f).
come (part.), *venu*.
come! *voyons!*
come back, *revenu*.
come in, *entré*.
to come down, *descendre*.
to command, *commander*
to commence, *commencer*.
common, *ordinaire*.
to compel, *contraindre*.
to complain, *se plaindre*.
complete, *complet*, *complète*.
to complete, *achever*, *terminer*.
completely, *complètement*.
comrade, *camarade*, *ami*.
to conceal, *cacher*.
to concern, *concerner*, *regarder*.
to condemn, *condamner*.
condition, *condition* (f)

conduct, *conduite* (f).
to confess, *avouer.*
conscience, *conscience* (f).
to consent, *consentir* (*à*), *vouloir bien.*
Constantinople, *Constantinople*
constantly, *constamment.*
construction, *construction* (f).
contented, *content, -e.*
continent, *continent* (m).
continually, *continuellement.*
to contradict, *contredire.*
contrary, *contraire.*
on the contrary, *au contraire.*
conversation, *conversation* (f).
cool, *frais, fraiche.*
copper, *cuivre* (m).
copy-book, *cahier* (m).
cordiality, *cordialité* (f).
corner, *coin* (m).
to correct, *corriger.*
to cost, *coûter.*
to cough, *tousser.*
to count, *compter.*
country (the whole territory), *pays* (m).
country (in contradistinction to the town), *campagne.*
in the country, *à la campagne* (f).
courage, *courage* (m).
courtier, *courtisan.*
course, *cours* (m)
cousin, *cousin, -e.*
Crœsus, *Crésus.*
cruel, *cruel, -le.*
to cry, *pleurer*
cunning, *malin, maligne.*
cup, *tasse* (f).
to cure, *guérir.*
to cure one's self, *se guérir.*
to curse, *maudire.*
to cut, *couper.*

Dainty, *difficile.*
to dance, *danser.*
to dare, *oser.*
date, *date* (f).
daughter, *fille.*
day, *jour* (m).
to dazzle, *éblouir.*
dead, *mort.*
deaf, *sourd.*
a great deal, *beaucoup*
dear, *cher, chère.*
decanter, *carafe* (f).
to deceive, *tromper.*
December, *décembre.*
to decide, *décider.*
to declare, *declarer.*
decidedly, *décidément.*
defect, *défaut* (m)
to defend, *défendre*
delicious, *délicieux, -se.*
to depart, *partir.*
departed, *parti.*
to descend, *descendre.*
to deserve, *mériter* (*de*).
detail, *détail* (m).
to detest, *détester.*
diamond, *diamant* (m).
dictionary, *dictionnaire* (m).
to die, *mourir.*
differently, *autrement, différemment.*
difficult, *difficile.*
difficulty, *difficulté* (f).
diligent, *appliqué, -e.*
to dine, *dîner.*
dining-room, *salle à manger* (f).
dinner, *dîner* (m)
dirty, *sale.*
to dirty, *salir.*
to discover, *découvrir.*
discussion, *discussion* (f).
disinterestedness, *désintéressement* (m).
to disobey, *désobéir* (*à*).
disposition, *caractère* (m).
distance, *distance* (f).
to disturb, *déranger.*
displeasure, *disgrâce* (f).
to do, *faire.*
doctor, *médecin.*
dog, *chien.*
done, *fait.*
door, *porte* (f).
to doubt, *douter.*
dozen, *douzaine* (f).
draught, *courant* (m) *d'air.*
drawer, *tiroir* (m).
dress, *robe* (f)
dressed, *mis, habillé.*
dressmaker, *couturière.*
to drink, *boire.*
to drive, *aller en voiture.*
drunk, *bu.*
dry, *sec, sèche.*
in a duel, *en duel.*
during, *pendant, durant.*
duty, *devoir* (m).
to dwell, *demeurer.*
dying, *mourant.*

Ear-rings, *boucles* (f) *d'oreilles.*

easy (things), *facile*.
easy (pers.), *tranquille*.
easily, *facilement*.
to eat, *manger*.
eaten, *mangé*.
Edinburgh, *Edimbourg*.
in effect (you are right), *en effet*.
effort, *effort* (m).
eight, *huit*.
eighteen, *dix-huit*.
eighth, *huitième*.
eighty, *quatre-vingts*.
either (after a negation), *non plus*.
elephant, *éléphant* (m).
eleven, *onze*.
eleventh, *onzième*.
emperor, *empereur*.
to employ, *employer*.
end, *fin* (f).
to end, *finir*.
enemy, *ennemi* (m).
engaged, *occupé*.
England, *Angleterre* (f).
English, *anglais, -e*.
engraving, *gravure* (f).
to enjoy one's self, *s'amuser*.
enough, *assez*.
to enter, *entrer*.
enterprise, *entreprise* (f).
to entreat, *prier, supplier*.
equal, *égal, -e*.
equality, *égalité* (f).
Ernest, *Ernest*.
error, *faute* (f), *erreur* (f).
to establish, *établir*.
even, *même*.
the evening, *le soir*.
event, *événement* (m).
ever, *jamais*.
every, *tout, -e, tous, toutes*.
everybody, *tout le monde*.
everyone, *tout le monde*.
everything, *tout*.
everywhere, *partout*.
evident, *évident*.
exactly, *précisément*.
to exaggerate, *exagérer*.
example, *exemple* (m).
excellent, *excellent*.
excuse, *excuse* (f).
to excuse, *excuser*.
exercise, *exercice* (m), *thème* (m).
to expect, bef. a noun, *attendre* ; bef. an infin., *s'attendre* (*à*).
experience, *expérience* (f).
to experience, *éprouver*.
to explain, *expliquer*.
to express, *exprimer*.
to extol, *vanter, louer*.
extremity, *extrémité* (f).

Face, *grimace* (f).
to fail in respect, *manquer de respect*.
faithful, *fidèle*.
to fall, *tomber*.
fallen, *tombé*.
false, *faux, fausse*.
family, *famille* (f).
famous, *fameux, -se*.
to fancy, *s'imaginer*.
by far, *de beaucoup*.
fat, *gras, -se*.
father, *père*.
favorite, *favori, -te*.
fault (defect), *défaut* (m).
fault (wrong), *faute* (f).
favor, *faveur* (f).
to fear, *craindre*.
for fear of, *de crainte de, de peur de*.
February, *février*.
fellow, *garçon*.
ferocious, *féroce*.
few, *peu*.
a few, *quelques* (adj.), *quelques-uns* (pr.).
fewer, *moins*
field, *champ* (m).
fifteen, *quinze*.
fifth, *cinquième*.
fifty, *cinquante*.
to fight, *se battre*.
to fill, *remplir*.
fine, *beau, belle*.
to find, *trouver*.
to find (a thing lost), *retrouver*.
finger, *doigt* (m)
to finish, *finir*.
fire, *feu* (m).
first, *premier, première*.
fish, *poisson* (m).
to fit, *aller*.
fit of anger, *accès* (m) *de colère*.
five, *cinq*
to flatter, *flatter*.
to flatter one's self *or* each other, *se flatter*.
flower, *fleur* (f).
fog, *brouillard* (m).
foolish, *fou, folle ; sot, sotte*.
foot, *pied* (m).
for, *pour*.
for (during), *pendant*.
for (marking the beginning), *depuis*.

to forbid, *défendre.*
forenoon, *matin* (m).
to forget, *oublier.*
to forgive, *pardonner.*
formerly, *autrefois.*
fortnight, *quinze jours, quinzaine* (f).
fortunate, *heureux, -se.*
fortune, *fortune* (f).
forty, *quarante.*
found, *trouvé.*
four, *quatre.*
fourteen, *quatorze.*
fourth, *quatrième.*
franc, *franc* (m).
frank, *franc, franche.*
free, *libre.*
freely, *librement.*
to freeze, *geler.*
French, *français, -e.*
Frenchman, *Français.*
fresh, *frais, fraiche.*
Friday, *vendredi* (m).
friend, *ami, -e.*
friendship, *amitié* (f).
to frighten, *effrayer.*
from, *de ;* from me, *de ma part ;* from thee, *de ta part*, etc.
fruit, *fruit* (m).
full, *plein.*
to fulfil, *remplir.*
fur, *fourrure* (f).

Game, *jeu* (m).
garden, *jardin* (m).
general, *général.*
generous, *généreux, -se.*
genius, *génie* (m).
gentle, *doux, douce ; gentil, gentille.*
gentleman, *monsieur.*
geography, *géographie* (f).
George, *Georges.*
Germany, *Allemagne* (f).
to get, *avoir, recevoir.*
to get rid, *se défaire.*
to get up, *se lever.*
gilt-edged, *doré sur tranches.*
girl, *fille.*
to give, *donner.*
to give back, *rendre.*
give me, *donnez-moi.*
given, *donné.*
glad, *aise, bien aise.*
Glasgow, *Glasgow.*
glass, *verre* (m).
glory, *gloire* (f).
glove, *gant* (m).
to go to bed, *se coucher.*
gold, *or* (m).
gone, *allé, parti.*
gone out, *sorti.*
good, *bon, bonne.*
good (in conduct), *sage.*
to be so good as, *avoir la bonté de.*
government, *gouvernement* (m).
grammar, *grammaire* (f).
grand, *magnifique.*
grateful, *reconnaissant, -e.*
great, *grand, -e.*
greatcoat, *paletot* (m).
greatness, *grandeur* (f).
Greek, *grec, grecque.*
on what ground, *à quel titre.*
to guarantee, *garantir.*
guardian, *tuteur.*
to guess, *deviner.*
to guide, *mener.*
guilty, *coupable.*
Habit, *habitude* (f).
a hair, *un cheveu.*
half, *demi.*
half-hour, *demi-heure* (f).
hand, *main* (f).
handkerchief, *mouchoir* (m).
handsome, *beau, belle.*
to happen, *arriver.*
happy, *heureux, -se.*
hard, *fort, difficile.*
harmonious, *harmonieux, -se.*
hat, *chapeau* (m).
to have, *avoir.*
will you have, *voulez-vous ?*
he, *il.*
he who, *celui qui.*
head, *tête* (f).
health, *santé* (f).
to hear (a noise), *entendre.*
to hear it said, to learn, *entendre dire.*
heart, *cœur* (m).
with all my heart, *de tout mon cœur.*
heedless, *étourdi.*
heedlessness, *étourderie* (f).
to help, *aider.*
Henry, *Henri.*
her, *la, elle.*
her (adj.), *son, sa, ses.*
to her, *lui.*
here is, *voici.*
herself, *se, elle-même.*
hesitation, *hésitations* (f. pl.).
to hide, *cacher.*
to hide one's self, *se cacher.*

high, *haut, -e.*
him, *le, lui.*
to him, *lui.*
himself, *se, lui-même.*
his (adj.), *son, sa, ses.*
(pr.), *le sien, la sienne, les siens, les siennes.*
historian, *historien.*
history, *histoire* (f).
hold! *tenez!*
holiday, *jour de congé* (m), *congé* (m).
Holland, *Hollande* (f).
at home, *à la maison.*
honey, *miel* (m).
honor, *honneur* (m).
to hope, (before a future) *espérer;* (before a pres. or past) *aimer à croire, aimer à penser.*
horse, *cheval, chevaux,* (m).
hot, *chaud.*
hotel, *hôtel* (m).
hour, *heure* (f).
house, *maison* (f).
at the house of, *chez.*
how, *comment.*
however, *pourtant.*
how long? *combien de temps? depuis quand?*
how many, *combien.*
how much, *combien.*
humanity, *humanité* (f).
hunger, *faim* (f).
hundred, *cent.*
hundredth, *centième.*
to be hungry, *avoir faim.*

I, *je.*
idle, *paresseux, -se.*
if, *si.*
ill (adj.), *malade.*
ill (adv.), *mal.*
to be ill, *être malade* or *se porter mal.*
illness, *maladie* (f).
illustrated, *illustré.*
imaginary, *imaginaire.*
impertinent, *impertinent.*
important, *important.*
to be important, *importer.*
impossible, *impossible.*
impudence, *impudence* (f).
in, *à, dans; en.*
incredible, *incroyable.*
indeed, *bien.*
indifference, *indifférence* (f).
indispensable, *indispensable.*
indisposed, *indisposé.*
indisputable, *incontestable.*
to induce, *engager* (à).
industrious, *laborieux.*
infinite, *infini.*
ink, *encre* (f).
inkstand, *encrier* (m).
innocence, *innocence* (f).
insolence, *insolence* (f).
instead of, *au lieu de.*
to insult, *insulter.*
interest, *intérêt* (m).
interesting, *intéressant.*
to interfere, *s'entremettre.*
to intimidate, *intimider.*
iron, *fer* (m).
it, *le, la.*
Italian, *italien, -ne.*
Italy, *Italie* (f).
its, *son, sa, ses.*

Jane, *Jeanne.*
January, *janvier.*
jealous, *jaloux, -se.*
John, *Jean.*
journey, *voyage* (m).
July, *juillet.*
June, *juin.*
just (adj.), *juste.*
just (adv.), *justement.*
to have just, *venir de.*
just now, *tout à l'heure.*
justice, *justice* (f).

to Keep, *garder.*
key, *clé* (f).
to kill, *tuer.*
kilogramme, *kilogramme* (m).
kindness, *bonté* (f).
to kiss each other, *s'embrasser.*
knife, *couteau* (m).
to know, *connaître, savoir.*

to Labor, *travailler.*
laborious, *laborieux, -se.*
labor, *travail* (m).
lace, *dentelle* (f).
ladder, *échelle* (f).
lady, *dame* (f).
young lady, *jeune fille, jeune personne, demoiselle.*
land, *terre* (f).
landlord, *propriétaire.*
language, *langue* (f).
large, *grand, -e; gros, -se.*
last, *dernier, dernière.*
last month, *le mois dernier.*

last night, *hier soir, cette nuit.*
at last, *enfin.*
late, *tard.*
Latin, *latin, -e.*
to laugh, *rire.*
law, *loi* (f).
lawyer, *avocat.*
laziness, *paresse* (f).
lazy, *paresseux, -se.*
to lead, *mener.*
to learn, *apprendre.*
learned, *instruit.*
learnt, *appris.*
at least, *du moins.*
at the least, *au moins.*
to leave, *partir.*
left (adj.), *gauche.*
leg, *jambe* (f).
to lend, *prêter.*
leopard, *léopard.*
less, (adj.), *moindre,* (adv.), *moins.*
lesson, *leçon* (f).
lest, *en cas que, de peur que, de crainte que;* after verbs expressing fear, *que.*
to let, *laisser,* (a house) *louer.*
letter, *lettre* (f).
liberty, *liberté* (f).
life, *vie* (f).
like, *pareil, -le; comme.*
to like, *aimer.*
to be like, *ressembler* (*à*).
likely, *probablement.*
lion, *lion.*
litre, *litre* (m).
little, (adj.), *petit, -e.* (adv.), *peu.*
to live, *demeurer; vivre.*
lively, *vif, vive.*
living, *vie* (f).
London, *Londres.*
long, *long, -ue.*
to be long in, *tarder à.*
a long time, *longtemps.*
no longer, *ne . . . plus.*
to look, *avoir l'air.*
to look at, *regarder.*
to look for, *chercher.*
to look ill, *avoir mauvaise mine.*
to lose, *perdre.*
to lose one's self, *se perdre.*
lost, *perdu.*
Louis, *Louis.*
to love, *aimer.*
low, *bas, -se.*
luggage, *bagage* (m).

Mad, *fou, folle.*
made, *fait.*
magnanimity, *magnanimité* (f).
magnificent, *magnifique.*
maid-servant, *bonne.*
malignant, *malin, maligne.*
mamma, *maman.*
man, *homme.*
manners, *manières* (f).
many, *beaucoup.*
March, *mars* (m).
to march, *marcher.*
market, *marché* (m).
to marry, *épouser.*
Mary, *Marie.*
master, *maître.*
May, *mai.*
it may be, *il se peut, il est possible.*
me, *me, moi.*
meadow, *prairie* (f).
meat, *viande* (f).
to meet (by chance), *rencontrer.*
to go to meet, *aller au devant de.*
to mend, *raccommoder.*
merchant, *négociant.*
merry, *gai, -e.*
metre, *mètre* (m).
Mexico, *Mexique* (m).
Middle Ages, *moyen âge* (m).
mile, *mille* (m).
milk, *lait* (m).
milliner, *modiste.*
million, *million* (m).
mine . . . , *le mien, la mienne; les miens, les miennes.*
minister, *ministre.*
minute, *minute* (f).
misery, *misère* (f).
misfortune, *malheur* (m).
to mislay, *égarer.*
Miss, *Mademoiselle* or *Mlle.*
mistake, *faute* (f).
to be mistaken, *se tromper.*
mistress, *maîtresse.*
to mock, *se moquer de.*
modern, *moderne.*
moment, *moment* (m).
Monday, *lundi.*
money, *argent* (m).
Mont Blanc, *le Mont Blanc* (m).
month, *mois* (m).
more, *plus.*
no more, *ne . . . plus.*
morning, *matin* (m).
mother, *mère.*
movement, *mouvement* (m).

Mr., *Monsieur* or *M.*
Mrs. *Madame* or *Mme.*
much, *beaucoup, fort.*
muff, *manchon* (m).
museum, *musée* (m).
muslin, *mousseline* (f).
must, *il faut que, devoir.*
mutton, *mouton* (m).
my, *mon, ma, mes.*
myself, *moi-même.*
mystery, *mystère* (m).

Name, *nom* (m).
naughty, *méchant, -e.*
near, *près de.*
necessary, *nécessaire.*
needle, *aiguille* (f).
to neglect, *négliger.*
neighbor, *voisin, -e.*
neither . . . nor, *ni . . . ni.*
Nero, *Néron.*
never, *ne . . . jamais.*
new (another), *nouveau.*
new-made, *neuf, neuve.*
news, *nouvelle* (f).
newspaper, *journal* (m).
next, *prochain, -e.*
night, *nuit* (f).
at night, *le soir.*
last night, *hier soir.*
nine, *neuf.*
nineteen, *dix-neuf.*
ninety, *quatre-vingt-dix.*
no, *non, ne . . . pas, ne . . . point.*
nobody, *personne . . . ne.*
noise, *bruit* (m).
no . . . longer, *ne . . . plus.*
no . . . more, *ne . . . plus.*
no one, *personne . . . ne.*
nor I either, *ni moi non plus.*
North, *Nord* (m).
nose, *nez* (m).
nosegay, *bouquet* (m).
not, *ne . . . pas.*
not at all, *pas du tout.*
note, *billet* (m).
nothing, *ne . . . rien.*
novel, *roman* (m).
November, *novembre.*
now, *à présent, maintenant.*
now that, *maintenant que.*
number, *chiffre* (m); *nombre* (m).
numerous, *nombreux, -se.*

Oath, *serment* (m).
to obey, *obéir* (à).
to oblige, *obliger.*
obstinate, *obstiné.*
to obtain, *obtenir.*
October, *octobre.*
of, *de.*
offence, *faute* (f).
offer, *offre* (f).
offered, *offert.*
office, *bureau.*
officer, *officier.*
often, *souvent.*
old, *vieux, vieille.*
omnibus, *omnibus* (m).
on, *sur.*
on *before a day or date is not translated.*
at once, *tout de suite.*
one (adj.), *un, une.*
one (pr.), *on, l'on.*
oneself, *se, soi.*
no one, *personne . . . ne.*
only (adj.), *seul.*
only, (adv.), *seulement, ne . . . que.*
to open, *ouvrir.*
opened, *ouvert.*
opera, *opéra* (m).
to oppose, *opposer.*
or, *ou.*
orange, *orange* (f).
order, *ordre* (m).
to order, *ordonner, commander.*
ordered, *commandé.*
other, *autre.*
otherwise, *autrement.*
our, *notre, nos.*
ours, *le nôtre, la nôtre, les nôtres.*
ourselves, *nous, nous-mêmes.*

Painting, *tableau* (m).
pair, *paire* (f).
palace, *palais* (m).
pamphlet, *brochure* (f).
paper, *papier* (m).
parasol, *ombrelle* (f).
parcel, *paquet* (m).
to ask pardon, *demander pardon.*
park, *parc* (m).
parents, *parents.*
part, *partie* (f).
to part from each other, *se séparer.*
to pass, *passer; se passer.*
passage, *passage* (m).
to pay for, *payer.*
pear, *poire* (f).
pen, *plume* (f).
pencil, *crayon* (m).
penknife, *canif* (m).
people, *gens, on, l'on.*
so many people, *tant de monde.*
pepper, *poivre* (m).
to perceive, *apercevoir.*
perfectly, *parfaitement.*

perhaps, *peut-être.*
perishable, *périssable.*
permission, *permission* (f).
personage, *personnage* (m).
philosophy, *philosophie* (f).
photograph, *photographie* (f).
physician, *médecin.*
picture, *tableau* (m).
piece, *morceau* (m).
pin, *épingle* (f).
to pinch, *serrer, blesser.*
place, *place* (f).
to place, *placer.*
play, *jeu* (m).
to play, *jouer.*
plaything, *joujou* (m).
pleasant, *agréable.*
to please, *plaire, faire plaisir à.*
if you please, *s'il vous plaît.*
pleased with, *content de.*
pleasure, *plaisir* (m).
plenty, *beaucoup.*
pocket, *poche* (f).
politely, *poliment.*
poor, *pauvre.*
pope, *pape.*
portrait, *portrait* (m).
positively, *définitivement.*
to possess, *posséder.*
possible, *possible.*
post, *poste* (f).
post-office, *poste* (f).
posterity, *postérité* (f).
potato, *pomme* (f) *de terre.*
pound, *livre* (f).
to praise, *louer.*
to predict, *prédire.*
to prefer, *préférer.*
preferable, *préférable.*
present, *cadeau* (m).
to pretend, *prétendre.*
pretty, *gentil, -le; joli, -e.*
pretty-looking, *joli, -e.*
pretty (before an adj. or adv.), *assez.*
priest, *prêtre.*
prince, *prince.*
princess, *princesse.*
principal, *principal, -e.*
principle, *principe* (m).
prize, *prix* (m).
to gain a prize, *remporter un prix.*
probity, *probité* (f).
professor, *professeur.*
to promise, *promettre.*
promised, *promis.*
to pronounce, *prononcer.*
proof, *preuve* (f).
proper, *convenable.*
to be proper, *convenir.*
property, *propriété* (f).
proposal, *proposition* (f).
to propose, *proposer.*
to protect, *protéger.*
protection, *protection* (f)
to prove, *prouver.*
proverb, *proverbe* (m).
to provide for, *pourvoir à.*
province, *province* (f).
Prussia, *Prusse* (f).
Prussian, *prussien, -ne.*
public, *public, publique.*
punctuality, *exactitude* (f).
to punish, *punir.*
punishment, *punition* (f).
pupil, *élève* (m *or* f).
purse, *porte-monnaie* (m).
to pursue, *poursuivre.*
put, *mis, placé.*
to put, *placer, mettre.*

to Quarrel, *se quereller.*
quarter (the 4th part), *quart* (m).
quarter (district), *quartier* (m).
queen, *reine.*
question, *question* (f).
quite, *tout à fait.*

Rabbit, *lapin.*
railway-carriage, *wagon* (m).
rain, *pluie* (f).
rainy, *pluvieux, -se.*
rare, *rare.*
to read, *lire.*
read, *lu.*
ready, *prêt, -e.*
reason, *raison* (f).
reasonable, *raisonnable.*
to receive, *recevoir.*
received, *reçu.*
reciprocally, *réciproquement.*
to reckon, *compter.*
to recommend, *conseiller.*
red, *rouge.*
to refuse, *refuser.*
to regret, *regretter.*
regular, *régulier, régulière.*
to reign, *régner.*
to relate, *raconter.*
relatives, *parents.*
to remain, *rester.*

remained, *resté*.
remarkable, *remarquable*.
remedy, *remède* (m).
to remember, *se souvenir*.
remembrance, *souvenir* (m).
to remind, *rappeler*.
to remit, *remettre*.
to remove, *déménager*.
to renounce, *renoncer*.
to repeat, *répéter*.
reply, *réponse* (f).
to reply, *répondre*.
report, *bruit* (m).
representation, *représentation* (f).
to reproach for, *reprocher à*.
to resign, *se démettre*.
resistance, *résistance*.
respect, *respect* (m).
to fail in respect, *manquer de respect à*.
to rest, *se reposer*.
to resume, *reprendre*.
to return (to give back), *rendre*.
returned (come back), *revenu*.
revolution, *révolution* (f).
reward, *récompense* (f).
to reward, *récompenser*.
ribbon, *ruban* (m).
rich, *riche*.
to be right, *avoir raison*.
ring, *bague* (f).
to ring, *sonner*.
to rise, *se lever*.
river, *rivière*.
road, *route* (f).
roasted, *rôti*.
Rome, *Rome* (f).
room, *chambre* (f).
rose, *rose* (f).
round, *rond, -e*.
rule, *règle* (f).

to Sacrifice, *sacrifier*.
sad, *chagrin, -e; triste*.
safely, *sans accident*.
said, *dit*.
salad, *salade* (f).
salt, *sel* (m).
same, *même*.
Saturday, *samedi*.
savage, *sauvage*.
Savoy, *Savoie* (f).
scandal, *scandale* (m).
scarcely, *à peine*.
scarf, *écharpe* (f).
scenery, *paysage* (m).
school, *école* (f).
boarding-school, *pension* (f).
science, *science* (f).
to scold, *gronder*.
Scotland, *Ecosse* (f).
scoundrel, *scélérat* (m).
sculpture, *sculpture* (f).
sea, *mer* (f).
seaside, *bord* (m) *de la mer*.
season, *saison* (f).
second, *second, -e; deuxième*.
secret (n.), *secret* (m).
secret (adj.), *secret, -ète*.
to see, *voir*.
see! *tenez!*
to seek, *chercher*.
to seem, *sembler*.
seen, *vu*.
selfish, *égoïste*.
to sell, *vendre*.
to send, *envoyer*.
sentence, *phrase* (f).
September, *septembre*.
seriously, *sérieusement*.
serpent, *serpent* (m).
servant (f), *bonne*.
service, *service* (m).
session, *session* (f).
seven, *sept*.
seventeen, *dix-sept*.
seventh, *septième*.
seventy, *soixante-dix*.
several, *plusieurs*.
severely, *sévèrement*.
she, *elle*.
she who, *celle qui*.
to be shipwrecked, *faire naufrage*.
shoe, *soulier* (m).
shop, *magasin* (m).
short, *court, -e, petit, -e*.
to show, *montrer*.
to show one's self, *se montrer*.
show me, *montrez-moi*.
shut, *fermé*.
to shut, *fermer*.
sick, *malade*.
silk, *soie* (f).
silver, *argent* (m).
simple, *simple*.
simply, *simplement*.
since, *depuis; puisque*.
to sing, *chanter*.
sir, *monsieur* (m).
sister, *sœur*.
sister-in-law, *belle-sœur*.
situation, *place* (f).
six, *six*.
sixteen, *seize*.
sixth, *sixième*.
sixty, *soixante*.
to skate, *patiner*.
to slander, *calomnier médire de*.
slate, *ardoise* (f).

slave, *esclave*.
to sleep, *dormir*.
to be sleepy, *avoir sommeil*.
slept, *dormi*.
slipper, *pantoufle* (f).
small, *petit*, *-e*.
to smoke, *fumer*.
so, *si*; after a transitive verb, *le*; after an intransitive, *ainsi*.
so many, *tant*.
so much, *tant*.
so soon, *sitôt*.
to soil, *salir*.
sold, *vendu*.
some, *du*, *de la*, *de l'*, *des*; *en*; *quelques-uns*.
somebody, *quelqu'un*.
something, *quelque chose*.
something else, *autre chose*.
sometimes, *quelquefois*.
somewhere, *quelque part*.
son, *fils*.
song, *chanson* (f).
soon, *bientôt*.
sooner, *plus tôt*.
sorrowful, *chagrin*, *-e*.
sorry, *fâché*, *triste*, *chagrin*.
to be sorry, *regretter de*, *être fâché de*.
soul, *âme* (f).
soup, *soupe* (f).
south, *midi* (m).
Spain, *Espagne* (f).
to speak, *parler*.
to spend, *passer*.
in spite of, *malgré*.
splendid, *magnifique*, *superbe*.

spoken, *parlé*.
to sprain, *démettre*.
station, *station* (f).
to stay, *rester*.
stayed, *resté*.
in his stead, *à sa place*.
steamboat, *bateau* (m) *à vapeur*.
stick, *canne* (f).
still, *encore*.
stormy, *orageux*, *-se*.
story, *histoire* (f).
stout, *gros*, *-se*.
straight, *droit*, *-e*.
strange, *étrange*.
strawberry, *fraise* (f).
stream, *ruisseau* (m).
street, *rue* (f).
strength, *force* (f).
strong, *fort*, *-e*.
stud, *bouton* (m).
studious, *studieux*, *-se*.
to study, *étudier*.
subject (noun), *sujet* (m).
subject (adj.), *sujet*, *-te*.
to submit, *soumettre*.
to succeed, *réussir*.
such, *pareil*, *-le*; *tel*.
to suffer, *souffrir*.
suffering, *souffrant*.
sugar, *sucre* (m).
sum, *somme* (f).
summer, *été* (m).
sun, *soleil* (m).
Sunday, *dimanche* (m).
support, *appui* (m).
to support, *appuyer*.
to suppose, *supposer*.
sure, *sûr*, *certain*.
to surprise, *surprendre*.
to surrender, *se rendre*.
sweet, *doux*, *-ce*.

Table, *table* (f).
to take, *prendre*.
to take to, *mener*, *conduire*.
to take a walk, *se promener*.
to take away, *enlever*.
taken, *pris*.
talent, *talent* (m).
tall, *grand*, *-e*.
tea, *thé* (m)
to teach, *enseigner* (*à*).
teacher, *maître* (m).
to tell, *raconter*, *dire à*.
temper, *humeur* (f).
temple, *temple* (m).
ten, *dix*.
tenth, *dixième*.
than, *que*.
to thank, *remercier*.
thanks, *merci*.
thanks to, *grâce à*.
that (adj.), *ce*, *cet*, *cette*.
" (pr.), *celui*, *celle*; *celui-là*, *celle-là*; *cela*.
" or which, *qui* (nom.), *que* (acc.).
" (conj.), *que*.
the, *le*, *la*, *les*.
theatre, *théâtre* (m).
thee, *te*, *toi*.
theft, *vol* (m).
their, *leur*, *leurs*.
theirs, *le leur*, *la leur*, *les leurs*.
them, *les*; *eux*, *elles*.
to them, *leur*.
themselves, *se*; *eux-mêmes*, *elles-mêmes*.
then (afterwards), *ensuite*, *alors*.
then (therefore), *donc*.
there, *là*, *y*.

there is, are, *il y a, voilà.*
there was, were, *il y avait.*
therefore, *donc.*
Therese, *Thérèse.*
these (adj.), *ces.*
" (pr.), *ceux-ci, celles-ci.*
they, *ils, on.*
they who, *ceux qui, celles qui.*
thick, *épais, -se.*
thimble, *dé* (m).
thine, *le tien, la tienne; les tiens, les tiennes.*
thing, *chose* (f).
to think, *penser.*
third, *troisième.*
to be thirsty, *avoir soif.*
thirteen, *treize.*
thirty, *trente.*
this (adj.), *ce, cet, cette.*
" (pr.), *celui-ci, celle-ci; ceci.*
those (adj.), *ces.*
" (pr.), *ceux, celles; ceux-là, celles-là.*
thou, *tu.*
though, *quoique, cependant.*
thousand, *mille.*
thousandth, *millième.*
thread, *fil* (m).
to threaten, *menacer.*
three, *trois.*
throat, *gorge* (f).
to throw, *jeter.*
thunder, *tonnerre* (m).
Thursday, *jeudi* (m).
thus, *ainsi.*
thy, *ton, ta, tes.*
thyself, *te, toi-même.*
tiger, *tigre* (m).
till, *jusqu'à, jusque.*
time, *temps* (m); *fois* (f).
a long time, *longtemps.*
by this time, *maintenant.*
from time to time, *de temps en temps.*
in time, *à temps.*
tipsy, *gris, -e.*
tired, *las, -se.*
to, *à.*
to-day, *aujourd'hui.*
together, *ensemble.*
told, *dit.*
to-morrow, *demain.*
to-night, *ce soir.*
too (also), *aussi.*
" (before adj. or adv.), *trop.*
too many, *trop.*
too much, *trop.*
towards, *envers.*
town, *ville* (f).
toy, *joujou* (m).
train, *train* (m).
to transmit, *transmettre.*
to travel, *voyager.*
treason, *trahison* (f).
to treat, *traiter.*
tree, *arbre* (m).
to tremble, *trembler.*
trembling, *tremblant.*
trial, *procès* (m).
trifle, *misère* (f).
to trouble, *déranger.*
troublesome, *fatigant, ennuyeux, -se.*
true, *vrai, -e.*
to trust, *se fier à.*
truth, *vérité* (f).
to try, *essayer, tâcher de.*
Tuesday, *mardi* (m).
turn, *tour* (m).
tutor, *précepteur.*
twelve, *douze.*
twenty, *vingt.*
two, *deux.*

Ugly, *vilain, -e.*
umbrella, *parapluie* (m).
uncle, *oncle.*
unfortunate, *malheureux, -se.*
unfortunately, *malheureusement.*
ungrateful, *ingrat, -e.*
unhappy, *malheureux, malheureuse.*
unjustly, *injustement.*
unwell, *malade.*
upon, *sur.*
us, to us, *nous.*
use, *usage* (m).
useful, *utile.*
as usual, *comme à l'ordinaire.*

Very, *très, bien.*
to vex, *fâcher.*
victory, *victoire* (f).
Vienna, *Vienne.*
to violate, *trahir.*
virtue, *vertu* (f).
visit, *visite* (f).
to pay a visit, *rendre visite.*
to visit, *visiter.*
voice, *voix* (f).
voyage, *voyage* (m).

to Wait for, *attendre.*
walk, *promenade* (f).
to walk, *aller à pied.*
to take a walk, *se promener.*

to go out for a walk, *aller faire une promenade.*
to be in want, *avoir besoin ; falloir.*
war, *guerre* (f).
warm, *chaud.*
to be warm, *avoir chaud.*
watch, *montre* (f).
water, *eau* (f).
to water, *arroser.*
way, *chemin* (m).
we, *nous, on.*
to wear, *porter.*
weather, *temps* (m).
in this cold weather, *par le froid qu'il fait.*
Wednesday, *mercredi.*
week, *semaine* (f).
to weep, *pleurer.*
to welcome, *accueillir.*
well, *bien.*
to be well, *se porter bien.*
what, *quel, -le ; quels, -les.*
when, *quand, lorsque.*
when (interr.), *quand.*
where, *où.*
which (nom.), *qui,* (acc.) *que.*
" after prep. or followed by *of, lequel, laquelle ; lesquels, lesquelles.*
from which, of which, *duquel, de laquelle ; desquels, desquelles ; dont.*
to which, *auquel, à laquelle ; auxquels, auxquelles.*
while, *en.*
whist, *whist* (m).
white, *blanc, blanche.*
who, *qui.*
whole, *tout, -e ; tous, toutes.*
whom, *que ;* aft. pr., *qui.*
why ? *pourquoi ?*
why ! *mais !*
wicked, *méchant.*
wide, *large.*
wife, *femme* (f).
wild, *féroce, sauvage.*
will you have ? *voulez-vous ?*
to be willing, *vouloir.*
window, *fenêtre* (f).
wine, *vin* (m)
winter, *hiver* (m).
wise, *sage.*
to wish, *désirer, souhaiter.*
with, *avec.*
without, *sans.*
woman, *femme.*
wonderful, *merveilleux.*
wood, *bois* (m).
wooden, *de bois.*
word, *mot* (m).
in a word, *en un mot.*
work, *ouvrage* (m), *travail* (m).
to work, *travailler.*
world, *monde* (m).
worse, *plus mauvais.*
to be worth, *valoir.*
worthy, *digne.*
to wound one's self *or* each other, *se blesser.*
to write, *écrire.*
written, *écrit.*
to be wrong, *avoir tort.*
wrought, *travaillé.*

Year, *an* (m), *année* (f).
last year, *l'année dernière.*
yes, *oui.*
yesterday, *hier.*
yet (again, still), *encore.*
" (however), *pourtant.*
you, *vous, on.*
young, *jeune.*
young lady, *jeune fille, jeune personne, demoiselle.*
your, *votre, vos.*
yours, *le vôtre, la vôtre, les vôtres.*
yourself, *vous, vous-même.*
yourselves, *vous, vous-mêmes.*
youth, *jeunesse* (f).

THE END.

www.ingramcontent.com/pod-product-compliance
Lightning Source LLC
Chambersburg PA
CBHW051123120726
47905CB00005B/1394

* 9 7 8 3 3 3 7 4 0 0 7 8 1 *